CODE WORD ROSE

Prologue

When the crushing blow lands, it strikes above her shoulders at the base of her neck and feels like the iron of a crowbar or a steel-toed boot this time, and not the meat of a man's fist. When she looks up, everything's red. She lurches forward and onto her elbows, clawing at the dirty concrete with her ragged fingertips. She gasps. There's too much pain to cry.

Another blow strikes her in the hip and she topples to the side. Their laughter reigns over her. The hideous laughter of these men; she doesn't know how many. She rolls from side to side, the throbbing pain rippling through her body. Lying on her back, she waits for the next blow to strike. The sky is dark, but her eyes are flooded with light from the tall street-lamp centered above the parking lot. There are no faces to be seen. Only shadows of men. But these shadows are tall and broad and terrifying, and she's not sure she recognizes any of them through the vapor of light. One of the shadows stoops over her. She winces, but the blow doesn't come. Instead, she hears a voice, deep and gravelly.

"*Now* you wanna tell us where Charlie is, bitch?"

She shudders, overcome by the hot, choking smoke

blown intentionally in her face from the speaker's mouth. She coughs. The man's face is lit momentarily by the cherry tip of his cigarette as he takes a long pull. Dark, callous eyes hooded by long bushy eyebrows, a square jaw. Not a face she recognizes. Probably a prospect.

The man stands, rejoining the shadows. "I guess she's not ready to talk yet, Gonz," he scoffs.

"She'll talk. Just needs a little help is all."

This voice she does recognize—Gonzo, a member of the gang she's had many occasions to meet. Recognizing his voice does nothing to calm her. In fact, the sound of his name invokes terror. She can hardly breathe, let alone think. She knows the wrath of this man. Especially with women.

"Look at the bitch," another man sneers. "She's turning blue!"

"Can't talk if she can't breathe," Gonzo says.

She rolls on her side, grasping at her throat. A row of heavy black boots surround her. Behind them the streetlamp illuminates the shimmery chrome of motorcycles. Choppers polished to a high shine. She is no stranger to the fury of these rides—the way their roaring engines seem to pound you from within.

"Remind her how to breathe," Gonzo barks.

One of the boots rears back and pounds into her rib cage. The pain travels in arcs of convulsive contractions down to her toes. She gasps for air, but cannot breath. She can only roll away from the blow, the blood beginning to run in little rivers from her nose. Her dry lips moistened with the metallic taste.

"You gonna talk, slut?" a voice screams.

She curls herself into a little ball, hugging her scraped knees to her chest, and groans softly. There's no hope for escape. She's penned by a heavy wall of men and a heavier wall of bikes. Gonzo bends forward with his hands on his knees, glaring down at her.

"Your punk-ass boyfriend ripped us off. You know what we do to thieves—and the cunts who hide 'em."

Her mind flashes to Charlie. She's strangled with fear. The shadows behind her inquisitor's head sway from side to side impatiently.

"Have it your way," the man says.

She hears the hissing of her own skin before she feels the searing pain. She looks down in horror to see that the man has put out his cigarette in the flesh just above her elbow. She screams.

"Listen, you fuckin' whore," Gonzo growls. "Nobody steals from Duke and gets away with it. You understand? Charlie's a dead man. One way or another, we'll find him. And you're dead, too, unless you give us what we want."

She feels a hand sliding in behind her head, gathering a large clump of her dirty-blonde hair. She winces at the coming strike. When it delivers, it delivers with a dull thud that she can hardly feel. A kaleidoscopic burst of red erupts from her closed eyes. The pounding ache within her head is such that it renders all other pain irrelevant. She can't feel her bones cracking or her hair tearing anymore, only hear it. Again and again, the sound comes to her as if from a distance. She's aware that several men are striking her now. Some with their boots, others with their fists. She longs to lose consciousness, but the release doesn't come. Her eyes merely glaze with a thin white light.

"Tell us where he is and we'll let you go!" Gonzo yells. "Where's Charlie? Where's the fuckin' money? Talk!"

Finally, the torrent stops. The thin white light slowly fades and is replaced by the darkness of the parking lot. She lies prone on the concrete, her head cocked to one side, toward the glimmering bikes. Charlie. She has a dream-like vision of Charlie there in the shimmering light, standing proudly over his own chopper with that silly tight-lipped grin of his. His muscular, tattooed arms folded at his chest; his black leather vest; the savage bullwhip he always carries slung around his neck; and his giant silver belt buckle emblazoned with the name. *Hells Angels*.

She feels the streetlight return to her face—the shadows looming above her close into a tighter circle.

"Let's see how you like the way ol' Mongoose here *makes* women squeal."

She gasps as she feels hands all around her. They clasp her wrists and pull her arms over her head, her elbows scraping heavily against the concrete. Someone grabs her hips and pulls her to her knees. From behind, she hears the unmistakable sound of a man loosening his belt and unzipping his fly. A low chuckle follows.

Mongoose. Just the name cripples her every will. She knows the evil of this man. He slides his hands from her hips to her belt. She tries to pull away but can't move, for all the hands holding her down.

Frantic. Hopeless. "Charlie," she whispers. Then the rip and jerk of her jeans and panties. She feels his warmth behind her before his touch.

Another picture bursts through her mind. Charlie. Emaciated. Hollowed, dark eyes and huffing mouth. Holed up in a motel.

"Wait!" she wheezes. The hands at her waist stop moving. They tighten to her hips. She feels Mongoose's manhood pressing against her. She shudders.

"I'll talk," she blurts, coughing up blood from deep in her chest. "Make him stop . . . I'll talk."

The hands holding her arms release, and she is allowed to rise up from her knees. Gonzo's face swoops in before her. He crouches low, glaring at her like a scolding father over a misbehaving child. "That's better," he says with a yellow grin.

"A motel," she gushes. "I checked him into a motel."

Chapter 1

The Big Break
San Diego, CA
June 22, 1996

Frank drives hunched over the wheel of the Crown Vic, his hands gripped tight, a Marlboro hanging from his dry lips. The smoke and ash disappear through the backdraft of the open window. Despite the heat of the Santa Ana winds, he's wearing his usual wardrobe: a god-awful brown tweed sport coat riddled with cigarette burn holes, polo shirt, corduroy pants, and his scuffed cowboy boots. He's still in pretty decent shape, as you'd expect for a former Marine gunny. His bulging biceps are tightly packed into the sleeves of his jacket, while his barrel chest and ample gut render the three front buttons useless. His ruddy, round face is scarred and rugged, with deep-set green eyes shadowed by heavy brows and a dark, reddish-tinged mustache that matches the color of his flattop. The tough-guy visage is softened somewhat by the wire-rimmed glasses. There's a lot of Irish in his looks, and he's quite proud of it.

"We're only going to get one chance at this, Nick," he says, his eyes fixed on the freeway racing beneath us. "And it's gotta happen right now. This is our break."

"I can't believe it, man, Stacey Ritt." I shake my head incredulously.

Stacey Ritt's a heroin addict, a full-on junkie, living each day for her next fix. My guess is she dialed the number on one of the San Diego PD business cards Frank's been laying on her for the past months. He'd schmooze her every time they crossed paths, uncommon kindness in his eyes as he'd tell her that if she was ever in trouble or needed to talk, she shouldn't hesitate to call him. I've seen him use this tact on probably hundreds of people. But the truth is, he really does care. He really does want to help. He practically bleeds "Protect and Serve."

Frank Conroy is San Diego PD. A former Marine gunnery sergeant with two combat tours in Vietnam. He's a relentless and tireless cop, and about as tough and disciplined as anyone I've ever met. His reputation within the department is legendary, but in an odd twist of fate, he's been partnered with me, an FBI agent about to be fired from the Bureau. Frank's assigned to the FBI's Hells Angels Task Force because of his extensive knowledge of this criminal organization. We've been working and practically living together for the past couple of months trying to build a case against the outlaw motorcycle gang, and to this point, we've had little luck gaining any ground.

We just lost the connection on the cell phone from a shrieking Stacey Ritt. Desperate and pleading, she's still reeling from a torturous beating she's taken from the Hells Angels. Disoriented and fragile, she mutters only a few words before we lose her.

"I'm bleeding, Frank ... You gotta ... you gotta ... Oh, God, they're gonna find him."

"Who are they going to find, Stacey?"

"Charlie!" she blurts. "They're lookin' for Charlie. Frank ... they ... they think he stole money from the club."

Frank and I lock eyes, acknowledging without a word the significance of the news. The "Charlie" that Stacey's referring to is Charlie Slade, and I can't believe the coincidence. Frank was just telling me about a run-in he had with Charlie over a briefcase when the cell phone rang.

"Stacey, where are you?" Frank urges.

There's a long silence like she's taking a look around and realizing she has absolutely no idea. She starts to cry in short, ragged gasps. "I'm scared, Frank—"

"We can help you, Stacey. Just tell me where you're calling from."

"They got me bad ... got me bad, I'm bleeding—"

"Who got you bad, Stacey?" I watch Frank's hand tighten on the wheel. "Who hurt you?"

"I ... I don't know ... Some prospects, I think."

"Club prospects? Are you sure?"

Stacey fall silent for a time. I can hear her sobbing. Sniffling. "Gonzo was there, I think," she offers meekly.

"That's good, Stacey," Frank says. "Tell me everything you can remember." He continues to hold the phone between us as the poor woman slurs and stammers through a list of vague details and possible names. The way she's wheezing, the way she takes long pauses to gather her breath for every detail, sounds as if it's causing her great pain to even speak.

"You . . . you gotta find him," she pleads. "Hurry."

"I understand that, Stacey," Frank says calmly. "But you have to tell me where he is."

"Motel—"

"Which motel?"

"I just can't...I gotta go—"

"Don't hang up, Stacey!" Frank barks into the phone. "You gotta stay with me. Which motel?"

"By the freeway . . ." she says, her voice now weak and drifting. "Off the freeway, I think. El Cajon."

"Are you in the room with him? Are you in the room with Charlie?"

"No—"

"Think, Stacey! There's got to be a name; a phone number."

"I'm scared . . ." She shudders. "They were gonna kill me."

"Nobody's going kill you, Stacey. You're doing the right thing here. Everything's going to be fine, but you have to tell me where Charlie is."

"Top hat...," she blurts. "There's a top hat."

"The Top Hat motel?" Frank asks and I can tell by his tone he's never heard of the place. He looks over at me, but I have to shrug.

When the line falls dead, it's the kind of dead that says we lost our signal. She's gone.

Frank slams the phone down on the seat. "Goddamn piece of shit!" he yells. "These fucking things are worthless."

He yanks the Crown Vic into a hard left turn onto Texas

Street, and within minutes we're flying eastbound on Interstate 8 toward the suburb of El Cajon. There's a wildfire burning in the Laguna Mountains to the east and the sun hangs in the smoky sky like a bad penny. He reaches for his two-way radio and calls PD dispatch. He puts out a query to all detective units for something, anything that might give us a lead on a location.

I scan the expanse beside the freeway, eyeballing the blur of passing hotels and motels that might qualify under Stacey's scant description. I'm also thinking about Charlie Slade, a man reputed to be one of the most dangerous and violent members of the San Diego Hells Angels. On the street, he goes by one of two monikers, "Crazy Charlie" or "Charmin' Charlie," depending, I guess, on his mood. In law enforcement circles, he's known as a first-rate asshole and cop-hater with a fierce loyalty to the Hells Angels.

Our most recent intelligence report, however, reveals a very different Charlie Slade: a desperate heroin addict who's become a vulnerable liability to the gang and a weak target of opportunity for law enforcement. He's also rumored to have been removed as sergeant-at-arms, a top officer of the club with intimate knowledge of all their dirty secrets. Add to that Stacey's claim about Charlie being accused of stealing. If it's true, then after months of all-night surveillances, street-level drug busts, and twisting low-level informants in an effort to leverage our way up to the top echelon of the Hells Angels, we may have gotten the big break we've been looking for dumped right in our laps. The invincible and impenetrable Hells Angels just might have a chink in their armor. All we have to do is get to him before they do.

A voice crackles over Frank's radio. Some guy in vice. The voice informs of a strip joint that just opened off Interstate 8 in the city of El Cajon in east San Diego County.

"I think it's called the Top Hat," the voice says.

"Figures you'd know all the skin joints, Creel."

"That's what they pay me for, Conroy." The voice chortles

smugly, revealing Creel's obvious delight that everyone else on this frequency can hear him.

I shoot a glance at Frank. "Strip joint? I thought she said a motel."

Frank grunts. "Keep your eyes peeled, Nick. Top Hat."

He jackrabbits back and forth between traffic, driving the Crown Vic like an Indy 500 race car. He's cruising one-handed, using his free hand to drag at his mustache. "I can't figure it, Nick," he says contemplatively. "Charlie wouldn't steal from the club. The club's his life—his family—no matter how desperate he might be. He's a Hells Angel, through to his soul."

"He's a junkie, Frank. Junkies steal to feed their habit, brotherhood or no brotherhood."

Frank squints at me, his bushy brow drawn tightly over his right eye. "Something like that happens, stealing from their own, betraying the brotherhood—these guys can make your average Saturday night ax murder look like a frat house hazing."

We're practically bumper locked on a beat-up VW bus with a rainbow-colored peace sign on the back window, blocking the fast lane. Frank lays on the horn and the wagon slides over. The bearded driver shoots us the finger. So much for peace and love.

I hear a click-click and look over to see Frank steering with his knees, cupping his hands over his Zippo and lighting up a fresh smoke, the Crown Vic shuddering beneath us. "There was this guy up in Ramona coupla years ago," Frank says calmly. "A Hells Angel. Reekin' Ray Randolph. I mean you couldn't get within a hundred yards of this guy without gagging." He chuckles as his hands leave the steering wheel again as he gestures to pinch his nose. "They took to that poor bastard with brass knuckles and pipes. When we found him, we'd have been better off scooping him into a bucket than putting him on a stretcher."

"Dead?"

Frank blasts a chalky cloud of smoke around the cigarette

dangling from his lips. "Might as well have been."

The exit comes into view. According to Creel, the Top Hat is somewhere up ahead, hard along the freeway.

"What'd he do to deserve that?" I ask.

"Lied to the club."

"Guess he won't do that again."

Frank snickers as he checks his rearview mirror. "They took that poor bastard and burned off all his HA tattoos with a blowtorch. The doc said he never saw anything like—"

"There!" I yell, jabbing a finger out the window.

Up ahead I see a pink and black neon top hat dangling from a pole on the other side of the freeway. Frank plows over to the right and slides into the number four lane, and we both crane our necks to get a look.

"That's gotta be it," I insist.

I brace myself for Frank to throw out the chutes and slow us down, but instead he guns it down the Main Street exit ramp, slams on the brakes, and blows through the red light at the bottom of the ramp. He makes a left turn back under the freeway and burns another red light, gunning the Vic back westbound onto the frontage road.

It's a hard curve to the right before the Top Hat returns to view. We can see it at the end of a row of rundown apartment buildings, sleazy bars, and abandoned storefronts. Seedy street dealers and desperate hookers pass by like wisps of rotten humanity until finally we reach the parking lot—a trash-strewn expanse of cracked asphalt just under the shadow of the elevated freeway overpass.

Frank wheels off the road, reduces speed drastically, and eases the car into the parking lot so as not to draw attention. We both know how fast things can break bad in situations like this. I unsnap the trigger guard of my holster and check my pistol and Frank does the same, examining the rounds in his little .38 snub-nose Detective Special.

We climb out into furnace-like heat. I'm wearing only a short-sleeve Mexican guayabera and khakis, but two seconds out of the car and I'm popping sweat. My shirt covers my side-arm. Frank's rumpled tweed jacket covers his.

The Top Hat sign is sizzling up there on the end of its pole, but the bar itself, a one-story box with bars on all the windows, looks closed for business. We walk over, try the front door, peer inside, but there's nothing. The parking lot's empty. No sign of anyone around. We skulk around the back, find another locked door.

"Great," says Frank. "Fucking Stacey, man."

We turn to walk back to the car and then I see it. It's about two blocks up the street in the shadow of the freeway—a peeling board with the word "Rooms" is just visible, daubed in flaking red paint. I tap Frank's shoulder, and without a word we hustle back to the car.

Two minutes later, we're walking through the main entrance of the Gold Coast Motel. The lobby is dark as we enter from the bright sunlight. When my eyes finally adjust, I see a counter made out of what looks to be cheap varnished bamboo. Tiki torches and a couple of palm trees are smeared on the wall. Behind the counter, there's a curtain-lined doorway leading through to what looks to be a residence or small office. The odor of the place is a mixture of cigarette smoke and Pine-Sol.

"Let's not mention Charlie," Frank whispers. "We're here for Stacey Ritt."

I nod and press a button on the counter, setting off a little ding-dong chime.

What sounds like a La-Z-Boy creaks, and a shriveled little weasel shuffles in from behind the dark, heavy curtain. He's a scrawny character with a stubbly beard and thin, graying hair, wearing a Felix the Cat T-shirt. He snaps on a little desk light and looks us over. As dazed as he is, it doesn't take more than a second for him to realize we're not here for a room.

Frank flashes his badge as he pushes a photograph across the counter—a picture of Stacey taken through a long lens about a month ago. She's wearing cut-off jeans, a tiny halter top, and a junkie's death mask as she's walking unaware toward our surveillance camera. The weasel picks up the photo. "What'd this bitch do?" His voice carries the gravel of a heavy smoker. His yellow-stained teeth suggest the same.

"Checked into a motel," Frank says.

The guy shrugs. "Not this one. Never seen her before."

"You sure about that?"

"Sure, I'm sure. Positive."

Frank grabs the photo out of the guys hand and thrusts it into his face. The weasel takes a step back, his hands raised.

"You own this place?" Frank growls.

The man nods, backing straight into the wall behind.

"Then take a closer look!" Frank's still holding the picture in the proprietor's face as he motions behind him with his free hand. "I count at least six code violations between here and the parking lot of this fleabag joint you call a motel. If you want to stay in business, I suggest you think a little harder."

With a sigh, the motel owner grabs the picture and holds it up toward a dim light bulb over the tattered bamboo counter, his eyes doing a little shimmy. Frank's attitude adjustment delivers the intended results.

"Karen," he says, handing it back. "She ain't in, though. Ain't seen her in a coupla' days—"

"Karen?"

He shrugs again. "What she said."

For the first time, I notice the strong odor of marijuana on his breath and clothes, but I'm too preoccupied to care. I'm watching through the tall, narrow window that opens to the mostly empty parking lot, listening for the roar of Harley engines. Depending on how much information they bled out of Stacey, we could be too late.

"She's in 6," the weasel mutters as he passes a large metal key across the counter, obviously preferring that we get on with our business and leave him alone. "Checked in last week. Paid cash."

"You check the room lately?" Frank asks. "I ain't been in the room, no," he says with an air of indignation. "I don't go into no rooms until the customer checks out. Ain't you guys never heard of privacy rights?"

"Anybody been here looking for her in the past couple of hours?" Frank asks.

"Look, Columbo. I ain't no babysitter. I mind my own business and stay back here in my little apartment. How should I know if anybody's come looking for her?"

"Where's 6?" Frank barks.

The proprietor points over his left shoulder with his thumb. I grab the key, then lean over the bamboo counter and stare directly into the weasel's reddened eyes. "Make that six code violations and one felony or misdemeanor, depending on how much marijuana you got stashed back there behind the curtain."

The weasel quivers.

"If anybody comes around looking for her, she was never here. Got it?"

The owner nods nervously as we push past him and head down the dark corridor, treading stained carpet that's sticky underfoot. When we find 6, we come to a halt and stand there listening for several minutes. There's no sound from inside. No TV, no flushing toilet, no running water, no movement. Nothing. But there is a smell. It's bleeding out from under the door. A dark fecal smell mixed with something worse. Something rotten.

Frank gives me the "ready" look, watches me unholster, then taps on the door.

"Charlie?"

Nothing. My hand tightens on the pistol grip.

"Charlie? It's Frank Conroy. San Diego PD. Stacey called us. I can't explain now, but we've got to get you out of here."

Nothing.

"Charlie? Can you hear me?"

Frank reaches under his jacket for his snub-nose, gives me a nod.

"We're coming in, Charlie. We're gonna come in real slow.

Don't do anything stupid now."

Frank inserts the key, turns it, pushes the door. The smell rolls out in a wave strong enough to make me step back.

"Charlie?" Frank says from behind his hand covering his mouth. And then he pushes the door back all the way.

Chapter 2

Thoroughbred
(*Four Months Earlier*)
Phoenix, AZ
February 7, 1996

I stood at the edge of a cliff overlooking the abandoned property and squinted through the dim light of dusk. Behind me towered a giant mesa cast in a blue hue from the setting sun. The engine of the old pickup truck we were using for this undercover operation grumbled off to my right.

It looked like the old farmhouse was abandoned, but would it be tomorrow afternoon when it mattered most? I'm not one to leave anything to chance, and would never walk into a UC deal without first studying the lay of the land. You never know when an observation might help if everything turns to shit: escape routes, dead-end roads, choke points, potential diversions. So I did what I always do before an undercover meet. I arrived early to do a little recon.

"What have you got?" Baird called from the pickup. Baird was my UC partner, assigned to me from the Phoenix FBI field office. He was monitoring the cell phone, waiting for a call from a couple of thieves named Evans and Sanders—a call confirming the deal was still on for tomorrow.

I reached for the binoculars hanging around my neck and pressed them to my face, panning over the valley below. There was no human activity, no cars, no sounds; nothing to suggest that this was anything other than a neutral meeting site selected by the crooks. The remoteness of this place made me uneasy and sorry now that I'd agreed to meet on their terms—never a good idea in undercover work.

"Nothing," I said, just loud enough for Baird to hear over the low rumble of the engine.

Baird grunted and leaned back into his repose.

A cool desert breeze traced down the mesa passing over the

back of my neck, bringing a chill to my spine. I scratched at my scruffy blonde beard I'd grown over the past several weeks to augment my cover. The ragged Wranglers I wore draped loosely over my scuffed Tony Lama boots. The white T-shirt covered with the day's dust and dirt completed my uniform; one that Evans and Sanders had grown accustomed to seeing me wear. Whatever it took to buy stolen horses in the middle of the desert.

Sanders and Evans, in one of their drunken stupors, had boasted of hijacking a tractor trailer loaded with five thoroughbred racehorses en route to Saratoga Springs in upstate New York. They bragged of beating the driver to death with a tire iron when he resisted, both getting a big chuckle out of it. As with every piece of information these two whack-jobs shared, we corroborated and confirmed their story. The good news was that the driver had survived the vicious beating—not so good news for Evans and Sanders. I wouldn't know a racehorse from a packhorse, but I did know how to bullshit these two morons and close the deal.

"You get anything yet, Baird?"

He answered by raising his left hand high out the passenger window, palm upturned. As I continued my recon over the valley below, I tried to envision how a cover team could get in place close enough to respond if everything went to hell. We weren't just dealing with petty thieves here. These guys were ruthless. Evans and Sanders were already suspects in a triple car bombing in the Phoenix area. Violent, senseless killings. And now add a poor truck driver and God knows how many other victims. This place was starting to give me the jitters.

Given that the property lay in a bowl of rocky terrain with only one road in and out, things could get dicey if they tried to rip me off. I would be carrying fifty grand of Uncle Sam's money for "show" to convince these guys to produce the stolen horses. When money and horses exchanged hands, we could take these idiots down.

Baird and I would have to make sure we were always in

sight of the cover teams deployed in the area and hope to hell the transmitter on my concealed microphone was powerful enough to reach them.

"Nick," Baird called.

I looked over to see my partner hanging out the window, gesturing excitedly at the cell phone. The call had come through. I jogged around to the driver's side of the truck and settled into the seat. "This is Quinn."

"Quinn?" An angry growl from a familiar voice. It hit me right away who the voice belonged to: Bob Klecko, my FBI supervisor in San Diego.

"That you, Klecko?"

"Where's Spence?"

"Klecko, it's me," I said incredulously. "Quinn's my UC name. You know that!"

Baird shook his head in disbelief.

"We're expecting a call from—"

"Listen, Spence," Klecko interrupted, "I need you back here right away."

"Come back there? What the hell for? We're about to—"

"Listen to me," Klecko said dismissively. "Your file review's overdue. You've done a good job of avoiding me on this case, and you were scheduled for a review last week. I want an update."

"What about the reports Johnson's been sending you?" I asked, referring to my contact agent in Phoenix, who's been faxing daily status reports to San Diego.

"I don't care about all that."

"Have you even been reading them?"

"Don't make me ask you again, Spence." And there was something there in Klecko's voice. Something I've heard many times before. The tone was threatening.

"But we got a deal set up for tomorrow! We'll lose—"

"Get back here immediately, Spence!" Klecko screamed. "That's a fucking order." He clicked the line dead before I could argue further.

Fuming, I looked over at my partner. "Klecko's ordered me back to San Diego."

Baird's eyes widened. "But the deal's tomorrow!"

I shrugged. "Fucking Klecko."

~~~~

The sign on the outer door to his office greeted me like a punch in the face. "Robert Klecko, Field Supervisor—Squad 4" in bold block letters, announcing to the world the importance of this egotistical prick. Here's a guy who never worked under-cover, only worked paper cases for a couple years in the field, and ass-kissed his way back to FBI Headquarters. In less than a year, this narcissistic phony was sent back out to the field as a supervisor. Pasty-faced and spindly with a pointed, pinched nose and perpetually pursed lips, Klecko has an Ichabod Crane look about him. His six foot frame carries only about 140 pounds, and his balding forehead is plastered with an oily swirl of hair that emanates from somewhere behind his right ear.

I pushed through the door, slamming it behind me.

"What's this all about, Klecko?"

"Spence, what the hell are you wearing? Look at yourself."

I looked down. I was in such a hurry to get back and get this ridiculous meeting over with that I didn't even bother to change before catching the last flight from Phoenix. "The buy's supposed to go down tomorrow. . . . Jesus, what could be so important?"

Klecko pressed his chin to his neck, his eyes wide. "When's the last time you shaved? You're still an FBI agent, Spence. Show a little respect for the job."

"You ordered me back here in the middle of an undercover operation just to tell me that?"

Klecko leaned back in his chair tenting his fingers and press-ing them to his lips. He gazed up at the ceiling as if pondering something deeply. Behind him, the late afternoon orange sunlight shimmered through his floor-to-ceiling windows, framing the cobalt blue waters of San Diego Bay.

"San Diego is the office of origin on Operation Cut Diamond," Klecko blurted. "It's our case. My case. So I'll ask you again, Spence . . ." He paused long enough to furrow his brow. "Why haven't I been kept in the loop?"

"What the hell are you talking about?" I said, feeling my face boil to red. "The reports Johnson's been fax—"

"You can't glean anything from those," Klecko interrupted. "I need hands-on control over these cases, Spence. You know that. I'm your supervisor, and as I said, we're the office of origin on this undercover op. Seems to me you've been avoiding direct contact with me since the case began."

Avoiding? My hands began to clench involuntarily to fists.

"Listen," Klecko said, as he leaned forward and placed both hands flat on his tidy desk. "I want you to move this deal to San Diego. I want the buy to go down here."

"How the hell do you expect me to do that?"

"Simple. You call the bad guys over in Phoenix and tell them there's been a change of plans."

I took a couple of steps forward, not stopping until I felt my thighs pressed to Klecko's desk. My supervisor leaned as far back in his chair as he could without tipping backward into the glass behind.

"You're crazy," I said furiously. "You just don't get it, do you, Klecko? You don't understand what it takes to do these undercover investigations."

"Now, Spence, remember who—"

"These guys are dangerous. They murdered people. They're unpredictable and suspicious of everything we do. Haven't you read any of the reports?"

"Spence, goddamnit!" Klecko barked, his own face reddening. "I don't give a shit who they are. When I order you to do something, I expect you to do it. You have a history of this kind of crap and I've had it with your insubordination."

I felt ready to explode inside. "Let me get this straight, Klecko," I said through clenched teeth. "Even though I'm standing here telling you how dangerous such a move would be to me and Baird and the rest of the team over there in Phoenix, you're still ordering me to make the call?"

Klecko nodded, his jowls wobbling. "That's right, Spence. Your days of running around making cases for the Phoenix Division are over. This is our operation and we're not sharing the stats with other offices."

"So that's it?" I shouted. "The stats? You don't think about anything but your own goddamned career."

Klecko sighed, shaking his head. "I guess you'll just have to trust my judgment, Spence. Now make this hap—"

"What judgment? Jesus, who cares about statistics, for chrissakes? We're all part of the same outfit."

Klecko looked suddenly dumbfounded. "You heard me. Move the deal. Now."

"Fuck you, Klecko. I quit."

"What do you mean you quit? You can't do that! I'll have you fired before you quit."

I smirked, letting my anger smolder. "Undercover work is voluntary. You should at least know that. I un-volunteer. I'm removing myself from the investigation."

"Then I'll have you fired for insubordination."

Standing there, watching the pasty bureaucrat mince around like some potentate, something snapped in me. I grabbed the closest thing I could get my hands on—a heavy file from the top of the stack on Klecko's desk—and fired it at my supervisor's face. "You can take this case and shove it up your ass, you stupid son of a bitch."

Klecko cowered away, both hands flailed in the direction of the flung binder. He knocked it to the floor and then stood up straight, his eyes wide, his face glowing with anger. He charged toward me. I grabbed him by the collar, bunching up his skinny black tie, my rage so intense I vaguely heard a scream from over my shoulder—a woman's scream. And before I realized that it was the squad secretary, who'd called for help, I was being pulled away by what felt like a dozen strong and unyielding hands.

"You dumb bastard!" I yelled, as I struggled against the agents trying to wrench my arms and wrists. At six-foot-three and 220 pounds, I'm big enough and strong enough to manage one last hook toward my supervisor. "You threaten me like that again, I'll throw your wimpy ass out that fucking window!"

"That's it, Spence!" Klecko howled. He seemed to be putting up far less of a fight, given that it took only one man to hold him back—one man to my three. "You're finished. Your FBI career is over!"

For a full minute, I continued to struggle, the fury overtaking me. But after a time, I felt myself cool, more out of exhaustion than any kind of resignation. Klecko attempted to gather himself and straightened his tie. The ruffled supervisor took short, raspy gasps as he made his way around his desk and returned to his seat, his vengeful eyes never tearing from me. I turned and pushed my way out of the room. My anger was immediately replaced with intense regret—not so much at what I'd just done, but at what I would now have to do—call Baird and tell him the deal was off. I'd be letting everyone down who worked long, tireless hours on Operation Cut Diamond.

Standing on the street outside the federal building, I took a deep breath of city air and exhaled with a gnawing sense of anxiety growing inside of me. I knew I had crossed the line with Klecko. Physical confrontation with a supervisor was an intolerable offense within the ranks of the FBI, and it wouldn't be long before the goons from the OPR would be paying a visit from FBIHQ. The headhunters from the Office of Professional Responsibility in Washington may not be as lenient with me as in the past.

Chapter 3

The Junkie Shell
San Diego, CA
June 22, 1996

The first thing that happens is I put my foot in something I don't even want to look at. The tattered, heavy curtains are all drawn and it's mostly dark, save for the muted light coming from the open door behind us. I quickly scan the room, picking up peripheral images: rotting food on the floor, cigarette butts, moldy pizza crusts, green shards of glass strewn about from broken bottles of Thunderbird wine. And there's someone on the bed, staked out like a renegade Apache in a Howard Hawks film, except that this guy is wearing Levis and heavy boots and instead of rawhide, his wrists and ankles are bound to the bedposts with electrical cords.

Frank walks over, looks down. "Jesus H. Christ, Charlie."

I yank back the drapes and push open a window.

For a moment, we both just stand there staring.

This can't be him. Hours and hours of surveillance flash through my mind depicting the hundreds of photographs and videos I've taken of the ruthless enforcer for the Hells Angels. A foreboding visage you would not soon forget: his strong jaw set upon a square dimpled chin; deep-set, dark penetrating eyes; jet-black hair pulled tightly back into a ponytail; prison-built muscles forming a V-shaped wedge in his upper torso; and those Herculean biceps. But this guy, the guy strapped to the bed, is something else altogether. The transformation is startling. He's gray—corpse-like gray—and he holds a gaunt, ghostly expression under his crown of matted, greasy, shoulder-length hair. His exposed and emaciated upper torso is covered with jagged scars and open cuts and marked here and there with tattoos, including the skeletal, hollow-eyed Hells Angels death head. Raw needle tracks run down the inside of his flaccid left arm.

I step over all the crap on the floor, which I can now see is crawling with cockroaches, and join Frank at the bed. It's a quiet, almost solemn moment. Standing over him in the rotten stench of the darkened motel room looking down at his drug-ravaged body tethered to the bed, it's hard to believe this was the once feared and vicious enforcer for the Hells Angels. His milky eyes are barely open, yet they are still able to convey the fury and hatred that has consumed him for most of his life. He opens his mouth as if to speak, and the stench billows out like a fog followed by something that makes my skin crawl: A cockroach scurries over his teeth and past his lips, darting down his chin and neck and out of sight between the mattress and headboard.

I have to clear my throat to speak. I'd been expecting a caged monster lying in wait, not this monstrous heap of humanity lying on the bed. This former badass hardly looks human. And the *smell*.

"We should call an ambulance." I say.

Frank's found a plastic cup by now and is trying to get a little water into him. He pours it slowly at the crease of Charlie's cracked and vomit encrusted lips, most of it spilling down his chin. "Who did this to you, Charlie?" he asks, sounding genuinely sympathetic.

Charlie tries to talk but can't. Frank gives him more water.

"Sta-cey," he manages after a couple of swallows, the name rolling out as something between a croak and a whisper.

"Your girlfriend tied you to the bed?"

"Scag, maan," Charlie groans. "Trying to ... *told* her to—"

"You kickin' the heroin cold turkey, Charlie? Is that it?"

Charlie manages a nod.

"Dead turkey, more like," Frank says. He stands and shakes his head. "You wouldn't have made it through the night, partner." He then shoots me a stiff glare, bending and busying himself with the knot binding Charlie's left wrist.

"She just *left* you here?" I ask.

"Told her to . . ." Charlie's eyes roll back in his head. He gasps for air, his jaw slackening and tightening involuntarily. "To leave."

"What about the club?" Frank asks.

"Fuckers . . . don't give a shit," he wheezes.

A menacing gaze comes to Charlie's narrowing eyes—a dark, kindling focus.

"Fuck 'em, man. . . . *Fuck* . . . *them*," he mumbles. "S'fucked up, maaan."

Frank straightens up again, looking down at the man on the bed. "So is this where it ends, Charlie? This is how you die? In a shithole motel with bugs crawling up your ass?"

Again the dark stare.

Both Frank and I feel the sense of urgency here, and as we bend over to hoist Charlie up into a sitting position on the side of the bed, I have it in mind about how heavy he'll be. But now, as we are lugging him, arms over shoulders, I'm amazed a man this emaciated can be so heavy. And the stench of him is nauseating. But at the moment, I'm not worried about all that. Right now, foremost on my mind, is getting him the hell out of the motel before all of us get stomped or killed. I can't quite figure how we managed to outrun a motorcycle gang with a mind for vengeance and a head start, but I do know one thing —they can't be far behind.

As we get to the door, we're already pulling and dragging Charlie more than we're aiding him. He gives us a step or two here and there, a moment of feeble support, but apart from that it's a wonder we're not tearing his bony arms out of their sockets. I make a move to grab the doorknob, but Frank pulls up to stop me. I see him grab his revolver, motioning for me to do the same.

"Remind me again why we're doing this?" I say, trying not to chuck my breakfast at the stench of Charlie.

"Just stay alert, Nick," Frank says. "We're doing the right thing here. Trust me."

My better judgment says otherwise, but with a junkie

in one hand and a gun in the other, I've got little else I can do. I imagine a huddle of Hells Angels waiting quietly outside ready to finish their business. I know that if they're out there, they'll react immediately. Their modus operandi is to strike first and strike hard. These guys don't concern themselves with collateral damage and sure as hell don't give a shit if a couple of cops stand in the way. I prepare for the option of dropping Charlie and defending myself if the need arises. I nod at Frank and we stumble out into the corridor. It's empty. I breathe a little easier. A little.

It's crazy how comparatively fresh the air smells in this otherwise dank hallway. Without the scrum of roaches crawling around, the drab and sticky carpet out here looks almost clean enough to dine on. We hobble with our human cargo down the expanse of shitty lighting and floral wallpaper, and I'm watching as best I can out the dirt-smudged windows we pass intermittently. My gun hand is sweaty.

My ears strain to listen for signs of danger outside. Raspy voices barking and raging. The harsh rumble of a bike at full throttle. But there's nothing. At least for now.

We make for the back of the motel to avoid the lobby and struggle to wedge Charlie through a small service door that empties out into the parking lot. The fresh air and hot sun feel cleansing as we reach the Crown Vic. Frank struggles to get the keys from the pocket of his tweed coat and passes them to me. I shift all of Charlie's weight onto him and run around to the driver's side. As I reach the door, I hear Charlie's shaky voice.

"What the . . . ," he groans. "What the fuck's goin' on, man?"

"We're getting you out of here, Charlie," Frank grunts, as he wrestles with the excess baggage on his shoulders. "We're saving your ass is what's going on."

I struggle to work the lock with the key. Then I hear it. The unmistakable, thunderous howl of Harleys on the freeway overhead. We've officially run out of time. I try the lock once more, but nothing's happening. The roar grows louder. They're close now.

"You have to jiggle it!" Frank yells.

I do as he says and the lock pops open like butter. I drop down into the driver's seat, leaning over to free the lock on the backseat passenger side. Frank opens the door, and before I can even get the engine started he's working to get Charlie shoved into the backseat. "Goddamnit, Charlie," he grumbles.

At that moment, we both hear the metallic roar of the Harleys throttling down on the exit ramp coming toward us. I glance back to see that Frank's struggling.

"Goddamnit, Nick!" He barks. "Gimme a hand."

I clamber out and open the rear door on the driver's side. Frank pushes Charlie while I pull. The approaching mayhem rings in my ear. Finally, Frank gets Charlie laid prone on the seat to the point where I can tug him through on his stomach. Feeling himself manhandled, he starts to panic; tries to sit up. We push him back down and finally stretch him out.

"Keep your fucking head down, Charlie!" Frank wails.

We both slam the doors behind us and scramble into the front seat. I throw the Vic into drive and punch the accelerator. We roar down the frontage road and I check the rearview mirror. Four or five bikers make the turn onto the road behind us and pull over in front of the Gold Coast Motel. As I steer the Crown Vic onto the westbound freeway ramp, I lose sight of them.

"Jesus, Frank," I gush, a little winded. "We did it." As soon as I say it, I'm wondering what in the hell we just did.

Chapter 4

The Case Explodes
San Diego, CA
June 22, 1996

As we roll back on Interstate 8 westbound toward the coast, I check my mirrors again and it looks like we're clear. No tail. I feel like we just stole the crown jewels, for chrissakes. I slow the Vic down and continue to snake my way through the shifty river of Southern California traffic.

My partner leans back with an eye on his side mirror. He lights up a smoke. "Well, Nick," he says, "he's ours for now—for better or worse."

"Yeah, well, what do we do for an encore, Frank?" I ask. "I mean, the whole damn HA chapter's after him. We can't just turn him loose."

Frank takes the cigarette from his lips and suspends it out the window, letting it settle just behind the side mirror—ashes blowing back all over his tweed coat.

"I was telling you about the briefcase incident," he says calmly. "Back when Stacey called."

"Yeah, Frank," I say, readying my self for another one of his long monologues.

Frank goes still for a second. Then he gives a tight little nod. "Right," he says. He takes off his glasses and rubs his eyes. He looks over at me in that wistful way he does when he's deep in thought. "So Charlie's got a cane gun. Thirty-two caliber. Loaded. In plain sight on the backseat. And he's also got rolls of cash stuffed in a grocery bag on the front seat, and this briefcase on the floor in the back," he says, adjusting his glasses back in place.

"When you pulled him over . . ."

He tugs at his mustache. Takes a quick final drag of his smoke. "And I'm thinking he's got more cash, right? I mean, you know, Charlie the drug kingpin. He's over in Ocean Beach driving a brand new, bright red Cadillac convertible. Kinda got my attention—a Hells Angel driving a new Cadillac. But this briefcase is real heavy and I mean it could've been guns, pipe bombs . . ." He kills his cigarette in the overflowing ashtray. "We'd already had the Hells Angels' bombing at that funeral parlor in Lemon Grove and I don't really *know* Charlie at this point, so . . ." He falls silent, staring out his window.

"So what did you do?"

"Ex-felon in possession—loaded firearm. I hook him up, impound his shiny new Cadillac, seize his money, the gun, the briefcase, and take him over to the PD sub-station in Pacific Beach for questioning."

"He's gotta be pretty pissed, huh?"

"It gets better," Frank says with a little smirk. "There's this guy from the bomb squad who happens to be there at the sub-station. Ramirez. He says a little C-4's gonna pop this thing right open—says we can have a little controlled explosion out back in the parking lot."

"Jesus, Frank, why not just x-ray it?"

"Well, what it was . . . I mean . . . I really just wanted to open the briefcase and Charlie's sitting there with his arms crossed like 'fuck you, get a warrant.' And so I tell him, 'No warrant, Charlie. I'm *opening* the briefcase.'"

"It's a standoff."

"A standoff, right, and—"

"So . . . what? You're just gonna blow the briefcase without a warrant?"

"I really didn't give a shit about filing any charges at this point, Spence," he says. "It was more like I wanted to let him know he couldn't fuck with me or hide behind any high-priced attorney, or the law, or any bullshit like that. I was sending him a message. I wanted him to know I *could* fuck with his stuff if I wanted and I *could* lock him up if I wanted and—"

"On the cane gun . . ."

Frank nods vigorously. "But that wasn't the point, Spence. The point was . . ."

Frank drifts a little, apparently trying to recall the point. I nudge the rearview mirror downward and take a look at our cargo. He's breathing shallow, but he's still breathing. The reality of what we've just done is really starting to settle in. We have an officer of the Hells Angels in the backseat and I have no idea what we're going to do with him, much less how he's going to react when he comes out of his stupor.

"A screwdriver, Frank," I say, snapping out of it. "A knife —to pry it open."

"Spence," Frank says, casting me a sardonic look, "if the damn thing's loaded with pipe bombs, I'm not jiggling at the lock."

I hit the brake pedal as a sudden flood of red lights appears in front of us and traffic slows to a crawl.

"So Ramirez takes the briefcase to the empty parking lot in the back of the sub-station and he puts a little C-4 on the lock—just a little. 'Pop it right open,' he says. And so we crouch down behind a Dumpster and Ramirez flips a switch and . . ." Frank flashes a wide grin. "KABOOM!"

He's laughing so hard, it's a few seconds before he can go on.

"The damn briefcase goes up about three hundred feet in the air. So now . . . so now it's raining quarters, and guys are running out of the station like what the fuck and—"

"Quarters? You mean like silver? Money?"

"Yeah, quarters." Frank shakes his head wistfully. "So I walk back into the interview room with what's left of the briefcase, which by now is this smoking chunk of Naugahyde, and I toss it on the desk in front of Charlie. And I say, 'Now I wanna look in your car.'"

"So, what'd he say?"

"He gives me that death stare of his and pushes the car keys across the table. He says, 'Fuck it, man. Go right ahead, asshole.'"

A guttural noise from the backseat interrupts my partner. He turns to get a look. In the rearview, I see our cargo's woken up, and he's working himself up into a half-sitting position. I can see the sweat beading on his gray face.

"When did you last score, Charlie?" I ask through the rearview mirror.

He stares at me blankly through the mirror for a long while, as if he's only just now registering my presence, unaware that I just helped drag him out of his personal hell.

"I said when did you last score, Charlie? Three days? A week?"

"Who the fuck . . . are you?"

"Spence," I say. "Name's Spence."

Charlie's eyes come into focus. Dangerous eyes.

"Spence's my new partner," Frank says over his shoulder.

Charlie keeps his dark eyes on me. "Ain't no fuckin' cop," he says.

"That's right, Charlie," Frank says. "Spence's with the Bureau." He flashes me a wry grin. My last glance at Charlie shows him growing very still as the information and whatever it represents for him sinks in.

"Fuckin' FBI . . .," he says in disgust.

Chapter 5

La Paloma
San Diego, CA
June 22, 1996

In my fifteen years in the FBI now, I've never seen anything like the current state of Charlie Slade. The last couple of hours have flashed by in a blur, and as we pull into the parking lot of the motel, I have to keep asking myself what we've gotten ourselves into.

For now, it's budgetary considerations that bring us to La Paloma Inn. Or to put it another way, it sure isn't the scenery. Reality is, this place shares many of the lesser qualities of the shithole we just pulled Charlie from. But at least it's a shithole we know. Having been in Charlie's company for a couple hours now, I reek. But despite all that, the night clerk takes my cash like always, and looks grateful to have my business. No questions.

Given the circumstances, it's all good at La Paloma, apart from a couple of downsides, like the motel's location under the interchange of two of San Diego's busiest freeways, and the steady rain of particulate solids, which discourages use of the not-so-scenic balconies. More important, it's the kind of place where the clientele go out of their way to be un-friendly and unnoticed.

I've taken two rooms side by side, as far away from the motel lobby and the eyes of the managers as possible. We haul Charlie up to the second floor, and as far as we know we've done all of this unobserved.

The first thing we do once we've gotten him into the room is get him cleaned up. There's nothing straightforward about this. For one thing, Charlie, in his confused state, is re-luctant to give up his boots or his jeans. So we abandon the idea of trying to get him undressed and back him into the shower the way he is, boots and all. As soon as I turn on the shower, he slides down the wall and sits there bundled up in the stall, shivering.

We still haven't been able to find out how long it's been since his last fix . . . or even if he's got anything else in his system that we need to know about. As far as we can tell, his plan was to go cold turkey, strapped to a bed.

"Methadone," Frank says after a couple minutes of watching Charlie shiver in the stream of warm water.

"And clean clothes," I counter.

"You doing okay in there, Charlie?"

He doesn't even look up. He just sits there, clinging to his knees.

"What're we gonna feed him?" I ask.

"Whatever he can keep down. Soup. Fluids."

Right on cue, Charlie throws up. It's a thin, spewy gruel that's immediately washed away by the shower. I'm amazed there's anything in his stomach left for him to puke.

"It's gonna be a long night," I say.

~~~~

Someone has to stay with Charlie, and since Frank's the one who knows him, I get the job of going to buy clothes and food. When I get back to the room, toting a Kmart bag containing a couple pairs of jeans, a plaid shirt, and as many cans of Campbell soup as I can carry, I find he and Frank in what appears to be a pretty one-sided conversation. Charlie's now wrapped up in sheets on the bed, nodding at the soft-spoken wisdom Frank's pouring into his ear.

They break off talking when they see me. Frank tells me Charlie's managing to keep down water and probably needs to eat something.

I warm up a little soup on the one-burner stove cramped into the corner of our small efficiency room. "Hope you like chicken noodle, Charlie."

Whether he does or not, he doesn't say. It seems like the

best he can do is cling to his knees and try to shut down his shivering. He gives me another one of his killer stares when I come over to the bed and offer to feed him some soup.

"Give me the spoon, man," he mumbles.

"Your hands are shaking, Charlie . . ."

"Give me the fuckin' spoon."

I let him take it from me, then watch him spill it over the sheets.

"Here," Frank says, ducking in and taking the spoon from Charlie's shaking fingers. "It's all good, Charlie. You did the hard part. You beat this thing in your head. Now all you have to do is get your body back on an even keel."

Charlie lets Frank feed him, swallows the soup like a baby, then wraps himself tighter in the sheets. And whether it's flat-out exhaustion or the psychological effect of knowing he's getting help, he starts to calm down, and within the hour he's out cold, breathing deeply.

~~~~

It's midnight, and for the first time I look around at the raunchy surroundings. The stained and ripped carpeting is a pea green color with some kind of reddish floral design barely visible beneath the dirt and grime. The furniture is upholstered in red plastic or vinyl, and strips of lamination are missing from the dresser and overhanging mirror. Cigarette burn marks line the edges of both bedside stands, and the dark and heavy draperies are identical to those at the Gold Coast Motel, emitting the same musty, moldy odor. Frank and I are each straddling dinette chairs backward while peering through the bathroom door as Charlie purges dinner. Frank's smoking and I'm sitting with arms slung over the backrest of the chair, trying not to puke from the reek emanating from our guest.

We both pull back and close the door for a little relief from the stench. I'm thinking about what I know about Charlie Slade. The sergeant-at-arms of the Hells Angels. In club hierarchy, this means that he's the chief enforcer, a role generally reserved for the guy with the most talent for scaring the shit out of people—a talent Charlie has in spades. The enforcer's job is manifold: provide security for the club's weekly meetings, throw down the gauntlet with rival gang members who threaten and challenge HA turf, and in general, intimidate or stomp the living shit out of anybody who disrespects the Hells Angels, a brother, or someone who messes with club business. And now here's this bad-ass sharing our bathroom, enjoying one of the many symptoms of heroin withdrawal and incapable of even standing on his own two feet.

"We got ourselves one hell of a prize here, Frank."

Frank cracks the door and glances in at Charlie, who's bent over the toilet bowl.

"I know what you're thinking, Nick, but under the circumstances all we can do right now is try and help the guy."

Frank puts out his smoke in the ashy soda can by his feet and then massages his red eyes.

"Point is, Spence, we don't have a lot of choices right now. I mean the guy just got dumped in our laps," he says, pausing. "Besides, Charlie's perfect."

"Mind explaining that, Frank?"

"Well, for starters, he's vulnerable. No Hells Angel I know is more fiercely loyal than Charlie Slade. It's family to him. He's strung out on junk and he's useless to them. More important, he's a liability. *But*, and this is a *big* but, he's also their money train. He's valuable to them. The guy has the golden touch. Hell, his drug operation brings in more money for the club than all the rest of the members combined."

"You think you can flip him," I say, getting straight to the point. "I just don't see it, Frank."

"Hear me out, partner." Frank slows down. He opens his hands and sets them on his knees, palms up. "Greed drives these guys, Nick. We've talked about this before. It's not like it used to be. This brotherhood thing is breaking down. In the old days, these guys would die for each other. It's not like that anymore. They're blinded by the greed. Besides, you heard him back there strapped to the bed when I asked him about the club. What'd he say . . . ? 'Those guys don't give a shit'—something like that. 'Fuck 'em,' he said."

"What about the money? Stealing from the club?"

Frank cracks the bathroom door open again and peaks into the bathroom at Charlie, who's slouched against the wall next to the toilet bowl. "We'll have to see how that plays out, Nick," he says. "Like I told you, I just can't see Charlie stealing from the club."

"Well, one thing's certain, they want him for something, the way they ripped his old lady." The bathroom's gone silent. For now at least, Charlie's done retching. I stand and Frank does the same.

"Frank, I know you got a feel for this guy and I trust your instincts, but I'm not sure everyone would agree with your assessment. We're looking at a long-term recovery to even get him where he *might* be useful to us, and we've got no assurance he's going to see things our way except for your hunches. I don't have to tell you, the Bureau is going to want a bang for their buck, and they're not gonna be *that* patient."

Frank walks out on the tiny balcony and lights up a fresh cigarette. He blows a lung full up toward the clamorous, congested freeways that seem close enough to reach out and touch.

"All I'm asking is for you to just stick with me on this and let it play out," Frank sighs.

"Look, Frank, even if I weren't in the shithouse with the Bureau, you know I'd stick with you. Reality is, I don't have a lot of choice right now . . . remember? I'm all yours until they put the rope around my neck."

Klecko, as expected, filed his complaint, and I'm instructed to have no contact with him. I've been temporarily assigned to the FBI's Squad 7, the Organized Crime Drug Enforcement Task Force. OCDETF. When Frank found out about my latest run-in with Bureau authority, he asked for me to work with him. The Bureau was more than happy to oblige just to get me the hell away from the office.

"I may have crossed the line on this one, Frank. Klecko's out to see me twist in the wind."

Charlie suddenly lets out a low groan and falls back hard against the bathroom wall. We pick him up and stumble toward the bed, lay him down on his side so he doesn't choke on his own puke, and cover him with a blanket. He's shivering uncontrollably, but within a couple of minutes he falls into a deep sleep, breathing heavily.

Sitting quietly in the darkened emptiness of this rancid motel room engulfed in the sweet smell of vomit, I wonder what's to become of him. Which way will he turn? Seemingly abandoned and betrayed by the brotherhood he has so fiercely protected, is this guy going to be pissed off enough when he comes to his senses to betray his betrayers?

~~~~

It's three o'clock in the morning by this time, and Frank and I are stumbling around, exhausted. I tell Frank to get some sleep, and he just grabs a pillow and lies down on the floor next to the bed.

"I meant in the other room, Frank."

"You go. You need it more than me. You look like shit."

I nod. He's right. Not an arguable issue.

"I'll call you in the morning," he says.

I stand there for a minute, looking at him down there on the floor.

"What?"

"What about Stacey?" I whisper.

Frank turns over on his side and bunches the pillow up under his head. "I've got some of our people looking for her. She'll be all right."

"No, I mean, what do we tell him when he asks about her?"

Frank turns back, staring up at me out of the gloom. He

doesn't answer. Maybe there *is* no answer. If we lie about Stacey, we'll break Charlie's trust before we even have a chance to start building it. But if we tell the truth . . .

"He'd go after them all, wouldn't he, Frank?" I ask.

"Nick," Frank says, "what do you think?"

I nod, too tired to ask just exactly what the hell that means as I glance over toward Charlie and the mound of blankets rising and falling in loose rhythm on the bed. It's hard to imagine *anybody* who knows Charlie. Not the *real* Charlie, anyway.

Chapter 6

The Clinic
San Diego, CA
June 24, 1996

Charlie slept a total of three hours that first night. Between us, Frank and I got about the same, as we struggled to get fluids into him, cleaned him up every time he vomited, and generally babysat him.

In the late afternoon of Day Three, we drive him to a methadone clinic a couple of miles from the motel. Charlie's a sorry sight, jammed down in the backseat of the car in his Kmart clothes, still shivering from time to time, and looking like a guy with a lot of bad things on his mind. But there are no roaches coming out of his mouth, and he doesn't stink anymore. I turn toward the backseat.

"Charlie?"

He looks up at me out of the gloom.

"You're going to have to walk in there under your own steam. You understand?"

If he does, he doesn't say so, just staring at me with the mute intensity of a cornered animal.

"I'm giving you some cash, and you're going to walk in there and sign up for treatment."

Frank half turns in his seat.

"They're gonna ask you a lot of questions, Charlie. They're gonna want you to fill in a lot of forms, pee in a cup. Think you can handle it?"

Charlie nods, and I reach over and push the money into his hand, then stretch further and open the back door. But he's too weak to get up. Frank jumps out and looks up and down the street. It's early morning and we're parked about a block from the front door of the clinic. Midway Drive is pretty slow this time of morning. The district that surrounds the clinic is a hodgepodge of commerce that obviously avoided the scrutiny of zoning regulators—a mixture of high-density residential apartments thrown in with tire shops, taco stands, strip joints, and warehouses tagged with artless graffiti.

The clinic is brick but otherwise fairly nondescript. The only way to know it's a methadone clinic at all is to know it already. It's a former warehouse turned house of desperate hope for scores of San Diego's ghostly men and women. The only entry lies down a long, narrow path of broken concrete strewn with cigarette butts and through a small wooden door at the back of the building. This provides cover for the people who might enter here, which, of course, in addition to the convenient location, makes it perfect for us. Charlie needs methadone, and he needs to get it as discretely and quickly as possible.

But the building itself is about where the discretion ends, given that Charlie still needs help to stand. Even with Frank pulling, it takes Charlie a while to get up on his feet. He props him upright outside the car and then jumps back into the passenger seat.

For what seems like a full minute, Charlie just stands there on the sidewalk with the bills in his hand, thinking I guess about what the hell he's doing here and what the hell he's getting himself into.

"Come on, Charlie," Frank says, willing him to take that first step.

Charlie doesn't move. A city bus roars past, heaving up a cloud of dust and exhaust. Charlie starts walking as if the backdraft is pushing him, taking it slow, head down, feet shuffling, the money still fluttering in his hand.

"Way to go, Charlie," Frank says softly, dragging at his mustache. "Way to go."

Chapter 7

Making Tracks
San Diego, CA
June 28, 1996

"It's fuckin' bullshit is what it is," Charlie says, propping a foot up on the edge of the tub so I can check between his toes for fresh needle marks.

"You think I like doing it?" I say, glaring up at him.

For a second, it looks like he's going to come back with some wisecrack, but I guess he thinks better of it.

I stand and hand him a towel. "Just procedure, man."

"Proceeedure . . ." He rolls his head back, exasperated.

"Gotta be sure you're clean, Charlie," I say. "Had a guy once who shot up in the john at the methadone clinic just before he got his dose—thought he'd get a double whammy. Guess he didn't know the methadone would kill any kind of high he'd get with heroin."

Covering his naked body with the towel, he offers me another of his sinister stares, shaking his head, hopefully contemplating what I just said.

We're four days into the treatment. We've got him into a "pay as you go" methadone program, which is pretty much all we can get for him right now. He needs the treatment desperately. It's risky taking him there, but until the Bureau comes through and approves our request for funds to take him to a private doctor, we have to continue sneaking him over to the clinic. To keep his slot, he's got to clean his sorry self up every morning, put a part in his hair, then piss in a cup when he gets to the clinic. Needless to say, he loves every aspect of this process, but not nearly as much as he loves me or Frank checking him over inch by naked inch when we get him back to the motel. Full body search. Procedure.

"Anyway, you're clean," I offer, as he turns and shuffles out of the bathroom.

I stand to wash my hands free of Charlie, then spend a little time in front of the bathroom mirror. I look like hell. Guys we've seen walking out of the clinic look better than I do. My blue eyes are swollen and sunken. I haven't shaved since we hauled Charlie into this dump, and my blond hair is oily and uncombed. I'm weak and drained and I feel like shit.

The combination of no sleep, trying to keep Charlie occupied, hours and hours of idle talk and debriefings, preparing daily logs, expense vouchers, and dictating reports have really taken a toll on me. We're almost a week into this and these are the longest days of my life—a roller coaster of emotional outbursts: anger, frustration, rebellion, reflection, and even occasional laughter . . . and very little sleep.

"I wanna go swimmin'," Charlie yells from the other room.

It's only the tenth time he's said this, and it's starting to get on my nerves.

"Like a spoiled brat," I mutter under my breath.

You'd think he'd give up the fight by now, as many times as we've told him no. Problem is, a corner of the pool is visible from our window, and Charlie spends a good part of his day peeking out through the blinds.

Frank sighs, comes alongside, and looks at his bloodshot eyes in the bathroom mirror. He's a shell of himself, too; it's almost as if the strength Charlie's regaining is being sucked straight out of us. "Ten minutes in the water," he says under his breath. "Probably set him up for the day."

By this Frank means to set Charlie up for three to four more hours of debriefing, which is what we're averaging now that he's lucid. The debrief sessions are all time and date logged and marked as evidence, as per Bureau protocol. Everything Charlie says is going into a couple of cassette recorders that Frank and I line up on the little vanity table by Charlie's bed, which is where he does his talking.

"The pool is visible from the street," I say. "Christ, it's visible from the *freeway*. What if someone sees him or someone here in the motel knows him?"

Frank pulls up an eyelid, revealing a tangle of inflamed capillaries. "We gotta ease off on the leash, Nick. Ease off or lose him."

He's right about this, of course. There's nothing to keep Charlie in this dump with us beyond the choices he makes for himself. He's free to walk anytime and he knows it. He doesn't seem in a big hurry to leave, which I find curious—if not suspicious—like he's testing us. Feeling us out. It's more like a cat and mouse game for him, and when he goes into one of his many mood swings and turns angry and hostile, we have to take a step back. He's still in withdrawal and edgy even with the help of the methadone. At least we've got him talking for now, and he doesn't seem to mind answering the questions we've asked of him.

"The fuck you guys doin' in there?"

Charlie's got this uncanny way of sneaking up on us. I look Frank in the eye, give him a nod.

"Okay," I whisper. "But you're the one goes in with him."

"Spence . . ."

"I'm not getting in that filthy cesspool."

Frank turns to Charlie. "Let's get through this next session, Charlie. We'll take a swim soon. I promise."

"Sure, Frank," Charlie sneers sarcastically. "But I'm taking a shower before we get started."

~~~~

Charlie's stretched out on the bed with a towel around his middle smoking a cigarette when I come back into the room. He looks relaxed enough, but his eyes have that steady pressure-cooker intensity as they follow me over to a chair. It's a look I'm getting to know real well.

"What about the reports?" he scoffs.

"What reports?"

"The reports you make me bring back from the clinic."

He's referring, of course, to the dosage reports and the receipts we ask him to bring whenever he's done with his treatments. We're giving him cash each time he goes into the clinic and it's Bureau money, and Bureau money needs to be accounted for. We've instructed him, if asked, to tell the clinic that his sister is paying for his treatment and that she wants the receipts to prove he was there. But so far, I've had to send him back twice to get the receipts and dosage reports, and Charlie's gone ape-shit each time. At first, I thought it was all about him not wanting to walk back into the clinic like a dumbass asking for a stupid piece of paper, but lately I've been formulating another theory.

"What about them?"

"I'm just saying, the thing with the receipts, I get it. But the reports . . . that's different. That's you checking up on me. That's you not trusting me."

And there it is, once again. Trust. It's a big thing for him and a common theme in many of our discussions.

"Charlie . . ."

"You think I'm lying to you, Spence?"

I can see in his eyes he's once again trying to pick a fight with me—thinks I should believe him when he says he paid and got treated. He's thinking "fuck the reports from the doctor." I guess it's humiliating to him. Like a school kid carrying a note home from a teacher.

"No," I say.

"Because if you're calling me a liar, man . . ."

"Charlie, I don't think you're a liar."

"What, then?"

As I stare him down, trying not to break contact with his unflinching glare, I know it isn't going to make any difference if I tell him that Bureau rules require a close accounting of all matters relating to an investigation. He doesn't want to hear it and really doesn't give a shit. But I tell him anyway. "Charlie, the medical records—they become part of the case file like everything else we do."

"Right," he says. "The case . . . the case. What the fuck *is* the case, man? I mean I been answering all your stupid questions about me and the club."

Frank comes out of the bathroom, and I know by the look on his face he's been listening. "You're helping us, Charlie," he says. "You're helping us understand the club."

Charlie thinks about this for a second, then kills his cigarette in a can of Coke. "I can tell you everything you need to know about the club in three minutes," he says. "About the drugs. About Duke. About the others. Where they get it. How they move it. How much they move. How Duke fronts the car business to cover his drug business. Everything."

"That's not how it works, Charlie."

Charlie sighs, folding his hands over his chest. "So how *does* it work?"

"We build a foundation for the case," Frank says.

"All you want to talk about is me. That's all we talk about. *Me.*"

"Because you're important, Charlie. If you're going to help us, it's important that we know about you. That we understand you."

"I still don't get it, Frank."

"You don't have to get it," I say impatiently, realizing immediately what I meant didn't come out right.

"You, either!" he shoots back, giving me that threatening, dark look. "I mean, you're fuckin' FBI, man. I don't even know what the fuck you're doing here."

"I'm here because—"

"Nick's here because he messed up," Frank interrupts.

It comes right out of the blue.

I guess the angry look on my face must be interesting because Charlie actually sits up on the bed. For a second he sits there, eyes cutting back and forth like he's waiting for the fight to start. I stare at Frank, who stares right back.

"Tell him about Phoenix, Nick."

I get to my feet and head for the bathroom. "Can I have a

word, Frank?"

"Sure," Frank says, but he stays right where he is. "Nick, tell Charlie about the Gecko and the jewel thieves."

"What the fuck's the Gecko?" Charlie asks.

"Klecko?" I say, keeping my eyes on Frank, trying to see where he's going with this. "My supervisor?"

"Ex-supervisor," Frank says with a snicker. And then, since I'm not offering anything, he starts right in, telling the whole sorry story of the robbery and burglary syndicate over in Phoenix, and how I never got to make the case. Charlie sits there, lapping it up. We're finally talking about something other than him.

When Frank gets to the part about racehorses, Charlie frowns. "Racehorses? I thought you said they were jewel thieves."

"Spence?" Frank turns to me.

"These were different crooks," I say. Frank waits for more, and I figure what the hell. I explain about the thoroughbreds—about the buy. About how we'd be in line to nail a couple of really bad guys for armed robbery and burglary—and, better yet, the murders.

Charlie lights up a fresh one, blows smoke at the ceiling. I watch his eyes go childlike-wide as I explain how Klecko botched the deal over a stupid file review. He twists on the bed when I tell him how I stormed the office. Just talking about it, I can feel the heat rising again in my face.

"That sucks, man." Charlie shakes his head in disgust, and it dawns on me that this is the first time he's expressed any kind of sympathy or real interest in what I have to say.

"So?" Frank says. "What happened then, Spence?"

Of course Frank knows exactly what happened then. I glare at him, searching for some sign of what the hell he thinks he's doing bringing this up in front of Charlie.

"I lost my cool," I say, trying to hide my anger.

"Spence . . ."

Charlie takes a hard pull on his cigarette. "What?" he

says. "Come on, man. What'd you do?"

"I told him he was a dumb son of a bitch—that he was over his head as an FBI supervisor."

Charlie chuffs. "Shit, man. Bet *that* didn't go over big."

"And you threw a file at him," Frank says.

"Yeah."

Frank holds his hands about a foot apart. "In his face. This big-ass, heavy binder."

The incident again flashes through my brain.

"And it hits him right in the face."

"What'd he do?" Charlie says.

I explain to him the confrontation. The yelling. The chest-bumping. The finger-jabbing. "Klecko starts screaming for help and half the squad comes running in to pull us apart."

Charlie's laughing, shaking his head.

"Nick threatened to throw him out the window," Frank adds.

"Fuck you, Frank. Not true." I give Frank my coldest stare.

Frank shrugs. "What I've been told."

"Well, it's not what happened."

Charlie's nodding, smiling his tight-lipped smile.

"I was out of line," I say.

"You fucked up," Charlie says, his dark eyes dancing.

"I fucked up."

"So they kicked you out for that?" Charlie asks, nodding, thoughtful. "They kicked your ass to the curb. Made you go work for Frank here."

Like it was some sort of punishment.

Chapter 8

Luscious Larry
San Diego, CA
June 28, 1996

"What was so important about that little show, Frank?" We're standing out on the little bookshelf of a balcony, watching sparse traffic zip by on the freeways above. It's some godawful hour in the a.m., and a rare opportunity to breathe something resembling fresh air. Behind us, Charlie's all twisted up in the sheets, sound asleep.

"I ever tell you about 'Luscious' Larry Cord, Spence?"

It's not clear to me that Frank's even heard my question, but I'm too tired to chase it. It's been a long day.

"First time I met Luscious Larry was at the parole office," Frank says. "I'm sitting there talking with Robby Ayala —you know, my friend there—and this guy comes in. Cord. He's like five-eleven, real muscular, a wide-bodied guy. Long, blond hair and these blue eyes like . . . like blue glass. He comes in for his first appointment, and Ayala, he doesn't even have a chance to start asking him any questions. This guy Cord just marches in and says, 'Ayala, I'm a blond-haired, blue-eyed, motherfucking devil and you'll never catch me doing a motherfucking thing. And if you come to my house and try to search it, you better bring the fuckin' SWAT team.' Then he stomps back out."

Frank shakes his head as if bewildered. "So Ayala turns to me and he says, real casual, 'So, Frank. How you think Larry's gonna do on parole'?" Frank looks wistfully up through the ozone, then takes a long pull on what has to be his fortieth cigarette of the day.

"So this is how Cord is," he continues. "This is a guy who lives to be a Hells Angel. Anyway, a few months later, I pull him over on his bike and he jerks out this little tape recorder. I say, what's with the recorder, Larry? And he says to me, 'Anytime a cop stops me, I'm recording him.'"

Frank chuckles to himself for a moment. "Now, right then, this young, buffed motor cop rolls up to cover me. He's heard me making the stop over the radio, and he walks up and he sees Cord recording me. He snatches the recorder out of his hand and throws it on the ground and stomps on it with his big, black motorcycle boots. And I'm like, whoa, okay . . . now the shit's gonna fly. But instead, Cord looks at his tape recorder just stomped to pieces on the ground and he busts out laughing. He says to the officer, 'That's fucking great, man. That's the kinda shit I'd do. You know what? Anytime you quit the cops, you come see me. You might make a good Hells Angel.'"

I blow air through my lips, exasperated. "What's your point, Frank?" I ask.

"Know what Pete Blair said to me when I asked if I could get you on our team?" he asks, lowering his voice. "Blair looks at me over his glasses. You know how he does." Frank demonstrates, in case I can't remember—his chin pressing to his neck and his irises dancing above the rim of his glasses. "He looks at me over his glasses and he says, 'Nick's in a little trouble right now.' You know how Blair talks, real serious, real low."

I can't help smiling. Frank's a good mimic, and his impersonation of my new supervisor is dead-on. He's a fair, reasonable, serious, and dedicated FBI agent intent on the mission of the FBI and not one to self-aggrandize . . . unlike Klecko.

Frank grins as he continues with his story. "'Well, what did he do?' I asked . . . and Blair tells me. 'Well, Spence threatened to throw a supervisor out the seventh-floor window.'" Frank chuckles again and then stops, suddenly serious. "And you know what I thought?" he asks.

I furrow my brow trying to make sense of his convoluted story. "That I'd make a good Hells Angel?"

Frank is still for a long time, staring at me over the burning end of his cigarette. "Exactly," he says softly.

I open my mouth to speak, but before I can even get a word in edgewise, he goes on.

"Spence," he says, "I need your help on this case. I need somebody with a strong backbone, somebody willing to stand up to these guys."

He lights a second cigarette from the first and flips the butt out into the darkness. I turn around and look at Frank's face in the moonlight. It's got to be after 2 a.m., but he's still fully functional. This is one of his many talents. He does not tire.

"Listen, Frank. I'll be upfront. I appreciate your confidence in me, but Charlie Slade is not as popular at the FBI as he is here on this tiny balcony. They're supporting this project with cautious optimism. I'm being constantly reminded that the Bureau's in charge of this investigation and will call the shots on how, or even *if*, we proceed with him as a potential cooperating witness. We're paying the bills. So, I have my marching orders. Federal rules of evidence. Move forward cautiously with tight command and control of the witness."

Frank turns away and walks back into the room and past Charlie, who's sleeping. He motions for me to follow him, and we go next door to the adjoining room. The place is in shambles: unmade beds, papers and reports strewn everywhere, and ashtrays overflowing with stale cigarette butts. No maid service for obvious security reasons, and it's becoming more depressing by the day. Frank pulls up a dinette chair and motions for me to sit down. He sits on the edge of the bed.

"We both want the same thing, Nick. We've got a great opportunity here, and you are the right guy for the job. That's all I was trying to tell you out on the balcony," he says, huffing as he yanks off one of his scruffy cowboy boots. He pauses for a moment, anticipating the ensuing struggle with the other boot. "I know you're under a lot of pressure. We'll just take it slow. Besides, we don't know how long we'll be able to hold onto sleeping beauty in there," he says, jutting a thumb over his shoulder.

"Agreed," I say as I move away from the newest foul odor in the room. "We'll keep it simple. If he decides to go to bat for us, we'll stick with hand-to-hand, controlled drug buys. "We'll keep it as basic as possible. No RICO. We'll target some fringe guys, get him used to working with us, do some team building, and then we'll hit the most violent gang members. Start small and build for quantity on every buy."

Frank rolls his head back, his eyes wide. "We'll gut 'em right under their own roof. We got the guy who can do it."

"We shall see, Frank. First, we're going to have to convince Charlie to wear a wire."

Frank leans in, lowering his voice. "Absolutely. We go for best evidence."

I think about this for a while. It all sounds good, but I still can't figure why Charlie is even talking to us, let alone why he might agree to wear a wire, risk his life, and go against the only family he's ever had. "You think he'll do it?" I ask.

Frank shrugs and blows out a stream of smoke. "I know a way to find out."

Chapter 9

Clubhouse
San Diego, CA
June 29, 1996

It's Thursday evening and Duke sits where he always does on Thursday evenings—on a tattered barstool set up in the corner of a dingy, smoke-choked room lit only by the red and white Budweiser lamp hanging low over the pool table. He waits impatiently for two members of the club who are more than late.

This is "church," a Hells Angels tradition. Weekly meetings. Attendance mandatory. And while Charlie, their wayward junkie of a sergeant-at-arms, hasn't made his presence known in more than five weeks, *nobody* skips church on Duke. Especially not Gonzo and Bull.

So Duke snorts hot air through his nose, reveling in the cigarette smoke encircling him. He sits at the head of the clubhouse for the San Diego chapter of the Hells Angels. The President. *His* clubhouse. *His* chapter. Beyond his pride and ego, there's the fact he also owns the building that now surrounds him and his gang. It's an old Chevy dealership on 35th and Adams in Normal Heights, shut down in the late '60s, only to be reopened by Duke Stricker, an audacious businessman with a keenness for cash operations and a penchant for keeping a high profile. When it isn't serving as his clubhouse, the building houses a limousine service, along with Duke's other pride and joy: a concert-promoting business that affords him the opportunity to rub elbows with rock stars and celebrities stupid enough to think that hanging with gangsters somehow makes them cool.

Celebrity Limo Service, the operation is called. It's an unusually prominent front for a Hells Angels clubhouse—most chapters tend to favor low-profile buildings in medium- to low-income neighborhoods—but it suits Duke's "see and be

seen" temperament perfectly. Inside, he can revel in his conspiratorial smoke and darkness, surrounded by stained furniture and hardass bikers. Outside, he graces the public with his
giant alter ego front as a legitimate businessman surrounded
by glittering signage, shiny limousines, and "celebrity" clientele.

"I'm tellin' you, Bad Eye," Duke says, his cigarette dancing between his lips, "I get more ass than a toilet seat with
these rock star groupies."

"I believe you, brother," Bad Eye says, chuckling. "You're
the man, Duke."

Duke nods pensively, his eyes surveying the room.
Everyone's arrived on time, save for Gonzo and Bull. Fucking *late* again. The president lifts his rather abundant ass off
the stool, putting a little distance between him and his vice
president. Tall and well-muscled, Duke has wavy brown hair
that's combed back in the James Dean pompadour style, a
break from the typically unkempt Hells Angels look. With
his neatly trimmed beard and deep-set, restless green eyes, he
looks more like a Vegas pit boss than the leader of an outlaw
motorcycle gang. As always, he wears his patch, a black-lea-
ther Hells Angels vest, a pair of jeans, and the requisite heavy,
black motorcycle boots.

"Fuck it, man," he says to no one in particular. "We better get started."

At that moment, the door swings open, and in walks
Jay "The Bull" Palac, followed closely by a wide-eyed Gonzo.
Gonzo, aka Brian Edwin Winters, is the club secretary. His
moniker was originally derived from his shady military service. A former Green Beret, Gonzo received a psychiatric and
dishonorable discharge following a tour in Vietnam for al-
legedly fragging his lieutenant's tent one night in Quang Tri
Province. It's a charge that was never proven, but that didn't
keep the shrinks from labeling him unfit for the uniform and
sending him packing.

He'd be insufferable and probably kicked to the curb

long ago if he didn't also happen to be the go-to member of the gang when it comes to all matters related to methamphetamine labs operating in the county. He might not be the most capable dealer—at least not nearly on the level of Charlie Slade—but he's a man with particular expertise on the supply side of the business.

"Jesus Christ, Gonz," Duke says. "Where the fuck you been?"

Gonzo shakes his head as Bull slinks into the corner, looking relieved to have not been called out. Bull's probably the man in the club who misses Charlie the most, given that the two of them had been best friends. And so it shouldn't surprise anyone that he's been a little unpredictable and edgy for the past several weeks.

Duke sighs and pinches the bridge of his nose. "Since we're already so fucking late, we'll skip the preliminary bullshit and just get to it," he says. "Gonzo's got a line on a lab in Jacumba. Rumor has it the Esposito brothers run it, right, Gonz?"

"The fuck is this . . . ?" Gonzo bellows, sounding furious.

"The fuck is what?" Duke replies.

Gonzo stands, his hands clenched into fists. "Fuck the lab right now, man. We still ain't found that rat fuckin' Charlie, and until we get our hands on him, we can't carve up his business. I want our money back. Finding that rotten fuckin' thief should be priority number one for everybody in this room."

Duke stares Gonzo down. Out of order and outspoken again about Charlie. Duke makes a mental note of Gonzo's outburst. "Sit down and shut the fuck up, Gonzo," Duke orders. Who's runnin' this outfit anyway?" As Gonzo slouches back in his chair and Duke regains control of the meeting, he turns to Bull, deciding to shift gears and address Charlie's absence. "Jay, anything at the morgue?"

Bull shrugs, looking almost relieved. "Nothin', Duke."

The president glares at Gonzo. "Okay, so we know Charlie ain't turned up wearing a toe tag."

Duke nods in the direction of his vice president, willing him to speak.

"Methadone clinics in El Cajon all say the same thing," Bad Eye offers. "They don't give no information on nobody gettin' the treatment."

Duke looks repulsed at this response. "Then I suggest you give them a little Hells Angels nudge, Bad Eye, for chrissakes. You forgettin' who we are? Duke's disappointed glare at his vice president is broken at the sound of a loud crash. He looks over to see that Scooter's fallen backward in his chair. Sammy "Scooter" Prevost stands wobbling drunk. The skinny, acne-scarred, toothless runt staggers forward a couple steps before regaining his balance. "Nothing at Sliver Stir . . . Silver Strer . . . Silver Stirrup, either," he stammers.

The Silver Stirrup. Charlie's favorite bar in Lakeside. As Scooter explains, no one's seen Charlie there in weeks.

Duke grins sarcastically, shifting back to Gonzo. "I guess since you brought it up, Gonz, you ain't found nothin' at Charlie's pad?" Gonzo's face has gone red and he's shaking. Normally, all the guy ever talks about at church is taking over drug labs, beating the shit out of everyone, and getting rich. Lately, he seems totally consumed with the business of finding Charlie.

Gonzo leans forward in his recliner. "I told you guys," he says, his eyes flashing from man to man in the room. "I been by his place a hundred times and the rat fucker ain't there. We're wastin' time lookin' for him there."

"Did you toss the place like I told you?" Duke asks.

Gonzo rises out of his chair, carefully eyeing Duke. "Yeah," he grunts. "Busted in a coupla nights ago. No sign of him. All I come up with is his bullwhip and these two guns." Gonzo holds up the bullwhip, a .38-caliber pistol, and a tiny .22-caliber derringer, then ceremoniously places them on the pool table.

Duke raises his eyebrows. "That *all* you found?"

Gonzo's head rolls back. He looks up at the ceiling as if

doing some heavy accounting in his head. "Yeah, man. Place is a shithole."

A few of the bikers who'd been to Charlie's pad rumble with the laughter of recognition.

"This ain't funny, man," Gonzo snarls. "That fuckin' thief is hidin' out somewhere with *our* money and you guys are laughin'?"

Duke snorts. "Bring me the whip, Gonzo."

The secretary does as he's told. Duke can feel the eyes of the gang on him as he fidgets with the whip. "What about his bike?" he asks.

"Out back with a tarp over it, man," Gonzo says. "Got barn disease—like it ain't been touched in weeks. Like the fucker's been beamed up by a goddamned spaceship."

A few in the club grumble.

Duke begins pulling at the frayed end of the whip. "Any cash?" he asks. He raises his eyes off the whip just long enough to assess Gonzo's reaction.

Gonzo seems intent to look at everything in the room but his leader. "Nah, man," he says.

Duke grasps the whip in both hands and glares at Gonzo. "Fucker *always* had cash," he says. "Whatever he had, we'll need to pay Silverman."

"I told you," Gonzo said. "Wasn't nothin' there."

Duke shakes his head and gets back to the whip. He's not sure if he buys Gonzo's story. It just doesn't seem likely that Charlie wouldn't have an emergency stash somewhere, considering all the cash he always carried, but he lets it die for now.

"All right then, Gonz," Duke says. "About Jacumba."

He watches as the club secretary goes rigid. And it's not like him. Not like Gonzo to do anything but jump at the opportunity to talk about scoring another lab. San Diego County has no shortage of meth labs. It's a target-rich environment, and no one knows this better than Gonzo, a man who's scouted the location of just about every meth lab from the Riverside

County line south to the Mexican border. He has all this information for good reason: He spends almost all his free time racing his chopper along the back roads, canyons, and desert highlands from Spring Valley through East San Diego County and the Mountain Empire—all the places where most of these clandestine labs are located. In his time running recon on labs, he's managed to construct an intelligence network that would put the CIA to shame.

But here he is now, looking pissed all over again at the change of subject.

"Gonzo," Duke says firmly, "I'm gonna have you run recon on the lab. You know the operation better than—"

"Fuck the Jacumba lab, man," Gonzo barks. "We gotta get Charlie, Duke, c'mon, man."

Duke's face turns fire red. He stands, the bullwhip falling to its full length by his side and snaking across the floor. He flexes his hand on the worn leather handle. "Look, man," he growls. "I'm orderin' you to get your ass out there and do the recon in Jacumba. We gotta take care of business. You got it?"

Gonzo falls back into the vinyl recliner behind him as if he just lost use of his legs.

"Jesus Christ, Gonzo," Duke says. "You'd think you got special interest in this shit." The president tweaks the handle of the bullwhip just enough to command the tip to fall atop Gonzo's heavy boots. He fires an unyielding glare toward his secretary. "I'll handle the Charlie matter. You handle the labs."

Then he turns a slow circle, addressing everyone in the group. "I want everyone to listen up. Long as we keep worryin' about Charlie, we're missin' opportunities. *Lucrative* opportunities. And I'll be goddamned if we're gonna let this Jacumba lab pass us by, Charlie or no Charlie. You said it yourself, Gonz. This lab's putting out excellent product. 'A gold mine,' you called it. So what we need is some recon." He opens his free hand to count out fingers. "Find out for sure who's operating it. Find out how much product they're puttin out. Find out about security."

When he's finished, Duke takes a seat on the edge of the pool table and sighs deeply. "We'll keep after Charlie and I promise you we'll find him."

"What about the cops?" Scooter blurts. He's sprawled out on throw pillows in the darkest corner of the room with his long, skinny legs splayed and his bony hands crossed over his chest.

"Word I hear was Charlie had a run-in with a coupla county mounties some weeks back. In Ramona. Was out of his mind, I guess. Drug rage. Punched a coupla the fuckers. The cops let him go's what I heard."

"He wasn't arrested?" Duke asks, dumfounded.

"Maybe he's workin' with the cops," Scooter mumbles.

The entire group seems to grow restless at the thought. The paranoia and blather reaches a crescendo as Duke grows more furious with every note. He lifts the handle of the whip up to his shoulder level and brings the thing cracking down. Everyone clams up.

"What the fuck's going on here?" he yells. "This still my club, ain't it?"

Nobody looks at their leader.

"Fuckin' Charlie Slade ain't workin' with no fuckin' cops. I known him longer than any of you."

"Then what about our money?" Gonzo asks.

"Jesus Christ," Duke says, slamming his hand down on the table beside him. "For the last time, I told you I'll handle it. Someone stole four hundred K from our safe and I'll . . ."

"It was *Charlie* stole the four hundred K," Gonzo shouts.

"Whatever the fuck," Duke says. "We'll keep up the search. We'll find his sorry ass."

Duke fumes. He throws his head back and blasts hot air through his nostrils. "We do as I say," he snarls through clenched teeth. "Jay, you keep checking morgues. County by county. Statewide, if you gotta. Bad Eye, kick some ass or bribe some clinic worker. I want some answers by next Thursday. Scooter, you *live* at The Stirrup from now on. Gonz, you get your ass to Jacumba. Take care of business."

Bull looks up at his leader with sad eyes. "Duke, you know I'm with you, man. Charlie wouldn't snitch out the club. But you know how he was when he left. We gotta cover our asses."

"I got a meeting with our greedy fuckin' attorney Silverman next week. Bastard's wondering what happened to his retainer. I'll get him churning on his Rolodex. Fucker's got contacts inside the cops up the ass. Charlie's been picked up, Silverman'll find him."

Gonzo starts nodding.

"That make you happy?"

Gonzo looks away.

"Everybody else keep your ears to the ground. Damage control."

Everyone nods.

"Now get the fuck outta here. Meeting adjourned."

Chapter 10

Space and Time
San Diego, CA
July 1, 1996

I'm on the line with Frank, who's calling from his cell on his way back from a meeting with Sergeant Ken Cantrell, his supervisor. I imagine Frank swerving between lanes on the freeway as he dials my number and the tiny phone pinched between his jowly cheek and shoulder, talking with only his cigarette hand on the wheel, windows open and ashes blowing everywhere. The thought of it makes me feel lucky to be here in this grungy motel room babysitting Charlie and not in the passenger seat of the Vic.

I'm here alone, sitting on the edge of one of the twin beds, scribbling out whatever I can glean from Frank's rambling monologue. When I left Charlie, he was taking a nap in the next room, so I figure he'll be fine on his own for a while. Anyway, I've left the door propped open so I can hear if he starts to stir around or break any of the house rules we've imposed on him, like using the phone or going for a walk.

I'm having a hard time keeping up because Frank's talking in circles like he always does when he has interesting news. And this news *is* interesting. It concerns Stacey Ritt.

"Uh-huh," I find myself saying over and over as I write down whatever I can fit on the little square notepad by the phone. "Yeah, I know, Frank."

The door's hinges squeak. I'm so engaged in my note-taking that I don't notice.

"Well, at least we know Stacey's alive," I respond to Frank.

I hear shuffling behind me. Boots shuffling over the shitty carpet. I turn and there's Charlie, his eyebrows raised.

"Where's Frank?" he asks, disregarding the fact I'm on the phone.

"He's right here," I say, pulling the phone's receiver from my head and sort of offering it up.

Charlie dismisses the offer with a wave of his hand. "I mean where's he at right now? Why'd he leave?"

"PD headquarters. Downtown."

Charlie sits down on the edge of the other twin. We're staring at one another across the gap between the beds, and the look on his face is sinister and threatening. Even with sleep still clinging to his eyes, the Hells Angel in the room is foreboding.

"What the hell for?"

I can tell he senses something's going on that he's not a part of, and I quickly try to think of something to say, something as noncommittal as possible. I don't know if he heard me mention Stacey, but for now I'm going to assume he didn't. "Cantrell wanted to see him," I explain with care. "On his way back now."

I'm so lost in the hypnotic aggression of Charlie's intense stare that I only just now realize that Frank's probably still listening through the phone's receiver I'm holding in the air beside my head. On cue, Frank starts barking through the phone. From here, it just sounds like warbling, but I can guess the point. I press it tight to my ear.

"Is that Charlie in there?" Frank asks, and he's urgent. Worried.

"Yeah," I say, real low.

"Did he hear anything?" Frank whispers.

"I heard you say something about Stacey," Charlie says to me. His tone is level, but it demands an answer.

"Uh...," I stammer.

"Did he just ask about Stacey?" Frank asks.

"Frank, I've got to go." I return the phone to its cradle, the sound of Frank hollering right up until I clack it down on the hook.

For a time, I just blink over at the rigid Charlie, whose eye contact never wavers. I find myself hoping this situation doesn't get out of hand, at least until my partner gets back. Until now, it's been a tag team, two on one with Charlie. Charlie and I don't share the rapport he shares with Frank. If he's going to hear about Stacey, it sure as hell would be better if Frank were here. So I just need to stall him until Frank gets back. Maybe five minutes, given the way he drives.

"You talkin' about Stacey *Ritt*?"

I consider lying. Apparently, Charlie can sense it.

"What you talking about Stacey for, man?"

I look down at my hands, folded over one another fidgeting, staring at the ragged carpet under my feet—whatever I can do to keep from looking him in the eye and giving away my awkward hesitancy to engage his question.

"Oh, I get it now. Frank's not here, you're not talkin'," Charlie says, and there's mockery in it, an unspoken threat. "I thought we was supposed to trust each other, you and me."

When I meet his gaze, his head's cocked to one side. He's gritting his teeth behind his lips, his square jaw gnawing his rage. All the while, that death stare remains fixed on my forehead. I can feel its heat.

Charlie stands up, hovering over me. "You guys keep talking about how we need to work together," he says. "Be a *team*. But now you're holding back on me. Hiding something. You know what that means, Spence?"

I look up into his dark, glaring eyes. "It means *you're* the one breaking the rules."

"Charlie, listen—"

"No, you listen, asshole," Charlie interrupts. He's like a wild animal. He can sense my weakness. "If you're breakin' rules, then I'm breakin' rules. That starts right now with the fuckin' phone."

I watch as he pulls the phone off the hook and then clasps the receiver between his ear and shoulder. He fires a challenge in my direction and then waits for me to say something. I'm not sure what.

"How'd you like that, Spence?" he asks. "Me using the

phone?"

I shake my head.

Charlie shakes the receiver in front of my face. "You said no phone. Period. Your rules. I agreed to them. If I break the rules, the damage will be done. That's what you and Frank keep tellin' me." He bends down to get right in my face—so close I can smell his breath, foul from sleeping. "Your words, man," he shouts.

He shoves the receiver back between his cheek and hunched shoulder.

"Fuck you and your rules," he says, starting to dial a number.

I lunge forward and press my finger to the hook and swipe the phone off the desk. It jangles to the floor, yanking the cord and receiver from Charlie's chin. Then I stand, Charlie looking incredulous. I'm five inches taller than him, but it does nothing to make me feel dominant. "Have it your way, asshole," I shout. "Fuck it. You're right. Maybe it's not worth it. Maybe *you're* not worth it."

I catch him off-guard. He appears baffled, and he calms momentarily. The fury in his eyes is replaced by a glazed, almost hypnotic stare, and his shoulders slump as he gently sits back onto the bed, his weight scarcely leaving a dent in the rock-hard thing.

"Listen, Charlie," I say with a sigh. "We *were* talking about Stacey Ritt. Frank had a BOLO out on her and . . ."

"The fuck's a BOLO?"

"A lookout. You know . . . if the cops pick her up, they notify Frank."

With every word, Charlie seems to grow a little more composed. It's enough to make me feel confident—in control of the situation. At least he's listening.

"PD narcotics picked her up last night on a DUI stop," I explain. "She wasn't the one driving, but she was obviously under the influence. So they took her downtown to police headquarters, sobered her up, and interrogated her for a while."

The phone starts belting its off-hook blare from the floor between us. Charlie calmly picks it up, replaces the receiver in its cradle, and sets it on the desk between the beds.

"They didn't have anything on her, so they let her go."

"Where's she now?" he asks, and I can hear the deep concern in his voice.

"She left PD headquarters on foot around midnight last night."

Charlie nods, dropping his head, loosening up. But then something seems to occur to him. He stares up at me again. "Why'd Frank have this, what'd you call it . . . lookout for her?"

I sink down onto the bed across from Charlie, checking my watch, wondering again what's taking Frank so long. I keep my focus trained on the watch for longer than I should. Charlie reaches over suddenly and smacks my wrist away from my line of sight. "Listen, man," he barks. "If you don't tell me what's goin' on, I'll go lookin' for her myself."

This is the first time he's touched me, and he's done it with anger. And I know what this means. Frank, or no Frank, if I don't give him something right now, he's out the door and I can't legally stop him.

"Listen, Charlie," I say. "Stacey's the reason we found you in the first place. She called Frank to tell us where you were because she was worried about your safety."

"My safety?" Charlie asks, confused. "That's why she tied me up in that room in the first place."

"No, I mean from the club."

"Why the hell would she call *you*?"

I sigh, looking him straight in the eyes. "Charlie, some of the guys from the club beat her up pretty good. She was worried they'd do the same to you."

Charlie leaps to his feet, his massive hands clenched to fists of rage. "What the *fuck* do you mean they beat her up?" he yells.

I try to keep calm, maintain eye contact. But I feel like

a lion tamer without a whip. "She's okay now, Charlie," I implore. "Narcs said she didn't seem too beat-up. Couple bruises here and there, but nothing serious."

"Couple fuckin' bruises?"

He's livid. His face is blood red, his temples pulsating. If he squeezes his fists any tighter, he'll start breaking fingers. "Motherfuckers beat up my old lady to get to *me*? That ain't right, man." He paces away from me, toward the door, and I'm glad for the space. "Who, Spence? Who did it? Which of those motherfuckers did it?"

"Only names she recognized were Gonzo and Goose," I say. There's no reason to offer up these names, but I figure that if Charlie's rage stays centered on someone other than me, we might just avoid a physical confrontation. In that moment, I see headlights pass through the darkness of the window behind Charlie, and hear the screech of tires.

"Fuck this," Charlie says, turning for the door. "I'm gonna waste those motherfuckers."

I leap to my feet, charging toward Charlie. Just as he gets to the door, my hands are on his shoulders. And just as quickly, he turns and pushes me back with a powerful shove. He's stronger than he looks in his still emaciated condition, so strong I topple back onto the bed a good six feet away.

"You've got no wheels, Charlie. No money!" I yell and he stops in the doorframe. "No way to get to them."

"I'll find a way," he hisses in a full-on rage. And yet he doesn't take another step. Something's holding him there. There's something odd and transfixing happening here. He's hell-bent for revenge, but it's like some kind of magnetic force is pulling him back into the room.

I stand and come up behind him, close enough that I can speak softly. "Think about how far you've come, Charlie," I say. "Think, Charlie . . . think about all you've accomplished between now and that day we found you strapped to the bed. I'm trying to help you here, for chrissakes. Look at yourself in that mirror, Charlie. You're on the mend. Don't go back."

His shoulders fall slack as he eyes himself in the mirror that hangs above the cracked, laminated dresser. "If you leave now, if you do what you want to do, you'll be throwing all that away."

His breathing slows. But when he faces me, there is no less anger in his eyes. The two of us stand there, toe to toe, sizing each other up, each man waiting for the other to speak. To make a move. Charlie is the first to relent. In his rage, he grabs a fistful of his jet-black hair in each hand and pulls as he steps around behind me. He howls. Tormented.

It is this moment that Frank picks to make his entrance. I feel him sidle up next to me, but I don't take my eyes off Charlie.

"No, no, I can't ...," Charlie grumbles, his back to Frank and me. "I can't let 'em get away with it." He straightens up again, his hands returning to fists as he straightens his arms down his sides. He turns and starts for the door again. "Outta my way, Sp—" He pauses when he notices that Frank is now standing next to me.

"Don't try and stop me, Frank," he says.

"This isn't the right thing to do, Charlie," Frank says sternly. "If you want to get back at them, the best way to do it is by taking them down."

"With us," I add.

Charlie's anger surges back to his face. "Fuck it," he belts. "I'm gonna rip those motherfuckers apart!"

He charges at the two of us standing between him and the door, centering on me. He lowers his shoulder into my chest, plowing me back into the wall beside the door. He jams his forearm against my throat, and his piercing eyes are filled with anger.

"I'll kill those motherfuckers!" he keeps yelling in my face. He's outside himself. Consumed by rage.

He pulls away from me and turns for the door, but Frank darts in front of him. Charlie stops and steps back. He starts to pace, looking like he's searching for a path around Frank. He's clearly confused. Seething.

"We can't legally hold you here, Charlie," Frank exhorts firmly. "You know that. But you also know you've come too far to blow it now. You gotta keep cool, calm down. Be smart."

"Rip those fuckers apart," Charlie mumbles, but he's listening. I can see it.

"Don't give up and go back to the way things were," Frank says. "Back to the way things were when you were a junkie."

Maybe it's Frank's calming tone. Maybe it's the bond he's always seemed to have with Charlie. Or maybe it's just the word *junkie*. Whatever it is, Charlie calms slowly and sits down on the bed, putting his head in his hands.

Frank and I just stand there for a while, trading glances. In time, we both lower our guard a little and relax.

"Wanna stay clean," Charlie mumbles. "No more drugs, man."

"That's good, Charlie," Frank says. He points at the other bed with his head, signaling for me to sit down there.

I do as Frank suggests, and I watch as my partner stands in front of Charlie.

In time, the Hells Angel looks up at him. "I don't wanna die no fifty-year-old junkie with a needle jammed in my arm, man."

"That's good, Charlie," Frank offers. "You're better than that."

Charlie nods, his brow furrowed. "Better than that," he echoes.

The three of us remain in our spots for what feels like ten minutes. I guess we each use the time to contemplate our own role in all this. For me, I've still got a lot of work to do to earn Charlie's trust. It's no small thing that he'd charge at me and not at Frank. I'm not sure how my partner's gotten to where he is with our potential witness, but I know that I'll have to get there too if we're ever going to make this case with Charlie as our witness.

Frank shoves his hands in his pockets. He's just watching Charlie, studying his mood.

As the silent minutes bleed away, Charlie seems to come back to himself. He's far less tense by the time he speaks again. "How's Stacey, man?" he asks. "I mean . . . is she hurt bad?"

"Just a couple of bruises, Charlie," Frank says.

"I'll find her for you, Charlie," I say. "Make sure she's all right."

The Hells Angel locks eyes with me. For the first time, he seems to hold some gratitude there. "You'd do that?" he asks.

If he's skeptical, he doesn't show it. He's a blank slate waiting for me to make my mark. I know that now is a good opportunity. If I make this promise to Charlie, that promise is binding, and it would go a long way to gaining his trust.

"I sure will," I say.

"But, Charlie, you have to give us your word you won't contact her," Frank says sternly. "Or anyone else. Let us handle it."

Charlie nods.

"It's dangerous. To you, to her, and to the operation."

Charlie nods.

"And to Nick and me."

Charlie nods. Whatever he's thinking, he appears compliant again. I don't know how we dodged this bullet, but somehow it feels like we dodged it and wound up better off in the end. We've touched a nerve here. No small thing.

Chapter 11

Finding Stacey
San Diego, CA
July 2, 1996

I just hung up the phone after speaking to Frank and Charlie about the Lakeside address that I picked up for Stacey from PD records. The address, 4950 Old Stagecoach Road, had sounded somehow phony, given the history of the woman in question compared to the upscale neighborhood surrounding the supposed residence. But Charlie confirmed it as the home of Stacey's sister, a place the junkie used to crash whenever she found herself in a jam with a dealer, strung out on heroin, or generally just hiding out. I asked Charlie if he thought his girl would ever go back there, and he expressed doubt.

"Her sister kicked her out the last time . . . said never again."

When I asked about paying a visit to the sister anyway, Charlie suggested I check out Stacey's work first, given the sister's tendency to spook at the sight of cops. As astonished as I was to hear that Stacey was actually employed, I had to agree with Charlie that spooking the sister would be a bad idea. So we established that Stacey's employer would be my best lead. Unfortunately, Charlie drew a blank on the exact name of the tire store in question.

"Chato's . . . Chappo's, maybe. Somethin' like that. Coupla Mexican brothers run the place. She does the books."

"Chappo's, Charlie?" I'd asked, surprised his junkie girlfriend could hold down a job—much less one as a bookkeeper.

"Fuck if I know. It's on La Mesa Boulevard, man."

~~~~

After several hours of watching the pair of Mexicans who run Concho's Tire Shop just east of San Diego in the small middle-class community of La Mesa, I come to two conclusions: first, the operation appears legitimate; second, these guys work their asses off.

There's a bus stop across the street from Concho's, and since I figure Stacey for a bus rider, I center half my attention there. The buses run on a thirty-minute cycle and prove pretty timely. They're crowded mostly with book-toting students, likely from San Diego State University about a mile away. So, as of yet, I've seen no pin-legged junkies in cutoff tops and ragged jean shorts. The hopeless gaze of a lost soul stares up at me from her last PD booking photo lying on the car seat.

The tranquilizing warmth of the afternoon sun is making it difficult to stay focused. I'm battling to keep my eyes open and feel myself drifting off.

The lankier of the two Mexicans drops his smoke to the cement, and I notice for the first time that I've dozed through closing time. The sliding door to the garage at Concho's has been slammed shut, and the owner is locking it from the outside. A kind of dread comes over me as I realize I've just burned a whole afternoon staking out a tire shop and have nothing to show for it. I'd kept my distance all day, wanting to avoid contact with Stacey's employer. That way, I wouldn't draw any unnecessary heat for her at work. But I don't have much time to waste on this little side project.

Before the lanky Mexican can even reach his pickup in the corner of the lot, I'm on top of him. "Excuse me," I say, "I'm looking for Stacey Ritt."

He cocks one of his bushy eyebrows. "Who wants to know?"

"Let's just say an interested party."

"I ain't interested in no interested parties, amigo."

I badge him, the gold patina glinting in the low light. The tire worker straightens up.

"She in some kind of trouble?"

"She's a witness to a robbery," I lie. "I need to ask her some questions."

"You gonna arrest her, then?"

"No. Just need to talk to her."

He sighs, his sloped shoulders slumping further. "She'll be here tomorrow morning," he says, and he's already turning for his truck. "Round 8—if she ain't late again."

I found nothing but gnawed pizza crusts and a pair of snoring lumps last night when I arrived back at La Paloma. Exhausted, I fell asleep on one of the twin beds, having managed to take my shoes off and little else.

After a decent sleep, I'm back on point at dawn before Frank and Charlie even wake. Hot coffee and a Winchell's donut and I'm good to go. The buses are running on their regular schedule and the traffic is heavy. It's the 8:30 bus that carries the payload. She's late, as predicted.

I watch Stacey Ritt amble down the bus steps and stand there on the curb for a moment. A pathetic sight. She looks like she's spent the past year in a Nazi concentration camp. Gaunt and bony, she takes an unsteady step off the curb and crosses the street. Her dark blonde hair is pulled back tight into a short ponytail. The early morning sun accentuates the heavy makeup and rouge covering her hollowed cheeks. Her tight miniskirt exposes rail-thin legs while a skimpy halter top crowns the outline of her ribcage. She's only thirty, but she looks seventy.

I jump out of the car to meet her as she reaches my side of the street. When she turns to look up at me, there is surprise in her expression. I flash my credentials and explain that I work with Frank Conroy.

"Yeah, I remember you," she squawks. "Guy always hanging 'round whenever Frank shows up buggin' me with those stupid business cards."

"You got a minute? It's about Charlie."

"Yeah," she says, taking a slow look in the direction of Concho's. "But you better not make me late for work."

I nod and lead her to the car, where she hops in without question. We wheel around the block, out of sight of Concho's near a grove of eucalyptus trees.

The first thing I notice when I turn to her are the scarred track marks on her right forearm. "You still using?" I ask.

She shakes her head with vigor. "Not since before the beating." She pauses. "I kicked the stuff about a week before Charlie . . ." Then she goes silent, shifting into a trance-like stare. Her vacant eyes began to tear up. "Where's Charlie? Did you find him?"

It's a question I should have expected and been better prepared for, but it still catches me off-guard. I know I have to give her something or she'll clam up. But I have to be careful here. The club came to her once for information, and I've got no reason to believe they won't do it again. Can't give her too much.

"We found Charlie at the motel," I say, winging it. "Just like you said."

I watch her soften some.

"He was in pretty bad shape, but he's doing better. Methadone. Wants to stay clean."

"Does he . . ." Stacey pauses, touching her jagged cheekbones with her fingertips. The bruises have faded, but they still look tender. "Know about me?"

I sigh to buy time more than anything. There's no way around it here, and I know it. I have to tell her the truth. "He didn't know at first," I say. "But when he found out, he went into this . . . rage. And he asked me to come check on you."

"What are you doing with him?" Stacey asks. She's shaking. Sallow-eyed. Haunted by her gnawing addiction and no doubt still recovering from the Hells Angels' special brand of justice.

"He's in medical detention," I lie.

"You're not . . ."

"He's being held pending possession of an illegal weapon," I lie again.

Strangely, this seems to calm Stacey. She loosens up. "Well, at least he's not out here. If the club finds him . . ."

"I know, Stacey."

My company falls silent for a time, shaking her head as if working through something that's bugging her. "You know ... I thought I was friends with some of those guys who beat me up. Gonzo especially. His girl, Bonnie, and me ... we go way back."

I have questions, but I keep silent because I can sense she's willing to keep talking for as long as I let her.

"But Gonzo, he been actin' strange lately. Always talking about how he don't trust Charlie. 'Bout how he thinks Charlie's a thief."

I nod, taking it all in.

"And he started *beatin'* on Bonnie." She goes wide-eyed, as if this is supposed to surprise me. "He beat Bonnie up so many times, she had to leave him. Beat her so bad sometimes I couldn't even recognize her face."

She's rambling now, getting off track, so I hold out a hand to stop her. "What were you saying about Gonzo not trusting Charlie?"

Stacey rolls her head back. "Oh, hell," she says. "It's *always* been like that. I think Gonzo was just jealous of all the money Charlie was makin'. Things back then, they were fine between him and me and Bonnie. But then Bonnie said one day he came home with this suitcase fulla money. Keeps it in his pad out in Ramona and—"

I arch my brow. Bells are ringing.

"Yeah. And ever since that day, he been beatin' Bonnie up, calling her a whore and a liar, shit like that."

Cash disappears unexpectedly from the Hells Angels' coffers. Suitcase full of money. Gonzo behaves erratically. Interesting.

"And this is unusual?" I ask. "Gonzo carrying a suitcase full of cash?"

She shakes her head again with vigor. "He ain't never had that kinda money before. Spending like a drunken sailor. Bought new pipes for his bike—a new car."

Then, as I watch, something seems to dawn on Stacey.

"Wait. You think it mighta been Gonzo who stole from the club?"

I consider my next words carefully. I ponder the best way to approach the question. I settle on ambiguity. "No way to know that, Stacey," I say.

She looks frustrated with me, but at this point, it doesn't matter. I've learned more about the situation than I'd ever anticipated. And I haven't told Stacey anything that will affect our position. It's a win-win. I can change the subject now and get away clean.

"Charlie's going to want to know, Stacey," I say. "Where are you staying?"

"My sister's," she says. "In Lakeside."

"That's good," I say, throwing the Vic into drive. "Just stay away from Charlie's place." I shake my head. "Actually, stay out of El Cajon completely."

I drive back to the spot where I picked her up and park. She climbs out of the car and turns back to me, and I notice she's crying. Her cakey makeup runs down her cheeks. We remain like this in silence for some time, with me sitting and staring at Stacey and Stacey leaning into the car and staring blankly at the little felt strip that supports the passenger window. I'd like to console her, but I'm not sure how. I can scarcely imagine the kind of world she lives in.

"You'll take care of my Charlie, won't you?" she asks.

She catches only the tail end of my nod, but it seems enough.

"Can I contact you at your sister's?" I ask. "You know . . . in case we need to get ahold of you."

She rifles around in her purse and shortly produces a pad of paper. She jots a number down and hands it to me.

"Just don't say nothin' to my sister about Charlie," she says. "Nothin' about no FBI neither. Just leave a message to call . . ." She furrows her brow. "What'd you say your name was?"

"Nick."

"Yeah. Nick. Just say Nick called."

I nod.

"Just call the number for the FBI in the phone book. They'll put you through to me."

"You gotta card?"

"I don't want you carrying around an FBI business card, Stacey."

"Yeah, guess you're right about that. I'm gonna start methadone tonight," she says with a teary-eyed smile. "Just like Charlie."

"That's good," I say. "You take good care of yourself, all right?"

"I'll be fine." And her smile widens revealing a mouthful of rotting teeth as she slams the door.

I take my foot off the brake, but she stops me with a hand slap to the open window's frame. "Oh, and . . . one more thing," she says leaning in, "one more thing. Charlie would never steal from the club. It's like his family."

I nod, then wave goodbye and head off. I feel somehow lighter. For the first time, I feel our case has a *direction*. This stakeout has produced more than one positive development. I'll be able to report back to Charlie that Stacey is doing okay and safe. With any luck, this will bring me closer to our potential witness—a critical next step. And better yet, I've uncovered information that suggests it was Gonzo and not Charlie who stole the money in question.

This is a positive turn with major significance. For one thing, if true, it clears Charlie's name on the theft. And that puts my mind at ease some. A Charlie who wouldn't steal from the men he calls his brothers seems far more stable and potentially reliable than a Charlie who would steal to feed a habit. And for another thing, if Charlie ever *does* find out about the money, we'll have something we can use to deflect his anger. He'll be less likely to storm away from the case—and, in fact, maybe even more likely to *ally* with us—if he thinks Gonzo's setting him up.

We're all sitting in Charlie's room, our impromptu interview quarters, and the tape recorders are off. Charlie's got his arms crossed over his chest and he's leaning forward on the edge of the bed. His dark eyes are fixed on the ground, contemplative, as I sum up what I've uncovered.

"She really gonna go on methadone?" he asks.

"What she said."

Charlie blasts a long sigh. He works one of his meaty hands over his jaw. Then, after a time he looks up and stares me square in the eyes.

"Thanks, Nick," he says.

I nod back at him nonchalantly.

"No, I mean it," he says, his brow furrowing. "You made good on your word and that's righteous."

"I'm glad she's okay." I glance over at Frank, whose eyes contain a glint of excitement.

"That's what we do, Charlie," Frank says. "We take care of each other around here."

Charlie lays back on the bed, laces his hands behind his head, and purses his lips. He's mulling it over. I watch as he lies there staring at the ceiling. For a time, we're all silent, figuring things out. And then Charlie practically leaps to his feet.

"Well, what're we wastin' time for?" he asks. "You fuckers got more questions for me or what?"

Frank smiles. I step over to the nightstand and fire up the tape recorder. My partner returns with a notepad. We sit. We talk.

Chapter 12

Reveries
San Diego, CA
July 4, 1996

We're standing on the little balcony, the three of us, straining to see the fireworks out over Sea World—hungry for a taste of the outside world. We barely manage to see anything over the top of the freeway directly in front of us and through the haze of a warm San Diego night. I just made some remark about my mother taking my brother and me to see fireworks over Lake Michigan when I was a kid. Charlie slowly turns and shuffles back into his room and plops down on the bed. He's lying there silently on his back with one arm draped over his forehead, shrouding his eyes. He's wearing a white T-shirt revealing the hideous image of the hollow-eyed, Hell Angels winged death head tattoo on his emaciated bicep. It's quiet except for the faint booming of the fireworks off in the distance. I come back into the room and stretch out on the other bed, and Frank takes a chair. No one says anything. He's in another place, and Frank and I have learned that it's best to leave him be at times like this.

"Trailer trash, man . . . that's what the other kids at school called me and Jake . . . trailer trash. All I ever wanted to do was play ball. I wanted to be a professional ballplayer . . . a pitcher. Robin Roberts, man. He was my hero. My ol' man hated baseball. Hated life."

He lifts his arm and turns and stares at me for a moment, breaking from his reverie. His eyes are moist and quiet. "Never went to no fireworks, Spence. No ballgames." He returns the arm across his eyes and goes silent for several minutes.

"Spent all his money in the bars . . . drunk on his ass, chasin' pussy. Always beatin' on the ol' lady. Then one day they came. The tall man with the stupid brown hat driving the big, black car. My ol' man signed some papers and my mother never came out to say goodbye."

Charlie's voice starts to crack, but he keeps his arm over his eyes. If there were tears, we weren't going to see them. His motionless soliloquy carries a sad tone. Frank glances at me and then looks back at Charlie. Both of us are stone silent.

"Just like that. No goodbye . . . nothin'. Never saw her again. My mother. But Jake and me, we stuck together. I took care of him. The orphanage tried to split us up, but I wouldn't let'm. I was eleven . . . Jake was eight. St Gertude's Catholic Orphanage. 'Wards of the state' was what they called us. Fucked up, man. Father Kramer . . . fucked up. Sister Marie. Jake was never the same after that place. Told me he was afraid of Father Kramer . . . kept saying Father Kramer hurt him. I never believed him . . . never saw no bruises. Never could get him to talk about it. We ran away, Jake and me. Lived on the streets until we got busted for shoplifting . . . petty theft they called it. Spent some time in juvie. Jake was always gettin' in fights. Fightin'. Seems like that's all we ever did. . . ."

His voice fades and then silence. Asleep. Frank and I sit there quietly reflecting in our own way.

~~~~

"The fuck you guys starin' at?"

I have no idea how much time has passed, but Charlie abruptly awakens and Frank and I are just sitting there gazing at him like zombies.

"Jesus, why don't you assholes go home? You're givin' me the creeps just sitting around here like this. I ain't goin' nowhere. It's Fourth of July for chrissakes."

Neither Frank nor I say anything. We're both about to fall asleep.

"I know Frank here's a two-time loser, Spence, but what about you? Ain't you got nobody to go home to?"

I shake my head. "Not really."

"You ain't married?"

"Was."

"What happened?"

It's the first time he's asked me anything personal, and I'm not keen on sharing my private life with him. Frank, on the other hand, has a different agenda. He leans forward on his chair, more alert than he looks.

"I thought you were a committed bachelor, Spence. I never knew you were married before."

"It's not worth talking about, Frank," I say, taking a deep breath.

"Well, in that case, it *is* worth talking about," Frank prods.

Charlie props himself up on the bed and stuffs the pillows behind his neck. "C'mon, Spence, tell us about it," he says.

I'm not comfortable talking about my marriage because it brings back a lot of painful memories and empty feelings. I roll onto my back, staring up at the sagging acoustical tiles above me. I'm exhausted, but since Charlie has just shared some of his personal life so openly and unexpectedly, it seems awkward to shut down and not share something about myself.

"We met at a bank robbery in Las Vegas. I'd only been in the Bureau a couple of months and was assigned to the bank robbery squad. She was working in loans at this bank where the robbery went down. Her old man was a big shot at the bank. She was a knockout . . . I mean stunning . . . drop-dead gorgeous. Had this beautiful, long, red hair and a body to die for. I was immediately in lust. She'd been out of high school a couple of years and didn't want to go to college, so her daddy set her up at the bank. We dated a couple of months and I just couldn't live without her . . . the sex . . . the excitement. I'd never been with anyone like her. She was wild and loved to party. We spent all our free time out on the town hanging out at the casinos . . . partying. It was a fast life and not exactly compatible with my job. About a year later, we get married and her old man's got connections, so we have this big reception at the MGM Grand. The old man pays for a two-week cruise to the Mediterranean and we come home and start our life together. She quits the bank and tells me she wants to start a family. We're not exactly rolling in the dough with my salary, but I'm so totally infatuated and in

love . . . or lust . . . that anything she wanted I was going to try to make sure she got. A few months go by and we were struggling. I couldn't keep up with her demands, and she had a lot of them. Clothes, jewelry, spas, hair salons . . . she was used to getting anything she wanted so she started hitting up her dad for money. I wasn't too comfortable with that arrangement, so I had a talk with her old man and told him I needed him to stop giving her money. I had this stupid image of myself as the provider, but I couldn't begin to provide for this woman. It wasn't long after my talk with the old man that I found out what she was spending most of his money on. Cocaine. I found her stash and confronted her and she told me to fuck off. I was shocked . . . tried to get her to go to rehab and she refused. Things fell apart quickly. I started working more and being at home less. I got transferred to the organized crime squad and volunteered for an undercover assignment. Somebody had a snitch inside the mob, and I got duped in as a driver for one of the underbosses. I worked at this guy's beck and call, mostly nights, driving him and his greaseball cronies around Vegas partying. This went on for a few months, and I was starting to gain the mob guys' trust. One night, we go to this strip joint in one of the seedier parts of town. I'm standing by the door watching this stripper through the choking smoke and haze. She's bumping and grinding to the pounding music, dry-humping the pole between her legs. I look down in front of the stage and see another dancer bouncing up and down on some drunken jerk's lap like she's fucking the guy. The girl has long red hair down to the middle of her back. When the music stops, she gets off the guy's lap, collects some bills, and turns toward me. It was Shannon . . . my wife. I was sick to my stomach. I ran outside and almost threw up. I got a cab and went home. That pretty much ended my undercover assignment . . . and my marriage."

"That sucks, man," Charlie groans.

"I'm sorry, Nick," Frank murmurs. "So what happened?"

"We got divorced, and the Bureau gave me a letter of censure and a transfer."

"For what?"

"They said I used bad judgment and compromised the investigation of the mob by leaving my undercover position that night."

Frank moves to the edge of his chair. "You gotta be shittin' me."

"True story . . . and that's not the end of it. A year later, she gets arrested for prostitution and heroin possession, and Las Vegas Metro notifies the Bureau that she dropped my name when she was popped. Claimed I was her source of supply."

"That *really* sucks, man," Charlie mutters, with a donkey grin on this face. "Were you?"

"Fuck you, Charlie."

"Shut up Charlie," Frank interjects.

I take a deep breath and drag myself up off the bed. "They wanted me to take a polygraph solely based on her accusations, and I told them to shove it. For that I got thirty days on the bricks for insubordination and another thirty days admin leave while they investigated her story."

"And . . . ?"

"Nothing ever came of it except I was put on daily reports and drug tested every week for a year. Let's just say it didn't exactly enhance my career."

Frank heaves a deep sigh and lights up a fresh smoke. "That sucks, man."

Chapter 13

Choices
San Diego, CA
July 7, 1996

Official FBI transcript (excerpt) dated 7/7/96

Nick Spence: Resuming the debriefings at 14:45, July 7, 1996. Present in the room, Special Agent Nick Spence, Detective Frank Conroy, and Mr. Charles Slade.

Charles Slade: Name's Charlie, man. I mean, if you're gonna fuckin' (unintelligible), okay?

NS: Sure thing, Charlie. We're . . . So, Charlie, on the previous tape, you started talking about how you got involved with the Hells Angels in the first place.

CS: Uh-huh . . .

NS: In San Quentin. How . . . how old were you?

CS: Eighteen, man. Catchin' the . . .

NS: You had been—

CS: I'm looking at ten years for armed robbery, and I'm catchin' the chain. You know, the bus out of San Diego that takes you to . . . It's a place called Chino—

NS: The California Institution for Men.

CS: Yeah. Where everybody goes before they get locked up and . . . I was scared, man. I mean, if you go to the joint, and you've never been there, everybody else knows it. I mean, they know it the instant you walk in. You can't hide the fact you've never been there. And you go into this big room and they strip you naked, which is fucked up right there, right?

And they line you up, you know, and (unintelligible) you get there, everybody breaks into groups. Because in prison, you're a nigger, a chincan, or a white boy; those are the three groups. And you never associate with someone of a different race and if you do . . . So it's a world that's just run totally different than out here.

NS: The fish tank.

CS: Say what?

NS: They call it the fish tank. The processing center. I guess they call it the fish tank because everyone there is the same . . . stripped down naked except—

CS: Except they ain't the same, Spence. Like I said, skin color is everything in the joint, man.

NS: Right.

CS: So I'm standing there naked and scared but trying not to show it and this CO—this corrections officer—comes up and looks at me and he just stares at me and says, "How old are you, kid?" Like he can't believe I'm in there and . . . well . . .

NS: So what happened to you?

CS: Well, like I said, they tell me I'm bound for San Quentin, lookin' at a dime, and the only way . . .

NS: A dime? Can you explain that for the record?

CS: You know . . . a ten-year sentence in the joint.

NS: So what was that like? Going to the pen for the first time?

CS: What was it like? I'll tell you what it's like, man. First day in the joint, I'm eating at the mess hall with this other guy, and this convict comes over and sits down next to me. And he says, you know, something like tonight I'm gonna come to your cell and fuck you. Just get yourself greased up and be ready about such and such a time, you know. Just sort of matter-of-fact, he says this. Grease yourself up, get ready, because we're going to have sex, man. So ...

NS: Whoa ...

CS: Right ... So I'm in my cell that night and the guy comes, and I ... There's a bucket on the tier with those rollers in the top to squeeze the mop dry and ...

NS: Uh-huh ...

CS: And it's real heavy and I just fuckin' beat this guy's fuckin' head in with it. Because (unintelligible) choice.

NS: Well ...

CS: Because if you don't do that, man ... I mean, you have to make that decision ... right then. I mean, if I'm an inmate and I know you're new, I'll say like, look, here's what's going to happen. You have to give me your whole canteen. When people send you money, whatever stuff you get from the store, that's mine. And if you don't do that, then you're—you're just going to be open season. So you have to make that decision. And there's only two choices: Give the guy your canteen or kill him, or hurt him so bad it sends a message to the other inmates that this guy won't stand for that and that's the way it is. So that's what I did, man. The guy had blood pumpin' out his ears when the COs pulled me off him.

All the domino tables, cards, TVs, everything's controlled by the inmates and the gangs that run the prisons: La EME, La Nuestra Familia, the Aryan Brotherhood, Black Guerilla Family, those groups. All those fuckers. Everything's controlled, and everything you do and every move you make is watched by the other inmates. It's like they got a magnifying glass on you the whole time.

NS: Uh-huh...

CS: I mean... (long pause)

NS: You okay, Charlie? You want a soda or something?

CS: Eighteen years old, man. I didn't talk to nobody for two years. That's how fuckin' scared I was.

NS: But you could handle yourself...

CS: That's not the ... I mean, sure, that helps, but it's like fuckin' insane in there, man. I mean, you can get killed in the joint over a chocolate chip cookie. You have to ask for everything you do. *Everything.* You have to leave everybody else's stuff alone. Just bump into a guy or ... look at somebody wrong. There's people sitting on the yard that can go like this and just nod at someone. They'll be dead that afternoon.

So what I'm trying to tell you is that's kind of how it was for me. And you can't tell me you can do that for ten or eleven years, come out and go, okay, I'm rehabilitated and I'm ready to meet society again and change my ways. You're punished, yeah, but when you come out, you're *conditioned.* You're trained to be different.

NS: And that's where... It was in San Quentin you got involved with the Hells Angels.

CS: Yeah. There was some HAs knew me ... noticed me, I guess... me and my brother, Jake. We sorta had a reputation.

NS: Jake was inside with you at the same time?

CS: Yeah.

NS: And the HAs—they noticed you?

CS: Yeah, because . . . you know, after a time I know my way around the place pretty good and people know me and I'm like . . . I was middleweight boxing champion four years in a row. I liked to box. Anyway, I helped a coupla these guys out in the joint and they was from Dago . . . you know, San Diego. And from then on, when a Hells Angel went to prison for whatever, drugs or whatever, they would stiff a message to me inside and say, "Charlie, this guy's coming up to the joint . . . kinda look out for him." And that's what I did. Because after a while, you're experienced, you know? I mean, you fuckin' live there, right? You got guys trying to fuck with you every minute of the day and night.

So after a while, I guess the word spreads around the Hells Angels that Charlie Slade's the one to hook up with in the joint.

FC: Charlie, I want to ask you something.

CS: Look out (laughter). Look out, man, Frank's got that fucking look in his eye.

FC: Did you ever take someone's life in prison?

CS: (long pause) No. I'm not . . . I saved a guy once, though.

NS: You saved someone's life?

CS: This one time.

NS: Can you tell us about that?

CS: Sure. There was a convict trying to throw a CO off a tier. The officer guy's clinging for his life, and if he falls, he's gonna die. The other guy was drinking pruno. You know . . . prison wine. Fuckin' shit man. Out of his fuckin' mind. And I told the convict, you don't wanna do this . . . you don't need this. And I was takin' a chance, you know, because the other inmates, they were yelling something like throw the fucker off and shit. I mean, they wanted blood, man. But I'd been there so long nobody really bothered me over it. You know, after a while, you get a reputation.

NS: And your brother. He was in there with you.

CS: (Unintelligible)

FC: Charlie?

CS: Tired, man . . .

NS: Your brother was in San Quentin, too.

CS: Yeah, man. But he killed his number before I did . . . got out about a year before me.

NS: I'm sorry about your brother, Charlie.

CS: Yeah, well, he was a hard case. Harder than me, anyways. Like I told you guys already, he was never the same after living at the orphanage in L.A. Always pickin' fights and shittin' on people, you know. Didn't have no friends. And then you guys had to go and (unintelligible).

FC: You want to take a break, Charlie?

Chapter 14

Squares and Regulars
San Diego, CA
July 9, 1996

Something's changed in Charlie Slade. Maybe it's the Stacey thing. Maybe it's the fact he now knows I'll smack a guy in the face with a binder if I think he's out of line, or that I had a wife who was a junkie. Whatever the case, his general attitude toward me has improved in recent days. The methadone treatments have been a lifesaver for him. While he's still testy and moody with sudden flashes of anger and contempt, I can at least move around the tiny room without his dark eyes tracking my every step. I've come to realize that his animal-like instincts were honed early in life out of necessity, and I'm beginning to see the guy behind the Hells Angel—to see what it is *Frank* sees.

As I sit and listen to his late-night reveries about his childhood, I can feel his pain and sadness. I don't think he's ever shared any of this with anyone, and it must be cathartic because he drifts into dreamlike trances recalling in such detail his voided youth.

Frank's slow pace and these grinding, long hours of debriefings are getting old, but I'm beginning to see that it's paying off. We're making slow headway in understanding the man behind the violent facade; slowly beginning to gain his trust.

"Charlie's a good guy," Frank tells me in his typical broad-brush manner. And when I point out the obvious ways that's a hard sell, he continues to insist that "underneath" there's goodness. I suppose I should trust his judgment, given that he's gotten to know Charlie over several years of misdemeanor detentions, DUI arrests, and cozy interview room encounters like the briefcase incident. Despite all that, he just flat-out likes him—or let's just say he's intrigued by him. It's as simple as that. For one thing, Charlie has a way of just *being* where he is at any given moment, which I find myself admiring. There's something cat-like about it. Like, give him a saucer of milk and some tuna, and he could care less about the rest of the world and its problems. I mean, here's a guy we've basically pulled out by the roots from his world of limitless cash, the respect and fear of everyone he meets, and the camaraderie of a kind that most people never get to experience outside a war zone.

A month ago, Charlie was living a life that was about as close to a superhero's as you can imagine for an outlaw: getting a blow job any time he walked into a bar, beating the shit out of whomever he felt like in the certain knowledge that no one in his right mind was *ever* going to fuck with him, and riding roughshod over people on his Harley with a bullwhip around his neck, for chrissake. And now he's sitting in this crappy little motel room with a couple of stiff cops, watching *As the World Turns* and *Days of Our Lives* and just waiting around to answer more stupid questions into a bank of tape recorders. And he's okay with it. He's handling it well.

I've come to realize the reason he can be this way is that his whole life has been this way. As long as he can remember, he's lived in strange rooms with strangers. The orphanage. The juvie halls and boot camps. Prison. He's seen it over and over and over. Charlie can look content in this shithole motel because he knows *exactly* how to do this kind of time, work this room, beginning with finding out who's the alpha and who's the omega, or in the parlance of ex-convicts, who's the square and who's the regular—because in his worldview, you're either one or the other.

Squares or regulars.

"You forgot to lift the seat again, Spence." Charlie stands in the bathroom doorway with a noticeably pissed-off presence about him, especially for so early in the morning. It's clear he's in a foul mood.

I look up from the report I'm writing and return his menacing stare. He's got his straight razor in his hand, his face half-covered with shaving lather, and a towel wrapped around his waist.

"Sorry, Charlie," I say. "It's a bad habit of mine."

"Well, I'm sick and tired of your bad habits, Spence," he sneers as he saunters into the room.

I look over my shoulder and he's standing behind me.

"What's *that* supposed to mean?"

He looks down at me casually waving the straight razor in the air and I'm thinking he's thinking how easy it would be to take me down. Beyond that, I believe he really wants to know how I'd react if it came to it. I don't like anybody standing behind me with a straight razor, especially this guy.

"This some kind of a test or stupid Hells Angels ritual or something?" I ask.

"Don't it ever worry you, Spence, being alone with a guy like me?" he asks, as he moves around to face me. "You know, I'm a Hells Angel, man—a mean motherfucker." He looks over at the razor in his hand as if noticing it for the first time. "I mean, I'm standing here with a blade, man. What makes you so sure this whole thing ain't a setup? Just me and the big FBI man...alone. You'd be a big score for me."

I do my best to look disinterested, but his tone and manner are disrespectful and it pisses me off. I flip my pencil onto the desk and stand to face him. "You pickin' a fight, Charlie, or did you just wake up on the wrong side of the bed?" I ask, and in a flash I reach and jerk the towel loose from his waist. He's stunned standing there naked. I draw my Glock and point it directly at his balls.

"Never bring a knife to a gunfight, Charlie."

"Jesus Christ, Spence, take it easy, man. I was just fuckin' with you, man."

"I'm in no mood to be fucked with, Charlie. Don't ever threaten me like that again," I say, as I angrily toss the towel on the bed and re-holster. I slam the chair back to the desk and sit down with my reports.

"Jesus Christ, Nick, settle down, man," he says as he retrieves the towel off the bed and shuffles to the bathroom.

Of course, it'd be easy to dismiss all this as prison yard bullshit—a rougher version of what most boys grow up with in the schoolyard and at some point *outgrow*, but I guess the truth is I don't see it like that. I think most guys make a kind of subliminal calculation about the size of the other guy's balls on first contact—especially in this particular environment. I think that stuff is pretty hardwired. This mano-a-mano evaluation comes to the fore in gangs because violence and intimidation is the business the gang is in. If you can't *do* the violence, you can't be in the business. But aside from that, each gang member needs to know that their brothers are going to stand their ground in situations where a guy might easily be tempted to turn tail and run. So the calculation is this: If this guy's scared of me, how's he going to stand up under pressure? And what's true of gangs is true of soldiers and is true of police and FBI agents. And in this line of work, to fail to recognize that crucial similarity would be a dangerous thing.

~~~~

As per the routine we've established, as soon as we get Charlie back from the clinic, we do the full body search, discuss his dosage levels and treatment schedule, go over his receipts for the day, and then set him up for another debrief. Charlie moans some when we get the tape recorders out, and it's obvious to me that just like Frank said, it's time to ease off on the leash a little. Either that or lose Charlie altogether, although he's deeper into this thing than I had ever anticipated. As though reading my thoughts, Frank tells Charlie it's pool time as soon as the debriefing session is done.

"No bullshit this time?"

"No bullshit," Frank says, giving me a thumbs-up. "You deserve it, Charlie. I know all this talk is getting to you. Believe me, I understand."

"I just don't see the point is all."

"You probably don't realize how much we're learning," Frank says, setting up the tape recorder. We've already agreed that Frank is going to take the lead in this session, and that we're going to try to get a sense of where Charlie's head's at with regard to the club, and in particular Duke. We need to know exactly how Charlie feels before we start talking about him wearing a wire and making drug buys.

Frank starts in talking about why Charlie decided to join the club in the first place. Stretched out on the bed, which is how he prefers to do the debriefs, Charlie stares up at the ceiling.

"They were there for me, man. As soon as I got out of the joint, they were there for me."

"What, like waiting for you at the gate?"

"No, but ... I mean, I'm a fuckin' ex-con, right? I'm looking at *maybe* getting a job flipping burgers. *Maybe* ... if I'm *lucky*. Some fuckin' nowhere minimum-wage bullshit job, but ..."

"You didn't want to do that?"

Charlie puts an arm across his eyes. "Would you, Frank? Come on, be honest. You're me and you're walking outta prison."

"I don't know, Charlie."

"I mean, I'm Charlie fuckin' Slade, man. Guys, they step *around* me in the joint. They give me room. I'm *somebody*. I don't flip no fuckin' burgers for nobody. And the guys, the club, they understood that ..."

"They knew how to value you," Frank says.

"Right on."

"But they weren't waiting at the gate."

"Not at the gate, but they'd said come on over, you know. I knew where to find them."

Like clockwork, a minute into the debriefing, Charlie reaches for his cigarettes and Frank fires one up for him. We're in for a couple hours of fog.

"So, what happened?" Frank says. This is Frank at his best, nursing along the conversation and putting aside his broad knowledge of the Hells Angels' culture and history.

"I hung out with them for a while. I mean, not like a 'hang around' . . . you know. I was . . . they knew who I was."

I look across at Frank, but he's watching Charlie intently, totally absorbed.

"What do you mean you weren't a 'hang around'?" I say.

Charlie gives me a slow look from under his right arm. "Fuck, Nick. Don't you know nothin'?"

Frank sits up in his chair. "So tell Nick how it works, Charlie."

"The Hells Angels, they don't go out and recruit people, man. Never. It doesn't work like that. If you want to be an HA . . . I mean, for starters, you gotta be twenty-one and own an American-made motorcycle, but you gotta also . . . I mean you gotta step up, man. You gotta have the balls to stand up and say I want to be a Hells Angel—me, Charlie Slade—and be able to explain why. And if you got those balls, they'll maybe say—I mean, if they like the look of you—they'll say to hang around. That makes you a 'hang around.'"

"But you didn't do that," I say.

Charlie covers his eyes with his arm again, settling back into his monologue. "Like I said, they already knew me. I helped out a couple of their guys in the joint. And they wanted me in the club."

"Because . . ."

"Because I'm a mean, tough motherfucker and I'm useful to them. The ones I knew wanted me to get to know the others. I mean there were nineteen or twenty of them at the time, but I had to sell myself to the others. So, eventually, I started to hang around, let the members get to know me and me to know them. I learned how they acted, how I was supposed to act. How to be a Hells Angel."

"So what happened then?" Frank says.

"I hung around for a month or so before they made me a prospect—which meant I was . . . I could be in on some club things, but I couldn't vote, go to meetings, you know. And then—this is like a few months later—I got my patch."

"Tell us what that means, Charlie."

"You can wear the club's patch, man, you know. *That's it.* You made it. You can now call yourself a Hells Angel. You can wear the club's colors. Go to meetings. Vote. Go on runs. Get the tattoos. The death head. Wear the patches. Top rocker. Bottom rocker. Everything, man. 'Hells Angels.' 'California.' 'AFFA.'"

"What's AFFA?" I ask, feigning ignorance for the sake of information to enter on the transcript.

Charlie fires another you-dumb-shit glare my way, puts his arm back over his eyes. "Angels Forever, Forever Angels," he grunts.

"Okay," Frank says. "And this whole process . . . from prospect to full patch . . ."

"Some guys wait years, man . . ."

"But not you," Frank says, checking his recorder, making sure the reels are still turning.

"For me, it's like two, three months." Charlie takes his arm away, I guess to check on our expressions. "That's right. I mean, three months after I walk out of prison I'm a Hells Angel and takin' care of business."

"What business, Charlie?"

"Come on, Frank. You know what I'm talkin' about."

"Tell me," Frank says. He snorts a long, slow plume of smoke through his nostrils.

"Nobody fucks with the Hells Angels, man. *Nobody.* Not the Mongols, Pagans, Outlaws, Joe Citizen, nobody. It's all about respect. Pride. Turf. Power. We have no peers, man. We're the Angels. Anybody fucks with us, they pay. I'm sergeant-at-arms. I'm . . . respected."

"You ever kill anybody, Charlie?"

Frank's question comes out of the blue. I stop breathing, intent on Charlie.

He just shakes it off and shrugs. "Naw, not really . . . none I know of anyways. Fucked some people up pretty good, though."

"What about drug dealing in the club?"

"What about it?"

"Who's the biggest dealer in the club?"

"Me!"

"Who else?"

"Duke . . . Sledge used to be."

"Tell us about your business, Charlie."

"I had my own distribution, man. I mean, I was king. They used to call me 'Cha-Ching Charlie.' I took care of my own business. I took care of the club. Nobody rips off the Hells Angels, man."

"What about you, Charlie?"

I make a statue of myself, glaring at Frank. There's a long silence. I'm not sure this is the time or the place to tell Charlie about what he's been accused of, but then Frank puts my concern to rest—and he does it without even looking at me.

"What about the people selling for you?" he asks.

Charlie nods, none the wiser. "I had different ways getting product to them. I'd get somebody to move my shit for me, you know, make the deliveries. Anyway, a guy . . . say, one of my dealers, would get a couple pounds and he'd be pushing that, and then each week I'd go see him to get the cash, see how much product he's got left, how much he needs. Some of these guys, I mean, these dealers, they're not . . . these are not always righteous people, and if they can stick it to you . . . like rip you off any which way, that's what they'll do. So you gotta . . ."

"Take care of business," Frank says.

"Exactly. And keep track of who's got what and what they owe."

"And what did that entail?"

"Entail?"

Frank bites his upper lip, moistening his ashy mustache. "How would you handle it?"

Charlie blows smoke at the ceiling, thinking about it for a while. "Well, first . . . they gotta fear you, man. Because fear . . .

fear brings respect. And for you to fear me, I gotta do certain things. Let you know that when I tell you something, that's how it is. I say 'meet me at 9,' I don't mean no 9:05. And if it *is* 9:05, I'm gonna stomp the shit out of you. I'm gonna break your fuckin' jaw. You understand? I'm gonna whip your ass."

Even though he's lying flat on the bed, Charlie's body language changes, his neck and jaw tightening as he jabs a finger at the gloom overhead.

"You ever whip anybody, Charlie?" I ask.

"Sure." He lifts his head, giving me validation with his menacing death stare. "What do you think, Nick? Why do you think I carry that thing?"

I shrug. "I mean, I've seen the bullwhip. I just figured it was a prop, you know, more for show. An act."

"Fuck that, man. I cracked that fucker and the motherfuckers, they shit their pants."

Frank gives me a look that says 'back off a little,' and I lean back in my chair. He wants to lead. He's headed somewhere with all this.

"So you were the sergeant-at-arms, this enforcer for the club," he says.

"Sergeant-at-arms, man. I'm an officer. And it's the same in Oakland as it is in New York as it is in Buttfuck, Pennsylvania, for all I know. HAs are organized. Crazy motherfuckers . . . but organized. It's like . . . like . . ."

"A corporation," Frank says. "President. Secretary. Treasurer. Weekly meetings to vote on business."

"Yeah. And it was . . . for me, coming out of the joint, it was like . . ." Charlie takes a long pull on his cigarette, drawing the tip to a little red cone. "You know that expression 'High on life'? Well, I was sky-high, man. I mean, shot out of a fuckin' cannon. And it wasn't just the parties and the . . . the pussy, and the money. It was the . . . the whole package, man. I found me a family."

"Love and respect," Frank says.

"Yeah, man. Love and respect. Trust. No lies. *Ever*. Not

inside the club."

"Right."

"Not to another Angel, man. Truth. Respect. And outside the club it's . . . I mean, I'm a fuckin' Hells Angel, man. It's like . . . it's like being a rock star except nobody, and I mean nobody's gonna fuck with you."

"But then . . ."

Charlie becomes still, listening—highly sensitive to changes in Frank's mood. He seems to pick up instantly on the tone of regret in Frank's voice. "Then what?" he asks eventually.

"Well, Charlie, you didn't exactly look much like a rock star when we found you strapped to that bed . . ."

Charlie has nothing to say about this, but he's clearly thinking on it, his dark eyes fixed on the burning tip of his cigarette.

Frank continues. "So Charlie, I'm curious. How did that . . . how did you get there? How did you get from being the Hells Angel, the guy with the bullwhip, kicking the shit out of everybody that crosses you or the club, all the women begging for your attention, to being the guy strapped on that bed?"

Charlie stares up at the ceiling again. We've come to the edge of something here, and we all three feel it. The next step takes us over.

He pauses, and the room is uncomfortably silent.

"You okay?" Frank asks

Charlie presses his chin to his neck. "Yeah, but we're going swimmin', right?"

"Right after we're through."

Silence. Charlie examines the dark crescents of grease under his fingernails, as indelible as tattoos.

"So, Charlie . . ." Frank keeps nudging. "Was it just . . . the drugs? You started using more than . . . more than you could handle? More than Duke was comfortable with?"

"*Fuck* Duke, man . . ." Charlie finishes his cigarette and angrily stabs it out in a saucer next to him on the bed. For a long time, he is silent, just staring up at the ceiling.

"I need to take a piss," he says eventually.

We break off for a few minutes while he does his business. I pause the tape recorder and open a window to let in some freeway exhaust fumes, hoping that by mixing them with the cigarette smoke and the room's rancid odors, we might get something almost tolerable to breathe. Frank stays right where he is by the vanity table, but his eyes are on me as I move about the room.

"Something happened," he says softly. "Something he doesn't want to talk about."

Chapter 15

Tarzan
San Diego, CA
July 9, 1996

"What the fuck, man?"

Charlie sits up on the bed to get a better look at Frank, who's standing in the bathroom doorway, wearing a pair of swim shorts that went out of style with the Cadillac tailfin. They're a kind of olive green with red contrast stitching, and they pinch the fat around the top of Frank's waist and thighs in a way the designers obviously didn't intend.

"Try these on, Charlie," Frank says jovially, flipping a pair across the room.

Charlie holds them up with a comical look on his face —somewhere between suspicion and disgust as he considers swaying palm trees silhouetted on orange polyester. "Come on, Frank," he grunts. "You gotta be kiddin'."

My partner looks aghast. "What's the matter?"

"Jesus, man, where'd you get these? You seen yourself in the mirror?"

"Very funny, Charlie," Frank says. "Come on, let's go. It's pool time. Last one in's a rubber ducky."

Charlie stands reluctantly, holding the swimsuit at arm's length as if it smells funny.

I watch as his expression melts to resignation. He fires a disgusted glance at Frank and then strips from the waist down. But by the time he pulls the shorts over himself, he looks like a new man. He gives himself a once-over, incredulous, but clearly exuberant at the anticipation of finally going swimming.

"Seriously, where the fuck you get these, Frank?"

"Home. Why?"

I watch the pair head down the landing, and Charlie's like a kid, hopping around and flipping his towel at Frank. He asks my partner how long it's been since his shorts actually fit him. Frank just shakes his head. When they get to the bottom, Charlie looks back up at me.

"You comin' or what?"

How they can will themselves to get into that swamp is beyond me. I decide instead to forgo the invitation and grab up an expense voucher I've been working on so I can finish in the sunlight.

La Paloma's pool is a cracked cement and stucco crater in tacky aquamarine. The last time I looked out at it from the room, a kid in coveralls was pulling a rat out of one of the filters; then I watched him pour in enough chlorine to sanitize San Diego Bay. Standing beside it now, I scan its surface. Through a rainbow-shimmery slick of what I guess is suntan lotion, I can see what appears to be a tampon floating on the bottom. Just looking at it makes my skin crawl.

I take a seat on one of the vinyl lattice and tubular steel loungers facing the motel and stack my pile of receipts on the tiled concrete. It seems safe enough, and I have to admit that it feels good to be out here in the sun. From here, I can observe anyone coming or going from the front of the building. So I unwind a little, realizing that the chances of Charlie being spotted in this setting are beyond remote.

Apart from his daily trips to the clinic, most of which involve being scrunched down in the back of the car, this pool will be Charlie's only real link to the outdoors. And to say that he looks happy would be a serious understatement. He whoops and starts plowing up and down the pool with a splashy but determined crawl. It's hard to believe that a little more than two weeks ago, he looked like he was on the brink of death. Frank is less of a swimmer, and after a couple of minutes of bobbing around doing a kind of half-assed breaststroke, he clambers out of the pool and flat-foots it over to where I'm sitting.

"Look at him go," he says, showering my documents with droplets as he slumps into a plastic chair. "Where'd he learn to swim like that?"

"Who the hell knows? Jesus, he looks like Tarzan."

For a minute, we just lounge there, soaking up the rays as we watch our star pupil carve up the pool. We're the only ones out here, and I hope it stays that way.

Taking advantage of one of the rare times we are alone without the possibility of Charlie eavesdropping on our conversation, I look over at Frank splayed out on the lounger soaking up the rays.

"Revenge is a strong motivator, Frank—revenge and retaliation. The way I see it, that's the only reason he's still with us. He sees a way to get back at them for not being there for him when he needed help . . . when he was down on his luck." The sun bouncing off the water makes Frank squint as he lights up a cigarette. He sends out a plume of smoke on a long exhale and then adjusts the lounger, pushing back against the plastic strapping. He looks more like a conventioneer playing hooky on the afternoon PowerPoint presentation than the obsessive cop he really is.

"I think there's more to it than that, Nick."

I watch Charlie swim. He's slowing down, taking a breather at the end of each lap now. "He's a guy with a grudge, Frank," I say. "He's angry about Stacey, but mostly he's angry about being betrayed by the brotherhood. If this project is going to get legs, that's the motivation we need to play on."

Frank nods. "Oh, he's angry all right." He takes a long drag of his cigarette, killing it off. "But I don't think that's why he's talking. . . ."

I wait for my partner to finish his typically dramatic pause. He spends his time rifling through the pack of smokes on the plastic table between us. He lights another one up, then talks through the exhaled smoke.

"I think the reason he's still talking . . . still with us is . . ." He rolls his cigarette hand in the air. "Well, shit. He wants out. He wants out and he wants to make things right. It's a moral thing."

I have to shield my eyes to see the expression on his face. To my surprise, he looks serious.

"I keep telling you, Spence. There's goodness in Charlie. I know it. I've *seen* it."

All I can do is shake my head.

"What?" Frank says.

"I guess I have trouble seeing how you get to be a Hells Angels enforcer with all this goodness inside you . . ."

"Spence . . ." Frank interrupts, projecting a long sigh. "Things start out bad for him. You heard his stories. Grows up using his fists. Before he knows it, he's in the system. Then he's shit out the other end with nothing. He walks out of San Quentin with *nothing*. Just a resume that guarantees a life of grinding, dead-end shit and misery. Like he said a while back, Spence—you're him, what would you do?"

I look across at Charlie. He's back to his thrashing freestyle. He touches the far side of the pool and then turns, pushing up a big wave as he heads back in our direction. I think about the hopelessness he must have felt as a young boy abandoned by his parents. What might he have become had someone cared for him early in life? Nurtured him and loved him?

"You know what I think?" Frank says. "I think he joined the club to belong. To be a part of something. A different guy might've joined a church, got religion. Just like a different guy would've let that convict fuck him in the ass first night in San Quentin. But Charlie's not that guy. Charlie's a fighter and he does *not* back down. He didn't need the Hells Angels to be a tough guy. He just needed a family and they wanted him. Probably the first time in his life he's ever felt wanted . . . except by the cops." Frank snickers at his own attempt at humor.

Charlie reaches the shallow end and stands up in the water, breathing hard. With his long, jet-black hair slicked back, he looks like Geronimo. He turns and finally notices that Frank and I are watching.

"What?" he says.

~ ~ ~ ~

"So, with Duke, you weren't getting along so great ..."

We're back in the room, eating meatball subs and he's unhappy about doing another debrief. He's very quiet, even somber, and once again I get the feeling we've reached the end of something, the edge of something. I think Charlie sees it, too, and I think seeing it unsettles him, forces him again to think about his options, which still include just taking off. Fuck our rules ... our bond. After all, what's holding him?

Stretched out on the bed in a white T-shirt and jeans, his wet hair combed straight back from his forehead, he looks ready to take a nap. But Frank's not letting him do that. Frank's insisting on just a few more questions.

"Is it because Duke ..."

"Duke's an asshole, man."

Frank waits. He knows when to be quiet.

"Yeah ... I mean, he's ... he's all about the club, but really everything he does is to promote hisself, to pump hisself up. I mean, you know, he got all kinds of heat from Oakland because he's like so upfront, bragging about being a Hells Angel and shit, wearing his colors out at these concerts, playing Mr. Big Shot—tough guy Hells Angel. You know he's a big concert promoter?"

"Right."

"Rock and roll shit. He gets all the stars, and he thinks that makes him a somebody. Like a celebrity, you know." Charlie chuffs. "All because he's hanging out with these people and he's got these groupie broads crawling all over him riding on his chopper and sucking his dick in the back of his limos, and pictures being taken and in the news and everything ... which is ... I mean, all this shit's real aggravating to Oakland because they don't want the attention ... the publicity, you know. Keep a low profile."

Charlie takes a breath and gives himself a moment to

calm down. Clearly just mentioning Duke sets him off. And he's not finished yet.

"And . . . but when someone close, someone we should protect and care for . . . gets hurt, he's like . . . he doesn't give a shit, man. I mean, the guy's got no feelings. He's an empty soul, man."

Charlie is completely still, just staring up at the ceiling. It's Frank who breaks the silence. His voice comes through in a low growl. "Did someone get hurt, Charlie?"

Charlie draws a hand across his mustache, keeps his eyes on the gloom overhead. When he finally speaks, there's sadness in his voice that I haven't heard before.

"Yeah . . ." he says. "Yes, they did."

"Who, Charlie?"

Charlie shakes his head. "Tired, man," he says. He rolls over on the bed, his arms crossed.

I'm shocked. The possibility that a man like this could feel sympathy or remorse . . . it just hadn't occurred to me.

Chapter 16

The Braid
San Diego, CA
July 10, 1996

"I'd like to get back to where we left off yesterday, Charlie," Frank says as he flips on the tape recorder. "Tell us about Duke."

Silence. Charlie seems to search for something up there in the gloom.

"I ever tell you about Becky?"

Frank shakes his head, looking confused, "Becky? Bulls old lady?"

"Jay, yeah. Bull," Charlie says.

"So . . . what happened?"

Charlie draws a long breath and massages the bridge of his nose. "Oh this is . . . it's like three months ago. We're coming back from a run."

"A run? Where to?"

"Out to Winterhaven."

"Winterhaven, California?"

"Yeah, just outside Yuma there on the California and Arizona border. We're on Interstate 8 heading west just outside El Centro." Charlie clears his throat, then sits up abruptly. He looks around the room like he doesn't know where he is, then grabs his smokes. He lights up, pulls in a shuddery breath, and shakes out the match. He's sitting on the edge of the bed now, looking straight at Frank, his eyes bright with a rawness and vulnerability that surprise me.

"It's beautiful out there, man . . . so clean . . . big and empty. I love the desert."

"Yeah . . ."

"And we're just . . . there's me and Bull, riding tandem, open road, sun goin' down. The big sky turning that golden orange color, like . . . just beautiful, man . . . hot desert wind blowing in your face and the roar of the pipes and . . ."

He shakes himself out of his trance. "So I've got Stacey on the back and Bull, he's riding with . . . with Becky. She's got this long, blonde hair, you know, that she . . . she ties it up in a . . . like a braid down to her ass. Then . . . anyway, up ahead on the road some guy slams on his brakes. We slow down from, like, eighty to about twenty-five because something happened. And after a while, I can see the accident . . . maybe a hundred feet up ahead. Fuckin' RV and this minivan in a fender bender, and traffic crawlin' past and all the exhaust and it's hot, man. I mean *hot*.

"Anyway, we finally clear the accident and Jay, I guess he just got real pissed off, and as soon as he's clear of all the shit, he opens the throttle and the bike, it . . . it jumps, the front wheel comes off the pavement, he takes off so fast, and . . . and it catches Becky off-guard."

Charlie looks down at his bare feet. For maybe a minute he sits like that. Then he scoots back on the bed and lies flat.

Frank has his eyes fixed on Charlie's face, studying him. "What happened, Charlie?"

Charlie takes a breath. He covers his eyes with his arm.

"Becky . . . she sort of rears back. And her hair . . . her braid, it gets caught in the . . . in the spokes or somethin', man."

Frank is completely immobile, the tape recorder clutched in his hand. Charlie squeezes tears out from under his eyelids and takes a drag on the cigarette.

"Happened so fast. It just . . . I mean, the back wheel, it just *rips* her . . . I mean it *rips* her out of the seat like she was . . . like a broken doll or something, you know? Wham. And Jay, he loses control, lays the bike down."

We all sit there blinking, I guess trying not to picture the horror of the scene.

"By the time I get up to them," Charlie continues, "Jay's getting to his feet and I can see Becky . . . her pretty face all smashed, and her scalp like . . ." Again he closes his eyes, shaking.

"Jesus Christ," he manages after a moment. "I mean, she's half fucking scalped, man. But she's . . . when I get off the bike and run over, she's still alive, and I can see in her eyes that she knows what's happening.

"'Becky?' I say. 'Becky?'

"And there's traffic, all these cars just driving past, people putting their headlights on to get a better look, but nobody stops to help, right? I mean, we're fuckin' Hells Angels, man. They're givin' us the finger and shit. Who's gonna stop for *us*? We're out there in the middle of nowhere and nobody's gonna stop."

Charlie looks at his hands. "And I . . . me and Jay, we try to pick her up, and we kinda have to drag her off the highway onto the dirt. And there's dust and dirt and shit and blood all over her pretty face. Jay tries to clean it off her mouth, but then she . . . she kind of . . . she just goes still. She looks up at the sky, and her eyes are so clean and clear. And I'll never forget it, man. . . . Her eyes. They just . . . and then she's gone."

It's so quiet in the room I can hear the tape cassette turning.

"We couldn't do anything," Charlie says. "Just sat there and watched her die. Becky. She was . . . she was good people, man."

Charlie's done. He stands and goes over to the window, looking out at the pool.

"You want to take a minute, Charlie?"

"And you know what Duke says?" Charlie asks. "He says, 'tough break, Jay,' when he hears about it, 'tough break, man.' Fucker didn't even go to her funeral. Told me she was a worthless piece of shit and a lousy fuck. A 'whore,' he called her. 'Good riddance,' he said."

Charlie turns. "Tough break. Like, whatever. . . . Because he don't give a fuck, man. Love and respect? I didn't see none of that. She's family, man, but Duke, he don't see it that way. And Jay, I don't know, he just kind of sucked it up, but I . . . I . . ."

"You didn't."

Charlie shakes his head. "It fucked me up, man. Me and Stacey. I mean, I couldn't even sleep. And then this one night, I just, I was like crawling out of my skin and . . . I just needed to . . ." He mimes injecting himself with a needle. "And all the badness . . . it just went away." He smiles, but it's more like a grimace than a smile. "And the next day I did the same thing. Hell, I'd been off the shit for a year. I just slipped up, man."

"All because of this accident . . ."

"Yeah. The accident. Other stuff."

"What other stuff, Charlie?"

Charlie shrugs. Whatever the other stuff is, it looks like we're not going to hear about it.

"That Thursday I missed church," he says. "You know, our church? Every Thursday we have this club meeting to . . ."

"Sure, Charlie," Frank says gently. "I know about church."

"Well, in the club you don't just miss church, so . . . so Duke calls me in . . . to the clubhouse, you know, and . . . and I'm not sleeping and this whole thing with Becky's got me fucked up, man. Anyway, so Duke, he really . . . he's pissed, you know? 'You gotta butch up, Charlie . . . shit happens, Charlie . . . get your fucking act together, Charlie . . . and . . . by the way, you need to get out there and be doing your fuckin' job . . . you're a Hells Angel. Gotta take care of business.'"

Charlie pauses, then looks over at me and Frank. "It's about the money, see? With Duke, it's all about the money. Fuck the money, man. What happened to love and respect?"

~~~~

As he sits in his office, Duke stares across the table at his sullen attorney, a bulging and balding shyster named Myron Silverman. Their conversation has stalled and Duke is incensed. He'd been under the impression that Silverman had come to the clubhouse—something highly unusual for him— so he could fill his client in on whatever progress he's made with his police contacts. But so far, he's done nothing but whine about his past-due retainer fee.

"Look," Silverman says, clearly uncomfortable to be in the bowels of the Hells Angels' clubhouse. "I don't get paid by the end of the week, I'm dropping the pending cases I'm working for Bad Eye and the others. You guys can get yourself another attorney."

Duke takes a deep breath and looks down at the solid mahogany desk separating him from his attorney. He knows better than to jerk the guy around here. As slimy as he is, Silverman's a capable attorney—he ought to be with a $500K retainer—so he'll know how to read through any bullshit and he sure as hell won't stand for being stiffed out of money he's owed. Duke takes his time coming up with a suitable response. He knows his position demands that he remain alert for deception and subterfuge—both from outside the club and within—and he's certainly not about to share or entrust any club secrets or club business with the likes of Myron Silverman, despite the thinly veiled protection of attorney-client privilege. Cautious to a fault, Duke leaves no stone unturned, which is why he insists that all private meetings like this one take place in his crowded, little office where it's safest. Apart from his surrounding army, Duke has reputedly taken it one step further by installing electronic counter-surveillance equipment implanted in the walls and doorframes, designed to signal an alert anytime someone walks in wearing a transmitting device of any kind. A wire.

"I keep telling you, Myron," Duke says, placating. "Reason we're looking for Charlie is we think it mighta been him who ripped off our legal fund . . . uh . . . your retainer. He just disappeared into thin air. This search should interest you as much as it does us."

Leaning forward in his chair, Silverman plants a firm index finger down on Duke's desk. "I did what you asked, Duke," he says with more than a hint of agitation. "I've called everyone in my Rolodex and Slade hasn't turned up in the system . . . anywhere. None of my cop sources have anything current on the guy, and if I keep asking around, people are going to get suspicious why I'm so interested in him. I'm not working pro bono for you guys. I've got expenses to cover, and I personally don't care where you come up with my retainer."

Duke heaves a sigh of disappointment, and his eyes project a heavy dose of his own brand of agitation. He decides it's better to stick to business here than react with a quick-tempered response to his corpulent counselor's insolence.

"Well . . . at least the cops don't have him. Maybe the fucker'll just turn up dead. Know what I mean?" Duke signals his message with wink.

The attorney leans forward as if whispering a confession to the Pope. "About that," he murmurs. "Just because Slade hasn't turned up with any of my contacts doesn't mean you don't still have a potential problem. He could be working with the feds. I mean from what you say, the guy's a walking time bomb for you."

Duke shakes his head slowly.

Silverman starts to fidget. "Duke," he whispers, "before you go off and do something you'll regret, you better think about how you're going to handle the situation."

"*Handle* it?" Duke blurts. "You tellin' *me* how to handle my own shit?"

If the attorney didn't look uncomfortable before, he does now. "I'm just suggesting that when you do find him —presuming he isn't dead—you better make sure he's clean. Then whatever you do with him," the counselor mumbles, "make sure it's handled . . . discreetly."

Duke chuckles, despite himself.

"Otherwise, you'll be giving the feds exactly what they want." The attorney's voice by now is scarcely audible.

"You got any suggestions . . . I mean, on the fed angle?"

Silverman leans closer, his eyes widening with conspiracy. "Allow him back into the circle," he whispers.

"How the fuck—"

"Hear me out, Duke." Silverman takes his time. "You let him back in. Cautiously. And you try to read him. You *know* the guy. If he's working for the feds, he'll be acting strange, nervous, anxious. Give him a . . . uh . . . you know . . . loyalty test."

Duke rocks back in his chair eying the beads of sweat popping from Silverman's forehead.

"You know . . . ," the attorney adds with more than a hint of darkness, ". . . see where it leads." He circles his hand over his head. "Shit, you got all this fancy electronic equipment, anyway. If Slade comes in here wearing a wire, you'll know it."

The president opens his mouth to speak but is interrupted by a head poking through the door. The club secretary.

"Got a minute, Duke?" Gonzo asks.

Duke motions toward his attorney, suggesting without words that he's busy.

As if waiting for the first opportunity to leave, Silverman practically leaps to his feet. "Should get going," he mumbles. "Gotta prepare for court in the morning."

"Fine," Duke says, perturbed by the interruption. "Keep to the fuckin' phones, man. In case somethin' comes up."

Silverman throws up his hands as he departs—an apparent sign of exasperation.

~ ~ ~ ~

"It's about Jacumba," Gonzo says, his voice just above a whisper.

"Great," Duke says, standing and patting his secretary on the shoulder. "You can brief us in church on Thursday."

Gonzo holds his ground in the doorway. "Hold on," he says. "I need a coupla minutes in private."

"Make it quick." Duke slides impatiently back behind his desk and flops down in his chair.

The secretary keeps to his feet. "Talked to my sources," he says, gesturing wildly, as always. "Jacumba lab's a gold mine. Fully equipped and pumpin' out huge quantities of righteous shit. Best part is, the cooks are a coupla crank heads who like to sample their product a little too often—know what I mean?"

Duke nods.

"Anyway, it's *ripe* for pickin' and security's weak."

"Whose operation?" Duke grunts.

"You ready for this?" Gonzo leans over the desk to ensure he impresses his leader. "It's the Esposito brothers, man. It don't get no better than this."

"You're jokin'," Duke says, reveling in the find. There's nothing the San Diego Hells Angels enjoy more than commandeering a lab from these two dagos. The president pushes back in his chair and clasps his hands behind his head. "So what's with the hush-hush?"

"Thing is, Duke," Gonzo says, stepping back scratching at his mangled beard, "I wanna get paid on this one."

"We're *all* gonna get paid, Gonz. Same as always."

"No," Gonzo sneers, leaning over the desk again. "I want a bigger percentage on this one."

Duke blasts air through his nose. "This is our brotherhood, man. You know that. Everybody gets an equal share."

"Not this time, man," Gonzo says, his head rollicking back as he straightens up. "This one's big and I found it, goddamnit, Duke. I feel like I deserve somethin' more. You know . . . a bigger piece of the pie."

Duke stands and walks slowly toward his secretary, who starts to back away from the desk. The president is angry at first, but the anger quickly fades as he contemplates the opportunity presented him here. His greedy eyes quickly turn conspiratorial as he takes Gonzo by the arm and leads him just to the edge of the door. "Let me handle this, Gonz," he whispers. "Maybe there *is* something we can work out here."

Gonzo nods with vigor.

"But only if this lab is what you say it is."

"Total profit center," Gonzo says with a wave of his hand.

Duke cranes his neck and offers a wry smile. "You got gambling debts or somethin', man? I never seen you like this."

Gonzo grins, exposing his yellowed teeth. "Nah, man," he mumbles. "Just feel like I got it comin'. I'm the one out there humpin', doin' all the work. What's the other guys contributed lately? Who's the guy makin' all the money for this outfit?"

The president pats the secretary on the back and makes for the door. He wears a jovial expression on his face, but inside he broods. As they walk down the hall, he considers what all this means. Gonzo. He just stood up in front of his leader and demanded the opportunity to sell out the club. Skim some profits. Though he's not one to turn away from an opportunity to enrich himself, Duke knows he's going to have to play this one close to the vest. He's not about to expose his own nefarious schemes by conspiring with a loose cannon like Gonzo.

Chapter 17

Rolex
San Diego, CA
July 10, 1996

Maybe it's the swimming or talking about how Becky died, but Charlie's out cold by the time I finish writing up my daily log and securing the tape transcriptions for evidence. Frank and I take the opportunity to go next door, leaving our door ajar.

We go back and forth on what exactly Charlie's latest disclosure represents for the case. Frank's excited—thinks Charlie's little monologue confirms his idea that Charlie's feelings about Duke and the club go beyond a simple grudge. But whatever the underlying dynamics, we're both pretty clear that our time at La Paloma has come to an end. If we want to take this any further, we'll need to bring in more agents, which will mean a place that accommodates a little more foot traffic —a house or an apartment, somewhere with more space—a place where we stand a better chance of keeping Charlie happy for a few months.

"I was thinking somewhere down by the beach," Frank says. "Not too expensive but . . ."

"Frank."

"What?"

"Before we even talk about taking things any further, we need to get something straight."

"What?"

I shoot an intense gaze at my partner. He's wearing the confused look of a basset hound, his mouth hanging open.

"The wire, Frank. If we're really moving forward, we need to know if Charlie will wear a wire. We need some kind of commitment from him. Is he willing to *do* these guys or not? Blair will want to know . . . and soon."

Frank goes pensive, his head drooping for a moment.

"Debriefings and intelligence reports only go so far when it comes to spending the Bureau's money," I say.

"Right." Frank continues to brood, stroking his mustache. "I'll talk to him about it."

"When?"

Frank thrusts his hands out, cocking his head. "I don't know, Spence. Today. Tomorrow. Jesus. I'd kind of like to hear more about the club. About Duke. I think there's . . ."

"He's had it with the debriefs," I interrupt.

"You think so? I don't know. I think this afternoon was a breakthrough for him. Could be he wants to talk more."

At that moment the door comes open. Charlie's standing there with a towel around his middle.

"Every time I turn my back, you guys go into a huddle."

Frank stands. "We thought you were sleeping, Charlie."

Charlie looks out on the landing, turns back to us.

"I was. I need to get out of this place, man."

"We were just talking about that," Frank says.

"Yeah?"

"Yeah. How would you feel if we got you into a house? Somewhere you could move around more."

"You don't get it, man. I'm talking about *now*. I've had it. I want to go back in the pool."

"You just got out of the pool."

Charlie roils into his death stare. "And now I want to get back in," he snorts. "Come on, Frank. Get your fucking shorts on."

It's late afternoon, but there's still plenty of heat in the sun. Charlie drops straight into the water from the side and starts plowing it up again. Frank and I take seats, both of us sizing up the sleazy guy reading a copy of *Penthouse* at one of the tables over by a rusting barbecue. He's acting like he didn't see us arrive, but he's obviously got us on his radar and I'm wondering what he's thinking, eyeing two stiffs and an emaciated junkie covered with tattoos hanging out by the pool. The guy's pretty typical of the clientele here. Shifty eyes, gold chains, black greasy hair, big Hollywood sunglasses, and "probable cause" stamped on his forehead.

"See, this is the thing," I say, keeping my voice down. "Now we let him out whenever he wants, he's not going to agree to be shut in anymore. It won't be long and the tail will be wagging the dog, if it isn't already."

Frank watches Charlie swim for a while.

"It's going to need outside space," he says, as if he didn't hear a word I just said. When he turns back to me, his eyes are pressed closed. "The house. The apartment. How much do you think Blair's gonna kick in for rent?"

"I'll talk to him," I say, my shoulders falling slack at the idea. "Just based on what we've given him so far, I don't see him approving more than five, six hundred a month. And even that will have deadlines attached."

Frank looks surprised. "Five hundred? That sounds a little tight." He starts pawing at his knees, fidgeting, as he turns back to watch Charlie. "Don't know if five hundred gets you a yard. One with a fence. Maybe a place with a balcony or roof terrace."

"I'll do the best I can, Frank. I'm not exactly leading a charmed life back at the office."

Frank nods. "What's the latest?"

"OPR's been out snooping around the office, you know, reviewing my personnel file, interviewing people. Took a statement from Klecko. I'll bet that was a zinger. I guess they'll want my statement soon. They usually move pretty slow on these things unless it's a matter of life and death."

Charlie comes to the edge of the pool, flops his arms over the side. "Not coming in, Frank?" he asks, sounding disappointed.

"Not this time," Frank says, and I can see he doesn't like Charlie saying his name in front of the eavesdropping greaseball any more than I do.

Charlie picks up Frank's chilly vibe and climbs out of the water. He comes over to our table and grabs a towel. Over on the other side of the pool, our company gets up and slithers back into the building.

"The fuck's this?" Charlie asks softly.

I turn and see him pick something up from under a pool lounger near where we are. It's a gold wristwatch with a chunky bezel, barely visible under the shade of the lounger. Charlie lowers himself into a lounger.

"Fuckin' Rolex, man. Must be my lucky day."

It's so bizarre, so unlikely, that I immediately think Frank must have planted it there. Some kind of practical joke. I mean, how often do you come across Rolex watches lying around on the ground, especially in a dump like this? I look across at him, but he's watching Charlie slip the watch onto his wrist and clip the bracelet shut.

Frank leans in to get a better look. "Is it real?" He taps a fingernail against the crystal.

Charlie's still shaking his head in disbelief, admiring the watch on his wrist. He tilts his head back, catching the last rays of sun going down behind the freeway.

It's Frank who breaks the silence. "Charlie," he says with a sigh. "You know somebody left that watch there—probably took it off to swim. They're probably in their room right now looking around and wondering where the hell it is."

Charlie just smiles his tight-lipped smile.

"How long do you think it's gonna take before they come back down here?" Frank says.

Charlie looks proud of himself as he holds his arm out, examining the watch. "You don't know that, Frank. You don't know any of that. Fuckin' thing's probably stolen."

"Charlie."

Charlie turns and shoots Frank an irritated gaze. "What? You want me to put it back on the ground? Pretend I never saw it? Leave it there for some other fucker to pick up? Fuck that, man."

Frank runs his fingers up through his mustache, dragging against the bristle. "I don't want you to put it back, Charlie," he says, his voice coming through in a whispery growl. "I want you to take it to the lobby. I want you to turn it in."

Charlie stares at Frank for a second, trying to make out if he's joking here. Frank returns the stare, stone-cold serious.

"Where I come from, it's finders, keepers," Charlie says.

"Well, where I come from, that makes you a fuckin' thief."

Charlie sets his jaw at this, but he doesn't say anything.

"Charlie," Frank says in the same low growl. "It's all different now. You're with *us*." He points at his barrel chest.

Charlie looks at the watch on his wrist, the gold lustrous against his dark skin. "Am I, Frank?"

"Yes, you are, Charlie. Because you're better than this. I *know* that. You're one of the good guys."

"Good guys," Charlie sneers, his chin pressed to his neck. "Who the fuck *are* the good guys, Frank?"

"We are."

"What . . . the fuckin' cops?"

"Fuck the cops," Frank says tersely. "I'm talking about me. I'm talking about Spence." He points back and forth between us. "Us."

Charlie's glaring at me now. I return his stare.

"You're with us, Charlie," Frank goes on. "And you can trust us. All the way down the line."

Charlie almost smiles at this. "What's this, Frank? Love and respect?"

"I don't know if I can give you my love," Frank says.

It's meant as a joke, and that's how Charlie sees it. He throws his head back, laughing, covering his mouth with his hand.

"But I guarantee the respect," Frank says, deadly serious now.

Charlie stops laughing, becomes thoughtful again.

"Respect and trust," Frank says. "If you're ready to earn it. And I'll work to earn yours."

I've seen Frank talk this way with guys before. If you

don't know him, it can sound kind of preachy. But there's no bullshit with Frank. It comes from the heart. Straight and strong.

Charlie thinks about it for a second, still eyeing the watch.

"Did you put this fucking thing on the ground?" he asks, after a while.

"No, I did not."

Charlie turns to me.

"Nick?"

"Jesus, where am I going to come up with a gold Rolex, Charlie?"

"There's a Rolex watch on the ground," he says. "It's right there on the ground and you guys don't see it?" Charlie shakes his head. "It's a fucking test. Some kind of bullshit test."

"Life's a test," Frank says.

Charlie unclips the bracelet and holds the watch up in the dying light.

"Do the right thing, Charlie. Take it to the lobby. Give it to the desk clerk."

"Fuckin' clerk's gonna put it in his pocket," Charlie says angrily.

"Maybe," Frank says. "But that'll be for him to decide. That'll be *his* test. But I don't think it'll play out that way. I mean, if I'm the owner, I come back out to the pool, and if I don't find it here, I go straight to the front desk to see if someone's handed in my watch."

"Frank . . ."

"I'm serious about this. This is the way we do things. You're with us now, and this is how it's got to be."

"Okay," Charlie says after a while.

"Okay *what*?"

"Okay. . . ." He pauses for a moment, shrugging as he looks away. "I'll hand the fucker in."

Chapter 18

Confrontations
San Diego, CA
July 12, 1996

The early morning sun is streaming through the large windows of the office of FBI Special Agent-in-Charge Norman Ziegler. Standing in the doorway, the first thing I see is Klecko's self-righteous image reflecting off the glassy sheen of the large conference table. I'm thinking that *one* of him in the room is plenty. Two other "suits" are sitting at the conference table as SAC Ziegler motions for me to approach the table.

"Good morning, Nick," he says. "Come in."

Klecko remains glued in his seat as the two others stand to greet me.

"Nick, these gentlemen are from the Office of Professional Responsibility. This is Inspector Donelan and his assistant, Special Agent Allhart."

I shake their extended hands and offer a cordial greeting to each before taking a seat across from my gloating former supervisor. Everyone sits except Inspector Donelan.

"You know the drill, Agent Spence. We've conducted a thorough investigation of the incident in question, interviewed pertinent witnesses, talked to some of your former supervisors and coworkers, and reviewed your personnel file. Unfortunately, this isn't the first OPR complaint against you, and it always seems to involve the same issues: insolence and insubordination. In the past we've tolerated your brash and impertinent behavior in deference to your exceptional performance ratings. But in this case, you have clearly crossed the line by instigating a physical altercation with your supervisor. This is unacceptable and intolerable behavior for a special agent of the FBI."

I glance over at a smirking Klecko, who's nodding in concert with Donelan's indictment. If I had any balls right now, and didn't value my career so much, I'd reach across the table and smack the arrogant prick.

"We are recommending a letter of censure and thirty days on the bricks without pay," Donelan deadpans. "Your personnel file will contain a letter from the director that any further acts of insubordination will be grounds for dismissal. Do you understand, Agent Spence? Do you have anything to add?"

I know it's a good time to keep my mouth shut, but I have never been much good at it, as evidenced by my current state of affairs.

"With respect, Inspector Donelan, I feel it would be a disservice to hardworking agents risking their lives working Bureau cases to not warn of the disconnect that exists between the field offices and Headquarters. Won't you people ever realize that MAP is a total failure?" I stand and gesture toward Klecko. "Here's a perfect example right here. You select a guy with very little field investigative experience, someone totally lacking interpersonal skills—not to mention a zero personality—and a narcissistic ego the size of Mt. Rushmore and put him through two weeks of your highly vaunted Management Aptitude Program. You shit him out the other end, make him a supervisor, and send him out to us here in the field presumably with direct oversight of the Bureau's biggest cases. And we're supposed to follow his lead. The program is a complete failure. Your selection process stinks. Street agents call your MAP the 'Make A Prick' program."

Klecko takes the bait and lunges out of his chair, knocking it over backward. He charges around the table toward me, his jowls shuddering in an aura of red heat emanating from his face. "I've had it with your bullshit, Spence. This is the last time you're going to insult me like this, you fucking . . ."

Everyone leaps to their feet, and Ziegler positions himself to block Klecko racing toward me. "Stand down, Klecko," he bellows. "This meeting is adjourned and *you* are excused." Donelan and Allhart have taken a couple of steps back, both with astonished looks on their faces. Klecko stands face to face with the SAC not moving, the bulging veins in his neck pulsating wildly. "*Now*, Klecko," Ziegler barks. "You're dismissed." Klecko collects himself, and as his shoulders slump he turns to leave. I still can't keep my mouth shut.

"There . . . there's a perfect example of what I'm talking about. You can't train someone how to react under stress . . ."

"Shut up, Spence. Get out of my office," Ziegler hisses.

~~~~

As I pull into the parking lot behind La Paloma, I sit there in the Bureau car assessing the morning's tribunal. Although my career is somewhat safe, for now, I won't be given any leeway the next time. Ziegler has negotiated with OPR to delay my punishment until the conclusion of the Hells Angels investigation. I figure Ziegler's got to know what an incompetent pinhead Klecko is. Ziegler's a stand-up guy and doesn't pull any punches, but he's still got to play it by the book. He has no choice. I fucked up and was clearly insubordinate. It doesn't matter that Klecko's a loser. I conclude that thirty days off would do me some good, but I certainly don't like not getting a paycheck.

~~~~

As I'm climbing the metal staircase that leads up the back side of La Paloma to the second tier, where our rooms are located, I hear loud yelling coming from one of the rooms down the corridor. It takes me a second to realize that the voices I'm hearing—angry voices—belong to Frank and Charlie.

I rush ahead and push open the door to Charlie's room. I find Frank and Charlie squared off under the florescent light fixture. Charlie is touching at a bleeding cut on his forehead.

"What the hell's going on?"

Charlie stabs out a finger. "He's fuckin' crazy, man," he screams. "Comes in here . . ."

Frank is tear-assed, standing there white-lipped with his fists clenched.

"He throws the fuckin' thing in my face," Charlie blurts.

"What thing?" I say.

"You fucking *lied* to me, Charlie," Frank growls through gritted teeth.

"What did you throw?" I ask of my partner. "What the hell's going on?"

Frank points at the floor. In among the tangled sheets is the Rolex.

I scratch the side of my head. "You threw the *watch* at him?"

"You're a fucking liar," Frank says to Charlie. He's heaving. Blistering mad. I've never seen him like this.

"Fuck you, motherfucker," Charlie says eloquently.

I push the door shut behind me. "Jesus," I breathe. "Calm down, you guys. The whole neighborhood can hear you."

Charlie dabs at the big welt that's coming up under the cut on his forehead and shoots me an ugly look. "Fuck you, too, Spence. I'll take both you motherfuckers down."

So here we are. It's that schoolyard put-up-or-shut-up moment. Squares and regulars. Despite the fact my heart is racing, I see it all like a fading dream, like some sort of slow-motion movie. This can't really be happening. Charlie's scary as hell in this mood, dark eyes blazing, steady as a rock, ready to rumble. He is, as they say, in his element here. I figure I can always try hitting him over the head with a chair. Shooting him is probably not a good option, although he's clearly fixing to kill my partner.

"Charlie..."

"Stay out of it, Nick."

Amazingly, this comes from Frank. He raises a hand to stop my traffic, keeping his eyes on Charlie.

"Come on, you assholes," I say. "Someone's gonna get hurt."

"Yeah, and it's gonna be Frank," Charlie blurts.

Frank doesn't seem to like this at all. A tight little smile twists his mouth as he presses his fists closer to his face.

Charlie cocks his head back. The death stare returns. "Take your best shot, motherfucker, 'cause I'm gonna kick your ass."

What happens next goes quick. Frank throws a punch as Charlie steps inside. With surprising control and power, the Hells Angel hooks two tight, hard shots into Frank's ribs, then snaps through an uppercut. Frank goes down like a stockyard steer. It's a matter of two seconds between Frank throwing his left and him lolling on the bed with his tongue sticking out. He's out cold.

I knee my way onto the bed, slap Frank's face. He coughs, groans. When I look up, I see Charlie's backed away to what I guess would be the neutral corner if this were a boxing ring. He's standing there, fists pressed together, snorting like a bull, ready to come back in.

"Charlie, for chrissake, get some water," I yell.

Charlie snaps out of it, as if in some kind of hypnotic trance, and goes into the bathroom. He emerges a moment later, carrying a plastic cup brimming with water. I splash a little over Frank's face and then empty the rest. He comes around, spluttering.

"Ohhhh . . ." For a second, he feels at his jaw, which is already starting to swell up under the point of his chin. "What happened?"

"It's okay, Frank."

"What happened?"

I can't help but smirk. "You told Charlie to take his best shot. So he did."

Frank sits up slowly, and he stays that way for a while, holding his chin.

Charlie's backed away into his corner again. "Sorry, Frank," he says, and he sounds like he means it.

Frank flips a dismissive hand at him. "Forget it," he says. "I asked for it."

"No," Charlie says. "I mean about the watch." He slides along next to the bed and scoops up the watch from the sheets. He paces back and forth for a while, holding the thing in front of his face.

"Do the right thing, Charlie," Frank says, his voice a low grumble.

Charlie stops and lets his arm fall to his side, the Rolex dangling. His shoulders slump as he stares down at the green, threadbare carpet under his bare feet, then turns and heads for the door. He slams it behind him before I can react. I look at Frank with a pair of eyes that say, "What the hell?"

"Let him go," Frank whispers.

"You've got to be kidding me," I groan.

"Trust me."

~~~~

After all we've been through to get this far, I'm despondent as hell as I sit alone in the next room. How could it have come to this? Frank just got the shit kicked out of him by our rising star witness and now Charlie's out there alone for the first time since we found him, carrying a $10,000 watch. He has every reason to put as much distance as he can between Frank, me, and the FBI and go find the nearest pawn shop. My thirty days on the bricks is going to come sooner than I thought.

Whether Frank believes in him or not, the realist in me knows Charlie's a goner. A half hour passes. Then an hour goes by and I'm thinking of packing up and going home.

I'm shocked when the door quietly opens and Charlie shuffles in, his shoulders sloped and his head down. He's got one of his hands jammed into his pocket and the other rubbing the ugly mark on his forehead. I watch him go around to the bathroom and grab a drink of water. He catches my look as he passes by. "What?"

"You okay?"

He shrugs.

"Did you give the watch back?"

Charlie nods, and there's a look on his face—a kind of serious, quiet, almost introspective look . . . a soft look that I'm not used to. This whole thing with the watch has obviously shaken him, and again I find myself puzzled. I try to put myself in his shoes, but I can't figure it. If I'm Charlie, I say fuck it; I keep the watch and ride off into the sunset. I try to think of it from Frank's angle—the notion that Charlie's feeling his way toward a better self—but I can't do that, either. So, *what the hell is it? What is it that's keeping him in our camp?*

"The fuck you staring at, Nick?"

I snap back into focus, assessing his now familiar riveting stare as he stands over me.

"Frank'll be okay," I say. "He's tougher than a two-dollar steak."

He says nothing, but I can almost hear him brooding as he takes a seat in the red vinyl armchair in the corner, thinking, no doubt, about Frank, who's lying on the bed next door holding a pack of ice to his jaw.

"You'll see," I say. "By dinner, he'll be his usual pain-in-the-ass self."

Whatever Charlie's thinking, he doesn't want to share it. Sitting with his elbows on his knees, he stares at the ground as he massages the cut on his forehead, which juts out in a lump.

"We should get you some ice for that cut, maybe."

He raises his head and looks me straight in the eye. "Why does he care?"

For a second, I don't know what he's talking about.

"Frank," he says. "Why does he care so much? About me doing the right thing, I mean."

I have to think about it for a second.

"We need you to be our witness, Charlie. We need you on our side. If you're not straight, truthful, and honest about everything from here on out, you're no good to us. You'll be vulnerable on the stand. The case'll fall apart. Frank wants you to—"

"The case . . . Jesus, Nick. Is that all you think about?"

"No, Charlie, I have a lot to think about," I say, knowing as I say it that he has no idea what I mean. "Sure the case is important, but . . ."

"That's the difference between you and Frank," Charlie says.

"What is?"

Charlie sighs. "Well, like this morning when he woke me up. I wake up and he's holding the watch in his hand, and . . . You shoulda seen his face, man. You shoulda seen his face when he threw that fucker at me."

"Frank's got a temper."

"No, it's more than that." Charlie shifts in his seat, trying to get comfortable. "It's what I was saying about you and Frank. With you, it's just a job, man. With Frank, it's . . ."

He doesn't know what it is.

"A crusade," I say, and I guess he thinks it's the right word, because he says it to himself a couple of times.

"It's all or nothing with Frank," I add.

Chapter 19

House and Paul
San Diego, CA
July 15, 1996

Despite the drama of the past few days, it's clear from a security standpoint that we've overstayed our time here at La Paloma. If nothing else, we're too close to the methadone clinic. The daily trips back and forth with Charlie are risky. Staying here in Old Town isn't safe any longer and, besides, Charlie hasn't been exactly invisible around the motel. I don't know what the Hells Angels have in store for this guy, but while he's with us, we owe it to him to do our best to keep them away from him, and that means to keep moving.

Since the Rolex incident, we've left Charlie pretty much alone, deciding to give him some space. The past couple of days, we've mostly holed up in the adjoining room catching up on reports, making phone calls, and getting some rest ourselves. We can hear him stumbling around next door. The television's blaring twenty-four/seven. Frank and I are eating a pizza at the dinette in our room when Charlie knocks and shuffles in barefoot.

"What? You guys don't like me no more?"

"Come on in, Charlie," I say. "How about a slice?"

"Nah," he says. "Sick of pizza."

He flops down on one of the twin beds and jams the pillow up under his head. "I've been thinkin'," he mutters. "We been here almost three weeks and all you guys do is talk. Ask questions. Don't you ever arrest nobody, you know, throw people in the joint?"

I sneak a glance at Frank, then turn to Charlie. "Well, Charlie, that's the general idea, but ..."

"But *what*, man?" he says. "Let's get out there and kick some ass. Come on. What'er we sittin' around here for? Let's have some fun."

~ ~ ~ ~

The following morning, I get a surprising call from Paul Rudnik saying he's found a place he thinks is going to work for us.

"Jeez, Paul," I say. "That was quick. How many places did you look at?"

"One. But don't worry, it's perfect."

Paul's right. The house is perfect in the sense that it's a two-bedroom dump of a bungalow with a garage facing the alley and a backyard surrounded by a high wooden fence. There's a door from the garage into the backyard and another door from the backyard into the kitchen, which means we can come and go with minimal exposure to the street—the kind of street where Charlie, if he ever *is* seen coming and going, will fit right in with all the surf bums and burned-out potheads that live in the neighborhood.

There are at least three cars jacked up on blocks in front lawns along the street. Chain-link fence is the preferred form of enclosure for the bald little lawns and weed-strangled gardens out front. A single palm tree struggling on the corner is really the only indication that we're still in Southern California—Pacific Beach, to be exact. PB to the locals.

It takes us a couple of days to get set up, but even with a little ant infestation problem and a temperamental shower, the place is a huge improvement on La Paloma. For one thing, we can turn around without bumping into each other, a significant advantage now that Paul Rudnik has joined our merry little band. My latest plea to my new supervisor for additional help finally bore fruit with Paul's full-time assignment to our project. Frank's ecstatic to get Paul on our team, as he's been insistent from the beginning that Paul would be the best man for the job.

Charlie doesn't know what to make of him at first, but after a couple of days he and Paul seem to click just like

Frank said they would. Six-foot-four, Paul has the wholesome look of a ballplayer, a star quarterback maybe, and there's a good-heartedness to him that Charlie really seems to respond to. Cheerful and outgoing, yet confident and firm, the young agent will help ease the load for Frank and me. Watching them through the kitchen window, pumping iron—Frank bought a set of rusty weights at a thrift store in the hopes of keeping Charlie amused and to build him back up—I can't help thinking about Charlie's brother, Jake, and how Paul might at some level be filling a void for Charlie. It's uncanny how they get along right from the start.

I find myself wondering how much of this dynamic Frank foresaw. When I see Charlie at his lowest and saddest, I sometimes feel a little uncomfortable with the idea of exploiting his weakness . . . his fragility. Like we're going to be his best buddies for the rest of his life.

But however else I look at it, as our key-witness-in-the-making, Charlie is coming along like an express train. We've finally been able to get approval for a physician up the coast to treat Charlie and administer the methadone as needed. This is a far cry from just taking him to that half-assed clinic and far less risky. Now we can more closely monitor his vital signs and get some professional advice about his recovery. Having decided that he's ready to wear a wire and go the distance, all he wants in the world is to get back out on the street—something we have to be very careful about, of course. Controlling Charlie in a house is one thing; controlling him out there in the jungle is another thing altogether.

"Why can't I just go score some dope for you guys?"

"It's not that simple, Charlie," I say.

We're sitting around in the kitchen, picking at the remains of some pizza on a Wednesday night. Me, Frank, Paul, and Charlie—a bunch of regular guys.

"How come you always say that, Nick?"

"Because it's true. For one thing, we've got to work out a way to get you back in the game. We need a story."

"What do you mean, a story?"

"Well, it's like . . . where's Charlie been . . . what's he been doing? We know Duke's been looking for you. We know he's pissed. And it may be even more threatening than that. We need to come up with something that gets you back in his good favor."

"Seems to me, where's Charlie been is the big question," Paul says, his mouth stuffed with pizza. "How come he disappeared?"

I look at Charlie for some kind of feedback to what Paul just said. If he stole the money from the club, you'd expect some kind of reaction, a nervous twitch, some sign of discomfort.

"Got myself a room in La Jolla," Charlie says calmly. "Put myself into that clinic. Wanted to get clean."

"La Jolla, Charlie?" Paul says, swallowing his food and cracking a big, toothy smile. "You fit right in there."

"Yeah, La Jolla, Paul," Charlie sneers. "*Where I don't know nobody*. You gotta better idea for a cover?"

"No, Charlie. Just picturing you in La Jolla, that's all."

Charlie flips a piece of pepperoni at him and delivers right between the eyes. He flashes Paul a harmless sneer.

"It's La Jolla because you don't know anyone up there," Frank says. "That's good. I like it."

"You knew if you were trying to get off the drugs, you'd have to do it somewhere where you couldn't just score some dope on a street corner."

Charlie nods, pulling at his chin whiskers with pizza-greasy fingers. "Yeah, and besides, it's not like the Hells Angels have a lot of contacts in La Jolla." He smirks.

"Okay," Frank snaps. "Let's go with it."

"Wait a sec," Charlie mumbles. "I went up there and now I'm back. But how come I'm here in PB? I mean . . . how come I don't just go back to my place in El Cajon?"

Frank ponders on this for a while, chewing through a slice. "You wanted to make a clean break," he says. "You wanted to change things. You're turning over a new leaf. Everybody knows where to find you out there. The temptation would be too much. Before you knew it, you'd be back on the spike."

Charlie's mood suddenly shifts. He looks down at his hands. For a moment, he sits like that, mulling things over. I don't know how much he's thought about leading a double life, giving up his apartment, lying to people who until very recently were the closest friends he's ever had, but I know this is weighing on him. Then, unexpectedly, he gets to his feet. "Gonna need to get my Harley," he says. Then, looking around at us, says, "If I'm back on the street, I ain't ridin' no bus."

"A car," Frank says after a moment. "Bike's no good for a wire, for meeting people. Too much engine noise, wind, ambient shit going on."

"Marty'd find a way," Paul says, and we all laugh because it's true. Marty Logan, our tech agent, would relish the challenge of wiring a Harley so that we could get clean audio.

"Who's Marty?" Charlie says.

Frank shakes his head, chuckling. "You'll find out soon enough."

Paul gets to work on the dishes and we head through to the living room, where the TV is on without sound. Charlie flops down on the couch, an ugly orange thing with a geometric design I already hate. Frank grabs the remote, and for a while we watch the evening news until Paul comes through from the kitchen and flops down on the couch next to Charlie. The news is the usual numbing drivel of talking heads, but I'm not even listening. I'm contemplating this question of how we get Charlie back on the street when a thought occurs to me.

"Charlie?"

"Yeah."

"I guess we can assume you still know how to drive a car."

"What?"

I stick out my hands, mimicking a steering wheel. "You

know, one of those things with four wheels?"

"What kind of question is that, Spence?"

"You got a license?"

"Sure, I do." Charlie frowns, then pulls out his battered leather billfold, which is on the end of a chain he attaches to the belt loop on his jeans. He flops it open, hands it to me.

There's a picture of Charlie under scratched plastic. He looks a whole lot younger. I pull the license out of the billfold to get a better look. "This expired five years ago."

"It did?"

Frank takes it from me and frowns. "Shit, Charlie. We're gonna have to get you tested." He fires a distressed look at Paul. "Can you set that up, ASAP?"

Paul nods.

Charlie grabs his billfold back. "Come on, man. I don't wanna go through all that bullshit."

Looking around at the other guys' faces, I get a feeling that even though we're sitting in the same room, we're talking to Charlie across a social divide the size of the Grand Canyon.

"The fuck difference does it make, man?"

Frank kills the TV, and for a moment sits there, looking at Charlie over his glasses.

Charlie raises his hands. "What'd I say *now*?"

"It's like with the watch," Frank says, using his softest voice. "You gotta be clean now, Charlie. You gotta be straight. You're no longer an outlaw. You're a law-abiding citizen."

Charlie shoots me a look, and I know he's thinking about the conversation we had a few days back.

Frank grabs a cigarette from Charlie's pack, lights up, blows smoke at the ceiling.

"I ever tell you about Rex Bower?"

"Look out," Charlie says, and he pushes back into the repugnant couch, putting his feet up on the coffee table. "Frank's got another story."

Frank enlightens everyone in the room who hasn't heard it before. He tells about Bower, about how he sacrificed everything for the ATF, risked his life as an undercover agent infiltrating the Hells Angels, and was able to gain their confidence by engaging in the same criminal activities as the gang. He wound up a useless witness because in running with the Hells Angels, he had crossed the line and broke the law himself.

"Yeah, but what's all that got to do with me?" Charlie says. "I ain't no fuckin' agent."

"Yes, you are," Frank says, leaning forward and looking up at Charlie. "You're one of us now. You're the man. See, the guys in the club, they know you. And as long as we can find a way of putting you back on the street, you don't have to *prove* anything, *do* anything, especially anything illegal. I'm saying you can be back in the club or on the fringe of the club making controlled buys, completely under our supervision, without ever committing another crime. And I mean *any* crime. Big or small. From here on, you are Mr. Clean."

"Why's that so important, man?"

"Because when you get on the witness stand and Duke's attorney is cross-examining you—ladies and gentlemen of the jury: Mister Slade, a convicted felon, motivated only by jealousy and a desire for revenge, turns on the very people who . . . etc., etc. He'll try to paint you ugly, sinister, blacker than black, Charlie." He shakes his head into a tight little smile. "But if you're clean, if you're beyond reproach, it'll be harder for him to do that. And it'll be easier for us to sell *our* story, the true story."

"Which is what?"

"That Charlie Slade is a good person. One who saw the error of his ways. And wanting to make right all the wrong he'd done, and all the wrong he'd been a part of, he came to us as a cooperating witness. He did the right thing for the right reason. And he changed his ways."

Charlie flops back against the couch, eyes closed. "Jesus . . . who's gonna believe that shit?"

For a long time, nobody speaks. Frank breaks it. "We'll

make sure you're never in the situations Bower had to deal with."

"How you gonna do that, Frank?" Charlie says, keeping his eyes closed as he massages the bridge of his nose. "I mean, what happens when Duke says, 'Hey, Charlie, there's this guy out in Lakeside that I need you to go fuck up?'"

"He won't."

Charlie opens his eyes. "Frank, I guarantee you he will. He'll try to test me."

"He won't," Frank says, hands out, "because you won't be around for him to say it. We're not putting you back inside the gang, Charlie. Not really. It's like I say—you'll be on the fringes. It has to be that way because that's the only way we're going to keep control. The buys are going to be in and out, in and out. Surgical. Strategic. We're going to keep you on the edge, Charlie. You're going to keep yourself on the edge."

Charlie pulls on his cigarette, letting the smoke roll out of his nose. "How the fuck am I supposed to do that?"

Chapter 20

Zippo
Jacumba, CA
July 17, 1996

Duke sucks in his gut and bares his hungry teeth. He flips his favorite lighter on and off, over and over, as he stands above his prey. To his right, Gonzo is so jacked up that he's actually bouncing on the balls of his feet like a prize fighter. To his left, Bad Eye and Scooter stand silent, arms folded. Executioners waiting to ply their trade. The focus of their attention is the pair of men groveling at Duke's feet.

"This is how it's gonna go down," Duke says—and he says it pleasantly, like maybe he's their best friend, like maybe he didn't have anything to do with the savage beating just laid on these poor bastards huddled in pain beneath him. "You're gonna put out twenty a week."

"Pounds?" the emaciated tweaker whines. "We ain't set up for that kinda quantity."

Duke motions to Gonzo, then points at the five-gallon can at the base of the tree. Gonzo scoops the can up and makes for the methamphetamine cook who's insolent enough to question his new employer. With a sneer, the secretary pours the contents of the can over the cook's squirming body. The assaulting smell of gasoline reaches Duke's flaring nostrils. The president flicks his lighter on and then off. Bad Eye and Scooter rumble with laughter.

"What's your name, punk?" Duke asks.

The cook's shuddering as he looks himself over, realizing with horror that he's covered with gasoline.

Duke snaps his fingers, bringing the cook to attention. "I asked you your name, asshole."

The cook's lips part. He's so frightened that even his teeth chatter. "R-r-r-russ," he stutters.

"Well, R-r-r-russ," Duke says, "You work for me now. And

I don't take no back talk from no fuckin' *cooks*."

"That's *right!*" Gonzo barks. "You tell those fuckin' dagos you work for us now!"

Duke raises a hand to silence his secretary. Then he gets down in the cook's face. "You know what I *do* take from my fuckin' cooks?"

The little tweaker stirs, firing a pleading glance at his partner, who's bleeding in the weeds beside him, his face so badly beaten he hardly looks human—just a corpulent lump quivering in the grass.

Duke snaps his fingers again, brings his new employee back to the moment.

"N-n-n-no," Russ says.

"I take his fuckin' *product*," Duke hisses. He flicks his Zippo on again, holds it just high enough over Russ's head to avoid combustion.

Bad Eye and Scooter roar with laughter. "He takes *product*," Scooter echoes.

Duke crouches down on one knee, gets eye to eye with the cook. "Any questions?" he asks.

Russ shakes his head so hard it threatens to twist off his neck.

Duke grins, still holding the flame in his hand. "Good."

~ ~ ~ ~

I'm watching through the open kitchen window into the backyard, Charlie and Paul lifting weights. It's Charlie on the bench and Paul spotting. I probably shouldn't be eavesdropping, but Paul just asked a question I feel like we've never gotten a clear answer to. At least not clear to me.

"You never told me why you left," Paul says as Charlie finishes his set.

Charlie stands and stretches his arms behind his back, revealing a physique that's come a long way in a month. I'm expecting him to deflect, but he doesn't.

"Yeah, I guess not," he says.

I slide up closer to the window above the kitchen sink and silently perch myself on the barstool. I can just barely see the two of them through the sheer café curtains. I wait for him to get into his story about Becky and her braid, about Duke, his greed, and his indifference, about how he was betrayed by his band of brothers when he was down and out, but I'm surprised when he goes another way altogether.

"There are some things you just don't do," Charlie says, his voice gravelly, sad.

"What do you mean?" Paul asks.

"We got this prospect," Charlie begins. "Name's Mongoose."

A picture flashes to my mind. Surveillance photos of Mongoose, a man aptly named. I see his long mouth and jagged teeth, his yellow eyes and greasy skin, the kind of photo you can practically smell. In the picture, he's standing over a fire, drinking straight from a whiskey bottle. Satan's disciple.

"So Duke sends the fucker with me on a collection run."

I hear Paul's voice, but it carries on the breeze only as a mumble. Whatever he's asked, Charlie nods.

"Anyway," Charlie says, "Mongoose is a psych job to start with, but around women he's savage, you know, *brutal*. And this guy, this dealer who owed us, he had a daughter. She was thirteen, maybe fourteen. I don't know."

Paul tenses up so hard I can actually see it from here.

"This guy'd been shorting us, you know? For the past couple of weeks, we'd get payments that were light. Not smart. You know the HA saying: 'Fuck with us and find out.'" Charlie finishes a stretch, then actually sits down in the grass cross-legged. I've never seen him do this before, but there he is. Like a Boy Scout in front of a campfire. The look on his face says it pains him even to talk about whatever it is that's on his mind.

"Tell me what happened, Charlie," Paul says, sitting down on the weight bench and setting his hands on his knees.

Charlie sighs and adjusts the ponytail on the back of his sweaty head. "We get to the guy's house and his old lady answers the door. We ask about the dealer and she makes up some story about him leaving town or being dead or somethin'." Charlie hunches forward, looking like he might put his head in his hands. He stops himself short, his hands hanging in the air under his chin like maybe he's pleading up at Paul. "And Mongoose, I mean . . . he just went *off*."

"Did he hit her or something?"

Charlie shakes his head. "Nah. He was yelling. You know, thought the old lady was jerkin' us around or something. And then the daughter comes to the door." He looks away, down toward the foundation of the house, his eyes closed.

"Why was Mongoose even there, man?" Paul asks. "I thought collecting was *your* job."

Charlie shrugs, and in one instant something occurs to me. Frank's been right all along. Charlie *has* been on the outs with the club. It comes so clear. It's like Duke looked at Charlie and realized this dog won't hunt anymore. So he sends Mongoose to back him up, learn the ropes, figure out how to *replace* Charlie when the inevitable came to pass.

"So Mongoose . . ." Charlie says, pausing and squinting up at the sun. "He gets out of control, grabs the woman's daughter." And now he does put his head in his hands. "I wanted to stop him, man. I wanted to make him stop."

"What happened, Charlie?"

When he looks back up at Paul, I can see he's determined now to get it all out. His voice carries without strain, like he's a man resigned to his torment. "Mongoose grabs the lady by the hair and then does the same to the girl. He drags them both into the, like, living room there and throws them down on the floor. They're both screaming, you know?"

Paul nods, hardly blinking. I realize after a moment that I'm doing the same.

"I'll never forget it, man. Mongoose is holding the mom down by the neck with his boot and she's starin' up at me with these eyes. Like she's beggin' me to stop him. But I just stand there and stare. It's like my feet are stuck to the ground."

"There was nothing you could do, Charlie?" Paul asks.

Charlie's face runs red. It's the look that says he's about to lash out at Paul. I've seen it before—clenching his teeth and pumping his fists—before he launches into a rage. But he just sits there shaking his head.

"Mongoose butt-fucked that little girl right there in front of her mother. I mean the kid is screaming for help. And me? I just walked out."

"But Charlie—"

"No, Paul," Charlie says. "You don't get it. I'm standing there watching this thing happen . . . and I just turn my back and walk out."

For a while neither of them speak. I can hear my own heart pounding in my chest.

"That's the day I decided I had to leave."

"Get out of the club, Charlie?"

"Had to find some place to crash and kick the juice. Cold turkey."

Paul nods.

"That ain't me, Paul. I was so fucked up on H, and . . ."

Paul nods harder, furrowing his brow.

"I joined the club for the brotherhood. Know what I mean, man? The pride of being one of them. But this other stuff—the business side of it, hurting innocent people—I couldn't take it no more."

"Makes sense, man," Paul says.

"I mean, it's only a matter of time before Duke orders me to do a hit on somebody," Charlie says. "And I don't care what you and Frank and Spence think, I ain't no killer."

"We don't think that, Charlie."

"Fucked some people up pretty bad over the years, but only when they had it comin', you know, disrespectin' me or the club. But . . . but hurtin' innocent people . . . kids . . . that ain't my bag, man."

He stands, shaking his head. And then he levels his eyes on the kitchen window. Sees me. Realizes I've heard everything. His eyes, they look sad—almost grateful—like it does him good to know that *I* know. It's a defining moment for me. Frank had it right. Charlie wanted out of the club, all right. He wanted to be clean of the junk in his system. But more than that, he wanted to be *clean* in the way he lived his life, free from guilt and a life of moral depravity.

I nod at him once and then look down at my hands. I try not to think about the little girl screaming and scratching and writhing beneath Mongoose. I try to think about that Rolex. About how Charlie eventually *did* take it down to the front desk. Frank had sent him alone despite every chance that Charlie would just keep walking. Find somewhere to score some dope and bail on our entire operation. But Charlie turned the watch in. And more than that, he came back.

Chapter 21

The Tweaker
San Diego, CA
July 18, 1996

It's pitch black and I stumble on a crack in the sidewalk I forgot was there as I fumble for my house keys. The motion-sensor light over my back porch is burned out, no doubt falling victim to the hoard of cats that patrol the small courtyards and alleys of North Mission Beach. The sound of the waves crashing onto the sandy beach and the fresh salt-air smell of the Pacific welcomes me home. I manage to unlock the deadbolt and the door lock and push the door open against the mound of mail that has accumulated below the mail slot cut in the door. The house is dark and empty with a musty smell you might expect of a small beach bungalow unoccupied for almost a month.

Built in the early '50s as a beach getaway for a farming family from La Mesa, east of San Diego, this small cottage is one of a dwindling number of such places along the beach that still exist from a long-ago era. These small, iconic places are being torn down and replaced by boxy three-story condos to maximize floor space and profits on the postage stamp-sized lots. The beach is my home and my sanctuary. My non-Bureau friends live here, and my Bureau friends think I'm crazy to live here. Of course, some of my FBI associates think I'm crazy anyway. I'm constantly reminded by my "establishment" friends that a thirty-eight-year old bachelor should have outgrown the beach scene long ago. Not so.

It feels good to be home after almost a month of living at La Paloma. With Paul's help, Frank and I can now get a little breather. At least that's what I thought. I'm not home ten minutes and the phone rings. It's my new supervisor, Pete Blair, sounding kind of groggy, like he'd just woken up.

"What is it, Pete?"

"Just got a call patched through from the sheriff's department. They're holding some freaked-out meth cook at the Pine Valley sub-station."

"Why do we care about a meth cook?"

"Guy came into the station scared to death. Says some Hells Angels doused him with gasoline and threatened to torch him. Something about the HAs taking over a meth lab in Jacumba."

My eyes go wide. "Where is he now?"

"Stinking up the sub-station in Pine Valley. I know you must be tired, Nick, but ..."

"I'm good," I lie. "I'll head back over to PB and see if Frank's still there."

Blair thanks me, reminds me that he still wants to meet with Charlie and then asks that I wait until the morning to call him with the details. I agree on all fronts. So much for a little R&R. I grab my coat, gun, and badge, kick aside the pile of mail still blocking the door, and head out into a heavy fog bank slowly rolling in off shore.

~~~~

Ten minutes later, I've picked up Frank at the house and we're headed east on Interstate 8, trying to ramp ourselves back up to full functionality with Winchell's coffee.

In and of itself, the club's move on the Jacumba lab is not at all surprising, and is simply an example of the club going about its business in the usual way. The Hells Angels don't cook meth themselves, preferring instead to rely on established clandestine manufacturers who, more often than not, operate out of remote shitholes in east San Diego County. They set up shop in places like Lakeside, El Cajon, Spring Valley, Jamul, Jacumba, Boulevard, Dulzura, and Ramona. A quality operation can typically produce around ten to fifteen pounds per batch using easily obtained chemical building blocks, precursors like P-2-P or pseudo-ephedrine, and ephedrine. The latter, of course, just happens to be the primary ingredient of commonly available cold remedies.

The typical lab is set up in a large trailer or mobile home, or maybe in an outbuilding on a ranch. It's the basic, no-frills, squalid living conditions you'd expect from these half-wits, with maybe a couple of sleeping cots, cases of Mountain Dew, cartons of Marlboros, Snickers bars, and all the chemicals and glassware needed to mix up their poison. The so-called cooks that run these operations are in most cases addicted users themselves, "tweakers," capable of staying awake for days doing a cook.

And this is where the Hells Angels and other rival gangs make their presence known. They seek out these well-hidden manufacturing centers and deploy the tactics they're famous for: They intimidate, threaten, and, if necessary, use physical force to overtake the operation—and they do this with the unquestioned confidence that no one in their right mind is ever going to fuck with them. Once they commandeer and establish a foothold on these profit centers, they set up their security to protect their newly acquired assets. It's a constant power struggle to stay in business, but the profits are staggering.

As sweet as this setup sounds, there are inherent instabilities that make it a tricky business to be in. This isn't exactly Mr. Roger's Neighborhood. For one thing, the labs have a tendency to blow up from time to time, due in part to the fact that they're run by heavy drug users who don't really know what the hell they're doing. It's the volatile nature of the ingredients that creates the explosive environment. Red phosphorus, for example, will spontaneously combust when exposed to moisture, burning up in a fiery explosion. And when red phosphorus boils dry in a flask—as it might whenever one of these tweakers takes an unscheduled nap—it produces phosphene gas, which is fatal when inhaled. Freon, a solvent often encountered in meth labs, when exposed to open flames, forms yet another kind of gas. This gas, called phosgene, was the lethal gas of choice in the trenches of World War I. And when cooks aren't getting blown up or gassed, they're often suffering horrible burns from hydriodic acid or lye.

There is constant pressure on these cooks to churn out a decent product in high volume. If they don't, the Hells Angels handle the matter in their typical cerebral manner, which generally means they beat the shit out of whoever's responsible, then torch or blow up the unproductive profit center and move on. I figure this is what we're likely to hear about from this Jacumba cook, and Frank seems to agree.

It's about forty miles to Pine Valley, an idyllic little place nestled in the Laguna Mountains in the Cleveland National Forest on old Highway 80. The sub-station itself is a one-story, gray modular building that looks like it's been nailed together out of packing crates. We pull into the lot at around two in the morning and enter to find a desk sergeant eating a Danish over a fly-fishing magazine. He knows who we are as soon as we walk through the door.

"Jesus Christ," Frank says, pinching his nose.

"We opened all the windows," the desk sergeant says. He's a tired-looking guy with thick, gray hair. "We got the fellah locked up in back, but the stench just seems to hang in the air. Don't light a match is my advice."

The desk sergeant stuffs in the last of the Danish and leads us into the back of the station, where we're introduced to Detective Rolf Nilsen, a big, melancholy Swede with eyes the color of wet slate. He stands up from behind his desk with a sigh when we walk in, asks us if we want coffee.

"It's Folgers," he says with another sigh, so it's hard to say whether he thinks that's a good thing or not, and we follow him through to a little kitchen off the squad room.

When we're all slurping fresh cups, I ask him about the cook they're holding.

"Came in around eleven o'clock," Nilsen says. "About as scared as anyone I've ever seen. Just reeking of gas, started jabbering about the Hells Angels. Tweaked out higher than a kite. Took him into the interview room. Tried to calm him down."

"You interviewed him?"

"No, sir. He was way too riled up. But he talked some about this lab in Jacumba and the Hells Angels wanting to take it over, and I figured it was something you feds should know about."

"A good call," I say.

Nilsen sips his coffee and lets out another sigh. "Agent Spence," he says, long and slow, "there's five patrol deputies and a detective out here in the mountains. And I'm the detective. We could use a little help from you feds from time to time."

"What's the guy's name?" Frank asks, ignoring the deputy's barb.

"Russell J. Young. Least that's what he says. He didn't have any ID on him. Gave us a DOB."

"Did you run him?"

Nilsen nods, explains that he ran Russell through ARJIS and NCIC—the Automated Regional Justice Information System and the National Crime Information Center—and that both inquiries came back with no hits.

"So you wanna talk to him?" he asks.

We go through to a holding pen at the back of the building. The gasoline smell is stronger here. We find Russ, or whoever this guy is, in a little lockup all to himself. He's sitting on the bench, clutching his arms close. I guess he's in his mid-twenties, but it's hard to be sure given the state he's in. Covered in streaks of filth, he looks as though he hasn't been near clean water in weeks, and hasn't eaten a decent meal in months. There's a big split in his bottom lip, which is swollen and as dark as an eggplant. He goes still when we enter the holding pen, all except his jaw, which continues to work with a steady chewing motion.

"Russ?" Frank says.

The chewing stops for a moment. Then starts right up

again.

"I'm Detective Frank Conroy, San Diego PD. This here is FBI Agent Nick Spence."

Russ just stares, his bruised eyes on Frank's hands as though he expects them to be the source of his next beating.

"We're here to help," Frank says, and the way he says it, with such complete sincerity, seems to get through at some level. For the first time, Russ raises his eyes.

Nilsen sets us up in a little interview room with three plastic chairs and a big metal table. Russ doesn't exactly calm down, but after some friendly chat and a glass of water, he's able to hold himself together enough to answer questions.

Frank and I have agreed that I'm going to take the lead, with him stepping in from time to time wherever it seems appropriate. He's also agreed not to light up any cigarettes during the interview in deference to the flammable condition of our interviewee.

All Russ wants to talk about is the Hells Angels. His version of what happened earlier tonight comes out in a rambling monologue I can't even make sense of, apart from a few nuggets, like somebody poured gasoline over his head and lit a Zippo.

"Russ," I say softly. "Back up a little, slow down. Everything's cool, everything's good."

Russ takes a breath and reaches for his water. "S'fucked up, maaan . . ."

"We're not going to let anything happen to you."

"But these . . . these guys, they said—"

"It doesn't matter what they said, Russ. You're with *us* now. You came to us and we're going to protect you."

Russ brings both trembling hands up onto the table.

"Russ," I say, "I know these guys. I know how they talk. And you're right, they're scary guys. And you know what? Someone pours gasoline over me and lights a match, I'm gonna be scared, too. But if they *were* gonna burn you, they'd have burned you already."

"Like those fuckin' monks I read about . . ." Russ says, his shoulders jerking involuntarily. "You know, like in Vietnam?"

I glance over at Frank, who rolls his eyes. "Sure," I say. "I know what you're talking about. So . . . Russ?"

Russ blinks, struggles to focus on my mouth.

"Where's the lab? The lab, Russ."

"Jacumba."

"Where in Jacumba?"

"It's in a . . . a house trailer. Parked off Railroad Road, south of Jacumba."

"Okay. What can you tell me about it? What kind of quantities you cooking up there?"

Russ scowls, twisting in his chair, showing me brown stumps of teeth in blotchy gums.

"Hey . . . hey, I thought this was about the Hells Angels, man."

I keep my voice level, calm. "It is, Russ. It is. But for us to understand their interest, we need to know a little more about the lab."

Russ blinks, I guess trying to process this, trying to see if he believes it. "We cook up . . . we'll maybe cook up ten pounds. Ten pounds maybe or . . ."

"Ten pounds a week? Ten pounds a month?"

"A week . . . maybe. It depends on what . . . they want."

"What who wants?"

Russ looks down at his hands. Clearly, he hadn't intended on getting into this.

"Come on, Russ," I say. "You know it's all over. There's no point trying to hold anything back. We're going to find everything out anyway. And you helping us, well . . . it'll make a difference down the line."

"I want a lawyer . . ." Russ says in a soft voice, his eyes now trained on the floor.

I look across at Frank. "Maybe we should just let you go," he says. Then turning to me, "What do you say, Agent Spence? It's clear Russ doesn't wanna help us catch these Hells Angels.

Maybe we should just cut him loose." He presses his hands to the table, readying to stand. "He's probably just making this whole story up, anyway."

Russ fires us a look, his tormented eyes cutting back and forth. "Esposito brothers," he blurts, the words coming out barely above a whisper.

"The Esposito brothers," I say.

"They're who we work for. They set us up. They tell us what they need."

Frank and I exchange another look. "And the Espositos... they didn't provide you with muscle? Security?"

Russ gets fidgety again. "There was this guy," he squeaks. "Carlo. This asshole in camo pants. You know, like those fuckin' shorts with the big..." He motions at his thighs.

"The pockets on the legs."

"Yeah... this, these pants... and this shotgun. Acted like some kinda mafia guy. But ... well, they jumped him. I mean, they really fucked him up."

"Fucked him up how?"

"The guy . . . the guy who poured the gasoline, he showed me this big mother of a ball-peen hammer. Says he broke Carlo's knees. Said he's gonna do the same to me if I give him any trouble." Russ starts shaking, his shoulders jerking in spasms.

"Keep talking, Russ."

"I was alone in the lab. Doin' a ... a cook when they ..." He closes his eyes, remembering it all, I guess. His body flutters and jolts, still in the grip of the drug.

"How many of them were there?"

"I don't know. Three. Maybe four. Big guys. Tattoos everywhere. One *really* big guy."

I take some photos from my briefcase and push one across the table. "Is this one of them?"

Russ nods. I push the photograph across to Frank.

It's Scooter.

I fan the pictures out on the table. Surveillance photographs accumulated over months—every member of the club. "Recognize any more of them?"

Russ squints. It takes him just a few seconds to pick out Duke and Gonzo. Then he hesitates for a while. Finally, he points to a photo of Ronald "Bad Eye" McClusky, vice president.

Then he separates the picture of Gonzo from the others. "He's the one poured the . . . the gasoline on me. But it was *this* guy . . ." He taps a finger on Duke's face ". . . this is the guy who . . . who lit the lighter."

Russ starts to sweat profusely. It seems to just pour out of him. For a second, it looks like he's going to pass out.

"Russ?" I smack my hand flat on the table, a metallic reverb echoing through the room. "Russ, stay with us. What did they want?"

"Take over," he says through gritted teeth. "Take it over. The lab."

"That's what they said?" I ask. 'We're taking over'?"

Russ jerks so hard he's practically sideways in his chair. It's like he's grappling with some unseen force sitting in his lap. "No, they wanted to know . . . to know how many pounds we could put out in a week. Shit like that, and . . . and they wanted to know who was putting up the money and who . . . who came to take the product away when we were done cooking. And then . . . and then . . ."

He scrunches up his eyes. "I was scared to . . . I didn't want to tell them about the . . . the Espositos, but they. . . . The big ugly guy. . . . This here guy." He points to the picture of Gonzo. "He punched me in the mouth. Kept hitting me. Said he knew where I lived . . . was going to kill my family . . . and then . . . then he pulled me outside." He starts pawing at his throat as he stares up at the ceiling. "He pushed me out there in the dark, and he made me get down on my knees and he poured it over my head."

"The gasoline."

"Yeah. And the other guy, the giant guy with the gut . . ."

He reaches for Duke's photo. "He had a lighter, you know, one of those Zippos. I'm telling you, man, when he lit that thing . . . I really thought . . ."

"So you told them. About the Espositos."

Russ flinches, looks me straight in the eye, his eyes welling tears. "I thought they were gonna torch me."

~~~~

"We have to shut the place down," I say.

We're back in the car, Frank and me, watching the dawning sky turn pale in the east as we discuss our next move. It's 4:20 in the morning and I'm sipping what has to be my twentieth cup of coffee in the last ten hours. We'll have to notify DEA immediately, of course, and get one of their lab teams out there to dismantle the operation and seize the evidence.

But right now, we've got a more immediate concern: There's a guy somewhere in Jacumba who may be dying or dead.

I look out at the woods ahead of us. The shapes of the indigenous Jeffrey pines are starting to emerge through the moisture of dawn. I'm wondering how shutting down the lab might impact our case with Charlie. We have an ongoing investigation and an informant to protect, after all. But I come to the conclusion that there's no connection. What's happened here has nothing to do with Charlie or how we plan to use him.

"It might actually help the case," I say. "Shutting it down, I mean."

"Duke's gonna be real pissed. That's for sure."

"That could work to our advantage," I say. "If they're angry, paranoid . . . whatever . . . maybe they'll get sloppy, do something stupid."

"Right," Frank says. After a moment, he turns to look at me.

"What?"

"What do you think happened to Carlo?"

The last Russell Young saw of the guard, he was crawling away through the weeds, groaning like a gut-shot bear.

I put the car into drive. "Let's go find out."

We make our way back down to old Highway 80 and then head east again, in the direction of Jacumba. Using the crude drawing Russell made for us, it doesn't take long to find the trailer house. It's parked at the end of an overgrown track and is barely visible from the highway. It looks like about a forty-footer tucked back in a grove of trees.

We drive right past the first time, looking straight ahead, but alert to the possibility of an HA lookout sitting somewhere there in the weeds. We pull off the road about 100 yards further on.

"See anything?" Frank says.

"Saw the trailer. Nothing else. No movement."

I drive into a small, overgrown grove of scrub pines and brush, going deep enough for the car to be invisible from the road. Getting out, I'm surprised by the freshness of the dawn air and the agreeable herbal aroma. We close the doors softly and make our way across uneven ground, approaching the trailer house from the north side.

There's no sign of life, other than a handful of quail that skitter off over the sage bushes as we slowly approach the house.

There are few things as sordid as a meth lab in the early morning light. This job gives you an inside look at places most people never see. When you think about it, when you enter into someone's private domain or sanctuary, you are most often invited or welcomed. That's what the Fourth Amendment guarantees. As uninvited guests with a warrant in hand, there's no telling what we in law enforcement are going to encounter behind these private doors. Dead bodies, violently sick people, unimaginable filth and squalor, hopelessly abused children . . . wasted lives on the edge of destruction. But there's something about meth labs. It's that combination of knowing that behind *this* closed door is an insidious, volatile, and inexact science project, producing a caustic and toxic byproduct that lowlifes and helplessly doomed people are actually going to put into their bodies voluntarily. It's truly diabolical to me, this idea of intense pleasure being squeezed out of the blackest of poisons.

At the screen door, we both unholster our sidearms. We're here under exigent circumstances, having just been told someone's life may be at risk. No warrant necessary. Frank softly pushes open the door, which, of course, squeaks loud enough to announce our arrival. We listen for a moment and then enter.

Moving into the interior, we see the usual debris of candy wrappers and soda cans mixed up with stained filter papers, tangled condenser tubes, and plastic hoses. We're careful not to touch or move anything. Strangely, there's a woman's shoe in the middle of it all. A single high-heeled shoe in shiny red vinyl.

Frank points to two fifty-liter flasks, a sure sign of serious production. There's also a row of one-gallon cans labeled "Red Phosphorus" and a couple of jars marked "Iodine." In the corner by what looks like a defunct stove, there's a gas cylinder that no doubt contains hydrogen chloride gas. Down on the floor in a beer crate, there's a stack of trichloroethylene cans and something else we often see.

"Acetone," Frank says softly, pointing to a big can. "Hotplates for . . ." He stops midsentence.

Something just shifted against the wall of the trailer. We both turn. The trailer shifts on its axles. It sounds like someone leaned against the wall outside. A hard scraping sound.

Frank takes a soft step toward the door, then another. I follow him, gun held down against my thigh, trying to steady my breathing.

Outside, nothing.

We step down from the trailer and make our way toward the back. The ground here is littered with broken glass and cigarette butts. Then I see it. Blood. There's fresh blood in the grass. Neither of us is moving now. We both stand there, listening. A weak coughing and gurgling sound like a person clearing their throat.

We come around the side of the trailer, weapons raised.

There's a guy sitting on the ground, leaning against the trailer. His face is so badly beaten, he can barely see out of his puffy eyes as he turns to look toward us. There's dried blood down his chin and over the front of his Led Zeppelin T-shirt. His long, baggy cargo shorts are covered in dirt, like he's been dragging himself around all night. But it's his knees that hold my attention. The left is swollen, big as a cantaloupe and darkly veined; the right is split across the front, the red mouth of the wound showing pearly white cartilage.

"Help, please . . ." he wheezes. "Help me."

He's got something metal in his right hand. Frank kneels down next to him and Carlo slowly opens his fist, revealing a Zippo lighter covered with dust and dirt. Frank takes it from him and shows it to me. My heart leaps at what I see: the Hells Angels death head logo inscribed on one side. He flips it over. Inscribed on the back side are the initials "J.A.S."

Frank looks up at me from his kneeling position. "Jason Andrew Stricker," he says. "Aka 'Duke.'"

Chapter 22

Meeting the Man
San Diego, CA
July 22, 1996

Frank drives a red and black Camaro into the garage at the PB house. We're all in there waiting as the door goes up—Charlie, Paul, and me—like a bunch of thieves in a chop shop, ready to strip the thing for parts. It rolls into the garage with the kind of throaty growl that even a car novice like me can appreciate.

Frank hops out of the driver's seat and waves his hand over the hood like a conquering matador. We each stand to one side, all of us biting our tongues, our hands shoved in our pockets. The paint job looks lousy under the naked lightbulb, and I can see at least three shades of red on the driver side door. There's a bullet hole in the trunk and a stylized Phoenix rising from the front of the hood. After our initial impressions, we all agree it's very Charlie.

Except Charlie, of course.

Standing with his back to the doorway that opens up to the yard, Charlie looks less than delighted with his new ride, Phoenix or no Phoenix.

Frank steps over and pats him on the shoulder. "Ain't she a beauty, Charlie?"

"I don't know, man."

Frank hops back over to the driver's side and pops the hood, again panning his hands through the air over the engine. "Come on. Two-forty horses. V-8. Thing's like a rocket ship."

Charlie offers a half smile, but that's it.

"You don't wanna get behind the wheel, at least?"

"Come on, Charlie," Paul urges. "It's a nice ride, man. At least give it a try."

"*You* give it a try," Charlie says.

Paul doesn't need to be asked twice. He folds his huge frame into the driver's seat and then sits there turning the wheel and checking out the dash. He looks every bit as enthusiastic as a sixteen-year-old with a new driver's license and a condom in his wallet.

It's infectious, I guess, because Charlie watches him only for a moment before stepping forward and tugging at Paul's sleeve. "Come on, man," he says softly. "Guess I better take a look at the fuckin' thing."

Paul steps out and Charlie gets in behind the wheel. He flips a couple of switches, but it's obvious he's just being polite. This whole thing with the car and now the driver's license issue has made him more surly than normal . . . whatever normal is. I know he'd rather eat glass than have to go down to the DMV to renew his license. He's been bitching about it for the past couple of days, complaining that renewing his expired license is only going to cost us valuable time and effort and whining about the fact that renewing isn't just a matter of handing over cash. There are tests to take, both written *and* practical. It's not going to be pretty. Frank gets into the passenger seat alongside him, gives the dashboard a tug. "Take a look, Spence," he says through the window.

I walk around to his side, check out the way the thing's snapped together. Hiding the wire is going to be a cinch.

"Marty's going to love this," Frank says, and the thought of Marty crawling around in the thing makes me chuckle.

"How come every time you guys mention this Marty guy, you all crack up?" Charlie says with a frown as he climbs out of the car.

"Marty's a character," I say. "A real piece of work. You'll meet him soon enough."

"How many fucking new guys I gotta meet?" Charlie asks.

~~~~

The other "fucking new guy" he's referring to, of course, is my supervisor Pete Blair. To this point, Blair's been approving my expense vouchers and cutting us checks without asking too many questions. It doesn't get any better than that in our line of work, but it didn't take a whole lot of foresight to realize that it was only a matter of time before Blair would want to get his hands dirty, to meet the Hells Angel we've been claiming we can turn cooperating witness.

It came two days ago, Blair's first request for an in-house visit with Charlie. And despite what I was anticipating, Frank was all for it. According to my partner, Charlie needs to start getting used to the idea that he's going to be a witness for the prosecution, and meeting with my supervisor is a reasonable next step.

"When's Blair getting here, anyway?" Paul asks.

I check my watch and realize that my supervisor's already a half-hour late. I glance over at Charlie, who's got a frustrated scowl for me. I can't say as I blame him. I've spent much of the past two days prepping Charlie on what a stand-up guy Pete Blair is and here the son of a bitch is late. This doesn't bode well . . . like Charlie's not important enough to be on time. Charlie always said never to trust a dealer who showed up late. I ask myself what that says about Blair.

Finally, a light tap on the front door. When I open it, there's Blair looking like a Fuller Brush salesman. In his late forties, he is balding with a neatly trimmed beard and tortoise- shell framed eyeglasses that permanently rest about halfway down his nose. He offers a flustered apology for being over an hour late. They're laying sewer pipe on Garnet Avenue, and he got stuck in a traffic detour from hell. We sit down in the living room—Frank, Charlie, Blair, and me. I've asked Charlie not to put on any fronts. Just to relax and be himself, which is a gamble under these circumstances. I'm surprised when he stiffly gets up off the couch and eagerly offers his greeting hand.

Blair receives the handshake graciously, turning on the charm, telling Charlie how much we appreciate what he's doing for us; what integrity it shows; what courage. Charlie shrugs this off as if the risks he's willing to take are no big deal. This is just Charlie being Charlie, of course, and I'm ready to move on, but Blair wants to dwell on it for a moment—wants to talk about Charlie's perception of the risk—and it becomes clear that one of the main reasons for Blair being here is to get to the bottom of Charlie's motivation.

"No, Charlie," he says, looking over the top of his reader glasses. "This *is* a big deal. It's not every guy that'll put himself in this kind of danger just because it's the right thing to do."

Charlie shrugs again and glances across at Frank, apparently seeking approval from the man he trusts most.

Blair holds out one of his meaty hands, palm up. "And I just want you to understand that there's a lot the Bureau can do to protect you," he adds. "So any anxiety you might feel ..."

"I don't feel no anxiety," Charlie says. "I mean, fuck it, man. Fuck 'em."

Blair looks down at his penny loafers, clears his throat. "Well, that's great, Charlie. I admire your passion. But there's going to be times over the coming weeks and months when you might feel a little ... exposed."

Charlie shakes his head distantly, then asks if it's okay to smoke—again looking over at Frank for an approving nod.

For the next hour or so, Blair asks questions about the Hells Angels, wanting to know how much crystal meth Charlie thinks they're moving each month and about who he considers to be the main dealers. He should know all of this stuff already, Blair should, given that it's all been well documented in the debriefing transcripts and reports I've been sending him, but I figure he just wants to hear Charlie talk. He's just trying to get a measure of the man.

As the questions trundle on, Charlie just gets more and more subdued. I find myself wondering whether this is because he's just bored or because he's finally starting to wonder what he's gotten himself into.

~~~~

I catch a ride with Blair back across town to the federal building. He's quiet in the car, not saying much until we're nearing the barrier that separates the street from the ramp that leads into the parking garage situated in the bowels of the building. Then, out of the blue, he says Charlie's an "interesting guy." I watch as he shows his ID at the barrier before heading down the ramp, which is isolated and fenced off with a floor-to-ceiling chain-link fence and only accessible through a gate that opens with a four-digit numerical code. The code changes monthly, and there's a line of cars stretched out before us. The agent in the car at the head of the line's obviously clueless on the new code.

"There's always one," Blair says through a sigh.

"I thought it went well with Charlie," I say.

Blair nods but says nothing. We sit there for a while, engine idling.

"I'm surprised he didn't speak up," Blair finally offers.

"About what?"

"About what he wants. Usually when I tell cooperating witnesses or informants about how we're ready to stand behind them, they want specifics—consideration of their service— lenient sentencing, money, witness protection, whatever. These people are always angling for something. Charlie didn't say a word, didn't ask for anything." He glances across at me. "Have you already talked about it with him?"

I shake my head. "It hasn't come up."

Somehow the guy blocking the entrance gets the code and we're moving again. Inside the secure area, Blair eases into the reserved parking slot marked "Supervisor Squad 7" and turns off the engine.

I unbuckle my seatbelt, but Blair makes no move to get out.

"So why is Charlie ... ?"

"Doing what he's doing?" I say. "Frank says it's because he wants to do something good. Something he can be proud of."

"Right," Blair says with more than a hint of sarcasm. "Frank's 'Noble Savage' theory."

I shrug.

"So we're supposed to believe this guy's made a decision about himself? About his life? Based on what? Frank persuading him it's a good idea?" Blair chuckles, but there's no mirth to it. "I don't know, Nick," he says, his hand flung over the wheel as he stares out the window at the brick wall. "I prefer it when I can see the quid pro quo a little clearer. I hope this guy's for real. I don't want to think about the blowback on this if he turns out to be taking us for a ride."

"I think it's a mixture of things, but I think Frank might be right about Charlie wanting to do good. I know it's a hard sell, but this guy is hard to put your finger on."

Blair cleans his glasses on his shirt then pushes them back on his nose. He makes a noise that's somewhere between a sigh and a cough. "Frank's gonna give me an ulcer," he says.

He steps out of the car, slamming the door closed behind him.

"Anyway, keep a close eye on him, Nick. You got a good feel for guys like this, and I trust your judgment. When the time is right, show him the carrot," he says, as we stand eye to eye. "We need Charlie to start thinking about what we're going to do with him after this case is finished, assuming we ever get started."

"You're talking about WitSec?"

Blair raises his bushy, gray eyebrows. "If we get convictions behind Charlie's testimony, he's going to be one hell of an unpopular guy. Don't mention the program specifically. Just let him know we'll be there for him. A clean start somewhere. No need to look over his shoulder at every turn."

As we make for the stairwell, I think about it for a moment, trying to fathom what the carrot might mean to Charlie. I try to picture him using an assumed name in some bumfuck town somewhere. I imagine him struggling to fit into society, get a job. I just can't see it.

Chapter 23

Entrapment
San Diego, CA
July 27, 1996

Official FBI transcript dated 7/27/96

Nick Spence: Today's date is July 27, 1996. This is an ongoing debriefing of Mr. Charles Slade. The time is 18:20 hours. Present in the room, Special Agent Nick Spence, Detective Frank Conroy, and Mr. Charles Slade.

Frank Conroy: (unintelligible)

NS: Sure, Frank. Stating for the record, we have determined that the most logical first target for this investigation is a convicted drug dealer named Donald "Spud" Jarvis. We have come to this decision based on Mr. Jarvis's prior arrests and convictions on particularly violent criminal acts. According to Mr. Slade—

Charlie Slade: Charlie, man...

NS: Yes, Charlie. According to Charlie, Mr. Jarvis sells methamphetamine out of a bar on El Cajon Boulevard. Is that right, Charlie?

CS: Yeah, that's right.

NS: The feeling here is that Mr. Jarvis is a particularly talkative dealer. If we're going to get information from a target, he is most likely to give it. He is also believed to be the most likely candidate to get word back to Duke and the rest of the Hells Angels, which would benefit...

CS: Let's just do this, already. Jesus Christ, you guys can't even fart without a three-part plan.

NS: Okay, Charlie. We'll cover the ground rules on the upcoming telephone call with Mr. Jarvis.

CS: You mean Spud?

NS: Yes, Charlie. Spud.

CS: Then why don't you call him that?

FC: We'll call him Spud from now on, Charlie.

NS: The first thing we need to establish is that we have to be careful, for legal reasons, about how we approach Spud . . . like initiating any conversations about selling drugs.

CS: You're saying I can't just roll up and score some meth?

FC: No, Charlie, because the defense is going to say you tricked the guy into a criminal act.

CS: What the fuck, man? It ain't no trick.

NS: What we're talking about here is entrapment, Charlie. And it's really not that hard to avoid. The key is that you can't induce someone to commit a crime if they aren't inclined or likely to do so without your help or suggestion. We're on solid ground with Spud because he has a prior criminal history for drug distribution. And he's conducted numerous criminal transactions with you in the past. But it's preferable if you don't say anything that could be read as inducement.

FC: Or suggestion.

CS: So what the fuck do I do, use sign language?

NS: You're going to call him. You're going to call him to set up a meeting. We're going to record the call. During this first call, you have to limit yourself to stuff like you're getting back on your feet, you know, getting back in business. Stuff like that.

FC: General stuff.

NS: Exactly. And then you set up a meeting. If Spud is the way you've described him, he's going to say everything we need him to say in the first two minutes. I don't anticipate you'll have to say much.

FC: What you can't say is, "Hey Spud, I wanna buy methamphetamine from you just like I've done in the past."

CS: I get it, man. I get it.

NS: Now we picked out a couple places we know we can cover you from . . . near the bar where Spud works.

CS: On El Cajon?

NS: Yes. We picked the locations, tested our communications and the transmitter in the Camaro. We know they work. Anything goes wrong, we can be on you in a couple of minutes.

CS: What's gonna go wrong? Fuckin' Spud, man. He shits a load when he sees me coming down the street.

(Silence, tape running)

CS: What'd I say?

FC: You don't wanna go into it like that, Charlie.

CS: Like what?

FC: The macho stuff. Mr. Tough Guy. I mean, it's important for you to be you, but just be aware of what's going on around you. You can't be reckless.

NS: We've got to ease you back into the circle if this is going to work.

CS: So what do you want me to say?

FC: You want to get back on your feet.

CS: So, what, like, "I wanna get back in business"? Like, "I've had kinda a rough time lately, been down on my luck"?

NS: That's right, Charlie. That's good. And once Spud starts talking drugs, meth, quantity, price . . . then we're in the game and past the entrapment issue.

FC: And once you're past the entrapment issue and he's talking freely, you can ask him about quantities and price.

CS: (Long sigh.) And that's not entrapment?

NS: No. You let Spud take the lead as far as possible. Then you can talk quantities and price and set a second meeting to do the deal.

CS: What a bunch of fuckin' bullshit, man. I mean, I get it. But I can tell you it's not gonna go down that way. I'm gonna meet with Spud and the first thing he's gonna say when I tell him I wanna get back in business is, "How much you want, Charlie?"

FC: Well, that's fine.

CS: Sure, but I'm sayin' you better send me packin' green if you want me buyin' drugs from him. There ain't gonna be no first meeting, no second meeting. It won't be like that. It's gonna be wham-bam.

(Silence, tape running)

CS: So, what kinda quantities you wanna go for? Dime bag? Teeners? Eight ball?

NS: Quantities sufficient for us to make good cases on these targets. To make a significant case on distribution and presumptive sale, we'd like to see anything from a half ounce to an ounce.

CS: An ounce? (unintelligible) The guy ain't fuckin' Sears, man. I mean, Spud's a little bit down the food chain.

FC: He can go an ounce, though. You do whatever seems natural, Charlie.

CS: (unintelligible)

FC: The bigger, the better, as far as we're concerned. We're gonna be giving you a grand to cover the buy with Spud. You negotiate as much quantity you can get for the thousand. We're not gonna expend any more than that on this guy.

CS: You're giving me cash?

NS: Buy money. Every bill photocopied, every serial number recorded.

CS: I guess that means I don't stop at the 7-Eleven for smokes and a six-pack with the dough, right?

NS: Very funny, Charlie.

CS: Okay, Nick. Okay. Let's do this thing.

Chapter 24

Marty's Wire
San Diego, CA
August 5, 1996

We've reached a critical point where we need to put our plan into action. No one's said anything about deadlines, but we all know there's a clock running as we work toward returning Charlie back to the streets. One thing's for sure, the longer he's out of circulation, the harder it's going to be to get him back in. But more important, we have no idea how long he's going to stick with us. He seems happy enough at the house, and we're busting our asses doing everything we can to keep him that way, but as the days drag by, he becomes increasingly edgy, blowing up at the smallest little thing. His methadone dosage is right on. So it's not about that. He's fit and getting stronger by the day and is mentally alert. He just seems overwhelmed by all the detail and preparation.

The last hurdle we need to clear is Charlie's body wire —getting the right equipment. We can't move until we have that sorted out because once he's back on the street, the word will filter through to the Hells Angels and there won't be any chance to call timeout. If Duke demands a face to face with Charlie, there'll be little we can do to stall him without arousing suspicion.

I'm glad I requested Marty Logan's help on the technical portion of this project. He's a meticulous and innovative FBI agent, and we'll need his expertise to lower the risks for Charlie. However, Marty tends to be a little rigid.

For this reason, I can't say I've been looking forward to introducing Charlie to Marty—two guys about as opposite as Felix and Oscar. Where Charlie is loose, to say the very least, Marty is retentive to the point of constipation.

So as Paul, Charlie, and I are playing gin in the living room, it's Frank who brings Marty to the table. A perfectionist in dress and manner, Marty is stiff socially and couldn't crack a joke if his life depended on it. His medium height, slender build, and youthful face belie his toughness and fortitude. As a former paratrooper and smokejumper, he has been there, done that, but you'd never know it when you meet him.

Marty shakes everyone's hand, and when he gets to Charlie he gives him the politician double-handed routine, grabbing his forearm while pumping his hand. Charlie twitches and takes a defensive step back, but holds his ground and stares at Marty, nodding while sizing him up. I guess he's trying to decide what's so funny or interesting about this guy who has us all chuckling every time his name comes up.

We move to the kitchen table, where Marty lays out a series of diagrams and flowcharts drawn in black marker pen. "Broadly broken down," he says, ruffling his nose, "the two main approaches for this type of investigation from the perspective of federal law enforcement, particularly the FBI, are consensual monitoring and wiretaps."

One of Marty's endearing little quirks is that he always talks as though he were addressing a convention full of interested people.

"As I understand it, there are no plans for wiretaps in this case at the present time, so I don't need to get into all the laws and rules and regulations that govern such matters."

Frank tilts back on two legs of his chair and heaves a restive sigh. He's already impatient with Marty's no-frills approach.

"That's right," Frank says. "What we're doing is consensual monitoring."

Charlie leans forward, an eyebrow raised. "What's that mean?" he asks.

Marty rakes at his scalp. He doesn't like being interrupted, I know, especially when he's delivering his introductory speech.

"It is in fact a federal crime to wiretap or electronically eavesdrop on the conversation of another," Marty says, upping the volume a notch to maintain control and keeping his eyes on the page in front of him. "Not without a court order or the consent of one of the parties to the conversation." He extends a hand, his fingers spread wide. "We're going to need to have you sign some consensual agreement forms, Charlie. I hope that's okay."

Charlie shrugs, then picks up one of Marty's wiretap diagrams. "How big is this thing, anyway?"

"How big is what?"

"The wire . . ."

Marty straightens up, which is difficult to do, given that he's a telephone pole rooted to the kitchen chair already. "Maybe we should . . ." He clears his throat again. "We should probably back up a little, talk about the basics." He simply refuses to be rushed, and starts in on how there are five primary categories of so-called bugs: acoustic, ultrasonic, RF, optical, and hybrid.

"Acoustic, basically refers to things like—"

"Marty . . ." Frank massages the bridge of his nose as he interrupts. "Maybe we can just focus in on—"

"Listen, Marty," I offer. "One thing we wanted to talk about—to have you and Charlie talk about—is Duke's counter-surveillance setup."

Frank lasers in on Charlie. "We were talking about it the other day, Charlie, remember?" he asks.

Charlie, still a little dazed by Marty's presentation, gives a bewildered nod. "Yeah . . . in his office and . . . and the club room."

Marty gasps. "What kind of counter-surveillance?"

Charlie shrugs. "I don't know, man. Duke got this PI guy, you know, private investigator, to install some shit. It's like over the doorframe. Duke says an alarm or signal or some fuckin' thing goes off if there's any bugs around. Like if someone comes into the office or the clubhouse wearing a wire."

"Is that even possible?" Paul asks.

Marty nods emphatically. "Most bugs put out electromagnetic radiation such as radio waves. Standard electronic countermeasure for bugs is to sweep the room with something sensitive to radio waves. A receiver of some sort." He paws at the diagrams in front of him, and I can see he's still a little miffed about not being able to get to them all in order. In time, he levels an eye on Charlie. "Do you know how much Duke spent on this equipment?"

Charlie cleans the end of his cigarette on a saucer, shaking his head. Marty convulses and erupts into a little involuntary shudder, obviously with a visceral hatred for the habit.

"Professional sweeping devices don't come cheap," he says. "Maybe you could find out what Duke paid. Give us a better idea of what he's got in there."

"You're fuckin' crazy, man," Charlie says. "If I start asking questions like that, he's gonna get suspicious."

"But maybe if you could just—"

"You don't fuck with Duke, man." Charlie snarls with that brooding, intense stare. "I mean, it's like fuck me once, shame on you, you know? But fuck me twice and I'm gonna fuck you up, man."

We all sit there for a while, waiting for Charlie to come back down and drop his defiant eyes from Marty, who looks increasingly uncomfortable at the table.

"We gotta have equipment that can defeat any of his dime store shit, don't we Marty?" I ask.

Marty ponders the question for a second and then shakes his head. "I'll come up with something, Spence," he says. "In fact, I've got an idea in mind already. There's this device that..."

"Bottom line," Frank says, cutting Marty off before he can build any momentum, "for now, I think we just need to monitor Charlie's telephone calls. And we need to set up some sort of body recorder for the buys we do outside the clubhouse."

"Right," Marty says, and he reaches into his attaché case, pulling out a little tape recorder. "Meet the Nagra." He pushes it in front of Charlie with a little flourish. "Reel-to-reel, built-in microphone *and* transmitter."

Charlie just stares at it.

Marty urges with his hands. "Go ahead, Charlie, take a look."

Charlie hefts it in his right hand. "Jesus," he says. "It's kinda big."

Marty frowns. "Three-by-five. About two inches deep. We tweaked it to boost the transmitter. Records and transmits at the same time. That means agents can monitor from a distance at the same time as the tape is turning."

Charlie puts the Nagra back down. "I thought you guys had, like, secret agent spy shit. I mean . . . small stuff. Like you can hide in a pen. Shit like that."

"But this *is* small," Marty implores, looking a little hurt.

Charlie grunts and disdainfully pushes the Nagra with the back of his hand. "It's gonna need to be a whole lot smaller than this fucker," he says. "I mean, if I'm gettin' it past Duke—"

"We're probably getting ahead of ourselves," Frank says.

For a moment, no one speaks. We're all staring at the Nagra, thinking, I guess, that it *does* seem pretty big.

It's Marty who breaks the silence. "These initial buys," he says. "What kind of scenarios do you envision?"

Frank blows smoke up at the overhead light. "Charlie's gonna be in a car."

~~~~

Marty doesn't want to bug the Camaro in the Pacific Beach garage, says it would be better to do the job at the federal building, where there's a proper "tech shop." Tech agents are a distinct breed within the Bureau. They're typically obsessed with spying and gadgetry and are really only comfortable in their spy shops, tinkering with and testing cutting-edge equipment they could never afford on their own salaries.

As promised, the next morning Marty returns to PB

with the Camaro. He must have worked all night on this little project. Paul, Frank, and I are standing in the garage as he pulls in and shuts down the throaty engine. As he gets out and struts around the vehicle, he proudly begins to take us through the alterations. A wire's been tucked under the windshield molding, up to a microphone that's been cleverly built into the rearview.

"The Nagra is accessible up under the dash," Marty says. He shows us an on/off switch under the steering wheel to activate the recorder. The Nagra's mounted on a platform that can be lowered and raised to facilitate changing the reel-to-reel tapes. Everthing is meticulously concealed. Anyone operating the Camaro would have no hint of the gadgetry hidden inside unless they knew where to look. We're depending on it.

"We modified the power source to run off the car battery so you don't have to mess with changing batteries," Marty says.

"Nice work, Marty."

"You haven't seen anything yet, Spence," he says with a broad grin.

Frank puts a flame to the tip of his cigarette, takes a drag, and blows smoke over the Camaro. "I'm glad we have this guy on *our* side," he says, as if Marty's not standing right behind him.

Marty tries and fails to mask the flattery. With a bounce in his step, he moves to the back of the car, where he fishes his attaché case from the backseat and starts fiddling around inside. "Here's what I wanted to show you," he says. He whips out a small plastic case a little smaller than a pack of cigarettes. "Behold the mini-Nagra."

Frank chuffs, blowing smoke. "The mini-Nagra?"

"Wow, Marty," I say, taking the thing from him and rolling it over in my palm.

"Careful, Nick, it's super-sensitive," Marty scolds. He takes it back as if retrieving his newborn son instead of a piece of FBI hardware. "It's state of the art ... the best the Bureau has.

We just got this from Headquarters last week. There's just one problem with it," he adds, staring at it in the palm of his hand.

I glance up at him and he's mincing.

"The good news is it puts out a very low frequency wave so it will be difficult to pick up by any counter-surveillance device, but the bad news is the transmitter and mike are almost *too* sensitive," he says. "Anything really loud—like a discharged firearm, for example—is going to overload the mike's tolerance."

"So if someone decides to shoot Charlie, we're not going to hear it," Frank says.

I fire a nervous glance around the garage, thankful that Charlie's taking a nap and not hearing this. Marty must sense the discomfort, too, because all he offers is a tight little nod.

"Let's hope it doesn't come to that," I say.

~~~~

A couple of days of trial and error would follow; Marty and Paul experimenting with where to secret the new mini-Nagra on Charlie so it won't show and be comfortable enough for him over long periods of time. They try putting it in the small of his back, which works well enough as long as he's not sitting down or leaning against anything. Taping it up under his arm or in his crotch is a disaster, with Marty becoming increasingly frustrated with Charlie's impatience and insults. While this fiasco is playing out, I decide to leave them alone to work it out . . . or kill each other.

When I get back the next afternoon, I find Charlie in the backyard pumping iron in his T-shirt and jeans. He's wearing a pair of cowboy boots that Frank bought for him at a swap meet a few days ago. They're Tony Lamas, nice-looking boots and beat up just enough to look like lifelong possessions.

"How'd it go this morning?" I ask. I'm referring to Charlie's second driving test, which I know he's finally supposed to have taken earlier this morning, after failing his first attempt last week. It was Paul's job to make sure Charlie walked into the DMV on time this morning. I look toward the house and don't see anyone around.

"Where's Paul?"

"Haven't seen him."

"So ... ?"

"So what?"

"Come on, Charlie, did you pass or not?"

"Aced the written test," he says, sitting up on the bench.

"I know, Charlie ... and?"

"Lady failed me again, Nick."

I look down at the ground and take a second to get a handle on my frustration. "Goddamnit, Charlie ..."

Charlie flops back on the bench and looks up at the bar. "This woman had to be three hundred pounds, Spence. Shoulda' seen her ... could barely get in the fucking car." He starts pumping the weight, grunting through his words. "She said ... it was ... for my ... own good."

"What was?"

He clanks the bar back into the cradle. "Failing me, man."

"So what did she fail you on?"

Charlie sits up and huffs. "Not turning around in my seat every goddamn time I change lanes. I swear she wants me to turn around in my goddamn seat to—"

"To make sure you got your blind spot covered."

Charlie fires out a hand. "And what happens while I got my eyes off the road, Spence? I'll tell you what happens. I rear-end the motherfucker in front of me."

And then it comes to me: his demeanor's all wrong. His lips turn up at the corners, stifling a smile.

"What's going on, Charlie?"

I turn as Marty comes out of the house, followed by Paul, both of them grinning like two mules in a briar patch. Marty's holding a tape recorder, hits the play button: "... sure you got your blind spot covered. And what happens while I got my eyes off the road, Nick? I'll tell you what . . ."

He turns it off and looks at me like he just won the grand prize at the high school science fair.

I can't help but smile. "You *recorded* all of that? How?"

Charlie stands up, also grinning, all lips. I look for the bulge of the Nagra under his T-shirt and jeans, but there's no sign of it anywhere. Then I look down at his boots and smile.

"I like it."

"Took Frank a while to stretch these wide enough to allow the Nagra to slip down inside."

"Is it comfortable?"

Charlie takes a few steps around the yard. He doesn't seem to favor it or break stride. "Not really, but it's okay."

"We tape it to his ankle," Marty says.

"Had to shave the fucker first," Charlie says, rolling his eyes.

By now, Marty's giddy. "Then we roll up his sock to cover it," he says, miming the act with his hands. "We slip on the jeans, then the boots, and pull the jeans down over the boots. I mean, even if they pat him down . . ."

"They don't," I say. I turn to Charlie, deadly serious.

"You *never, ever* let them pat you down, Charlie. Gonzo, Scooter . . . any of those other fuckers try that kinda shit, you get in their face, challenge them about trust . . . brotherhood. If they can't trust you . . . you don't want any part of them or the club. You gotta take the offense. Got it?"

Charlie flinches, then shrugs. "You say so, Nick. Jesus."

Marty pulls up the leg of Charlie's jeans. "We had to leave access so we could punch the activator switch to engage the reel-to-reel. But once it's running, there's no reason to touch it."

"Where's the wire?"

Marty turns Charlie around and lifts his shirt. The wire is taped along his spine. Strong as he is, Charlie's spine sits in a groove between two bands of muscle, making the wire easy to conceal.

"And the mike?"

Again, Marty turns Charlie around. I can't see any tell-tale bulge on his chest. I pat his breastbone. Charlie smiles. Finally, he lifts his left arm and pulls open the sleeve of his T-shirt, revealing the microphone, which is taped right under his shaved armpit. With his arm down in a normal position, just the end of the mike sticks out in a little bud.

"How long does it take to set up each time?"

"It's pretty awkward," Marty admits.

"'Specially when he runs the wire up my ass," Charlie says.

I laugh out of relief as much as anything; glad to see him joking about it all. "Great job, guys," I say eventually.

"Has Frank seen it?"

"Loves it," Marty grins. "He thinks he's ready. Time to put Charlie in play."

"How about it, Charlie?" I ask.

"Let's rumble, man."

Chapter 25

Spud
San Diego, CA
August 7, 1996

Charlie makes the call on a Wednesday night. Apart from Charlie himself, there's only me, Frank, and Marty in the room and we're all pretty tense. We've been through what Charlie needs to say at least ten times, and Marty's about to set the tape recorder running when Frank says, "Remember, Charlie, the tape is evidence. We have to hand over the full reel unedited and completely tamper-free."

Charlie rolls his eyes. "Jesus, Frank, how many times you gonna tell me that?"

"It's just important is all, Charlie. *Very* important. Once Marty hits the button, you're on the air. If shit gets mumbled, it'll be useless as evidence. If the guy says something you don't think is clear, you ask him to repeat it."

"And the same goes for you," Marty adds. "No mumbling, Charlie."

"Okay."

"And no cursing."

"The fuck you talkin' about, man?"

This gets a big laugh and I revel in it. The energy in the room is good. Focused and positive. After all the weeks of preparation, we know we're finally going to nail some righteous crooks.

"Charlie, I understand you have to curse," Frank says. "It's just your nature. But you have to think about the little old ladies in the jury box."

Charlie nods, and I can see that the mention of a jury drops like a stone into some particularly deep, dark waters. He appears pensive, his eyes vacant.

Frank looks at me over his glasses. "Anything else, Spence?"

I shake my head. "Let's do it."

Marty presses a button and the recorder starts to roll.

I look Charlie straight in the eye as I start the preamble: "This is Special Agent Nick Spence, FBI. Agent Marty Logan, FBI, also present, as is Detective Frank Conroy, San Diego Police Department. We are in San Diego, California, at 17:35 hours on August 7, 1996, and we're recording a consensually monitored telephone call by Charles Slade, a cooperating witness, calling Donald Jarvis, aka 'Spud,' the subject of an ongoing narcotics investigation. The telephone number being dialed is 646-2556."

Frank dials the number, and we all lean forward, listening for the dial tone. It comes through nice and clear and clean, and then someone picks up.

"Yeah..."

Charlie nods. "Spud, it's me, Charlie."

"The fuck..."

"Spud, it's Charlie."

"The fuck it *is*. Charlie! Where you been, man?"

Charlie closes his eyes, trying to focus in, trying to get it right. "Been around, man, you know. Here... There..."

"You been gone like fuckin' months, man. Guys lookin' for you, man. We thought you was fuckin' dead!"

"Nearly was, man. Nearly was. Nearly OD'd."

"Get the fuck outta here..."

"But I'm good now. Better anyways. Trying to..."

"You seen Duke?"

"No, man."

A long silence follows, and a dreadful thought suddenly occurs to me. As wrapped up as we've been with getting Charlie straight on how to conduct himself on this call, I completely forgot we'd be calling someone who might know about the missing money and the accusations against him.

"Uh," Spud says slowly. "He's, uh. .... Well, he's lookin' for you, man. They's *all* lookin' for you. Duke, Gonzo, that big fucker Jay. Scooter."

Charlie fires a glance at me, and I nod as confidently as I can.

"Yeah," he says. "Yeah, well, you know—"

"They're, uh. . . . They're *worried*, man. You know what I mean?"

"Yeah, sure," Charlie says, rolling his eyes. "I know how they *worry*. But I'm back now, man," he says. "That's what I wanted to talk to you about."

"What?" Spud asks.

"Getting back on my feet. Getting back in business."

Spud cackles—raspy and crackbrained. "That right?" he says. "You lookin' to buy or sell?"

Charlie furrows his brow. For the first time, I notice he's got his fists clenched. He's nervous. Something I've never seen before.

"Maybe we should meet," he says.

"Damn right," Spud says, and he sounds excited. "Come see me at the bar, man. I'm still bouncin' heads at Tink's on the boulevard."

"Nah, man. I'm tryin' to keep a low profile for a while."

"You runnin' or somethin'? Hidin'?"

"Just wanna ease myself back in," he says. "How 'bout the lot in the alley back of Tink's?"

"You wanna talk business in the parkin' lot? You crazy, man?"

"Not in the parking lot, man. In my car."

There's a silence at the other end, and for a second I think we've lost him. "Spud?" Charlie says.

"Your car?" Spud says. "You're fuckin' with me, man. Since when do you drive a fuckin' car?"

~ ~ ~ ~

We're standing in the small guest bedroom we now refer to as "Paul's room," and we're here because it's the only place in the house we figure we can enjoy full privacy. I close the door quietly. Frank's looking at me wide-eyed, but I can tell he knows why I've dragged him in here in such a rush.

"We're on thin ice here, Frank," I say.

Frank nods, pats at his chest for his smokes, which thankfully he's left in the living room.

"Something's gotta give here," I say. "If Charlie's going into this thing, he's *got* to know the club's pissed at him. More than just because he hasn't been around; the addiction thing; missing church. He's got to know the whole story."

Frank's bushy eyebrows rise. "I know," he says. "But we need to buy a little more time, Nick. Every day he's a little stronger, and that makes a big difference. The stronger he is, the better he'll be able to handle it. If he really flies off the handle, we have no way of stopping him and it'll be too late to bring him back into the fold."

"I'm just telling you, if he's going to hear about the stolen money, he'd better hear it from us."

My partner nods, sitting down on Paul's bed and throwing his palms up. "We're gonna get it from both barrels, partner," he says with a sigh. "He'll be pissed at us for withholding information, and pissed at the club for thinking he stole money."

"Yeah," I say. "But who'll he be pissed at *more*?"

Frank sighs.

It's a question with no answer right now, a question on which our entire investigation hangs.

Chapter 26

First Buy
San Diego, CA
August 8, 1996

Quarter to nine on the following night. I'm riding with Charlie through fluorescent-lit streets, eastbound on El Cajon Boulevard, where the hookers and johns are just starting to play out their nightly mating games.

I'm slouched down in the passenger seat of the Camaro with an Oakland Raiders cap pulled down over my eyebrows. Charlie's at the wheel. When he switches lanes, he makes a mockery of keeping with the official traffic laws he's so recently learned, turning almost completely around in his seat to look back over his shoulder.

"Cut the shit, Charlie, enough of the bullshit. Watch the road."

He's quiet in the car, but there's no sign of second thoughts about what we're about to do. At the corner of 28th, I tell him to make a right, then another right a block off the boulevard. He does as I instruct and we pull into the entrance of a one-story, light-industrial unit with bars on the windows. The building was recently used in an FBI undercover sting operation. We're putting it to use again because the lease is still good to the end of the month. A couple cars are parked out front alongside a white Econoline van.

The back door of the van opens up as we pull in next to it. Marty hops out, grinning like a kid, with a bundle of equipment in his arms.

"Jesus," Charlie says. "Marty looks psyched."

"We all are, Charlie," I say. "It's a big night for us."

I climb out and take a look at our surroundings: a few scrubby eucalyptus trees, overhanging power lines, a Dumpster full of discarded boxes. Charlie gets out on the driver's side. He looks pretty scruffy, his long, black hair draped down over his shoulders, chin dark with a couple days' growth of beard. His black T-shirt has a rip in it, and his jeans are blotched with grease stains at the knees. It's a look calculated to evoke the Charlie that Spud knows, the Charlie who doesn't give a shit. He's also wearing the cowboy boots Frank game him, despite the fact he's not going to be wearing the Nagra and wire on this buy. It's important that we establish them as part of his new look.

We walk in through a fire exit around the side of the building held open by a cinder block. I hear Frank before I see him. He's pacing up and down, pontificating in the middle of a funny story, a cigarette burning between his fingers. He breaks off as we enter the room—a big, gloomy space that smells of cardboard and bubble wrap. Light filters down from fluorescent fixtures high up in the ceiling, picking up the shadowy mass of boxes stacked on palettes and three guys standing with Frank by a forklift. They turn as we walk in, curious eyes settling on Charlie, someone they've all heard about but are meeting here for the first time.

I do the introductions, tell Charlie the guys are from Squad 7, handpicked by Pete Blair.

"They're our backup for the evening," I explain.

Mike Dove, a fitness nut who cycles into the office with bricks in his backpack, shoves out a muscular hand for Charlie to shake. "Mike Dove. Good to meet you, Charlie."

Charlie nods, shakes the offered hand, and then awkwardly shakes with Agents Ryan and Clouser. He seems a little embarrassed to be the focus of so much attention. There's an awkward pause. Frank asks Charlie if he's ready to catch some bad guys.

"Sure," he says, shrugging, "but . . ."

"What is it, Charlie?"

"I don't really see why we need so many guys. I mean, it's Spud we're talkin' about here. The guy's a fuckin' pussy."

In the midst of raucous laughter, Frank steps on his cigarette, shakes his head, and heaves one of his long sighs. "It's not Spud we're worried about, Charlie."

Everyone's quiet now. Charlie instinctively turns and gives me a nasty look.

"There somethin' you ain't tellin' me, Spence?"

I raise my hands. "No, Charlie," I say. "We just prefer to be safe over sorry."

Charlie's eyes linger on me for longer than I'd like. I try to keep myself expressionless, show him I'm telling the truth, even if I'm not. When he finally directs his gaze elsewhere, I fire a look at Frank, who shrugs. We can't keep holding this stolen money thing from Charlie. If he finds out from Spud, we're screwed.

"Fuck my safety," Charlie says. "I don't give a fuck about safety. I can take care of myself. Somethin' goin' down here I don't know about?"

"Far as I know, this is all going to run smooth and sim—"

"We just have to consider the possibility of some sort of a setup," Frank interrupts, stepping forward. "Spud may be working for Duke now. You know he's always wanted to prospect for the club. So . . . there's a chance he called the club and told them about the meeting. Thing is, Charlie, we really don't know where Duke's head is at on all this. The way they went after Stacey to find you. You were the enforcer for the Hells Angels. You don't just walk away from the club and disappear. They have to consider you a liability. We all know Duke's a paranoid, crazy bastard and he's capable of pulling anything."

Charlie mulls this over for a second, then shrugs. "Whatever, man . . ."

"We're all going to be monitoring the meet," I say, as much for the other guys as for Charlie. I list off our positions and logistics. We'll be operating on Channel 4 on our radios. Frank, Marty, and I'll be parked in the van on the corner of Orange and 46th. "We want radio transmissions kept to an absolute minimum so we can concentrate on the dialogue between Charlie and Spud."

"You got it," says Clouser.

"In the event something happens and we have to move in to rescue our witness, I will be the only one to give the command. Have your raid jackets with you just in case, understood?" The guys nod, all eyes on Charlie. I turn to him. "If things go bad, we'll be within striking distance. If Spud tries anything, or if any of the club shows up looking to fuck with you, we're gonna jump in."

Charlie smiles.

"What?" I say.

Charlie holds his hands out and shrugs. "Hey," he says, "if shit goes down, it'll go down fast. Unless you guys are standin' right next to me . . ."

Frank nods, reaching for a cigarette. "That's why we're gonna use a code word, Charlie. Anytime you feel like something's not right, tension's starting to build, you feel like your life is in danger, you say the word 'rose' or 'roses.'"

Charlie looks at Frank like he just asked him to gut-punch his grandmother.

"'Rose' is our code word, okay?" Frank says defensively.

"Fuckin' *rose*," Charlie says, rolling his eyes. "That's some stupid fuckin' shit, man. Code words, for chrissakes. Jesus, Frank."

Frank cracks a smile. "You start talkin' about roses. Like, 'How come you boys didn't bring me no roses?' or 'You boys shoulda brought me some roses.' Anything with the word 'rose' or 'roses,' and we'll be there before you can say 'Glock 9.'"

Frank lights his cigarette, the smoke drifting through his grinning lips. "It'll kill our little project stone dead, of course, us jumping in like that . . . but if someone pulls a gun or whatever, you start talking roses. It's your lifeline, Charlie, and it's no bullshit. Remember, we can't see what's going on . . . only hear."

Charlie nods and looks at the floor and shuffles a foot, smiling his I-can't-believe-this-shit smile. "I hear you, Frank . . . I hear you. But I'm tellin' you . . . Gonzo, Duke. . . .

Those fuckers ain't gonna try nothin' with me on the street. If they're gonna try somethin', they'll try and grab me somehow, you know? Surprise me. Shove me in a car or van and take me someplace where there ain't no witnesses."

We all kind of stew on this for a moment.

"But I ain't gonna let that happen," Charlie adds.

"Spud's got two priors using a gun during the commision of a felony," I say.

Charlie spits on the floor, shaking his head. "Nick, Spud pulls a gun on me, I'm just gonna shove the fuckin' thing up his ass." He looks around at the guys, smiling his tight-lipped smile, meeting stares that acknowledge the stone-cold simplicity of what he just said. Charlie's not bragging here, and we all know it.

It's Frank who breaks the silence. "Okay for shoving it up his ass, Charlie," he says. "Just don't pull the trigger."

~~~~

I've just finished our procedural search of Charlie and the Camaro and briefed him again for at least the tenth time about how legal protocol and chain of custody means he can't depart from the plan, can't drop in to 7-Eleven for smokes. I've given him the thousand dollars—an envelope stuffed with a skinny wad of marked and photocopied bills—and wished him good luck.

So as Charlie pulls out in the Camaro, I get in the back of the van with Marty. Frank's up front driving. The ride we're using to monitor the buy is a Ford Econoline with tinted windows and a big dent on the driver's side door. It's nothing fancy, but it meets our basic requirements for space and privacy.

Marty's set us up with some portable monitoring equipment and a backup tape recorder in case the Nagra recorder in the Camaro fails. We do a little test in the street in front of the warehouse—have Charlie drive up and down a couple of times to make sure we're a go and the transmitter is putting out a clear signal. Everything works as it should, so with twelve minutes to go before showtime, we head east on El Cajon Boulevard, about half a block behind Charlie, listening to the low growl of his voice over the wire.

"Got you in my mirror, Frank. Feel kind of... feels stupid talkin' to myself, but ... well, that's what you said to do, so I'm doin' it. I'm drivin' east on El Cajon Boulevard, passing Texas Street."

Frank makes a right turn on 45th, south toward Orange Avenue about a block southeast of where Charlie's set to meet with Spud.

"I see you guys peeling off," Charlie says. "Bye, guys. See you on the other side ... don't fall asleep on me."

Frank turns into the alleyway, and almost as soon as we park, Charlie goes quiet.

I look up at Marty, who's watching the tape turn on our recorder. "What?" I say. "We just lose the signal?"

"Come on, Charlie," he says under his breath. "Keep talking."

Then Charlie's voice comes through, louder than before. I guess he's sitting forward over the wheel, maybe looking for a place to park.

"Son of a bitch," he says, his voice going introspective, sad. "I can't believe Tina's still here on the same corner, wearing that same stupid fake fur jacket. Its eighty fuckin' degrees out, man ... she's still on the spike ... still hookin'. This street, man ... I used to come down here on my Harley every Christmas Eve wearin' a Santa Claus outfit and give each of the girls I was friendly with a coupla grand, told them to go home, be with their families for one night outta the year ..."

His momentary reverie snaps and he's back with us ... "You guys' ... uh ... still hear me?" He coughs loudly into the mike and hawks a big loogie out the window. "There ... there's Spud out front of the bar, talkin' to some fuckin' tweaker." We hear Charlie toot his horn. "Gonna pull 'round the back to the parking lot and wait for him . . ."

The Bureau radio crackles, and Clouser comes through loud and clear: "I'm set up and I've got an eye on our guy. He's parked on the east side of the lot in the alley behind the bar, facing east against a building. White, male subject, long hair, ponytail, walking toward the car, light-colored shirt and dark vest."

"Roger that, 710."

The others acknowledge. "Copy, 710," and we hear the door of the Camaro open and then Spud's voice, booming loud. He's either cranked up or drunk, laughing as he says how great it is to see his old friend Charlie back on the street. Charlie stays quiet through all this, and I can picture him sitting there, his hands on the steering wheel, playing it cool, restless.

"So, this is your ride?" Spud says in a tone of utter amazement.

"What?" Charlie snarls. "You don't like it?"

Spud's laugh comes through loud and phony. "Just ain't used to seeing you on four wheels is all."

"Yeah, well, get used to it, man."

Then there's a long silence. So much silence that Marty leans in close, checking dials on the recorder.

"Okay, man," Spud says. "It's all good. All. . . . So . . . so where you at, what can I do for you? You goin' small or large? Lookin' to buy a gram, eight ball, teener, what?"

Bingo. Drugs and quantities right from the get-go. I stick up a thumb at Frank, who's nodding, smiling. I knew Spud wouldn't let us down.

"Don't want no fuckin' teener," Charlie growls.

"Eight ball, then. One-twenty-five, Charlie. I can sell you two right here, right now. Two-fifty. Two-forty, since we're old—"

"Need an ounce."

"An *ounce*?"

"That a problem?"

"No . . . but . . . I gotta go back inside for that."

"So go back inside, Spud. I'm kinda in a hurry, okay?"

"Sure thing, Charlie. Relax. Ounce is gonna cost you a grand."

"Nine, if it's any good," Charlie blurts.

"You won't be disappointed, okay? For you, nine. Nine hundred it is."

The Camaro door closes with a heavy *thunk*.

Clouser crackles in. "710 to all units. Subject is out of the vehicle and walking west in alley toward the back door of the bar. Our guy's still in the car. Just lit up a cigarette."

I close my eyes, focusing on what's coming through the wire. Think I can hear Charlie blow smoke on a long, shuddering exhale. "It's okay, Charlie," I say to myself. "You're doing good. Doing great."

I'm saying these things for my own reassurance more than anything. I know if something bad's going to go down, it's going to go down right now. I'm thinking of the possibilities, getting a flash of images: Spud, faking his euphoric high, checking Charlie out, assuring himself that maybe Charlie isn't armed and is vulnerable. I see him coming back out with Duke and a couple of Hells Angels to settle the score with Charlie, or maybe Spud's prospecting for the club. He always wanted to join. Maybe this is his chance to prove his worth and he comes out with a gun, puts a round in Charlie's head.

The silence wears on. It all seems to take forever, but in fact only five minutes pass before Clouser's voice breaks the silence: "710 to all units. Subject just exited the back door of the bar and is walking toward our guy's car."

The Camaro's door opens and slams shut.

"Crazy in there, man. You should come in . . ."

"Yeah . . . maybe next time . . ."

I hear rustling sounds.

"One ounce," Spud says. "Excellent product."

More rustling.

"What the fuck is this?" Charlie says, his voice going flat and ugly. "This looks like shit, man."

"What?"

"The color, the texture. What the fuck did you cut it with?"

"That's some righteous shit, Charlie. Never been stepped on. Pure as the driven snow."

"*Yellow* snow. Don't fuck with me, Spud."

"Charlie, you know color of product can vary."

"Sure, Spud . . ."

"Charlie, it's crystal meth, as good as you're gonna—"

"Eight hundred."

"Come on, Charlie."

"Eight hundred."

"There goes my fuckin' margin," Spud says.

"Who you kiddin', man?"

More rustling and shifting sounds from inside the Camaro.

"Good doin' business, Charlie."

"Count the fuckin' money."

"S'all good, Charlie."

I look up at Marty, who's pumping his hands in the air. It is indeed all very good.

~~~~

When Charlie pulls back into the warehouse, Frank, Marty, and I are already waiting for him, holding up three sets of thumbs and grinning like idiots.

I get on the radio and tell the other agents to discontinue. "The bird's in the cage. Thanks for your help."

Charlie gets out of the car, nodding, smiling.

Frank's the first to shake his hand. "You're the man, Charlie."

"Did you get it all?"

"Everything, Charlie. Good job."

It's high-fives all around as I take the keys from Charlie and slide into the driver's seat. I clear my throat, look into

Marty's dual-purpose mirror, and record my epilogue statement on the tape recorder to pronounce the operation closed.
Then I reach under the steering wheel and switch off the
Nagra. I remove, initial, and bag the reel from the recorder,
prepping it to be filed into evidence.

"Where's the meth, Charlie?" I ask through the driver's
window.

Charlie nods in the direction of the passenger seat. I turn
and find it on the floor in a plastic Ziploc bag. I pull on a pair of
evidence gloves to protect for latents, then reach down, bring
it up into the light.

Frank opens a liquid-filled vial labeled "Presumptive
Field Test Kit-Methamphetamine." I take the tiny spoon that
comes with the kit, crack the vial, and sprinkle in a small
amount of the yellowish white powder. I snap the vial closed,
give it a couple of shakes, and watch it turn a purplish blue.
Frank conducts a complete search of the Camaro while I
search Charlie again head to toe.

"Man, I can't believe the bullshit you guys go through,"
Charlie says.

I shrug, smile. "You got anything else for me, Charlie?" I
say, putting out my hand.

Charlie frowns, then remembers the two bills he still
has in his pocket. He hands them over. "So, what did that
fucker sell me, man?"

I put out my hand again, for him to shake this time. "One
ounce of a Schedule 1 controlled substance, Charlie. You did
good."

Chapter 27

Rent Comes Due
San Diego, CA
August 11, 1996

"I gotta pay my rent, man."

It's a few days after the buy with Spud, and Charlie's getting antsy again. Things are going well, but for Charlie they need to go faster, further. Like us, he knows the time is coming when he'll have to face the club—and I guess he just wants the talking and the planning to be over. We're sitting in the living room of the Pacific Beach house. I'm trying to catch up on my daily logs and expense vouchers while Charlie reads the paper and frets about his rent.

I put down the report I'm holding. "You pay rent, Charlie?"

"What do you think, man?"

"I don't know. Just picturing you writing a check every month and . . ."

"Don't pay no check, Spence. It's all cash with my man Eugene. Cash on the nail, six months in advance."

I fold my hands in front of me. "And it's due?"

"*Past* due. And I don't wanna lose that place, man. It's my home."

Frank comes in from the kitchen and glances over at me. I know what he's thinking because I'm thinking it, too. At some point, Charlie's going to have to face up to the reality of his situation. Moving back into his apartment after all this is over won't be an option. Whatever kind of case we build against the San Diego Hells Angels is probably not going to put every last member of the club in prison, and even if it did, they could still get to Charlie. His only chance for a future is somewhere far from El Cajon or San Diego, somewhere no one will find him.

The Federal Witness Security Program, or "WitSec," as

we call it, is a possibility, but it's certainly not a given. Common perception of the program is that it's available to any threatened witness for the federal government, but that's not the case. The U.S. Department of Justice and U.S. Marshal's Service, who administer the program, are selective about who gets in, and they're selective for good reason. It costs a lot of money and man hours to protect a person from danger and harm. So after intense screening and testing, if the Justice Department or the marshals think a person is an unlikely or unfit candidate to play by their strict rules, they reject them.

"And I need to pick up my stuff," Charlie says.

"What stuff?"

"I don't know, man. My shit. My bike, clothes, colors."

"Why do you want your colors, Charlie?" Frank asks.

"Say what?"

"You're not in the gang anymore."

"I know that."

"So?"

"Well, if they're gonna trust me . . ."

Frank steps over to Charlie, staring down at him. "You wear the colors, they're gonna suck you right back in," he says. "Like I say—you gotta stay on the fringe, man."

Charlie shrugs, nods. "Need my shit anyway," he says, going back to his paper. "My clothes. Sick of wearing this thing." He pulls at the plaid shirt he's wearing, one of the first things I purchased at Kmart after we found him in the motel. For a moment, nobody speaks. Then a thought comes to me.

"How are you going to pay the rent anyway, Charlie?"

"Like I said."

"With cash?" I ask cynically. "*What* cash? I mean, where is this cash, Charlie? It's not like you have a bank account . . . at least one that we know about."

Charlie gives his paper a defiant rustle. "Don't worry about it, Nick."

So now, of course, I *do* worry about it. I shoot a look at Frank, whose eyes reflect my own concern. Money. *Cash*. Given what we know about Charlie's current standing with the club, it's a touchy subject. I put my papers aside, giving Charlie my full attention.

"What?" he says.

"Come on, man, you know I have to ask about this stuff. I've got to because of the—"

"Because of the case," Charlie interrupts. "I know, I know."

"So ... this money," I say slowly. "Where is it?"

Charlie lights a cigarette, brushes ash from his thigh, clearly thinking about how he should answer the question.

"Charlie ..."

"In the apartment."

"What?"

"It's in the apartment."

"Okay." I offer a pair of placating hands in the air. "How much is there?"

"Enough to pay the rent."

I wait for more.

"What?" Charlie says.

~~~~

Charlie's sudden urge to go back to his place in El Cajon presents a new set of problems. For starters, telling him he can't go back there will only fuel his resolve to do just that. Second, there are obvious security reasons, the most significant of which we haven't even shared with him yet. As far as we know, the club still has reason to believe Charlie stole from them. And the more Frank and I discuss it, the more it becomes clear that despite our growing sentiment for our witness, we still have no evidence to doubt their suspicions. There's a devastating question that hangs in the air every time the subject comes up: What if he *really did steal that money*? If he did, then any plans we have for sending him back into the clubhouse would be a death sentence.

Still, we've both agreed that his request is somewhat reasonable. But only on two conditions. First, I get enough time to conduct a thorough counter-surveillance in the area of his apartment before Charlie goes there; and second, that Charlie lets Paul go along with him. At least, with this new disclosure about this stash of cash, we get to find out what kind of money he's talking about.

Since the recent controlled drug buy from Spud, we can assume that our talkative target has done just what we expected him to do . . . tell the world that Charlie Slade's back on the street and doing business. This news would no doubt redouble the club's efforts to find him, and his apartment would certainly be ground zero in their search.

Aside from the security concerns, we have to worry about Charlie himself. There's always the possibility he's maybe kept a stash of drugs at his place, and would be tempted to use them once in the privacy of his own home.

~~~~

As I make the left turn at the end of the exit ramp off Second Avenue in the City of El Cajon, heading toward Charlie's apartment, I keep having the same nagging thought . . . are we really certain that we *can* trust him? He's been doing well on methadone. The treatment continues, but at much reduced doses, and Charlie seems determined to stay clean, strong, and healthy. It's a Tuesday afternoon and I'm driving a borrowed undercover vehicle on loan from SOG, our Special Operations Group. One of nine squads that comprise the San Diego FBI field office, SOG is mainly a surveillance squad. They're our eyes and ears in the field, and as such, put a huge premium on protection of their identities. They do business out of an off-site undercover location, they never come into the downtown offices, and their vehicles are never brought into the FBI garage.

The other squads from the office, like mine, Squad 7,

can call on them to take pressure off investigative case agents with regard to time-consuming surveillance. SOG teams are well trained and expertly proficient at surreptitiously following people, and they have aerial surveillance capabilities with light aircraft, though I won't need any eyes in the sky on this occasion.

With Blair's sanction, I've requested an SOG surveillance team on site in the vicinity of Charlie's apartment since late yesterday, when Charlie first argued his way into a trip back to his old place. The team's job is to look for any kind of sign of Hells Angels surveillance in the area, and given the importance of this job, it felt right to leave it to the pros.

After a short meeting with the SOG team leader, I'm assured all's clear in and around Charlie's apartment, so I call Paul, who's waiting at the house for the go-ahead. Half-hour later, he and Charlie drive past me in a U-Haul truck and I head back to the house. At my request, SOG will remain in the vicinity until Paul and Charlie clear the area.

Just before dark, I hear the truck pull up in the alley behind the house. Charlie stomps in through the garage, clutching a bundle of clothes to his chest, his face clenched in anger. Frank's gone and this looks like one of those times he should be here.

"Charlie?" I'm in the backyard, taking a break, a mug of coffee in my hand.

He stalks past, barely glancing in my direction.

"Charlie, what's wrong?"

He comes to a halt, clutching the clothes and a couple of plastic grocery bags to his chest. "Those motherfuckers ripped me off, man."

Rather than have the details broadcast to the neighbors, I tell him to come into the house. He follows me in, stands in the middle of the kitchen, shaking his head, a distant gaze in his eyes that makes it look almost like he's never been here before.

Paul comes trailing into the kitchen. "Someone took his

stuff," he says.

My heart skips, sensing what's coming next.

Charlie hawks, leans forward, spits in the sink. "Duke, man," he says bitterly. "Or Gonzo. One of the guys."

"How do you know?" I ask.

He shoots me a vindictive look. "Nick, who else gonna take my shit?"

"We got the bike," Paul says, clearly straining to ease the tension, trying to cheer Charlie up with a reminder about his ride. "It's in the truck."

Charlie shakes his head, too angry to speak. Then he tromps off to his bedroom. The door slams like a gunshot.

This is another one of those moments—flight or fight— and with or without Frank, it requires immediate confrontation.

"Jesus, Nick," Paul says. "He wanted to head over to the club. Kick some ass." He goes wide-eyed. "I think if his bike had started, he would've and I would not have been able to stop him. I had to talk him down in the truck."

"What the hell happened?"

Paul grabs a soda from the refrigerator, pops it, takes a drink. "We get there, park in front, and I go around the back to get Charlie's bike. Course, the thing's been sitting out there for a while, and it doesn't start. So I'm pushing it around the side of the building..."

"Where's Charlie while you're doing this?" I interrupt.

"Went inside." Paul notices my look. "What?"

"I told you to stay with him."

Paul gets defensive with his eyes. "Figured we'd be quicker in and out if we divided the work."

I nod, decide to let it go. "So Charlie..."

"Went inside. And then after a couple of minutes, he comes back out, like . . . I mean, he was white. Like *chalk*. I've never seen him that angry. Says the place was ransacked, totally turned upside down. Most of his stuff's there, but his stash is gone."

"His stash?"

"Of money. Of cash. He says he kept it in an old beat-up suitcase."

~~~~

Charlie's sitting on the bed when I come into the room. He's got the drapes pulled together and is still holding the bundle of clothes and bags in his arms, just staring at the floor.

"Charlie?"

He doesn't look up, even when I close the door behind me. For a second, I just stand there, thinking about what to say. Seeing him like this, I can't help thinking of him the way he must have been as a little boy, sitting in empty rooms like this, nothing on the walls, nothing but bad things in his head.

"Least they didn't take the bike," I offer.

"Yeah..."

He slowly opens his arms, letting the clothing and bags fall to the floor. There's a belt with a big silver Hells Angels buckle, a couple of T-shirts, some underpants, flannel shirts, socks, and a pair of old sweat-stained boxing gloves. I slide down with my back against the wall resting on my haunches so I'm eye level with him.

"What about your patch, Charlie, your colors?"

"Uh-huh. But Frank told me to leave it. I ain't in the club no more."

"But it was there?"

"Yeah. It was there. With my belt." He picks up the belt and passes his thumb over the shiny buckle. "I'm keepin' this fucker, though..."

With my eyes, I sift through the pile at his feet. I notice the ragged boxing gloves. "And the gloves?"

"They're mine. The only thing I brought with me when I left San Quentin. What I won the championships with."

I nod, remembering Charlie's stories of prison in an oddly fond fashion. But I know I can't dwell on these things—

know I can't keep skirting along on the fringes—keeping him in the dark. Whether Frank would agree with what I'm about to do or not, I feel like I have no choice but to do it. Charlie looks like he'll crack at any moment. I've got to tell him *something*.

"Paul says they took your money," I say reluctantly.

"Motherfuckers ripped me off, man."

"How much?"

"All of it. Every last fucking dollar . . ." He reaches for his smokes, fires one up.

"Charlie," I say firmly.

"Yeah?" he grunts.

"How *much* money are we talking about?"

Charlie huffs. "What the hell's it matter?"

I'm trying to make eye contact with him, but he's not cooperating. "Just curious."

"I don't know," he says. "Maybe three, four hundred."

"Thousand?"

"Yeah, thousand." Charlie stands up, starts pacing. "The fuck you think I mean, man?"

"Charlie . . ." I say, faltering a little now. "There's something you need to know."

"Jesus Christ, Spence," Charlie barks. "What's the matter with you? Spit it out."

I sigh and stand, looking him straight in the eye for the first time since entering the room. What I'm going to tell him is now clear. So rather than ruminating on my words, I consider the actions I'll need to take as soon as I speak them. I'm expecting the kind of eruption I got back in the motel, expecting to trigger a rage in Charlie that will send him plowing over me and roaring straight for the clubhouse.

"Listen, Charlie," I say. "Frank and I have picked up some rumors through sources close to the club."

"Rumors?" he asks darkly.

"Yeah," I say. "The rumor is the club's after you."

"No shit, Spence. You don't just walk out on the Hells

Angels and expect them not to come looking for you."

"It's not like that, Charlie." I glance at the floor. "They're looking for you because they think you stole money. Ripped them off."

I brace for the violence, but it doesn't come. Instead, Charlie submissively sinks onto the bed and drops his head into his cradled hands. He rubs his eyes and shakes his head.

My fingers go numb when I realize what this means. "Is it true, Charlie?"

He slowly lifts his head revealing moist, red eyes. The look he gives me cuts to my core.

"Jesus, Spence."

I slide down against the wall again, squat there like that, giving him time to chew on what he's just learned. I can't believe we're both sitting here like this; can't believe he didn't explode and run for the Camaro; can't believe he's just mulling things over in silence. Several minutes go by. Totally quiet. A car with a busted muffler roars past in the street. In the distance, I can hear music playing. His eyes are filled with sadness, not anger. I certainly know the difference by now.

"I ever tell you about the time I went to buy a Corvette, Nick?"

I shake my head, taken aback. "No, Charlie," I say softly. "No, you didn't."

He takes a deep breath. When he speaks, he does it in a wistful way that's more like Frank than Charlie. "I had all this money," he says. "I don't know, I guess I wasn't keeping count. And then suddenly I had this fuckin' *pile* of money. More than I knew what to do with. And I thought, fuck it, I'm gonna buy me a car."

"I thought you didn't like cars."

"I don't. But you know . . . a nice car is a nice car and I thought what the fuck? It was like lighting a cigar with a hundred-dollar bill. You do it because you can."

He smokes for a moment, thinking things through. "So, anyway, I put some of the money in this old briefcase and walk into a dealership. I'm with my old lady."

"Stacey?" I ask.

He nods. "I'm with Stacey and we're lookin' at this car —this red Corvette. We're standin' there and nobody comes over to see what I want, you know, like to wait on me. And I'm wearin' my colors, and I'm just . . ." He breaks into a distant smile, all lips. "I guess I'm kinda testin' these squares. A little bit. And there're all these sales guys just sittin' there, starin' at me. They're sittin' in their little cubicles in their suits and their aftershave lotion, just lookin' at me—the bad guy."

To my surprise, he laughs. It's a mirthless laugh, but a laugh all the same.

"Anyway, not one of them chickenshit motherfuckers would get up, Nick." He shakes his head incredulously. "Now, I understand if they're afraid or intimidated, but I'm a fuckin' customer, man. And I got the money and I wanna buy a fuckin' car. It's their job, man. Sell cars."

He stands, pumping his open palms before him as he paces. "I got this briefcase full of cash. So I open it and I say, 'You had a chance to make a sale here, you dumb bastards. A cash fuckin' sale.'"

He lights another cigarette and draws deep, shaking his head. "So I go across the street and I buy a brand new fuckin' Cadillac convertible, biggest one on the lot, bright red. I didn't even want no Cadillac. I wanted a Corvette. Anyway, I drive it back across the street with the top down and my old lady sittin' next to me, and give those fuckers the finger, and I drive off."

For a moment, he says nothing. He just sizes me up. I nod like I get it, but I don't. Is it about how important money is or how unimportant? It can buy you a car, but it can't buy respect? I really don't know what to think.

For the longest time, neither of us says a thing. Then I ask him the question I have to ask.

"So they came and took their money back from your apartment, Charlie, or what?"

He sighs. "You don't get it, do you Spence?" he says.

I nod. He's right.

"I didn't steal no money from the club, for chrissakes. Why would I do that?"

"But, Charlie, why do they think—"

"How the fuck do I know, man. Gotta be some kinda setup . . . somebody inside."

I stand up from my squatting position against the wall, eyeing him with enough confusion to garner a response.

"Gonzo, man. Gotta be fuckin' Gonzo took the money and pinned it on me."

"What makes you so—"

"That asshole's always grubbin' for cash. He ain't got no honor. Besides, me and him don't see eye to eye. He's an officer of the club and only the officers supposed to have the combination to the safe. The money in there's supposed to pay our fat lawyer."

I take a deep breath and consider the situation. This is all starting to make sense now. Or is it? According to Paul, Charlie's money from his apartment is kept in an old suitcase. And according to Stacey, Gonzo's former old lady, Bonnie, told her that Gonzo's been acting strange and talking shit about Charlie since the day she discovered a suitcase full of cash in his room out in Ramona.

But if Gonzo ripped Charlie off, who ripped off the club?

For now, I can't help but believe in Charlie. If he'd been angry at learning about the club accusing him of stealing, that would've been one thing. But he's not angry. He's *devastated*. I can see it in his eyes. And the more I think about it, the more I believe it's true. He wouldn't act this way if he wasn't telling the truth.

"I'm tellin' you, Spence, if that fuckin' Gonzo took it . . . that motherfucker shoulda never been an Angel, man. Outta all the guys, he's the one I never fuckin' trusted. If I find out he's the one took my shit . . ."

He doesn't finish the sentence, but I can tell he's thinking thoughts that it's probably best I know nothing about.

He stares at his hands for a while. "Took my whip, too," he says. "You know? My big ol' bullwhip. Why would somebody take my fuckin' whip, man?" He looks straight at me. A kindling dark look that I've come to know well.

"Maybe they took it to piss you off. So that you'd come after them. You know, flush you out."

Charlie shrugs as I consider the implications of what I've just learned.

"So what do we tell Duke?" I blurt.

Charlie looks at me like I've just asked him the strangest question he's ever heard. "The fuck you mean?"

"I mean when you see him again for the first time."

Charlie plops down on the bed and then takes another long drag from his smoke.

"Everything we're doing is building up to the time we can send you back into that clubhouse," I say. "And if we're going to do that, the only way is to convince Duke that you didn't steal his money."

The witness nods.

"So how do we do that?"

I wait for him to go back into his shell, roll over onto the bed, and lie down, tell me to fuck off. But he doesn't. Instead, he picks up his head—and what I see is totally unexpected. He looks bewildered, as if I'm stupid for not seeing the answer from the beginning.

"We tell the truth, Spence," he says. Simple as that.

Chapter 28

Whispering Death
San Diego, CA
August 18, 1996

Things change after Charlie loses the money. I think that, at some level, it makes it easier for him to be part of our team. Not that he isn't already, but the realization that the gang, or at least some members of the gang, are ready to steal from him as soon as he's down on his luck only refuels his anger and disappointment about his former band of brothers.

Whatever's going on inside Charlie, outwardly he becomes more relaxed with us, more one of us. The tighter we are with him, the better it is for the case. But I think it goes beyond that. Certainly for me anyway, and I think for the other guys, too. As twisted and warped as his life has been, there's a straightness to him I can't help but admire. Listening to him talk, I come to a deeper understanding of the forces that shaped him: the indifference, the casual violence, the callous brutality, the crushing poverty as a child.

It comes out in the stories he tells—and he tells a lot of them—talking late into the night about his parents abandoning him and his brother; about the severity of nuns and priests at the orphanage where he was raised; about his struggle to survive in San Quentin.

But it's not all darkness. There are laughs, too. Crazy exchanges across the social void that separates us. Yet there are times when we all get together in a room, it's like a group of old friends catching up. More and more so as the weeks go by.

For all the complexities of the situation, all the vested interests that Frank and I have in this investigation, and all the white-hat/black-hat issues that divide us, when we're in a room together, hanging out and chewing the fat, there are moments in which I realize we're chewing the same fat, the same rind, and the same gristle. We're just not that different in a lot of ways. But there are differences. Most notably, we have a life outside the case and he doesn't. We are acutely aware at all times that what we're doing is part of an official FBI investigation with an informant, regardless of our growing camaraderie. Neither of us is about to take this guy home to dinner. Introduce him to our friends. Also, I'm conscious of the fact that getting too close to Charlie can be bad for the case. It's the kind of thing defense lawyers can turn against you in court.

There's one night I remember in particular. We'd just returned from another controlled drug buy in Ocean Beach where Charlie bought two ounces of meth from a very righteous drug dealer . . . a significant target. Anyway, we're all back at the PB house, unwinding, when Charlie starts talking about the cash again. He says it used to lie around his apartment, crammed into shoeboxes, shopping bags, and laundry baskets. It's nearly one o'clock in the morning. We're dog-tired and Frank and I are looking for a right time to leave. But there's something about Charlie—a kind of fragile intensity as he tells his story of untold wealth that holds me there, and I guess it's the same for Frank. I sense that it's not about the money again but mostly that he doesn't want to be alone . . . that the more he holds our attention, the less lonely he feels.

"It used to . . . I mean, you know that thing they say about money burnin' a hole in your pocket?" Charlie says, looking across at Paul, who's beginning to fall asleep on the couch even though he just arrived for the midnight to eight babysitting shift. "Well, this cash . . . all this cash layin' around, it used to keep me awake. Like it was burnin' a hole in my brain, man. It was like it was talkin' to me, tellin' me to go out and spend it."

"I know that feeling," I reply, trying to offer support to wherever he's going with this. "I mean, when I've got money in my pocket, I'll go looking for something to buy sometimes."

"Money in your pocket? I'm not talkin' about money you can put in your pocket, Spence. I'm talkin' about telephone book wads of hundred-dollar bills. *Boxes* of money."

There's no pride in the way he says this. He's just telling it like it is.

"So what did you do with it all?" Frank says. "I mean, you lived in this shitty two-bedroom apartment, rode around on a Harley. There's only so much money you can spend, right?"

"I did . . . I did stupid shit," Charlie says. He passes his big hand through his dark black hair. "Crazy shit. This one time, I went out to Vegas." He taps a finger to his temple, staring at nothing. "See, the money, it was on my mind. So . . . so there's this guy in the club named Stump, big old psycho guy. He's dead now. Mongols killed him."

"Stump," Frank says with a knowing nod.

"Stump," Charlie says, chuckling. "Now there's a motherfucker you couldn't push around."

"Unless you had a tank," Frank says.

"What?" I ask, breaking into smile.

"I didn't ever tell you that story, Nick?"

"I guess not."

"I know that story," Charlie says. His eyes twinkle.

Frank waves us off. "It's a long story. Go on, Charlie."

Charlie doesn't waste any time. He leans forward, elbows on knees. "I ride by Stump's place one night and I beep the horn on my Harley and Stump comes out in his underwear and I yell to him like, 'Hey, Stump, what's your favorite number? I'm goin' to Vegas . . . I'll play it for you.' And Stump tells me to play number seven." Charlie shakes his head, smiling. "So I ride out to Vegas, and I'm playin' roulette. I put a thousand down on an inside bet on number seven. And it hits. Fuckin' *hits*, man. So at thirty-five to one, I pull in thirty-five grand. And I'm thinkin', *Shit, man. I can't even* lose *money*. So I tell the guy to let it ride." Charlie chuckles. "And the guy's like, 'Sir?' He calls the pit boss, tells him this guy's bettin' thirty-six grand. So the slimeball pit boss gives me the look . . . you know. I'm sittin' there wearin' my colors and maybe he don't like the way I look. He says to me, 'Five thousand-dollar limit.' Asshole. So I let the five Gs ride, the wheel spins, and it hits again—seven."

Frank starts giggling. "You gotta be kiddin', Charlie."

"This is . . . *impossible*, man," Charlie says. "I win 175 Gs. The casino's goin' crazy. Big crowd gathers around. The pit boss is in shock and I flip him the finger as I walk out. I head back to San Diego, but now it's early the next morning and I'm in front of Stump's house, revvin' my engine. He comes chargin' out like a hyena in heat. 'Hey, motherfucker! What the fuck do you think you're doin',' he yells. So I tell him I bet the number he gave me. 'I don't give a rat's ass, Charlie. Let a man sleep, for chrissake.' So then I give him the money, and his face . . . you shoulda seen his face, Nick." Charlie nods, smiling with his lips. "Stump, man . . . he was one ugly motherfucker. But he smiled at me, Stump did, and he's missin' quite a few teeth, you know, but I don't know . . . it was kind of a cool thing to see. You know what he says to me? He says to me, 'Thanks, Charlie. Thanks, man'. I gave him like a hundred grand."

Again, I get the feeling I had when Charlie told me the story about the Corvette. I have no idea what this story means, if it means anything at all. The money was a burden? The money was a release?

"Seems like the only time you really liked the money was when you were giving it away," I say. Charlie nods at this, falls silent. I figure it's a good time to leave, but then Frank starts in on a story of his own.

"Frank," I say. "I gotta go home and get some sleep."

"Only take a couple minutes, Spence." Frank lights up a cigarette, curls his lip to blow smoke. He's clearly revived himself at the prospect of telling a story.

"First time I met Stump, I was investigating an aggravated assault that happened out in Ocean Beach. What happened was Stump's girlfriend's dog gets into a fight with another girl's dog, and instead of separating the mutts like an ordinary citizen would, Stump takes out a claw hammer and beats the other dog to death."

Everyone laughs . . . for a moment. It's the story of a brutal assault, and must've caused real anguish for the dog owner, but I find myself chuckling, too. It's the Hells Angels—something about the way they take care of business.

"A couple days later, the owner of the now-dead dog is in a liquor store with her boyfriend when in walks Stump. The boyfriend, who happens to be on the Ocean Beach town council, makes the mistake of going over and getting in Stump's face. And Stump, he takes out his claw hammer and smacks the guy in the skull, damn near killing him in the process."

"So, did you arrest him?" Paul asks.

"I did. We get a warrant and find him working on his bike in the front yard, and I walk in through the gate and I say, 'Stump you're under arrest,' and I start naming off the charges: attempted murder, aggravated assault, assault with a deadly weapon..." Frank lists off the crimes on his fingers. "I read him his rights, and Stump, he just stands there, stares at me. Nothing. No reaction. He's just glaring at me with this crazy look in his eyes.

"'You finished?'" he asks.

"I think so," I say.

"Okay, now I'm gonna read you *your* fuckin' rights, cop. You gotta right for me to give you a fuckin' whack across the head as we speak. You have the right to have me stomp the living dogshit out of you," he says.

"By this time, I've unholstered my revolver. And as he comes toward me, I aim it straight at his head and tell him to stop the fuck where he is. But he just keeps on coming."

"Sounds like Stump," Charlie says, shaking his head.

"Luckily I've got backup," Frank says. "This big Samoan detective from our unit, Lomo, jumps out of the car and races toward us. Great street cop ... liked nothing better than wrestling assholes like Stump. But it takes both of us to get the cuffs on him."

Frank chuckles some more and looks down at the carpet.

"I bet he was really pissed," Charlie says.

Frank nods. "Yelled something like 'you ain't seen the last of me, cop' as Lomo shoved him in the back of the patrol car."

There's a pause and I know if I don't get up and get out of the house, I'm falling asleep right where I sit. I'm about to stand when Paul says, "I want to hear about the tank."

Charlie's all excited and pushes at Frank with his foot. "Come on, Frank," he says. "Tell the story."

Frank looks at me. He can see I'm wiped out, but he smiles.

"So," Frank continues, "Stump skips bail on my arrest there in his yard, and stupid bastard that he is, gets himself involved in the kidnapping of a Mongol gang member named Rockwell Charles Prefontaine, aka Rocky. It's Stump and this other Hells Angel, name of Sledge."

"Sledge, Stump, Rocky," Paul says, chuckling. "What is this, *The Flintstones*?"

"Interesting you should say that," Frank says, "because Sledge's real name is Thomas Joseph Stonemaker. A first-class asshole..."

"Sledge is okay," Charlie interrupts, cocking a half-smile. "Guy's not too bright is all."

"Always gave me the hardest time," Frank says.

"Like I say ... not too bright."

"Anyway, Sledge and Stump grab this Mongol, and I guess everything gets a little out of control and they're on the run, and San Diego PD is looking high and low. The Mongols and the Hells Angels are at war, and this little act of kidnapping is about to cause a full-scale riot."

"Is there a tank in this story?" I say, trying to expedite the storytelling. I look over at Charlie and he looks like a kid watching his first western on TV.

"I'm coming to that," Frank says. "So we're looking for these guys and I get a tip from an informant that they're in Northern California, around Monterrey. And they're driving around in a green Pontiac.

"Next day, I'm going over the case file and see that Rocky's old lady who lived with him when he was kidnapped drove a green Pontiac GTO. I'm thinking this is too much of a coincidence. I run the plate and get a hit on a stolen report filed by Rocky's girlfriend. The car was reported stolen two weeks after the kidnapping. We contact her and she says the car was actually stolen the same night as the kidnapping, but she was afraid to report it."

Frank rocks forward in his chair. "So I put out a state-wide BOLO, and sure enough, I get a call a couple of days later from a detective from the Monterey PD that the car had been located parked and ticketed in front of a residence in Monterey. So I went up there, and we drove a tank into the frontyard of this house where we knew Sledge and Stump were holed up with the kidnapped Mongol."

"Whoa, whoa, whoa . . ." Paul says, laughing. "Back up, Frank. You got a *tank*?"

Frank shrugs like it's just another day on the job. "I don't think we needed it, really," he says. "But I just thought it'd be interesting to do that."

This gets the biggest laugh so far. Frank grins, clearly as amused by his own storytelling as we are.

"What kind of a . . . of a tank?" Paul sputters.

"You know, Paul, a regular . . . big, giant tank."

Paul's really into it now. He sits up on the edge of the couch. "Where did you get a *tank*?"

"National Guard Armory," Frank deadpans coolly. "It was near the house Sledge was in with these guys. I saw it and I said, 'Well . . . okay!' I was with a couple guys from the U.S. Marshals Service, and there were probably five or six local cops, and I thought this tank would demonstrate to the guys in the house that we have the necessary firepower, and that resistance would be, uh, futile."

By now, we're all rolling.

"The marshals contacted the National Guard and they were eager to help. Obviously these guys never heard of the Posse Comitatus Act of 1878, which prohibits this kind of shit." Frank's now standing and gesturing with his hands. "They rolled out their shiny M1 Abrams Battle Tank with the 120mm rifle cannon and rumbled down the street about a half-mile to the house. So we drive this tank into the front yard and point the muzzle of the cannon at the front door, and I had the guys on the phone inside the house, and it's Stump's voice I'm hearing. All the drapes and blinds are closed and he says, 'We're not comin' out.'" Frank stops and offers one of his theatrical pauses while crushing his cigarette out in the ashtray. Paul bites at the long pause.

"Come on, Frank, what the hell happened?"

"I say, 'So what now, Stump? Because when I fire this tank, the house is gonna be gone. What do you want to do?'

"Anyway, we see the drapes part in the front of the house and they get a load of the U.S. Army's Whispering Death parked on their front lawn, and they surrender immediately."

I can hardly breathe, I'm laughing so hard.

"I put the cuffs on Sledge myself," Frank says. "He's cursing me up and down. Not happy. Not happy at all."

Charlie's laughing so hard, there are tears in his eyes. And I'm laughing with him. And we're all just a bunch of guys, hanging out.

Chapter 29

Pointing Fingers
San Diego, CA
September 5, 1996

Spud's down for two drug buys, and in the weeks following, we set up several more buys with dealers we singled out as most likely to fall hard—those with prior convictions and violent criminal histories. Charlie's presence back out on the street was getting the kind of attention we'd hoped for. He has become increasingly adept at avoiding entrapment issues while at the same time getting the dealers to talk business, weight, and price. Of course, his reputation as a cop-hating badass precedes him, so the idea that he would become a snitch—that he would wear a wire—would never occur to anyone.

As much as anything, these buys were set up to get Charlie comfortable with carrying the mini-Nagra in his boot. He's cool with it, and the audio we've been getting from his body mike is clear and clean. We've watched him carefully while wearing that contraption in his right boot, and he walks effortlessly without breaking stride or favoring that side in his gait. We know we are going to be seriously upping the ante when he finally walks into the clubhouse, which is what we plan to do at some point. We're hopeful that by the time it comes to that, he'll be so used to having the wire on him, he'll be able to concentrate on appearing normal, on being Charlie.

Meanwhile, we spend quite a lot of time tossing around ideas about the best way to edge Charlie back into the gang. The PD has a reliable informant who is pretty close to the club. She told us Duke and other members have been asking around for Charlie, pretty riled up and curious, wondering how it is he could be back in business and remain so out of sight and out of touch. So our message has reached its intended target. We've accomplished the first phase of our operation. Now it was time to move to phase two. Time to walk Charlie into the lion's den.

~~~~

"What kind of a plaque?"

It's the first week of September, and we're all sitting around in the kitchen.

"A nice plaque," Frank says. "The Bureau will spring for a nice plaque, right, Nick?"

I shrug, a little bewildered.

Frank turns to Charlie. "You like the idea, right, Charlie?"

Charlie purses his lips and blasts air through his nose. "I think Duke would go for it, man. Yeah."

"A plaque, for chrissakes!" I say. "Sounds like something you'd give to the head of a lawn bowling league."

"It's the club's thirty-year anniversary," Charlie says. "It's perfect. They'll be throwing a big party, for sure. Duke likes shit like that. Feeds his ego." He rifles through the front pocket of his shirt. "I made a drawing..."

I look across at Frank, who's got sort of a smug look on his face as Charlie pulls out a crumpled piece of paper. He spreads it out on the table. There's a finely drawn picture of a winged death head set between the top and bottom rockers, as they'd appear on a Hells Angels patch, "California" on the top rocker and the moniker for the San Diego chapter, "DAGO," on the bottom rocker. Below it all, Charlie's scribbled the dates "1966-1996." He's also added an inscription that reads, "To my friend Duke Stricker, from Charlie Slade."

When I'm done sizing it up, I offer another baffled look at Frank and Charlie. They've been hard at work on this.

"Maybe painted nice," Frank suggests. "Or etched in copper or something."

I smirk. "You guys are jerking me on this. You really see yourself walking into the club carrying that thing, Charlie? I mean...come on."

"Sure," he grunts. "Why not? I gotta offer somethin', right? And I sure as hell can't keep duckin' and divin' out there. It's better I go *to them*, you know. Walk through the front door. Show 'em I ain't got nothin' to hide." He crosses his arms and nods contemplatively. "That's the way to do it. Better I go straight at them than for them to find me, you know, see me on the street or somethin'."

I pace away from the table, taking a long look out the kitchen window as I think it over. I can feel Charlie and Frank staring at me. Paul gets up and heads in the direction of the can. I turn with a wary expression. "This is like offering a bouquet of flowers to a Comanche war party. Am I missing something here? There's still the matter of Charlie's alibi about the stolen money," I say.

"We already talked about that, Spence," Charlie blurts.

I offer a calming hand. "I know that, Charlie," I say. "And I agree. The truth is best."

Charlie nods, but I can see he's still not satisfied.

I sit down across from him, Frank standing over my shoulder. "There's still the matter of Gonzo," I say.

"Fuck Gonzo."

"That's exactly what I mean," I say, fully expecting his response. "You can't go in there with that attitude."

"The motherfucker rips me off and . . ."

"Charlie," Frank interrupts, "you'll wanna listen to what Spence has to say."

Our witness waves a hand grandly over the table, signaling for me to proceed.

"We can't have you pointing the finger at Gonzo at this point," I continue. "You do that, and all hell will break loose."

"I'd take that fucker down, man."

I smile. "I'm sure you would, Charlie. But that's not the point. Point is we don't want unrest in the gang right now. That would only lead to difficulties in the case going forward."

Charlie furrows his brow, turns away. "Fuckin' *case,* man."

"I'm serious," I say. "You can't go in there trying to set Gonzo up to take the fall."

Frank sits down next to me, the chair backward, his legs clamped on either side of the backrest. "Pointing the finger at Gonzo would only weaken your alibi, anyway," he says.

Charlie looks skeptical.

"You go in there accusing someone else, what's to keep Duke from thinking you're a liar?" Frank says. "And besides, you gotta think like Duke. On one hand, he's got a guy who left the club without warning, whacked out on heroin. Just walked out. On the other, he's got Gonzo, who's been there all along, you know, takin' care of business."

Charlie stews. I can see this burns him up.

"No," Frank says, taking a long drag. "The best way to handle this is to appeal to Duke's reasonable side. You're going to want to tell him what you told us. Tell him you were down and out. Strung out. Remind him about past times. That whenever he or anybody else in the club needed money, you were always there to help. Remind him you *gave away* more money than you ever spent. No matter how bad off you were, you would never, *ever* steal from the club."

Charlie starts nodding. We're making progress.

"Tell him you think stealing from the club would be like stealing from him," I suggest.

This gets him on board. He looks me straight in the eye, and I can see there's understanding. He's with us. He's ready.

"So," he says, "when do we set him up?"

~~~~

The following day, Frank and I go down to the Federal building for a meeting with Blair, Frank's supervisor; SDPD Sergeant Ken Cantrell; and Assistant U.S. Attorney Mike Barrett, the attorney assigned to our case. We fill them in on our plan going forward, and the consensus view is that the buys we've made on significant midlevel drug dealers have served the purposes intended and that it's now time to move up. It's time to establish direct contact with the gang itself.

Everyone agrees that Charlie's proved reliable and trustworthy. The time has come to put him in where he can do some real and lasting damage—to hit our elusive and volatile target dead center—under their own roof.

Chapter 30

Calling Duke
San Diego, CA
September 8, 1996

Official FBI transcript dated 9/8/96

Nick Spence: This is FBI Special Agent Nick Spence. Agent Marty Logan, FBI, and Detective Frank Conroy, San Diego Police Department, are also present. We are in San Diego, California, at 16:15 hours on September 8, 1996. We are recording a consensually monitored telephone call by Charles Slade, a cooperating witness, who will call Jason Andrew Stricker, aka "Duke," the subject of an ongoing drug investigation. The telephone number being dialed is 643-2020.

(Sound of numbers dialed)

Andrew Stricker: Yeah?

Charles Slade: Duke, its Charlie.

AS: What the fuck . . . Charlie? Jesus Christ, where the fuck you been, man?

CS: I know I let you guys down.

AS: Fuckin' A.

CS: I just want you to know, Duke . . . well . . . this was something I had to beat on my own.

AS: Didn't mean you gotta go drop off the fuckin' radar, Charlie.

CS: I know it. I guess I wasn't thinkin' straight there for a while.

AS: You gotta watch that shit, man. We figured you was dead in a ditch . . . OD'd in some fuckin' fleabag motel.

CS: Gotta be honest with you, Duke. For a while there, I didn't think I was gonna make it. But I got it under control now. I mean, I'm sober now. Takin' it one day at a time, but I'm doin' better.

AS: You on methadone?

CS: Not now. Not no more.

AS: But you was . . .

CS: Yeah . . . for a while. Tried hittin' it cold turkey, but I couldn't do it. Checked myself into this place . . . you know."

AS: Yeah?

(Delay, silence, tape running)

AS: So, what you been doin', Charlie?

CS: You know, man. Hustlin'. Tryin' to pay the rent.

AS: You still got your place in El Cajon?

(Delay, long silence, tape running)

AS: Charlie?

CS: No, man. Moved out.

AS: You did? Why's that?

(Silence, tape running)

CS: Just wanted to turn the page, man. You know? Make a fresh start.

AS: New place. New wheels?

CS: Huh?

AS: I heard you was drivin' 'round town in a Camaro. I said no fuckin' way. Not my Charlie, man. Not the Charlie Slade I know.

CS: I know, I know ... it's ...

AS: It's what?

CS: Thing is—what happened—I dumped the bike, laid it down, man.

AS: Get the fuck outta here.

CS: I'm tellin' you, man. It was fucked up. Got high one night, damn near killed myself. It shook me up.

AS: Fuck it, Charlie. Never thought I'd see the day ...

CS: Yeah, well ...

AS: Gotta get you back in the saddle, man.

CS: I guess. Anyway ... so ...

AS: Yeah?

CS: Listen, I got something for you ...

(Silence, tape running)

AS: That right?

CS: It's a gift. From me to you.

AS: Yeah? You got me a gift. Wow. I don't know what to say, man.

CS: It's no big thing, man. Just somethin' to show my 'preciation. My respect. I was thinkin' I could swing by, present it to you in person.

AS: You wanna come *here*? When?

Chapter 31

Stomping Charlie
San Diego, CA
September 8, 1996

Duke slams the phone down. In less than an hour, he's got an audience with Bad Eye, his vice president; Gonzo, the club secretary; and Scooter, the treasurer.

"How come we got no sergeant-at-arms at this meeting, Duke? Why ain't Mongoose at this meeting?" Gonzo asks.

Duke arches a brow. "The fuck you mean?"

"It's like I been sayin'. . . . We need a new sergeant-at-arms now that Charlie's gone. You been draggin' your feet, Duke. This is an officers meeting, man. We shoulda voted on Mongoose a long time ago . . . patched him in. Mongoose should be our guy."

"Jesus Christ, Gonz—"

Duke rocks back in his chair, crossing his tattooed arms over his bulging chest. He glares at Gonzo, waiting for the secretary to break rank again. It takes a good long minute, but the snarling goon breaks from Duke's officious stare.

"You know damn well Mongoose ain't no Charlie Slade."

Bad Eye and Scooter chuckle. Gonzo does not.

"Besides," Duke continues, "Charlie ain't dead."

"How you know that?" Gonzo asks.

Duke's lips part into a wide smile. "'Cause I just got off the fuckin' phone with him, that's how, Gonz."

Everyone seems to lose their breath at the same time.

"I hear you right, Duke?" Bad Eye asks.

Duke nods solemnly. "Charlie's alive and well." He looks from man to man. "And he's comin' in."

Gonzo starts licking his lips. "Here. To the *clubhouse*?"

"That's right."

Silence reigns.

"Where's the fucker been?" Bad Eye asks after a time.

"Rehab, he says. Methadone."

"Why ain't he come in before now?"

"Claims he didn't think he could kick the junk unless he went it alone."

"Bullshit," Gonzo spews. "You gonna believe that thievin' asshole, Duke?" He's gripping the arms of his chair so tight his knuckles are white.

"All I know for sure is he sounded great on the phone. Says he's got somethin' to present to me."

"Present to you?" Bad Eye says. "The fuck's that mean?"

"Hell if I know."

"He's gotta be real pissed about Stacey."

Duke nods. It's a possibility that can't be ignored.

"You know how . . . how whacked out Charlie can be," Scooter says, looking nervous.

And Scooter's right, of course. If anyone's crazy enough to pull a one-man vendetta on the club, it's "Crazy" Charlie Slade.

"I don't like this, Duke," Bad Eye says.

"Fuck him," Gonzo urges. "Let him come down here."

Duke hard-stares the secretary, doesn't like what he sees in his eyes. "Well, I already told him to come in, so it's on."

Gonzo fidgets, already obviously scheming how this is going to go down.

Duke holds his stare on the secretary for a moment, trying to send the message that he better damn well listen to what he's about to say. "I want everybody on standby," he says. "And I mean *everybody*. When Charlie gets here, I want a full house."

Gonzo nods with vigor. He clearly likes the idea—but Duke suspects he likes the idea for different reasons than he'd intended.

"I don't want *nobody* to make a fuckin' move on Charlie," he barks. "Not without my order."

Gonzo nods sarcastically, but it's obvious he's not really listening.

"Gonzo, you hear me?" Duke barks. "Charlie comes in here *untouched*. I'm gonna be the one sizes shit up. I don't like what I see, we take care of business."

The secretary grins.

"But *not* until I give the order."

The secretary's grin fades.

"You got that shit, Gonzo?"

"What if..." Scooter says, and his addled brain begins to drift. He glances at the ground the moment Duke hard-stares him.

"Spit it out, Scooter," Duke demands impatiently.

"What if . . . what if we set up a meeting with Charlie away from the clubhouse, you know, like . . . ?"

"The fuck you mean?"

"We set him up, you know? Grab him. Pump him. You know . . . like we'd do with anybody who . . . betrayed the brotherhood."

"Right on, Scoot," Gonzo erupts.

Duke leans forward and sets his elbows on his desk, shaking his clenched fists. "Jesus Christ, am I talking to myself?" he mumbles.

"Shut up, everybody!" Bad Eye commands.

"Listen, assholes," Duke says, leveling his gaze on Scooter, who quakes. "Like I been sayin' all along, we don't *know* Charlie betrayed the club." He stares now at Gonzo to show him he means business.

Gonzo fumes, grits his teeth. "Why would he just fuckin' disappear if he wasn't the one who stole from the brothers?" Gonzo asks.

Duke shoves himself back from his desk, exasperated. "Brilliant logic, Gonzo," he says. "So, if Charlie stole that money, why would he come back *here* to the fuckin' clubhouse?"

Gonzo draws a quick breath to speak, but whatever he had to say it dies on his lips.

"Yeah," Duke snaps. "That's what I thought. Look, I don't

know what to make of this shit either. All I know is Charlie's comin' in. And we're *all* gonna play it nice and easy until I say otherwise. I'd rather have the guy inside the tent pissin' out than outside pissin' in. Meeting adjourned. Now get the fuck outta here."

Chapter 32

Hit the Brakes
San Diego, CA
September 9, 1996

Monday dawns bright on a beautiful Southern California morning. Under a flawless blue sky, I drive down to the federal building, where Paul is already there waiting for me. We have an eight o'clock with Felix Ritter, who's heading up the SOG surveillance support for our operation.

We'll be using the team's aerial capabilities on this one to assure maximum surveillance coverage. In the event anyone grabs our star witness and tries to leave the clubhouse, we'll be able to track their movements from the sky. There will also be an SOG team on the ground in communication with us on a coded and voice-scrambled radio channel. No one is going to be tuning into our conversations that shouldn't be.

Ritter is all business during the briefing, and we're out of the office in half an hour. I make a call to our attorney, Mike Barrett. I want him to come over to the house in the afternoon to give Charlie his support and to make sure we're all on the same page as to how the meet should go down. Barrett says he'll be at the PB house at three.

On the way out the office, I stick my head around the door into Pete Blair's office. He's already wading through a mound of paperwork, but he breaks off for me to bring him up to speed. I take him through the latest version of the plan, and he nods approvingly.

"Give Charlie my best, Nick. He's doing a hell of a job for us."

Around ten, Paul and I get back to the house where we find Charlie pumping iron in the backyard, watched by a preoccupied Marty Logan. I can hear Frank inside on the phone in the middle of what sounds like a mostly one-sided conversation. I look at Marty for information.

"Cantrell," he says.

The name is all I need. So far, Sergeant Ken Cantrell, Frank's boss, has proven to be something of a pain in the ass on this case. The SDPD is supposed to be a partner in the task force, however Cantrell has been lean on contributing manpower and financial resources to the project. He barks plenty of orders but seems to have little grasp of the delicacy and difficulty of what we're attempting to do with Charlie. It goes without saying that if and when we finally bring down the club, Cantrell will be pawing his way to the front of the line, looking for credit. I hear Frank hang up with a curse.

"How you feeling, Charlie?" I say, hoping Frank's anger doesn't mean things are turning ugly in some way at this late stage.

"Good, man," Charlie says. "I feel great."

And he looks great. He's got two hundred pounds on the bar, and he's benching steady reps. Watching him work out, it's hard to believe this is the same guy we dragged out of that motel just a month and a half ago.

Frank comes out of the house, scowling. For a moment he watches Charlie pump iron, then looks sharply up at me. "Can you come inside for a second, Nick?"

As soon as Frank closes the kitchen door, he gets into it. "Cantrell wants Charlie to wear a wire today," he hisses. "Insists on it."

I shake my head and follow him into the living room and take a seat on the recliner. "Come on, Frank. We've been through all this."

We've talked it through at least a dozen times, and have decided that putting the wire on Charlie the first time he walks into the clubhouse is just too risky. There's every chance that Duke or Gonzo or one of the others is going to pull Charlie into a big welcome-home-brother hug while feeling for a wire, or worse, give him a full body search. We've talked with Charlie about making sure the Hells Angels don't try any sort of a pat-down, and he says he won't let it happen.

Of course he would say that, but we've tried to drill into him that this is a reality and how dangerous such a confrontation would be, so he'd better damn well be prepared for it. We've instructed him if it looks like someone is going to try to pat him down or challenge him, he must immediately react with a strong offensive. Go into one of his angry tirades. Start ranting about trust and explode into his Crazy Charlie mode that his brothers know so well and most fear. Tell them they can all fuck off if they don't trust him, then get the hell out of there. It's a huge concern. Charlie doesn't retreat very well.

"Cantrell's worried about continuity of evidence," Frank says.

This, too, is a problem we've discussed at great length. Put simply, during all these previous midlevel drug buys, Charlie's been wearing a wire and we have recordings of every single buy and meeting; but, the first time we send him into the clubhouse, he's not wired. No recording. Exculpatory evidence. A good defense attorney would dance on our heads over something like that.

"No," I say after a moment.

"No what?"

"Charlie's not wearing a wire today. It's too dangerous."

Frank waits for more.

"We're going to keep it real short," I say. "He's in and out in twenty minutes. Thirty minutes, tops. Down the line, we explain to the jury we had more than enough justification to fear for our witness's safety for this first meeting. We're testing the waters."

Frank starts nodding.

"We've got Barrett's approval on this," I say, "and as far as I'm concerned, he's got the biggest stake in this case. He's the one who's got to prosecute it. Fuck Cantrell."

Frank smiles at me. "I love it when you get excited, Nick."

~~~~

Mike Barrett shows up at three o'clock sharp. When Charlie emerges from his bedroom, he's dressed and ready to roll, but he looks surprised to see our federal prosecutor standing there in his three-piece suit. This is only their second meeting, but it's important, I know—to both Charlie and the investigation as a whole—that Barrett came down here to show his support.

Barrett takes a moment in sizing up the witness. "How do you feel, Charlie?" he asks. "You ready to kick some ass?"

Charlie shrugs. "Let's get it on, man."

Barrett stiffens his back and tugs at his collar. "What you're doing here, Charlie, is honorable but very dangerous. Don't take any chances. If anything doesn't feel right or you feel your life is in danger, you *walk*—you get the hell out of there, got it?"

Charlie nods.

"We want to get a feel for how you're accepted back into the club, that's all. Get a sense of where you stand before we make any decisions about moving forward on this, okay?"

Charlie nods, actually paying attention.

Barrett shoots a quick glance in my direction.

"But if anybody tries to pat you down," I interject, "you know the drill, even though you're not wearing a wire this time. You set the rules, man, not them."

Marty gets up from the kitchen table, where he's been tinkering with the Nagra. "If you get a chance, Charlie, I want you to look out for any kind of wiring or gadgets in and around doorways. Anything you can tell us such as: are there exposed wires, the color of the wires, where the wires run to and disappear to, any evidence of newly drilled holes—anything like that will be a real help. Also, any kind of infrared beams, you know, red beams of light between doorways or entryways—we need to know about that."

Charlie heaves a heavy sigh. "Okay, Marty."

"Just keep it real simple," Barrett says. "You deliver the

plaque, say a few hellos, and then leave. Tell them there's something you gotta do across town."

"Keep an eye on the time," Frank says. "You stay no more than half an hour. Got it?"

Charlie throws up his hands. "Okay. Jesus, guys. Would you just relax a little. It's all gonna be fine."

~~~~

"Okay. Showtime. This is it," I say.

The shadows are lengthening and the sun flames red in the rearview of the Econoline as we follow the Camaro eastbound from PB onto Midway Drive. We're taking surface streets to avoid rush hour traffic on Interstate 8, our progress tracked from the SOG's plane, a Cessna 172 High Wing buzzing around at 3,500 feet, doing orbits about a quarter-mile away. Bob Anders at the controls and Chick Reinhardt eyeing the target.

"Hot in this jacket, man. . . . Way too fuckin' hot. . . ."

We're running the Nagra and transmitter in the Camaro to stage the meeting for future testimonial support, and we've told Charlie to keep talking to us as he heads for the meet, urging him once again to try to keep it clean for the sake of the future jurors who will be listening to these tapes.

"I'm takin' the fucker off," Charlie rumbles. "Gonna look like an asshole if I show up sweatin'."

"Remember to put it back on, Charlie," I say, as if he could hear me.

It's just me and Marty in the back of the van. Frank's up front with our assigned driver for the day—a brash, talkative former Texas Ranger named Hank Kinney. Kinney's a solid, dependable agent from SOG.

Swooshing sounds echo through the radio, which I guess is Charlie struggling out of the jacket. He spits out an agitated curse as I guess he gets an arm caught. Up ahead, I see the Camaro drift toward the middle of the street.

"Drive the goddamn car, Charlie."

"Sounds nervous," Frank says over his shoulder, and he's right. As calm as Charlie seemed back at the house, he's coming through real anxious now.

"Probably coming home to him," Marty says.

"What is?" I say, glancing up.

"What he's about to do. It's a hell of a thing. Takes a lot of balls."

Marty's right, of course, walking into a room full of guys who'd happily cave his head in and slit his throat for good measure if they knew he'd turned snitch. I listen as I watch the reel turning on the recorder, and now I pick up the tension in his voice as he continues to spew about the jacket. For all his bravado, he's now facing the moment of truth.

But if things turn to shit, we'll be moving quickly. In addition to the four of us in the van, there are nine guys from Squad 7 ready to rumble, including Ryan, Clouser, and Dove, who are all in position as near as they've been able to get to the clubhouse without getting burned. The four SOG guys handling ground surveillance on Charlie to and from the meet will not be part of any cavalry charge, as that would blow their preciously maintained cover. If needed, we can always have Frank call for SDPD backup if things turn really ugly.

"Making a left," Charlie blurts.

I watch the Camaro turn, heading north toward Adams, a broad east-west boulevard lined with low-rise commercial buildings.

There's a crackle of static. Chick Reinhardt comes on the radio from the plane overhead: "904 to all units. Our guy's turning north onto 30th."

I clear my throat.

"Copy that, 904. What's the traffic like up ahead?"

"Clear sailing."

I radio Clouser. "705 to 710."

"710, go 705."

"Any new arrivals?"

"Negative. All quiet."

Clouser's got the eye on the clubhouse and has been in place for over an hour. He's parked in a discreet location about a block from the clubhouse in a nondescript white van with a ladder strapped to the top and placards on the side that say "Western Electric." The van has tinted windows, and Clouser has a pair of high-powered binoculars to peek out the back of the van. He's in a prime spot to call out the action in front of the clubhouse. So far, he's reported the arrival of Bull Palac, Scooter, and several other gang members. They're all flying their colors and standing around the parking lot in front of the clubhouse. There's been no sign of Duke or Gonzo, but I'm guessing that means they're already inside talking about Charlie and how to handle him. As we suspected, it looks like Duke has called a "special" church meeting for Charlie's return.

"710 to all units: We have a new arrival pulling in on a chopper."

"Can you identify the subject, 710?"

"Looks like Stonemaker. I thought he was still locked up."

Frank blows smoke at the rearview. "Welcome to the party, Sledge."

"He must've just got outta the joint," I say to Frank. "How much time did he get on the Prefontaine kidnapping?"

Frank shrugs his shoulders, doing the math in his head. "Seven to ten years, so, yeah, with good time, he'd just be getting out."

"You got a description, 710?"

"Big, bald, and *bad*. Six-two, two-eighty, three necks."

"904 to all units. We got more bikers coming westbound on Adams. Looks like maybe five, six . . ."

"Roger that, 904," I say.

Charlie comes through on the other channel. "I'm turning right on Adams."

"904, you got him?" I radio.

"Roger, 705. We're on him eastbound on Adams."

Kinney wheels into the parking lot of a small strip mall and finds a space next to some shopping carts.

"710 to all units, our guy's pulling into the target location."

I close my eyes, trying to visualize it . . . Charlie surprised and off-guard seeing Sledge—trying to get his shit straight. I'm convinced now more than ever we did the right thing not wiring him up.

The sounds from inside the Camaro suddenly go dead. Charlie remembers to turn off the Nagra and transmitter. He's thinking.

"Our guy's out of the car," Clouser reports. "Stonemaker's going over . . . giving our guy a big hug."

Here we go. Game on.

"904 to all units. We have six bikers eastbound one block west of target location. You should be hearing them by now."

"Roger, 904. We got em'."

We're two blocks from the clubhouse and I can hear the seismic roar of the Harley tailpipes, and it's a chilling sound. I try to focus on what's coming through the radio.

"710 to all units . . . there . . . there's a pack of them coming into the . . . into the parking lot . . . throttling down. It's . . . it's . . ."

Clouser's voice is drowned out by the deafening howl of the bikes as some of them roar past him. But then he's back, sounding anxious.

"We've got a lot of people here . . . too many to identify . . . they're all around our guy . . . but the . . . stand by," he says. After a long pause he breaks back on the air. "I got a guy coming out of the clubhouse. I've got one subject . . . looks like . . . Gonzo, uh, Winters, coming out of the office. He's walking over to our guy . . . smiling . . . laughing. Looks like a family reunion."

"Here it comes," I say, still keeping my eyes closed. I can visualize him perfectly, Gonzo: six-five, long and lean upper torso bare, as always, covered only by his black leather Hells Angels "cut" or vest, wearing his trademark grease-spattered jeans and massive-sized motorcycle boots giving him a towering presence over a five-ten Charlie Slade. His sinewy arms are covered with a combination of gang and military tattoos, his large head adorned by a crusty tangle of streaked blond hair, and his eyes locked in a perpetual "Here's Johnny" look made famous by Jack Nicholson in *The Shining*. He's a weird-looking dude, and his military record speaks for itself.

"Gonzo's got his arms wrapped around our guy," 710 radios.

"Feeling him up for the wire," Marty says. A long pause ensues with no radio traffic.

"What's our guy doing, 710?"

"Talking to Gonzo. Other guys are parking their bikes. Lots of smiling, high fives. Now they're going into the . . . in through the front door."

"Is our guy wearing his jacket?"

"Affirmative. He grabbed it out of the car."

"The package?"

"In his hand."

I nod. This is good. Charlie's still thinking.

"Everyone's inside, doors closed."

"Roger that, 710." I check my watch—5:15 p.m. I lean back against the side panel of the van and heave a deep breath.

"710, all units. Someone's coming back out. Confirm Gonzo. We've got Gonzo jogging toward the Camaro. He's . . ."

"*What?*"

"He's climbing in the Camaro, starting the . . . he's on the move."

My heart races. "You got him, 904?"

"904. Confirm, we see him. He's backing out. Heading up the alley behind our target location."

"*What the hell's going on?*" I blurt out to everyone inside the van.

Frank looks back at me from the front, his eyes reflecting the same alarming brand of confusion I'm feeling.

"He's pulling into the back, 705, under a covered parking bay. I've lost visual . . . standby."

"710, can you see him?"

"Negative."

I slam down the pen I'm holding and it clatters across the van's metal flooring. We've gone over *everything* with Charlie—everything we could think of. But here we are in the heat of it and something comes up that we never considered. How did Gonzo get his keys? And why would he move our car?

I've had some pretty tense moments in my life, but the next thirty minutes are riveting as we sit there in more or less complete silence, listening to the occasional status updates from Reinhardt and Clouser. Clouser can only see the front parking lot, so Reinhardt's keeping his eye from the sky on the back where only a few vehicles can be seen outside the parking bays. There has been no movement and the Camaro is still parked in back of the clubhouse. Frank's cigarette smoke hangs in the air. The second hand on my watch looks suspended, like it's moving through molasses.

At 5:55, I'm beyond apprehensive. When I look over at Frank, I find him staring back, thinking, I guess, similar thoughts.

"Nothing we can do, Nick."

"We said a half-hour."

Frank shrugs. "It's Charlie. We gotta allow a little leeway for 'Charlie time.'"

"What if he's—"

"Let's hold off," Frank says with a grimace.

At 6:05, I'm flashing horrid images in my mind: Charlie taking the beating of his life, a blowtorch searing the death head tattoo from his right forearm, the "AFFA" tattoo from his upper left, a gang of Hells Angels burning our witness then smacking him around brutally until he's near death—all while we sit out here twiddling our thumbs.

"705 to all units," I radio. "Heads up. Everybody. Be alert

to any vehicle departing from the back of the building. No mistakes. We gotta cover *any* vehicle departing from under those bays."

As careful as we've been, running through my head are all of the possible scenarios of how they could've tracked us to Charlie or vice versa. Maybe they found Stacey and tortured her again for information, or they surveilled us without our knowledge back and forth to the clinic every day. I mean, these guys don't just sit around and do nothing when they think they've got a problem. They take care of business.

"*Come on,*" I say. I check my watch, stir in my seat.

"That's it, Frank," I say, reaching for the cargo door. "We gotta make a move. It's been almost an hour. We gotta go in. Fuck the case."

"710 to all units. Stand by. Our guy's coming out the front door." Clouser's voice comes over the radio filled with relief.

"Confirm that," Reinhardt radios. "Our guy's walking around behind the house . . . now he's under the parking bay. He's got something around his neck. Looks like a big snake."

"705 to 710. Anybody with our guy?"

"Negative. He's alone. And that's a bullwhip around his neck. . . . The Camaro's backing out into the alley . . . turning westbound onto Adams. You got him, 904?"

He's heading our way. Kinney starts the engine. We back out of the space and almost plow into an old guy pushing a shopping cart. The guy comes to a startled halt, gives Kinney the finger. Kinney raises a hand in apology, then moves out.

Charlie drives past as we get to the intersection with Adams. We see him reach down and hear the transmitter click on and hear the whir of wind blowing through his window. He glances across toward us as he rolls by but makes no sign that he's seen us sitting there.

Kinney has to wait for a couple of cars to pass and then pulls out, getting behind Charlie.

"904 to all units. We've got our guy westbound on

Adams, and we got you right behind him. We're looking good."

Reinhardt is set to follow us back to the PB house. The rest of our guys and the SOG team are going to be checking for a possible tail.

"What the hell?" Frank says.

I peer through Frank's smoke, see Charlie racing for an intersection. The light changes to amber.

"No way he can make that," Kinney says. "What's his hurry?"

"Shit."

Charlie rockets straight through the red light. Traffic careens. A big Lincoln swerves to a halt, horn blaring.

"Son of a bitch," Charlie blurts into the mike.

"Jesus, Charlie," I yell to no one. "What's he doing?"

"What do you want me to do?" Kinney asks.

"Get on his ass!"

Kinney guns it past the car in front of us. Tires squeal. A van almost identical to ours, with the words "Pacific Florist" scrawled on the side, rolls into the intersection at the same time. Horns blare. I close my eyes, gripping the back of Frank's seat. We swerve, rock up on two wheels, and slam back down hard on the pavement.

When I open my eyes again, we're roaring down Adams, coming up behind the Camaro. Charlie veers to miss a car pulling out of a parking spot. He fishtails back into his lane.

"What the fuck's he doing?" Frank says.

"Goddamnit. Son of a bitch," Charlie bellows through the mike.

Up ahead, we see his arm sticking out the window and he's waving frantically for us to come up alongside. Kinney shoots up beside the Camaro and we hear Charlie yelling out his open window, "Shit! Fucking brakes, man! Can't stop!"

"Brakes gone," I say.

Kinney floors it, and we shoot past Charlie, who's cutting his left hand across his throat, screaming, "No brakes! No brakes, man!" He's rolling at maybe forty miles per hour.

Kinney swerves, gets right in front of the Camaro, then eases up on the gas. "Hold on tight!"

The Camaro hits us in the rear with a deep *thunk*. Kinney touches the brake. There's a screech and then grinding of metal on metal. He eases it down and it's like stopping a train. There's a release, then we pick up speed again like maybe our own brakes have failed.

"Kinney, Jesus Christ!"

More crunching. Kinney lays on the pedal and our brakes hiss like a locomotive. And then we finally roll to a halt.

It's over.

"Fuck," I say. "I can't believe this shit."

Frank pops the door, jumps out.

"904 to 705. What the hell you guys doing down there?"

I can hear Reinhardt chuckling, and I guess from their perspective, it all must look like the Keystone Cops. But I'm not laughing. Not one bit.

"What the fuck happened?" I yell again, clambering out of the van.

"You okay, Charlie?"

Charlie kicks open the door, white-lipped, more angry than shaken up. "Fuckin' piece of shit."

"What?"

"Fuckin' piece of fuckin' *shit*!"

"What the hell happened?"

Charlie gives the door a solid kick shut.

"Charlie?"

"It's the brakes, man. Fuckers just gave out."

Frank comes alongside and immediately starts pushing the Camaro toward the curb. We all pitch in, clearing the street as fast as we can. Cars are going around us, drivers staring. We push Charlie into the back of the van to get him off the street. He's mad as hell and ready to lash out. Frank tells Marty to grab the Nagra from the Camaro, and as soon as Marty's back in the van, we pull down the street behind a Jack in the Box to put some distance between us and the abandoned car. I put an epilogue on the tape to close it out with the date and time, and I pull the reel off the Nagra.

One glance at Frank tells me he's fuming. He takes a deep breath, and the look in his eyes is scary. I mean Marine Vietnam scary. "Gonzo," he mouths toward me, no sound escaping his lips.

I nod. Frank's absolutely right. Gonzo had the motive, means, and opportunity to cut Charlie's brake lines. And I know Frank's thinking what I'm thinking. This only confirms our suspicions. From day one, Gonzo's been setting Charlie up to be the fall guy.

Chapter 33

Suspicions
San Diego, CA
September 9, 1996

It's been a couple hours since the clubhouse fiasco, and I've already gone back under the cover of darkness to have the Camaro towed to the FBI garage. We just got word from our mechanic confirming our suspicion. There's clear evidence of tampering—several small punctures along the brake lines creating a slow leak of fluid.

Charlie's in his room with the door closed when I get back, cooling off I guess, but he shuffles into the living room when he hears me come through the kitchen door. We all sit in the living room.

"We heard Gonzo grappled with you outside the club," Frank begins. He's waited for me to return to debrief Charlie.

Charlie drinks water from a smeary glass, nodding thoughtfully. "Fucker's like . . . 'Hey, Charlie, great to see you, man.' Grabs me with those skinny long arms of his, gives me the big bear hug, you know. Then Duke does the same damn thing inside, saying how great it was to see me . . . feeling me up real good."

He lights up a cigarette, laughing.

"But nobody tried to pat you down," I say. "I mean, nobody just balls-out says, 'Charlie, we gotta shake you down,' right?"

"Nah. I guess they thought they'd be sly about it," he sneers.

As he empties the glass, I notice that his hands are trembling slightly. The day has left its mark on his nerves.

"Charlie," I say slowly, "Why did Gonzo move your car?"

He gives me a foul look. "The fuck you mean, *Gonzo*?"

"We watched him right after you went inside," Frank says. "He came out and moved the Camaro from the front to the back. Parked it in that parking bay where you found it."

Charlie stands, his brow furrowed, his hands clenched to fists. "Mother*fucker*!" he barks.

"Charlie?"

"You sure it was Gonzo moved the car?"

"We're sure."

Charlie's eyebrows rise. "So that's it. It's been him all along! He fucked with the brakes, didn't he?"

"Charlie ... yeah, the brake lines were punctured, but we don't know ..."

"That rotten motherfucker. It's all there. It all fits. Settin' me up, man. *He's the one* stole from the club, trashed my pad, ripped me off, and fucked with my old lady. Now tries to kill me." His face is crimson red as he paces back and forth in the small living room.

I try to deflect him. "Charlie, why'd you let Gonzo have your keys?"

The look in his eye tells me I've done the opposite of deflecting him. "The fuck you think, Nick?" he growls. "I *didn't* let that asshole have my keys. Duke didn't want my car parked out front. Was worried about the cops. Asked if he could move it around back, he said."

"But Gonzo ..."

"Look, Nick," Charlie interrupts, "Duke tells me to give my fuckin' keys to Sledge, all right? *Sledge*. I don't know what happened with the car after that—only that Sledge came back with the keys like ten minutes later."

We all stew on this for a while. The room's so silent I can hear the old refrigerator humming in the next room.

"So you gave Duke the plaque?" Frank asks, subtly shifting gears.

Charlie offers a slight snicker, settling down on the couch and putting his boots up on the table. "Fucker loved it, man. At first, they're all lookin' at the package thinkin' ... I don't know what they're thinkin' ... but they were kinda nervous, you know. Like what the fuck is Crazy Charlie gonna pull now. They sorta handled the package like it was a bomb or somethin'." He cackles.

"So I says, open it, and Duke says, 'You want me to open it *now*, Charlie?' And I says, yeah man, open it up while everybody's here. You shoulda seen the looks on everybody's faces. So Duke, he acted a little nervous, but when he opened it, he's like ... 'Fuck me, Charlie.' He says, 'What the fuck? It's beautiful, man.' But he's checkin' it over, right? Lookin' at the back and shit, and I can see he's tryin' to figure out if there's a mike hidden in it or somethin'."

"Really?"

"No shit, man. I'll guarantee he's gonna have that thing X-rayed."

Frank nods. "How'd Sledge look?"

"Fuckin' Sledge, man. Seven to ten, right? What they gave him?"

"That's right."

"And he's out after five. Guess he didn't stomp nobody in the joint."

"How's he look?"

"He's big, man. I mean, Sledge has always been huge, but pumpin' iron at San Quentin for five years really packs on the muscle. Next time you arrest him, Frank, you better take two tanks."

Frank rubs at tired eyes. "So you gave Duke the plaque," he says. "What happens then?"

"Well, like you told me: I said I had to be across town, that I had stuff to do, that I just wanted to drop by and pay my respects, and that I was feelin' better, you know. But Duke's says, 'Wait up, Charlie. You just fuckin' got here.'"

Charlie thinks about it for a second or two, remembering, I guess, exactly how it played out.

"So he says to me, 'I got somethin' for you, too, Charlie,' and I look around the room and they're all lookin' at me and smilin' kinda weird like, and I'm thinkin' *this ain't right, man.* If things are gonna go bad, it's right now. I gotta be honest ...

I had a hard time readin' everybody. I mean, the way they looked and stared at me. Nobody's sayin' nothin'. So I says to him, 'You got something for me, Duke?'"

"'Fuckin' A,' he says. 'Step into my office.' So I walk through there and—"

"Did you get a chance to look at the door?" Marty interrupts. "Any sign of new plaster or wires?"

Charlie holds up a hand. "I'm walkin' just behind him, so, yeah, I take a look around. There's somethin' there. Some wires. Like skinny little blue and red wire clippings on the floor by the door, and there's a place been plastered over. No paint."

"Duke probably wanted to test his new toy," Frank says. "See if you triggered any alarms."

"This is very disturbing news," Marty moans.

"Anyway . . . ," Charlie continues, drawing on his cigarette. "So he takes me through and I'm right behind him and it's just me and him, and he sits down behind his desk. Then he gets up and closes the door. He sits back down and he opens this drawer . . ."

Charlie takes another pull on his cigarette, thinking. This is another moment for him, a moment he needs to chew on for a second.

"He opens a drawer, and I'm thinkin' here it comes, man. I mean, I'm kinda expectin' a gun or somethin'. I know he keeps one there loaded in his desk and I'm kinda expectin' him to say somethin' like, 'I know all about it, Charlie. I know all about you and the cops,' and *bam*, you know." Charlie makes a gun with his finger, presses it to his head. "So we're alone, no witnesses, doors closed, he could make up a story that it was self-defense or somethin'."

"But it wasn't a gun," Frank says.

"It was my. . . . Fuck." Charlie jumps to his feet. "My bullwhip, man. I left the fucker in the car."

"Paul's picking it up at the FBI garage later," I say.

"Yeah, but that's *my* whip, man. If one of those greasemonkey motherfuckers gets hold of it . . ."

"Charlie, *our people* have the car. Nobody's gonna take it. I'll give Paul a call," I offer. "Make sure he picks it up."

He nods, sits back down.

"Your whip," Frank says.

"Yeah, man. Duke, he puts it on the desk."

"So what did he say? 'Hey, Charlie, we tossed your place and . . .'"

Charlie shakes his head, becoming very still. "He said it was there in the clubhouse. Said I musta left it there . . . in my fucked-up, drugged-out haze." He's fuming again.

"So? Did you call him on it?"

"No, man. I mean, what's the upside? I coulda said a lot of things to him, man. Coulda jacked him around about Stacey. But then what? I get into a big argument about him ripping me off? No, Spence, that ain't what I was in there for. I was in there to set this fucker up."

This is a huge step for Charlie. He's even starting to *think* like a cop.

"I just let it slide. I said, 'I guess I musta just dropped it, man.'"

"That was a good call," Frank says. "You did right, Charlie."

Charlie looks down at his lap, and I can see it's all starting to sink in. Duke having the whip is pretty much proof that one or more of his "brothers" broke into his apartment and ripped him off.

"Bastards," he growls after a moment. "They picked me clean, man. Beat my woman. And Duke has the balls to sit there and tell me my whip was just *laying around* the clubhouse. He musta been thinking *you dumb fuck, Charlie.*"

Frank shakes his head. "Listen, Charlie," he says carefully. "It's water under the bridge. And you didn't react angrily right at a time when it could have hurt us the most. You played it perfectly and you were thinking clearly and in control of your anger at the moment, and I can't tell you how important that is to us."

He stares at Frank without a word, then shrugs. It's clear he's not going to let this betrayal go.

"He never said anything about the money missing from the clubhouse?" I ask.

"Nothin'," Charlie says as he slides down further into the couch.

"So what did you do when he gave you the whip?" I ask.

Charlie suddenly rises off the couch as if timing his next answer. A slow, angry smile curls his lips.

"I jumped up outta the chair kinda excited, you know, and grabbed it and gave the fucker a big crack about six inches over Duke's head. 'Yee-haw!' He just about shit, man. Guys came chargin' in from the clubroom, and I started laughin' and everyone started laughin' with me."

I'm astounded. "Jesus, Charlie. You *are* crazy."

"So then what happened?" Frank says.

Charlie eases back down on the couch. "Duke orders everybody out of his office and he sits back down and he's kinda red in the face, you know, kinda jittery, and he says somethin' like how he missed me and how the club missed me, shit like that. And I'm thinkin', *You motherfucker . . . you steal from me and tell me to my face you miss me.* But I don't wanna get all pissed off again, so I change the subject and ask him about his house."

"His house?"

"Yeah, he gets off talkin' about his house. Said he'd been doin' some work on his house. See, he tells everybody he wants to build this big addition on his house. Told me he finally *persuaded* his neighbor to sell his house to him so he'd have room to build the addition."

Charlie pushes forward to the edge of the couch again. "There's this old couple lives next door, see . . . like in their eighties or somethin' . . . refused to sell their property. So Duke, he started parkin' his chopper on their front lawn, which the old guy really keeps nice, you know. I mean, it's a beautiful lawn and Duke does a couple wheelies on it, tells me he tore the hell outta this guy's lawn. Anyway, that didn't get no results, so Duke orders a load of dirt and has that dumped on the old guy's front lawn, too. So now there's no fuckin' grass what-so-fuckin'-ever."

"Nice guy."

"Oh, Duke's a prince, man. So anyway, I guess that wasn't enough to intimidate the ol' man into sellin', so Duke's tellin' me he called the *San Diego Union Tribune* and made up an obituary for the old man's wife, sayin' she died 'unexpectedly.' Had an accident. Finally, the guy sold to Duke. So he's pretty pleased about that." Charlie shakes his head in disgust.

"I can't figure why he wouldn't confront you about the stolen money," I say.

"Look, man," Charlie says. "It's like this. Duke's smart, you know. Street smart. He's got nothin' on me. No proof. And here I am walkin' right back into the clubhouse like I don't know fuckin' shit about no fuckin' stolen money. I mean, if I took money from them, I'd be a stupid motherfucker to go back there."

Charlie takes a long pull on his cigarette and pauses, looking at no one in particular. "So anyway, we go back out into the clubhouse, and the guys, they're all talkin' about the Jacumba lab bein' taken down by the DEA. They're super pissed, man. Especially Gonzo. Guess they were countin' on a big score there."

"How was he with you?" I say. "Gonzo."

"After all the smiles and the hugs? Just watchin' me, you know, starin' with those weird eyes."

"Our surveillance team detected no effort to follow you away from the meeting," Marty interjects. "What do you make of that?"

"I don't know, man. Me and Duke, we talked a lot about trust and friendship, I guess."

"Love and respect," I say.

"Yeah, man, love and respect."

We talk some more, but then decide we'd better get this conversation in the form of a recorded debriefing. In the end, the debrief runs for about an hour, and at ten o'clock Paul returns and reports to Frank and me in the kitchen that the Camaro will be back in business tomorrow afternoon. He walks into the living room, where Charlie's stretched out on the couch, one arm across his eyes listening to Merle Haggard on the radio. Paul tosses the whip onto the coffee table. Charlie takes a peek from under his arm, smiles tightly with his lips, then sits up. When he takes the whip in his hand, it's like a family reunion, like he's getting back with a brother he hasn't seen in months.

Chapter 34

Wire Tension
San Diego, CA
September 11, 1996

So now we're down to the wire in both the literal and figurative sense. Charlie's going to have to walk into the clubhouse wired for sound, and there's no way we can be sure some asshole won't try to shake him down. Similarly, we can't guarantee that the transmitter Charlie's going to be wearing won't set off whatever gizmos Duke's implanted in the wall above his office door, or anywhere else around the clubhouse. Marty's warned us time and again that without knowing what kind of equipment Duke's using, there's no way to be sure.

So we're pitting the Bureau's state-of-the-art equipment against what in all likelihood is over-the-counter spy store stuff installed by a two-bit PI. The consensus view—the view expressed by Blair and AUSA Barrett—is that it's highly unlikely that we'll be compromised. I try not to think about the number of times I've seen "highly unlikely" shit happen. Murphy's Law is no stranger to the FBI. Whatever *can* go wrong, *will* go wrong.

~ ~ ~ ~

"Put a soda can on that chair."

It's two days after Charlie handed Duke the plaque and we're standing in the backyard at the PB house, watching Charlie giving a demonstration in the art of bullwhipping. His whip is oiled up and ready to go. He's strutting around the backyard like Lash LaRue.

"A soda can?" Paul says. "Come on, Charlie. I thought you were good with this thing."

Charlie smiles with his lips, takes a breath, then straightens up, giving the whip a good, solid crack. The thing zips and bangs like a clap of lightning and fills the air with a pungent, leathery tang.

"Jumping Jesus," Frank says admiringly.

It certainly is an impressive sight.

"Took out a lightbulb once at the Silver Spur, Frank," Charlie says, recoiling the thing in his restless hands. "Like a bomb goin' off."

"Maybe you could whip that cigarette out of Frank's mouth," I say.

Frank wedges a freshly lit Marlboro between his lips; sticks out his chin. "Go for it, Charlie. Give my nose hairs a trim while you're at it."

Charlie chuckles, his dark eyes on Frank. "Soda can's good enough," he says. "Paul, come on."

Paul finishes his Tab and sets the empty can on a plastic chair propped against the fence.

Charlie's all business now, uncoiling the whip and laying it along the ground with the flared end touching the chair. Then he coils it up again, clearly enjoying the creak and feel of the oiled leather.

"Are we taking bets?" Frank says, smiling.

"Sure," Charlie says. "What you wanna bet?"

"I bet you five dollars you can't hit the chair."

This gets a laugh from everyone except Charlie.

"I'll take your five," he says, and he lines himself up, standing about six feet from the chair now. "But I'm hitting the can, okay? I don't hit the can, I give you five bucks."

He holds the whip in front of him, aiming along the handle. We all take a step back.

~~~~

We don't want Charlie to appear too anxious to do business, so we wait five days before having him call Duke again. Like the other calls, this one's consensually monitored; Charlie sitting at the kitchen table when he makes it and Marty's tape recorder right in front of him.

Duke sounds more relaxed this time, but when Charlie talks about needing to get back into business, Duke fails to take the bait. Duke's no Spud. He's going to be a whole lot more cautious and discreet. But he does agree to meet Charlie at the clubhouse on Friday. This gives us just one day to set things up with SOG, but as it turns out, things fall into place pretty smoothly. The same team we've been using happens to be available on short notice, so we'll go in with familiar guys.

The one big difference on this second meet is the wire, of course, and Charlie's the one who feels the full weight of that. He doesn't say much about it, but I can see it's eating at him.

Thursday morning, I find him standing alone in the backyard, holding the whip loosely in his hands. There's five or six empty Tab cans, unscathed and lying on the ground under the plastic chair, which is by now missing most of the plastic. It turns out that Charlie's overestimated his prowess. He's currently twenty-five dollars in the hole with Frank, who refuses to take further bets until Charlie starts showing results. That said, there's no doubt about Charlie's ability to crack the thing, and his accuracy is improving now that he's spending so much time practicing. He keeps saying he's just a little rusty.

"I don't know how they do it," he says as I come out of the kitchen. "Snapping a cigarette from between the woman's lips like that. In those . . . circus acts or whatever. I seen it on TV."

"You think that's what they do, Charlie? You don't think the girl just kinda spits it out when the guy cracks the whip?"

Charlie thinks about this for a second and then goes into a crouch and lets fly with the whip. It smacks the chair hard enough to send the aluminum frame flying across the lawn.

"I think a lot of it is in the stance," I say. "You want to reduce the number of moving parts. Like when you serve a tennis ball."

"That right?"

"Ever watch McEnroe serve? Blocks himself almost backward on the baseline; puts himself into a kind of strait-jacket."

"Not really a tennis fan, Spence. Always thought it was kind of a sissy sport." He shoots me a sarcastic look. "Do you play?"

I grin. "I do play, as a matter of fact. And what I'm saying is you lose accuracy when there are too many moving parts."

"Moving parts, huh . . ."

Charlie goes quiet now, disconnecting from our conversation as so often happens, slowly coiling the whip in his hands. From the look on his face, I can see he's not thinking about tennis.

"You know, Charlie," I say, "you can back out of this anytime."

He glares, clearly offended. "Fuck that," he growls. Then he braces himself and lets loose with the whip again.

"Fuck that," he says again, softer this time, and again with the whip.

I look down at his cowboy boots. "How's the Nagra?"

Charlie shrugs. "Good. It's good. I'm getting to a point I don't know I'm wearin' it."

"You wearing it now?"

"Wha'dya think, Spence?"

I size him up for a second. It's impossible to say.

Charlie smiles, lifts his shirt, showing the wire taped along his spine.

"No way are they going to know, Charlie. Unless someone grabs you and feels the mike under your arm."

"Or a buzzer goes off in Duke's office," Charlie says with a solemn stare. I return his stare, nodding. We're at ground zero here, the focus of all our fears.

"I ain't afraid, Spence. I'll take all those fuckers on if I have to."

I can see he means it. I can see also that he's not talking about winning. He's talking about going down fighting.

"Just remember 'roses,' Charlie, and we'll be coming from all directions."

Charlie smiles, lips tight.

"I'm serious," I say. "If he pulls that gun from his desk..."

"If he shoots me, you won't hear it. I know."

"Exactly. The gunshot will overpower the transmitter and we'll hear nothing. I guess Marty told you. So say the word 'rose' anytime you think things are headed south. We'll be there..."

Charlie nods, smirking. "That right, Spence? You got my back on this?"

"Yes, I do, Charlie. I'm behind you one hundred percent. So's Frank. So's everyone else. We're a team and you're our quarterback."

~ ~ ~ ~

The day has a blank, stalled feel. Then at some point in the afternoon it seems to pick up speed, and suddenly I'm back in the SOG van, riding up front next to Kinney this time. Frank and Marty are stuck in the back, listening to Charlie over the wire.

The witness's gravelly undertone sounds more *intense*, more focused, with an edge of hostility in his voice that's a little scary.

"These fucker's are goin' down," he says, his voice rumbling barely above a whisper. "We're gonna take these fuckers *down*."

It's like he's pumping himself up before a boxing match.

"Atta boy, Charlie," I find myself saying.

A burst of static. "904 to all units. Our guy is making a left on 30th Street."

"Roger, 904."

Chick Reinhardt's voice comes through strong and clear, exuding the kind of confidence you'd expect from a former Navy fighter pilot. He's seen his share of action in the air, but even so, these surveillances are no cakewalk for our guys up in the plane. I picture them jammed, side by side, in the Cessna's cramped cockpit, Bob Anders manning the controls and Reinhardt looking down at the sprawling city through a big pair of Zeiss binoculars. They hardly have room to fart, and if they have to piss, they do it in a bottle. Until a month ago, Chick was struggling with a gyroscope designed to cut out some of the motion in the plane, but it made him sick when he looked through it. So now he's gone back old-school with the binocs. His job—to monitor the exterior of the clubhouse while Charlie's inside and, above all, to pick up and follow anyone who might think about taking Charlie by force away from the clubhouse.

We in the van will be the only ones monitoring the wire off a different frequency, while maintaining radio contact with the others on the surveillance channel. We'll keep Reinhardt and Anders apprised of the activities inside the clubhouse as necessary.

At Adams, we peel off and head for the second of the positions we've singled out as most likely to offer good reception: a Denny's parking lot two blocks south of the clubhouse. It's pretty crowded and Kinney has to drive around for a while before finding a space. But then we're in and parked.

Kinney switches off the engine. Only now is the full richness and clarity of the audio coming through from Charlie apparent. There's a certain amount of rubbing noise where his clothing comes in contact with the mike, but beyond that, all is clear, including the sound of his steady, deep-drawn breaths.

"Nice job, Marty," I say. "It's like he's sitting here in the van."

"I'm pulling up to the clubhouse." Charlie's bass rumble comes through, silencing us. Through the bug-smeared windshield, I see a few drops of rain starting to fall.

"This is it . . ." Charlie says. "This is where the rubber hits the road."

"904 to all units. Our guy's turning into the clubhouse

parking lot."

"Copy, 904."

I do a quick roll call radio check to the Squad 7 agents positioned around the clubhouse. Everyone's in position. I close my eyes and try to visualize.

"Hey, Charlie!" comes a voice. "Good to see you, man! Get in here!"

"Hey, Scooter," Charlie replies. "How they hangin'?"

"Good, Charlie, good. It's good to see you, man."

There's more of this friendly back and forth, and then I hear the front door open with a distinctive squeak. Charlie's going inside, and we're going inside with him—acoustically, at least.

There's a sudden rush of static—I pray it's not interference from electronic counter-surveillance—and then the echoey sounds of what I'm guessing is a corridor.

Scooter comes through louder inside. "So how's business, Charlie?"

"Could be better, man. You know."

"Yeah, I know. It's hard out there, man. Fuckin' cops everywhere. Fuckin' *snitches*. Hey, I heard about you being broke into, man. That fuckin' sucks, man. Got any idea who did it?"

"Nah, man. But when I catch up with them, they're gonna regret touchin' my shit."

"I hear you, brother."

"Where's Duke at, man?"

"He's waiting for you, man. In his office."

I close my eyes tighter, hearing Charlie's heavy footsteps. If Duke's counter-surveillance is top-notch, this is where it all comes crashing down. There's another wash of mixed sounds—chairs being moved, a radio or TV in the background.

"Catch you later, Charlie."

"Right on, Scooter."

There's a rap on a door. Then the door opening. Then

Duke's voice, loud and brash, welcoming Charlie in. I try to visualize the office, finding it easy to imagine a little red light flashing under Duke's desk—something only he can see.

"Come in and take a seat, Charlie."

"Thanks, man. And thanks for . . ."

Silence. Nothing.

I look over at Marty, who's frowning at the tape recorder. It's suddenly unbearably hot in the van.

"Did we just lose the signal?" I say.

Marty's shaking his head, tweaking knobs, tapping gauges.

"Marty? What the fuck just happened?"

Marty holds up a hand and leans forward until his ear is touching one of the speakers he's rigged up.

"Marty?"

"Wait a second, Spence."

"Maybe a wire came loose," I say.

Marty's now more or less doubled over the amplifier.

"No way, Nick. My wires don't come loose. Unless someone ripped them out."

I look at Frank.

He returns my gaze, frowning. "Give it a minute," he says.

"Quiet," Marty says. "I'm trying to listen."

I reach for the radio. "705 to all units," I say, just above a whisper. "We've lost the audio. Stand by."

I blink sweat from my eyes . . . it's hotter than shit in here and the tension is mounting.

A minute passes. Five. I instinctively check the gun in my holster and turn in my seat.

"Marty?"

"Wait!" he says. "Wait."

I climb over the seat, get into the back with Frank and Marty. We're all leaning forward, heads almost touching, trying to hear something, anything. There's a soft rushing sound, like a page being turned, then something else.

"What *is* that?" I say.

"Whispering. They're whispering."

"Who's whispering?"

I check my watch. Twenty minutes have passed. My shirt clings to my back, soaked all the way through.

"Doesn't make sense," Marty says.

"What doesn't?"

"The equipment's working fine, but no one's talking. No voices . . . at least no audible voices. If they were making a move on Charlie, we'd surely hear them at least moving around. At least no one's yanked the transmitter."

A shrill noise takes us all by surprise. A screeching, scraping sound. It comes through so loud, we all jump back from the amplifier like it was on fire.

Then I hear Charlie's voice. "Thanks, Duke," he says. "Thanks, man. Let's talk some more."

"You got it, Charlie."

"How 'bout tomorrow?"

"Why don't you call me in a couple days?"

I flop back against the side of the van.

"Jesus Christ," I say. "Jesus Christ. What was that all about?"

~ ~ ~ ~

"Notes, man."

We're back at the house—me, Frank, and Marty around the kitchen table.

"What kind of notes?"

"Like notes. Little notes. As soon as I walk in there, he holds up a piece of paper with 'DON'T TALK' on it in big red letters."

I fire a troubled look at Frank, who squints, I guess trying to visualize the scene.

"I walk into his office and sit down across from him at his desk," Charlie continues, talking with his hands. "And he takes out a notepad and writes, 'What do you want?' Like that. We're pushing notes back and forth the whole time."

Frank looks at me and we both start laughing.

Charlie looks perplexed. "What's so funny?"

"The guy's so paranoid that he supposedly goes to all the trouble to wire the room with electronic sensors and then passes notes," Franks says with a chuckle.

Charlie now joins in on the laughter. "That's Duke, man. Paranoid motherfucker."

"Did you keep any?" I ask.

"What?"

"Notes."

"He burned them. When we was done. Struck a match and just burned them all in the trash can."

Frank calmly returns my stare. Nailing Duke is going to be harder than we thought. The best news is, of course, that the most worrisome barrier has been broken. Charlie didn't send off any signals inside the clubhouse. At least none we know of.

"So how'd it go down?" I ask.

Charlie rolls his head back, triumphant. "I told him I was getting my old crew back in order, you know, puttin' things straight again, but needed a little help getting back on my feet. Said I had some housecleaning to do, you know, guys ripping me off while I was on the juice." He glances proudly at both Frank and me.

"He bought it."

"Great job, man," Frank says.

"Did you talk quantity?" I ask.

"I told him I had enough to cover half a pound . . . told him I needed enough to get me jump-started again," Charlie says.

"That's good, Charlie. Half pound's a good start," Frank says.

"Perfect," I say. "How much?"

"Nine hundred an ounce," Charlie says with a sneer.

"Goin' rate, he tells me."

"Nine hundred?" I say. "That's street price. What, no discount for old friends?"

Charlie gives me his deadpan look. "I told you, man. With Duke, it's all about the fuckin' money."

"And that's what's gonna bring him down," I say. "His greed."

Chapter 35

Boxing Day
San Diego, CA
September 18, 1996

Paul and I are on our way back from the federal building to the
PB house after bringing Blair up to speed. For most of the ride,
we've been talking about Charlie—his state of mind, his feelings about the case. Paul's telling me he thinks Charlie could
probably be left more on his own now and has no need for full-
time babysitters anymore. I'm not so sure.

"If he was gonna screw up, he'd have done it by now,"
Paul says.

"Maybe," I say, looking out at the glistening blue waters
of Mission Bay as we cross the Ingraham Street Bridge.

What Paul says is true to some degree. Charlie's had a
number of opportunities to go sideways on us and has so far
shown himself to be worthy of our trust. Not that we've been
giving him much leeway. Mainly, it's been a question of spotting him some pocket money to go out and buy cigarettes and
shaving cream from the nearby 7-Eleven. His personal use of
the Camaro is strictly off-limits, so any trouble he can get into
would have to be within walking distance, and we've asked
him to stay out of the bars, movie theaters, and local restaur-
ants. We've also told him if he goes out, we'd prefer it would be
after dark, so he's less likely to be spotted on the street. Given
our restrictions, it's hard to imagine why he'd go out at all except to get some air and get out of the house.

Personally, I'd rather he not go out at all, but he's not
our prisoner, and everything he's doing for us he's doing voluntarily. Also, telling Charlie he can't do something is just a way
of guaranteeing he'll do it, so the situation has to be handled
with a certain amount of psychological finesse. So far, we've
been able to keep him on task by talking about the risks of
jeopardizing the case and undermining all our hard work if

somehow his relationship with us is compromised.

"We'll talk more about this with Frank," I say.

The idea of Charlie being left alone at the house would certainly relieve some pressure on our team, but the fact is, he thrives on people being around. It probably stems from all the loneliness he's had in his life. In any case, loneliness might explain why, even when everyone's around and things are upbeat and loose, he often reverts to telling stories about his past. They're stories that, for the most part, contain a healthy scoop of darkness and ashes.

"I guess those nuns can be pretty cruel," I say. "My dad was pretty liberal with the back of his hand, too."

Charlie stares at me, shaking his head. "You don't get it, Spence."

"What?"

"I'm not talkin' about that kinda shit. There was plenty of that, yeah. I'm talkin' weird stuff, man."

It was quiet in the house. Paul's in the living room, reading. Charlie's sitting there, staring at me with a hollowed-out, wistful look on his face. And I'm stunned by the accusation. He's once again recounting his dark years in the orphanage.

"I'm like twelve, thirteen years old," he says softly. "A couple of them would do it to me. You know . . . jerk me off . . . make me touch them. Stuff like that. But there was one—Sister Marie—the one who liked to hit me with the edge of the ruler. She got on top of me."

"Come on, Charlie . . ."

"What?"

"You sure you're remembering it right?"

He shrugs and shows me a side of him I've never seen before—a brittle version of Charlie Slade that can't quite seem to look me in the eye. "Sure, I'm sure," he says. "Those nuns fucked with me, man. Why would I tell you a story like that if it wasn't true?"

I just sit there, shaking my head. Charlie rakes at his scalp a couple of times, then becomes still.

"They were supposed to look after me, man," he says softly. "Protect me."

~~~~

Paul's had enough waiting, I guess. "C'mon, Charlie!" he howls from outside. "You chickenshit bastard."

He's yelling so loud we can hear him in the living room where Charlie, Frank, and I are playing gin. Paul had gone out about an hour ago to do what he called some "grocery shopping," which struck all of us as odd since we order takeout for every meal. In any case, he hadn't even announced his return, save for this screeching from the backyard.

I go to the kitchen window and push back the curtains. I see Paul pacing the yard. He's wearing a new pair of boxing gloves with the price tags still dangling from the drawstrings, beating his clenched fists together as he practices his own version of the Ali shuffle.

I'm chuckling to myself as Charlie slides in next to me, poking his head over my shoulder. He smells like cigarettes and cheap shampoo, his wet hair let loose from its usual ponytail. He snickers through a little scoff. "Crazy fucker," he says.

"C'mon, Charlie!" Paul yells, and I guess he can't see us in the window, owed to the reflection of the late afternoon sunlight. "I'll tear you limb from limb."

Charlie steps back and shakes his head at me. "Crazy fucker," he says again.

Frank comes in and asks with his eyes what's going on. I nod in the direction of the window, then take a seat on the counter opposite. Frank peers out, laughing heartily at what he sees.

"Crazy fucker," he says.

"Beat you with one hand, Charlie!" Paul yells.

This has been building for weeks. Paul's been taunting Charlie to spar with him. They've joked back and forth for so long about who's the toughest that this moment was bound to come sooner or later. Charlie looks at Frank and me. We've discouraged this from the start, but Charlie insists it's all in good fun.

"On two conditions," Frank says with a sigh. "One, you don't take his head off; and two, you know when to quit."

Charlie nods and darts for his bedroom. In a flash, he's out the kitchen door and into the backyard.

"You take it easy on him, Paul!" I yell.

Frank chortles as we follow Charlie out into the sunlight. A beautiful day for boxing, I guess. Paul reverses his shuffle and ungracefully begins prancing backward, tripping on his heels as he makes the turn.

We all bust out laughing.

Paul leaps to his feet, still talking trash. "Beat you like a rented mule, Charlie," he says through a mischievous smile.

Charlie just nods through all of this. We watch as he takes great care to unlace his most treasured possession: his San Quentin championship gloves. He senses he has an audience as he performs what looks almost like a ritualistic ceremony—
slowly slipping each large knuckled hand into the soft, sweat-stained leather mitts. He uses his teeth to tighten the strings and tie his knots. I guess in prison you don't have a trainer. When he's finally finished, Charlie beats his gloves together and then does a little stretch, lifting one arm over his head and bending to the side, then lifting and stretching in the other direction.

"Quit stalling, you pussy," Paul barks. "I'm ready."

Charlie lets out a dark little laugh, then turns to me with urgent eyes. I assume this means it's my job to officiate, to call the match to a start.

"Ding, ding, ding," I say. "There's the bell."

Charlie charges at Paul in a flash. Paul's so taken aback by his opponent's quickness and aggressiveness that he stumbles over his feet again. He topples to the ground, stopping himself with both elbows in the clumpy grass.

Frank and I burst out again.

"Knockdown," I say.

"Your ass, Nick," Paul says, getting back up.

"You sure you don't want a mouth guard?" Frank asks, wiping tears from his eyes.

"Charlie ain't wearin' one," Paul says defensively.

They start to circle clockwise, jabbing and ducking and weaving until Charlie connects a light blow to Paul's chest. Paul returns the favor with a brushing glance against Charlie's right ear. Charlie quickly answers with two taps to Paul's chin with his right and then cracks him with a stiff left jab. Paul topples back, falling to the ground, again tripping over his own feet. We all laugh again. Charlie stands over his opponent, looking down at him with a blank stare.

"Well, *that* one counts," I say.

Paul gets a determined look in his eye. Stands. Locks his gloves in front of his face. He's ready now. "Just warmin' up, Charlie," he says.

Charlie fires a right cross that's so fast it's a blur, and I'm surprised when Paul ducks it and lands a quick jab into Charlie's ribs. The blow would double me over, but Charlie brushes it off like it's a stiff breeze. He weaves to his right, switching stance to southpaw, coming around with a kind of grace I never would have expected. He cracks Paul in the jaw, sending him to stumble. But Paul stays on his feet.

"You fight like my brother Jake," Charlie snorts. He dances around so Paul comes between him and me, and I can see Charlie's wearing a hungry sneer.

"That so?" Paul says.

Charlie snaps him with another hard left. "Yeah."

"Well, then he must fight like a fucking raging *bull!*" Paul yells, as he suddenly unleashes with a whirlwind of completely uncoordinated punches.

Charlie ducks most of them. The ones he doesn't wind up as glancing blows, they're so misguided. Charlie's sneer deepens. "He *did* fight like a fuckin' bull," Charlie bellows.

"Bullheaded and stupid." He unloads a three-punch combo that ends with an uppercut that would send a lighter man flying through the air.

Paul's left blinking; his knees wobble. His arms slump down for a moment before he cranks them back up to his face. "I guess that's not a compliment," he says.

"No," Charlie grumbles. "Ain't no compliment, man." He cracks Paul in the nose and a wet, fat sound erupts.

A small trickle of blood emerges, running into Paul's mouth. "All right, Paul," I say, stepping in. "That's enough."

But Charlie stops me with his gloved right hand. "Let him be, Spence," he says with a dark intensity. "I ain't through with him yet." The tone of his voice is all wrong. And then it occurs to me. Charlie's not fighting Paul anymore. He's fighting the ghost of his brother. I picture him doing this same thing to Jake, over and over again, as he struggles to tame his brother's incorrigible belligerence. And then I picture Jake lying in his own blood on the steps of the First National Bank in San Jose. I had nothing to do with the standoff that got Jake killed, but I've seen pictures.

"I can take care of myself," Paul interrupts, but I can see he's more than a little woozy. "C'mon, Charlie."

"It's over," Frank interjects. "We've had enough fun for one day."

Paul waves a gloved hand dismissively at Frank, grunts his disapproval. But I can see now that even Charlie's not into it anymore. Whether it's the topic of his brother or his remarkable willingness to go along with just about everything Frank has to say, I'm not sure, but there he stands with his gloves at his sides staring at the ground as if staring through it.

Frank strides over to Paul, helping him remove his gloves.

"I coulda taken him, Frank," I hear Paul say—and he says it so softly, I wonder if Charlie heard it, too.

Charlie's expressionless.

"Had him right where I wanted him."

I guess it doesn't take Paul long to see there's no joy left in the yard.

"What?"

It's Charlie who speaks. "I'm sorry, Paul," he says. "I guess I just lost it."

"What're you talking about?"

"About Jake, man."

"What about him?" Paul asks.

The three of us look at one another as if waiting to see who will be first to take the lead. I'm surprised when it's Charlie—and even more surprised to hear him sound so level about it all.

"He's dead, Paul," he says. "FBI killed him."

Paul blinks wide-eyed like he's startled.

"And I guess I was just takin' it out on you, man."

Frank finishes unlacing Paul's gloves, and Paul chunks them to the ground and shakes out his hands.

"Jesus, Charlie," he says. "I didn't know . . ."

"Yeah," Charlie says. "I figured."

I've never seen Paul so affected. It looks almost like there are tears in his eyes—though it's hard to tell if it's from sympathy or from getting wailed on. "What happened?"

Charlie chuffs. Looks away. "He got caught robbin' a bank and they executed him."

Paul's eyes dart to Frank, then to me. "Is that *true*?"

"San Jose," I say. "Couple of years ago."

Paul looks incredulous. He raises his hands to either side as if to ask why he wasn't informed.

"Hey, even *I* didn't know about it until after we started this case," I say. Then I turn to Charlie, looking him directly in the eyes. "And they didn't execute him, Charlie. He drew a weapon on our agents while fleeing a bank after a robbery. The agents had no choice. You know that."

"Geez," Paul says. "I'm sorry, Charlie."

Charlie stares down at the ground again and there's a long silence that follows. A skateboarder clatters down the alley on the other side of the fence as Charlie slides off his gloves with his teeth.

"Forget about it, Paul," he says. "My brother was an ass-hole anyway." He shuffles toward the door, heading inside, cradling his gloves like they were newborn babies.

Chapter 36

Gonzo Bites
San Diego, CA
September 22, 1996

As badly as the scene played out in the backyard, it somehow resulted in a kind of catharsis for everyone. Releasing his aggressions on Paul, Charlie seems ready to put his feelings about his brother aside, even if he's not completely ready to forgive the FBI for what they did to the only true family he ever had. Either way, the air feels clearer, like we're all ready to get back into the business of taking down the San Diego Hells Angels.

And all of that starts and ends with Jason "Duke" Stricker.

If we want to nail Duke with the best evidence, we know we have to get him talking quantity and price on tape. We realize that the best we can hope for is that Duke's going to get more comfortable, become less cautious. But it's not like we have forever with this. At some point soon, Blair, Cantrell, and Barrett are going to want to see results.

Four days later—again, timing it so that Charlie doesn't look desperate—we have him make a consensually monitored call to Duke. We want to schedule a second meeting, try to get Duke to say a few words. Charlie's just getting into his prepared speech when Duke says, "Hey, Charlie, come on over. I got something for you."

Charlie glances up at me with a deer-in-the-headlights look.

"What?" he says.

"Something I know you'll like."

Before I can even react, Charlie mumbles, "Uh, yeah . . . okay. Right on, man."

I stand, give him a thumbs-down. We can't just go in at a moment's notice. SOG responds to all kinds of requests for support on a daily basis. They're not sitting around waiting for me to call.

Charlie frowns, clearing his throat. "Damn it," he says. "I forgot."

"What's the problem?"

"Fuckin' brakes, man. Car's in the shop."

"What about your bike?"

Charlie looks up at me. Again, thumbs down.

"Bike's in pieces on the kitchen floor," Charlie says. "How 'bout I come by tomorrow?"

"Okay, in the morning," Duke growls.

"Give me a chance to get my car back."

"Come by at ten."

~~~~

With short notice, we manage to bring together a team for another shot at Duke. At eight o'clock the following morning, Marty's wiring Charlie up and Paul's photocopying hundred-dollar bills in the living room.

I search Charlie while Frank and Marty search the Camaro. Everything's clean, and at 9 a.m. we're ready to go.

"I want you to try to get him to talk this time, Charlie. We need conversation," I say.

"Or if you can't do that, you just say some words while you're in there," Frank says, urging with his eyes. "*Anything.* Just so we know we're picking you up on the wire."

"What do you want me to say?"

"Like 'okay, Duke' or 'sure thing.' Shit like that. It's just so that we know you're okay, okay?"

Charlie nods.

"And I want you to count the bills," I say.

"What?"

"When you're paying him. Count out the hundreds. Put them in stacks of ten. Make a big deal out of it. Like you want to make sure he knows you're not screwing him. I want to get it on tape. Think you can do that?"

"Christ, Nick."

"Charlie, work with me on this."

"I'll try."

~~~~

But he doesn't try. For some reason, in the heat of the moment or whatever, it all goes out of his head. We spend the next hour sitting in the van, trying to work out what the hell's going on inside. It's not as bad as the first time, but still bad. He does manage to mutter a few syllables, enough to let us know he's still alive.

In the meantime, I know there are a dozen agents out on the street, ready to leap into action, and a Cessna 172 burning up fuel 3,500 feet above the city. We're running up a hefty tab for—in the final analysis—just a few hundred feet of blank audio tape.

Charlie's chipper as he pulls into the garage. When he sees our faces, his lips fade from their smile. "What?" he says, getting out of the car.

"You were supposed to talk, Charlie," I say. "We got nothing on tape."

I ready myself to do the search of Charlie and the vehicle in the presence of Frank. I'm not really prepared to get into an argument here, but the words just come out.

Charlie sets his jaw. "I talked, man."

"Well, we sure as hell didn't hear it," I say loudly with angry frustration.

Charlie becomes very still, and for a second I feel like we're back in the Paloma, playing that old squares and regulars game.

"Don't fucking yell at me, man."

"Charlie."

"Don't fucking yell."

"Charlie, I'm not yelling."

"You're not in there, Spence. You're not sittin' there with Duke mad-doggin' you with his killer stare."

"Charlie," Frank says, raising his hands.

"Anytime I went to say something, the fucker scribbled a note. *'Don't talk.'* Don't talk means don't fuckin' talk, Nick. He was real clear on that."

I feel my face run red. "We don't have a clue what happened in there, Charlie," I say, ducking inside the Camaro to search under the mats. "Did you score? You were supposed to count out the bills like I told you."

"Why am I gonna count the fuckin' bills, man? Here's Duke sayin' don't talk and I'm countin' bills? It's bullshit, man. It's stupid fuckin' FBI bullshit. What do you want me to say to him, 'Speak up, Duke, so my newest pals out in the van can hear you?'"

And he storms out of the garage. By the time I climb back out of the car, I can already hear him cracking his whip in the backyard . . . with a little more punch than usual. Frank's standing there in the doorway looking at me with one eye on Charlie. He's as frustrated as I am. He opens his mouth to speak but loses his train when Charlie storms back in, looking like he's going to start with me again.

Frank cuts him off. "Nick's under a lot of pressure, Charlie," he says. "We know you're the one taking the risks."

I nod, hold up my hands—guilty as charged. Still, I can't give him a pass on this. "Charlie, I know it's tough what you're doing," I say. "It's just that . . . well . . . we need some results here. Truth is, this all costs money and I'm getting heat from my office."

"So? It ain't your money, Spence."

"No, but I've got to account for it, Charlie. I'm burning a lot of manpower. I have to show results."

Charlie reaches into his pocket and tosses a large plastic baggie onto the Camaro's hood. "So show that," he says.

My heart leaps as I see the baggie's full of white powder. I pull out a pair of latex evidence gloves, do the presumptive field test, and weigh the bag. Frank begins the procedural search of Charlie while we all watch the test turn purple-blue.

"There's just under eight ounces here."

"That's points on the board, Spence," Charlie says.

Frank finishes searching Charlie, gives him a high-five.

"Looks like we scored one for the good guys."

I give Charlie an apologetic look. He seems stoked that he's done well, but he's still clearly pissed at me.

~~~~

So we've got our first hook into the biggest fish, but knowing the quantities the club deals in, we know we've got more work to do. We can certainly do a whole lot better than a half-pound of crystal meth, but it's a start. We've got our foot in the door. It takes a few days for Charlie to come down off his indignation, but eventually he gets over it and we're a fully functional team again. A week after his first meeting with Duke, he's back in the big man's office, and this time it goes a little different.

All week, Frank, Marty, and I have been reminding Charlie that he has to talk, that without someone saying something on tape, we're going to be struggling in court. The first time I know he's been listening comes three minutes into the now familiar and frustrating-as-hell silence of Duke's note-shuffling routine.

In response to what I guess is a written question, Charlie blurts out, "I'm gonna need another pound, Duke."

There's an audible hiss, which I figure is steam coming out of Duke's ears.

"What the fuck, Charlie?" he says loudly.

"Sorry, man," Charlie says. "I forgot."

It goes quiet again for a while, and then, maybe four minutes later, Charlie says, "Is that a three or a five?"

"Charlie, fuck!"

"You write your fives weird, man."

This time Duke says nothing, but I guess he's giving Charlie his mad-dog stare because Charlie comes back with, "Fuck it, Duke, I'm just ... I guess I'm just tired, man."

And maybe it's Charlie's famous charm, or maybe it's Duke just starting to relax a little, but he starts to talk now, or mumble, anyway—whispering sounds. I can't make out what they're saying, but there's something there.

~ ~ ~ ~

Back at the house I do my best to look happy, but in reality I doubt we've picked anything up on tape of any real value. The only thing we've really accomplished is to clearly put Duke in the same room with Charlie. I'm starting to wonder if we're ever going to get the kind of solid evidence we need to secure a conviction.

Charlie could generally give a shit about what I think, but he's sensitive as always to the slightest signals put out by Frank.

"It went great, man. What's the problem?"

"Charlie," Frank says. "We need ..."

"Duke to talk," Charlie interrupts. "I know that, Frank. Jesus. But he *did* talk. He talked *plenty*." He looks from Frank to me and back again. "You didn't get it? I mean, he was whisperin', but it was sorta loud. I thought this equipment of yours was high-tech?"

"What did he talk about, Charlie?"

"All kinds of shit. He said he's got like a hundred pounds of meth stashed in one of his limos there. He's sayin', 'I got product out the ass.' You tellin' me you didn't hear that?"

I look at Frank. I sure didn't.

"I don't fuckin' believe you guys," he snorts, as he reaches under his shirt and retrieves a large plastic baggie full of white powder and tosses it onto the kitchen table. In a gesture of frustration and defiance, he turns and heads for the backyard and his favorite diversion—his bullwhip.

~~~~

We do the presumptive field test in the kitchen on the meth Charlie bought and it comes up positive. I'm about to drive over to the federal building to log it into the evidence vault when Marty comes out of the second bedroom.

"We got something," he says.

"What?"

"Better if you listen yourselves."

We follow him into the bedroom and sit down at a little desk where he has set up his equipment. Once we're all settled in, Marty reverses the tape, watching the tape counter, then hits play.

"It's not great," he says as the reel begins to turn. After a few seconds, he boosts the volume using an audio filtering device attached to the recorder. The sound from the tape is an echoing cacophony of whirrs and hisses, the ambient sounds noticeably enhanced from the first time we listened to it, but I'm still not hearing anything.

Then Duke's voice comes through. He's whispering, but loud and clear enough for us to hear most of what he's saying. Of course, without tone and tenor, the whisperer could be anyone. But at least it's something.

Marty is grinning. "Listen," he says. "Right here." And he turns up the volume just a little. "Here, you can hear him say it."

Then we do hear Duke say, "You kiddin', Charlie, I got a hundred pounds . . . got a hundred pounds of that shit."

Then Charlie whispers, "One hundred pounds? Jesus, Duke."

It's brilliant, what he does there. He's feeding Duke's ego, and repeating for our benefit.

Then Duke responds barely audible. "Yeah," he says. "Stashed right here in a limo . . . righteous crank."

"This is good stuff," I say, patting Marty on the shoulder.

"Nice goin', Marty. This is *huge*. This is our probable cause to search the clubhouse."

"He's using his business in furtherance of criminal activities . . . stashing drugs in his limos. It doesn't get any better than this. Way to go, Marty." Frank says.

I nod, smiling. "Forfeit all those fancy vehicles owned by Celebrity Limo Service . . ."

"Asset seizures," Frank says, grinning back at me. "I think it's time to call in Joe the Jew."

~~~~

I phone Mike Barrett the next day, and we set up a meeting for the afternoon. Marty comes, too, and plays the audio we have. Attorneys have a way of dampening enthusiasm, so I'm half-expecting Barrett to dismiss it as unusable, but instead he nods. He likes it.

"Hey, the audio's not optimal," he says, "but backed by Charlie's testimony, your surveillance, the physical evidence, I think it's enough to go on. Maybe we'll get lucky and get Duke's prints on the baggies. For sure we can charge him with possession and sale, and he's conducting drug trafficking out of the clubhouse within a thousand yards of a schoolyard, which gives us the chance to double his sentence. That's a pretty good start."

"What about asset forfeitures?" I say.

"I'll get some of our people to take a look at this. Good job, guys."

"Great," I say. "Blair's going to assign Joe Bernstein to assist on the seizures."

Barrett reels back in his chair. "Jesus, just when things are starting to come together, he wants to throw Bernstein in the mix?"

A call comes through on Barrett's phone. He takes it, says a couple of words, and hangs up. "So, how do you guys want to proceed? Spence, what say you?"

"We've just got our foot in the door, Mike," I respond. If we believe what we just heard, there's a hundred pounds of crystal meth sitting in a limo somewhere on the property . . . maybe more. Given the scenario we've created with Charlie, we're going to need some time to get close to that kind of quantity. Duke's no fool. He's not about to trust Charlie like in the old days. He's going to slowly feel him out. If we try to go for all the marbles now and hit the place and come up empty, then all we got is a couple of small quantity buys from Duke and a valuable witness burned to the ground. We need to continue to slowly get Charlie back into the fold and build on the quantity of these buys. As Duke and the others become more relaxed around our witness, we should be able to develop valuable intel on the locations of their labs, ongoing criminal activities, and corroborate prior criminal acts."

Barrett rolls his pencil between his lips, staring blankly at the three of us. "These are my concerns," he says after a prolonged silence. "You've had your guy out there a while now and time is *not* on our side on this project. Every time he goes into that clubhouse or around those guys, it's like waiting for the hammer to fall. Our witness is volatile and unpredictable. One mistake or one slip-up and he's a dead man. He *is* our responsibility. Secondly, making multiple drug buys from the same person has its limits. If the guy's a drug dealer, he's a drug dealer. Increasing the size of the buys when you're dealing in ounce quantities of meth is not going to give us a bigger bang for our buck. We have to be prepared to justify these expenditures of government monies. I know we all want to develop sufficient evidence to prove the Hells Angels are an ongoing criminal enterprise, but right now we're not in a position to spread our witness out among the other gang members. I'm worried it might raise suspicions if Charlie were to solicit other members. I mean, Duke's providing Charlie with the quantities Charlie supposedly needs and can afford right now, and we all know Duke's a greedy man. If he gets wind that Charlie's hitting up some of the other guys, it's not going to fly.

What say you, Detective?"

Frank stiffens in his chair. "I don't disagree with anything you said, Mike, but we're in a high-risk business and we need to push on with what we've started here. I want to go back to Duke for another buy. Let's say a couple of pounds. It'll show that Charlie's building up his client base, increasing capacity. If Duke sees the potential for some real money, he should loosen up—want Charlie closer to him like in the old days. We try to get him talking more about club business, as Spence says. We keep it simple and stick with short-term goals. This is not just about drugs. We've got several unsolved violent crimes on the books that we know the Hells Angels are responsible for. If we can buy enough time on this project with our witness, I'm confident we'll corroborate our suspicions and bolster existing evidence by hearing it straight from the horse's mouth. Duke likes to brag. "

"Third time's a charm," Barrett says, getting to his feet. "See if Blair will go along with it and let me know. Tell him I don't have a problem with the plan."

~ ~ ~ ~

"I'm telling you, man. I got my old crew back up and running. It's just like old times. We can kick some ass out there, Duke."

I'm sitting in the back of the SOG van with Marty and Frank, listening to Charlie on the wire. After an awkward start —Duke telling him to keep his voice down twice—Charlie's talking pretty much normally, albeit in his usual low mumble, feeding us some beautiful audio in the process.

"Third time's the charm," Frank says under his breath.

I nod, but it seems to me that the real charm is Charlie's. The more Duke is exposed to it, the more relaxed he gets, and Charlie's really been working him, feeding his ego. Combined with the possibility of some potentially lucrative business, it's all just too much for Duke. Charlie's a proven commodity and Duke knows it. He's made more money for the club than all the others combined. His distribution network is, or was, huge, and Charlie controlled the business with an iron fist. Now that he's back and sober, everything can go back to the way it was.

"Just tell me what you need," Duke whispers into Charlie's mike. "You know I got no problem with supply."

We're stumbling over each other in the back of the van, fist-pumping and high-fiving, but the celebration is short-lived. Duke abruptly wraps up the meeting and Charlie's on the move.

He's on his way out the front door of the clubhouse when we're all caught off-guard. We stare at each other as he gets drawn aside by a voice we don't recognize.

"Hey, Charlie, get over here . . ."

There's long silence over the wire. Nothing. Just some shuffling and rubbing sounds.

"I hear things are goin' righteous for you out there."

"Yeah, man," Charlie says.

"Look, man, if you need anything, like, you know . . . If you're buyin', I'm sellin'."

"Right on, man," Charlie snorts.

"Just between you and me, okay?"

"Whatever," Charlie says. "You still in Ramona?"

"Ramona?" Frank whispers. "It's Gonzo."

"Still in the same place, man," the voice says. "Same phone number."

Chapter 37

Shorting Dope
Ramona, CA
October 5, 1996

I call Blair and Barrett to fill them in on the latest develop-
ments as soon as I get back to the house. Through the doorway,
I can see Charlie pumping iron in the backyard. He's about as
keyed up as I've ever seen him. Like us, he's finding it hard to
believe that Gonzo would approach him like this.

By the time I hang up, I'm as excited as I've been since
we started this operation. Blair and Barrett give the green
light to move on Gonzo after careful consideration of the fact
that Gonzo solicited Charlie and not vice versa. With Gonzo in
the boat, we're moving in the right direction to prove our conspiracy theories against the Hells Angels.

After trying to get evidence on Duke, Gonzo seems like
a walk in the park. The next day, when Charlie calls him, he
talks openly about drugs. It's so easy it feels like a setup or
trap. Lure Charlie out to his place in Ramona and settle the
score once and for all between them. There's also the possibility that Gonzo's a snitch for another agency. It wouldn't be the
first time snitches have crossed paths. And, of course, we have
to consider Gonzo trying to rip Charlie off.

"Just tell me what ya need, Charlie, and I'll see if I can't
help you out," Gonzo says.

"Half a pound."

"Whoa..."

"That a problem?"

"No ... no ... I just wasn't expectin' it, Charlie. You're
doin' better than I thought, man. It's gonna put a little air in
my fuel line. You know ... supply and demand. But I guess I can
live with it."

"Can you do it or not?"

"I'm sittin' on a couple pounds, but most of it's spoken

for."

"I need a half now."

Gonzo sighs. "Done . . . but I'll need the goin' rate. And you'll have to come out here to pick it up. I don't do deliveries."

"The goin' rate?" Charlie says, raising his voice. "So what are we talkin'?"

"Grand an ounce."

Charlie shakes his head in disgust, but I give him the thumbs-up. We want this deal to happen.

"You're rippin' me, man. That's too fuckin' much."

Gonzo snorts. "That's the fuckin' price, man."

Again, Charlie shakes his head. "Better be good shit, man."

"The best, Charlie. For you, my brother, only the best."

"Okay, brother," Charlie sneers. He pulls the receiver away from his ear and gives it the finger, ceremoniously sending it down the line to Gonzo. "Tuesday. Can I get it on Tuesday?"

"Good enough."

"Say three o'clock?"

"Three's good. See you then."

Charlie hangs up and shows me the edge of his dirty smile. "Only the best," he repeats. "Motherfuckin' bastard."

"You think he's snitchin' for somebody, Charlie? That was too easy."

"Gonzo? Naw, he's just greedy, like all of 'em.

"You ready to take a ride out to Ramona?"

"Let's do it, Spence. Let's take this fucker down."

~~~~

By now, preparing Charlie for a controlled drug buy has become something of a routine, with me searching both the car and Charlie in the presence of one of the other members of the team before sending him on his way. This buy is different for a couple of reasons: first, the remoteness of the location; and second, the nature of Charlie's relationship with the target of the buy.

So we've spent more time than usual prepping Charlie, talking about the importance of staying cool and, above all, of continuing to think about what he's doing moment to moment. We remind him that everything that happens has consequences and will eventually play out in court.

In the garage, I hand Charlie $8,000 stuffed fat into an envelope. "Try not to get mugged."

"Gonzo ain't gonna try nothin' with me," Charlie says with a cold stare. "Not without an army behind him."

"Just do the deal and come on home," I say. "But whatever you do, Charlie, don't forget, as you come into Ramona, pull off to the side of the road and activate the Nagra in your boot. We can't let that thing run from here or we lose an hour of recording time while you're driving up there. So you have to remember. If you forget, we lose our best evidence."

"Jesus, Spence, you've told me a hundred times. I won't forget."

~~~~

At 2:30 we're rolling into the tiny Ramona Airport parking lot to set up. Kinney is at the wheel of the SOG van he considers his own; Marty and I in back, both sweating in the afternoon heat.

The airport is just as it was the day before when we ran a recon for this operation—kind of sleepy and neglected, a few cars coming and going. Our arrival seems to go unnoticed. The rest of our Squad 7 backup crew is spread out around the airport. We're about a mile from Gonzo's house, but it's the closest place where we can stage without drawing attention. Our response time to get to Charlie if he's in trouble is only marginally acceptable.

Chick Reinhardt is again our spotter in the Cessna, and

the plane has followed Charlie from the PB house up through the remote, steep mountainous canyons to Ramona. No sense risking someone tailing Charlie and seeing us along for the ride.

"705 . . . 904, what's your 10-20?"

"We're just coming into Ramona, 705."

"Let me know when he pulls over."

Reinhardt is aware that Charlie has to stop and activate the Nagra.

"904 . . . 705, he's made the turn northbound on Montecito, no stops."

I grit my teeth. "Goddamnit, Charlie," I bark. "I knew it. I *knew* it. He forgot to turn the damn thing on. Son of a bitch."

The silence is deafening until Reinhardt's commanding voice booms over the radio. "Our guy's making an eastbound turn toward the target location. I thought he was supposed to make a stop?"

"Fuck it." I glare at Marty, who's sitting there helplessly turning a few knobs on the amplifier. "I can't believe this shit. I should've never given him that responsibility. Son of a bitch."

"904, all units, our guy just pulled over on the dirt road. He's about a quarter-mile from the target."

"Gonna knock the fuckin' bottom outta this junk heap," Charlie blurts, his voice coming through loud and clear on Marty's amplifier.

"Jesus H. Christ, Charlie." I look at Marty and he's got this big grin on his face.

"Take it easy, Spence," he says. "Everything's going to be fine."

"Fuckin' shocks ain't worth a damn," Charlie groans.

"705 to all units, we've got audio. We're picking up our guy loud and clear. 904, what's the status at our target location?"

"All quiet. I'm counting three cars out front."

"Three?" I say, glancing up at Marty. "Can you confirm three cars, 904?"

"Three cars. I'm looking at a reddish orange Trans Am, a green Mustang, and a black pickup—possibly a Ford. All parked in the driveway."

Marty returns my stare, frowning. "Green Mustang?"

"Scooter?"

Scooter is certainly the only club member with a green Mustang. Metallic green. We've often commented on what a horrible paint job it is.

"What the hell's Scooter doing out there?" I say.

"Comin' up on Gonzo's place," Charlie grumbles. "What the fuck . . . ?"

"904 to all units. Our guy just pulled up at the bottom of the drive."

"What's with all the cars, man?" Charlie asks rhetorically. "Looks like some kinda convention."

I don't like any of this. It smells like a rip-off, Gonzo luring Charlie out here for some sort of a reckoning. But it's too late to try to pull him out. All we can do is sit tight and listen to his deep-drawn breaths. It's sweltering inside the van.

"Okay, I'm goin' in," Charlie reports in a ragged whisper. The car door creaks open and slams shut, then footsteps crunching dirt.

"Charlie!" The first voice booms through the amplifier so loud Marty winces. Then some thumping, shuffling noises . . . like someone just grabbed Charlie, gave him a hug.

"Talk to me, Charlie," I say under my breath. "Give me some names."

"What the fuck, Scooter?"

"Hey, Charlie . . ."

"The fuck you doin' here, man? Where the fuck's Gonzo?"

"It's cool, Charlie," another voice says. "Everything's cool." The voice is familiar, but I can't put a face to it. Definitely not Gonzo. "Scooter's old lady kicked him out. How's it going, man?"

Footsteps, shuffling, back-slapping sounds.

"705 to 904."

"904 . . . go."

"Can you see what's going on?"

"Our guy just went inside the house with two unidentified subjects. One of them may be Bull Palac. I think we've seen this black pickup before."

Down Charlie's wire—more rustling, thumping sounds.

"How you been, man?"

"Good, Jay. Good."

Jay Palac. Bull. Confirmed. Charlie's best pal in the club. I don't know what to make of it.

"Your old lady gave you the boot?" Charlie asks.

"Three weeks ago," Scooter says. "Fuckin' bitch. And she didn't *kick* me out. I walked out on that fuckin' whore."

"She was up here yesterday," says a deeper voice. I recognize this one instantly as Gonzo. "On fire, man . . . lucky Scooter wasn't here. She'd have wasted his skinny ass. Hey, Charlie."

"Gonzo."

"Grab a beer, brother. Sit down."

I close my eyes. I hear echoey sounds, chairs scraping, plates rattling. They're in the kitchen, I'm guessing. For the next few minutes, there's some small talk. Gonzo tells Charlie all about Jacumba—how it got raided, how the feds shut it down. It seems that Gonzo still can't get over it.

"I'm gonna waste that little fuckin' cockroach cook," he hisses. "Weasel musta ratted to the feds. I'll take care of him all right."

I look up at Marty and give him the thumbs-up. Charlie waits for a pause in the conversation.

"So what've you got for me, Gonzo?"

"All business, eh, Charlie? Like always. Okay, man. But before we get into it, I want you to understand that this here's our little deal, okay? Ain't no reason Duke's gotta know about everything, right?"

For a moment, there's silence. I hope it's the sound of

Charlie getting his ideas straight about how to proceed.

"What you tell or don't tell Duke is your own fuckin' business, man."

It goes quiet again, and this time it's a silence I know well, a silence in which merchandise is being brought out for perusal. Someone clears his throat.

"Good shit, brother," Gonzo says. "Uncut. Righteous shit."

The long silence returns. This time I look across at Marty. He frowns, shaking his head.

"There a problem, Charlie?" Gonzo says.

"Looks a little short."

"Short?"

"Short the weight. This ain't no eight fuckin' ounces of crystal meth, man."

"Charlie. I'm tellin' you, man, it's eight ounces."

Again the silence.

I can picture Charlie giving Gonzo his death stare. "It looks short," Charlie says, putting a little steel into it this time.

"Just buy the fucking dope, Charlie," I say softly.

"Charlie . . ." Gonzo comes through in a low growl. However much of an asshole Gonzo may be, he's certainly not a coward, and if a guy's going to push him, he's going to push right back.

I close my eyes again. The last thing we want is a stupid mano-a-mano.

"We agreed to half a pound," Charlie says. "I got eight grand in my pocket lookin' to buy eight ounces."

"I know what we said, Charlie. And I'm tellin' you it's the full weight."

"The full weight . . ."

"Just buy it, Charlie," I whisper, almost pleading now.

"Okay, Gonzo," Charlie snorts. A chair screeches on the hard floor. Sounds like our man pushing away from the table. "I wanna weigh the fucker . . ."

"Come on, Charlie," I mutter. "Let it go. Jesus, it doesn't matter."

"Bring me a scale," Charlie says.

"I don't have a scale, Charlie."

There's a dry little laugh here. A snicker I know well. "You don't have a *scale*?"

A different voice: "Charlie, the weight's good."

"How the fuck would you know, Bull? You weigh it?"

"No, Charlie," Bull says. "But I got a piece of the action. An ounce of it, anyway. Gonzo asked me to kick in on the deal. He was coming up short on product."

"Wait a minute," Charlie says. "You told me on the phone that you were sittin' on a couple pounds."

Another chair scrape over the hard floor.

"That was then, Charlie, this here's now," Gonzo groans. "Shit sells fast. Lotta demand, you know. We knew you wanted it today, so we put the deal together, me an' Bull."

"Come on, Charlie," Bull says. "You know I ain't gonna try and screw you."

Again, a long silence. Something's wrong.

"Buy the fucking shit, Charlie," I say. "For God's sake, quit playing games."

"Friend or no friend, Bull, I weigh the dope or I walk."

"Jesus Christ," Gonzo says. Then . . . "Scooter, get the fuckin' scale."

"You said you didn't have one," Charlie snarls.

"Well, I do, okay? But it's under the fuckin' sink."

"So what, man? Get the fucker out here."

"Lucy's under there," Scooter whines. "I ain't stickin' my hand under there."

"What?"

"A fucking rattlesnake, Charlie."

"So kill the fucker, man."

"It's *my* snake. I keep it for the cops. 'Specially for the feds. Anybody comes snoopin' around."

"You keep it under the sink?"

"She likes it under there, man. Eats crickets and roaches and shit."

"You're fuckin' crazy, man," Charlie sneers. There's less tension in his voice and I can hear him lightening up.

I sit back against the side of the van. It's all going to be okay. There's some banging around in the kitchen. Scooter complaining.

"Here."

"You see her under there?"

"She's in there, man. Looks asleep."

"Okay," Charlie says. "Let's have a look at this fucker. Weigh it."

There's another long silence. Familiar silence. Merchandise being examined and weighed.

"Satisfied now?" Gonzo says.

A chair pushes back hard. Someone just stood up. Charlie growls something completely incoherent.

"What?" Gonzo says.

"It's fucking *short*, man," he yells. "Just like I said . . . *It's fuckin' short!*"

"Easy, Charlie, for chrissake."

"You fuckin' tried to short *me*, man?"

Another chair screeches back, falls over.

"Jesus Christ, Charlie, put the fuckin' knife down, man," Bull yells.

"Cool down," Scooter says.

"Fuck you, Scooter!"

"Charlie!"

"I got a stash," Scooter says. "Hold on . . . in my bag in the bedroom. How much is missin'?"

"Charlie?"

"You fuckers' tryin' to rip me off, man."

"How much is missin'? I'll make it right, man. Just put the fuckin' knife down."

"A *knife*? Jesus," I shout.

"A quarter-ounce."

"A quarter-ounce? Is that all? We're arguin' over a quarter fuckin' ounce? I can make up the difference, man. It's cool."

"The *fuck* it's cool."

Another long silence and I'm blinking the sweat out of my eyes and praying that Charlie has enough sense to let this go. What the hell's he doing with a knife? Where the hell did *that* come from? God Almighty!

After a minute, Scooter comes back gasping. There's more rustling.

"There. My quarter makes it eight. Are we good now?"

"Charlie," Bull says softly, "Come on, man, now put the knife down. Gonzo wasn't tryin' to rip you off, man."

Silence.

"Come on," Bull says. "We're brothers. You know. Love and respect, man. Love and respect."

Charlie mumbles something inaudible, then chairs screech again and we hear Charlie start counting bills. Thinking. He's back on track. Doing the job he was sent here to do. "One hundred, two hundred . . ."

I nod, relaxing a little. "Attaboy, Charlie."

"Sorry 'bout that, Charlie. . . . You know . . . the weight."

The deal is done. More rustling sounds. Eight grand in marked bills just changed hands.

~ ~ ~ ~

We're ecstatic inside the SOG van—euphoric to have nailed three Hells Angels in one controlled drug buy. Unrehearsed as it was, Charlie's little outburst over the weight turned out to be the perfect device to get everyone present to open up, although the knife incident is very troubling. Gonzo, Scooter, and Bull have all now said more than enough on tape for us to get convictions in court on the sale *and* conspiracy. We also place Gonzo at the scene of the Jacumba lab, or I should say he put himself there.

I'm high-fiving Marty in the back of the van as Kinney

backs out of our slot when we start to hear Charlie over the wire, raving, screaming into the mike about his brothers trying to screw him over. He sounds furious to a level I've never heard before.

"Jesus," Marty says.

Reinhardt calls in from the plane: "904 to all units. Our guy's heading south on Montecito at a serious rate of speed."

A sinking sensation comes over me. Charlie's lost it.

"Son of a bitch," I say, grabbing hold of the radio mike: "904, has he got a tail?"

"Not as far as I can see, but I can't see much with all the dust he's kicking up."

"Let me know when he gets to the main highway."

By the time we get Charlie in our sights on the road out of Ramona, he's calmed down some and slowed down considerably, his furious tirade reduced to the occasional expletive. We make a slow pass in the van and see Charlie gripping the wheel. The sweat streaming from his face is the only outward sign of the recent meltdown. I wait for him to look across as I stick two thumbs up against a window.

~ ~ ~ ~

Back at the PB house, we gather around him in the garage, immediately shut off the Nagra, and start the process of searching the car. Charlie's still agitated. Jaws gnashing and fists pumping, he angrily tosses his cigarette butt to the floor and crushes it under his cowboy boot.

"Way to go, Charlie," I say softly. "You did great. *Better* than great."

He shrugs, hands me the baggie.

"You hear Gonzo try to fuck me over, man?"

"Don't worry about it, Charlie. You nailed the son of a bitch real good. But what's with the knife for chrissakes? Where did *that* come from?"

He shrugs and dismisses the question with a wave of his

hand. "It was lyin' there on the kitchen table, man. Just pissed me off, I guess. I sorta lost it for a minute . . . thinkin' about Stacey . . . what that fucker did to her. But I got it right, man."

I take a sample of powder from the bag and field test it, eying Charlie as he continues to brood.

"Motherfucker, man. He beats up my old lady, tries to kill me, steals my shit, then shorts the weight on the dope he's already stiffin' me for. Disrespectin' me, man. If you guys hadn't been listenin', I'd a killed the motherfucker right there."

I ponder the significance of what he just said. No small thing.

"We get three Hells Angels in one meeting on conspiracy, possession, and sale of narcotics," Marty interrupts, trying to get back on track. "Gonzo, Scooter, and Bull. It's truly outstanding, Charlie."

At the mention of Bull's name, all the rage seems to go out of Charlie. He looks down at the floor, spits, then draws a shaky hand across his face. "Tired, man."

"You should be tired, Charlie, after a day like this."

"Fuckin' tired," he says again. Then he lifts his arms limply, waiting for me to search him per our procedure.

"You did good, Charlie," I say.

I expect at least a nod, but he just stands there like a statue. There's something in his eyes. A deadness I haven't seen before.

Chapter 38

FotoMat
San Diego, CA
October 5, 1996

Frank comes by the house in the early evening. He walks into the kitchen, where I'm working on the report of today's activities. He's been in court testifying all day on another case, which is why he couldn't make it up to Ramona. It takes a few minutes to fill him in on the essentials of what went down at Gonzo's place.

"We're going to have to remember to warn whoever searches the house about that snake," I say, but I can see Frank's no longer listening. He's leaning against the sink, a disconsolate expression on his face.

"What's wrong?"

"Where is he?"

"Charlie? In his room, I think. He's wiped out."

Frank nods, pulls out his cigarettes.

"What?" I say.

"It's the first time I've come here and he's not come out to say hi."

"Like I said, he's tired."

Frank nods, puts a flame to the tip of his cigarette, blows smoke at the ceiling lamp. "What'd he say about Jay?"

I put down my pen, shrug. "It's not like we planned on Bull being there, Frank."

"I know that, Nick. But I'm betting Charlie was pretty upset."

There's no denying this. I lean forward, elbows on the table, massaging my tired eyes. "Yeah. I don't think it really hit him until we got back here."

"Burning his buddy like that," Frank says in a low rumble. "Hard for anybody, but especially Charlie." He leans forward under the light, which reflects smeary marks in his wire-frame glasses. "And the knife thing. What the hell was he . . ."

We both become aware of Charlie at the same time. He's standing there in the doorway, can't have been there for more than a couple of seconds, but maybe enough to catch the tail end of our conversation. There's a despondent look on his gaunt face. Frank goes over and shakes his hand.

"Way to go, Charlie," he says softly. "Nick told me all about it. Sorry I wasn't there to see it go down."

Charlie nods, looks down at the floor. "I need to get some air," he says. "Sick of being cooped up in this place."

"Want me to come with you?" Frank says, glancing over at me. "Take a stroll around the block?"

Charlie shakes his head, then looks at the papers spread out in front of me on the table. "No, I'm good," he says. "I just need to get some air is all."

~ ~ ~ ~

I drive home that night, unable to shake off a vague feeling of anxiety. I know I should be ready to pop the champagne, but Charlie's reaction to the day's events, particularly to Bull's involvement, and the knife incident, have got me worrying about all the things that can now go wrong from here on in.

What lies ahead for us was always going to be hard to negotiate, whatever the circumstances. Preparing Charlie for trial, getting him to be the kind of rock-solid witness we need —those things were never going to be easy. But with Jay Palac, one of his best friends, maybe the best friend he's ever had apart from his own brother being one of the defendants on the stand, there's no telling how Charlie will now react. And regardless of his explanation for grabbing the knife off the kitchen table, any defense attorney will jump at the chance to shred the credibility of our witness and portray him as a crazed, out-of-control, knife-wielding maniac.

I'm restless lying in bed listening to the sound of the waves cresting on the sandy shoreline outside my bedroom window. The sounds, smells, and sight of the Pacific Ocean are usually my antidote to nervous tension and stress. I finally manage to drift off to the rhythmic drone of the distant fog-horn out on the jetty at South Mission Beach. The jangling phone on the nightstand rattles me awake.

"Can you get over to Garnet and Ingraham in PB?" Frank asks, his voice shaky.

"What's up?"

"It's a little strip mall about a half-mile from the house. Know the place I'm talking about?"

"Yeah. What's the problem?"

"Charlie did something stupid."

~ ~ ~ ~

It's raining, and a heavy fog shrouds the empty parking lot when I pull in. There's an SDPD cruiser parked over by a Dumpster at the back of one of the stores, its red lights turning silently in the mist. I see Frank standing with a couple of uniformed patrolmen, smoking a cigarette, deep in conversation.

I get out of the car, feeling numb, feeling sick, trying not to think about what all this might mean. The dome light is on inside the police cruiser, and I can see someone in the back, know it has to be Charlie, but nothing prepares me for the jolt of seeing him scrunched down in the backseat with his hands cuffed behind his back. There's this pitiful look on his face—a look of despair and shame as he glances up to meet my disbelieving gaze through the rain-spattered window. There's some swelling and discoloration on his face. His shirt is torn open at the neck. I walk past him without saying a word.

"Nick..."

I look up and see Frank beckoning me over to join him and the other cops. Frank does the introductions, letting the two officers know what a solid guy I am, FBI or not. Like Charlie, the officers are showing signs of a recent scuffle. The smaller of the two, an officer by the name of Lennox, sports a nasty split in his bottom lip—a cut he keeps dabbing with the back of his hand.

"Charlie broke into the old FotoMat kiosk out front," Frank says.

"He did *what*?"

"Officer Lennox? Maybe you can tell Special Agent Spence exactly what happened."

Lennox looks at the blood on the back of his hand, and I can see how pissed he is.

"We're rolling through the intersection, and we see this guy trying to break into the old FotoMat," he says, turning to point at the kiosk out in the center of the parking lot. "Place has been closed down for a few years but never changed the name. Used to be a drive-thru deal. People drop off film and then pick up the pictures a day later. Twenty four hour processing. They went out of business. Now some guy sells cigarettes and who knows what else out of the tiny place. Too lazy to change the signage and fix the place up, I guess. Anyway, it's got one of those trays that come out when you press a button, like a night deposit at a bank."

"Charlie's stealing cigarettes?" I say, still not getting it.

"Anybodys guess," Lennox says. "Maybe he thought they left deposits inside the kiosk overnight."

Officer Lennox holds up a screwdriver. "He was using this to pry open the drop drawer." He glances across at the other officer, who so far has said nothing. "Anyway, when we roll up, he turns on us. I mean, the guy goes fucking ape-shit and he's holding up this screwdriver like it was a knife."

I let out a groan, look down at the cracked asphalt covered with slick, oily water. Charlie breaking into this little shit hole and then assaulting a couple of officers is all discoverable before any trial, and will inevitably emerge in court as the defense team seeks to discredit Charlie Slade as a witness. Charlie can no longer be sold as a man who's seen the error of his ways. I can hear the defense attorneys now: "So, Agent Spence, how many other crimes did your informant commit when you were not around?"

We're fucked six ways to Sunday.

"He was like a wild animal," Lennox says. "I mean, we had our guns drawn, we're ordering him down on the ground, but he keeps on coming. In the end, we had to fight him. It was like wrestling a fucking alligator or something. Finally, I get the cuffs on the son of a bitch and he starts talking about Detective Conroy. Told us to call you. Which is what we did."

Frank gives me an empty look. I can see he shares my assessment of the mess we're in here. The rain stands in beads on his glasses. Images begin to flash through my mind of us entering the room and Charlie strapped to the bed, Charlie clocking Frank in the room at the Paloma Inn, us talking with Charlie late into the night, bonding like a bunch of regular guys. I can't believe it all ends here in the rain in this dumpy strip mall.

"Nick?"

Frank's voice brings me back into the moment.

It comes to me that he's called me here for a purpose, not just to hear what a gigantic fuck-up Charlie is capable of being.

"These officers want to file charges against Charlie for attempted burglary and assault on a police officer."

I clear my throat, nod. "Understandably," I say. "You officers have every right to be angry. It's indefensible what he did."

"Anger doesn't come into it," Lennox says stiffly. "Guy needs to be locked up."

"You're right," Frank says. "In any other situation, I'd agree with you one hundred percent. But in this case . . . the thing is . . . and I say this confidentially, Mr. Slade is a witness in a case that Agent Spence and I have been working on for the past several months. A case we're hoping will result in shutting down a major methamphetamine organization." Frank waits a moment for all this to sink in, then takes a slow pull on his cigarette. "So I would consider it a personal favor if you officers would release Mr. Slade to our custody."

"As would the Bureau," I say, kind of dumbfounded by Frank's approach. "This is a significant long-term investigation that we're ready to take down in the next couple of weeks. And Mr. Slade—Charlie—despite his behavior tonight, has played a key role in the investigation, done everything we've asked him to, and put his life on the line for us."

The officers look at each other, then look at Frank. This is what it all comes down to. Frank being Frank, as Pete Blair would say. Frank Conroy, the living legend in the SDPD, known and respected by all.

"We're going to have to write this up, pass it on to the sergeant," Lennox says. "There's damage to property. Owner's going to want to know what happened. That means follow-up investigation, too."

"I understand all that," Frank says. "Do the reports and submit them as you normally would, and include in your report that you turned over custody of Mr. Slade to me. I will contact your sergeant and give him the heads-up and take responsibility for this. We need a little more time to take this case down. He will *not* be out of our custody and control again, and we'll leave it up to the DA to decide whether to file on Mr. Slade. We'll ensure he appears in court, if necessary."

Lennox dabs at the cut in his lip again, then offers a reluctant nod. "He's all yours."

~~~~

None of us says a word until we're on the way back to the PB house in my Bucar. I realize it's probably better to wait until we're inside the house before getting into it, but I just can't contain myself.

"What the fuck, Charlie? What were you thinking?"

He's slumped over in the backseat, staring out at the rain, a posture adopted by just about every criminal I've ever arrested.

"Do you even realize what this means for the case? I

mean—this is months and months of work, Charlie."

"I know about the work, Nick. I been working, too, re-member?"

"So how the hell can you..."

Frank, sitting next to me in the passenger seat, puts a hand on my arm. He wants me to take a breath, to hold my tongue. We drive the rest of the way in complete silence.

Back at the house, Charlie cleans up in the bathroom—washes his face and hands, changes into a clean T-shirt, and comes out in his underwear. Under the light in the living room, I can see how beat up he is, his mouth puffy and red, his left eye beginning to close, and both legs have been pummeled blue by the officers' nightsticks. He's limping noticeably and looks so miserable I start to feel sorry for him, as stupid as he is.

"Charlie," Frank says. "It's okay. We're okay. Those cops, they're gonna file their report. They have to just cover their asses, but not every report ends in charges being filed by the DA."

"But it's still going to come out in the trial," I say.

"Why?" Charlie says in a barely audible murmur. "I mean, can't you guys fix it? Get other guys to sit on it?"

"No, Charlie," Frank says. "And we wouldn't even if we could. The defense has a right to question prior to trial. It's called 'discovery.' One of the questions they're gonna ask is whether or not you've committed any crimes while under our control and supervision."

"But I haven't," Charlie says. "I mean, I was tryin' to break in, but I didn't actually steal anything."

I look at Frank in disbelief, force myself to shut my trap.

"Charlie," Frank says softly. "Attempted burglary is a crime. Resisting arrest is a crime. Assaulting a police officer is a crime."

Charlie looks down at his hands, a new weight seeming to settle on his shoulders. "I fucked up," he says softly.

"You sure did, partner," Frank says. "But we're still in

good shape. The evidence you've helped us accumulate is devastating. The defense can question your integrity, but they can't make the tapes go away. But we've got to know where your head's at on this," Frank says.

Charlie slumps down on the couch, and after a moment or two, Frank sits next to him. I take a seat in the old leather recliner facing Charlie.

"I fucked up," Charlie repeats, rubbing at his jaw.

Frank turns toward him on the couch. "Damn straight. But that's not the important thing. The thing we have to understand is *why*, Charlie. What were you thinking?"

"I don't know ... I just ... I get to a point where ..."

He leaves the phrase unfinished, but both Frank and I know what it is he's trying to say. He gets to a point where getting high looks like the best and only option, either to enhance a state of euphoria or to soothe and salve a sense of sadness and loneliness.

"What did you need the money for, Charlie?"

Charlie tries to smile and then shrugs, turns over his left arm. In a hopeless gesture of resignation, he slaps the thick vein running up inside his elbow.

"You were going to get high?" Frank says softly.

"Yeah," Charlie says, looking up at the ceiling. "I mean, no. But that was why I was trying to break into that thing. I wanted to get some money and score some dope, but ... but if I woulda got some, I wouldn't have ... I wasn't going to shoot up, Frank. Honest."

Charlie stares sharply over at me—a naked, vulnerable look, challenging me to question his words. I look over at Frank, who's sitting there, shaking his head. For a second, I think he's going to pursue the point, but when he opens his mouth to speak, what comes out stuns Charlie and me both.

"That's good, Charlie," he says, "because I don't want you ending up like Stacey."

I blink through a moment of confusion. When I look over at Charlie, I see he's doing the same.

"What do you mean, Frank?" he asks.

Frank sighs, rises off the couch, and turns to look him in the eye, man to man. "Charlie, I got another hit on my BOLO on Stacey last week from the PD."

Charlie nods, his face lined with worry. "You mean you kept the lookout for her even after Nick found her?"

"Yeah, I did," Frank says, and even I'm surprised to hear it. "Because I wanted to make sure she was staying out of trouble."

Charlie's eyes squint nearly shut. "What happened, Frank?"

"They found her in a junk house," Frank says.

"A shootin' gallery?" Charlie asks breathlessly.

Frank nods. "Charlie, she's in bad shape. She's in the hospital, barely hanging on."

Charlie's head drops into his hands. He goes stiff, his breathing slow.

"That's why you gotta stay clean, Charlie," Frank says. "You go back now and . . ."

"It's like I told you guys before," Charlie interrupts, looking up at both of us. "I might be a fuck-up, but I ain't dyin' no fifty-year-old junkie with a needle jammed in my arm."

We all stew in the words for a minute, trying to come to terms with all that's happened and all that might.

Frank folds his arms against his chest and heaves a big sigh. "Charlie, for what it's worth, I believe you. And I know it's a battle you fight every day. And as bad as this was tonight, it was just a stumble. And we all stumble. The important thing is whether you get up afterwards."

I watch Frank talk and I wonder why he never told me about Stacey. Maybe he thought it wasn't important to the case. Until now, anyway . . .

"Now I know you're gonna pick yourself up, Charlie," Frank says. "Because you're a fighter and that's what fighters do." Frank sits back down and the three of us sit in silence, as we've done so many times before. After several minutes, Charlie gathers himself up and stiffens on the edge of the old couch, and I see a sudden transformation—a kind of resurrection before my own eyes. Gone is the pathetic look of self-pity and shame. His eyes brighten with some restored hope, and his shoulders rise and he looks like the old Charlie again. There's a tear in his eye and I suspect it's for Stacey. It's for Stacey or it's for himself—but either way—Charlie's found his resolve again. He's found his reason to keep going. Frank should have been a preacher.

Chapter 39

Up to Speed
San Diego, CA
October 25, 1996

Despite Charlie's resolve, we know our train is starting to roll backward on us and we need to come up with an end game. The fragility and unpredictability of our witness is on everyone's mind. Barrett is anxious to shut the operation down and deal with the damaged goods as best he can, and any thought of continuing the project with Charlie leading the way are out the window as far as he's concerned.

I'm sorry for Charlie. In his mind, he hasn't done anything wrong... at least *really* wrong. Trying to explain to him his credibility issues is like scolding a dog and putting him out on a cold winter's night. Instead, we focus on his positive contributions while we set a plan in motion to bring the case down. We've agreed to attempt to set up a buy-bust scenario with Duke. We send Charlie back into the clubhouse to negotiate a large quantity purchase of meth, something that will really get Duke's attention without arousing suspicion. When Duke makes the delivery, and the money and drugs change hands, we take him and the rest of the operation down simultaneously.

~ ~ ~ ~

The next few weeks are a blur. It's not just a question of getting together all the paperwork, filing our complaints, getting our warrants signed, and deciding on a strategy for the bust; there's also the matter of the forfeitures and seizures we plan to make. If we're going to be ripping assets out of Duke's greedy hands, everything we do needs to be unassailable from a legal point of view. To make sure this is the case, we call in Special Agent Joe Bernstein.

Known affectionately as Joe the Jew, he's a fast-talking,

aggressive young agent from Philadelphia, a lawyer by train-ing and an expert in all federal laws pertaining to asset forfeit-ure and seizure of "ill-gotten gains." As detail-oriented as he is, Joe loves to play the street cop. So it was a big thrill for him when we first brought him over to the Pacific Beach house to meet Charlie.

They hit it off immediately. Charlie, always quick at reading people, picked up on Joe's peculiar mix of aggression and vulnerability. They got along so well, in fact, that after a couple of days we decided to bring Joe in on babysitting du-ties. Since the FotoMat incident, we're not about to let him out of our sight. There's not much we can do with Charlie now except keep him positive and focused on reaching the finish line. With Paul and Joe carrying most of the load—keeping Charlie not only entertained but motivated for our last major move on the club—we've got to borrow some time now to get everything in order.

~~~~

Joe is sitting beside me as I stare out over a room full of agents and police officers assembled to hear my briefing about the overall raid plans and how the buy-bust at the clubhouse is going to go down.

"There will be raid teams for each location where ar-rests and searches are to be carried out," I explain. "That's twelve locations including the clubhouse and Tinks Bar on El Cajon Boulevard."

The faces turn in my direction, then go back to the lu-minous rectangle made by the overhead projector as I draw a circle around the diagram of the clubhouse. We're up on the sixth floor of the federal building, and the large combined Squad 7 and Squad 8 office space is uncomfortably hot with all the crammed bodies. We've removed all the partitions that separate each agent's "bullpen" space so we can accommodate everyone. The projector adds to the heat in the room and gives off a smell of burnt plastic.

"Each team has a designated team leader who will maintain radio contact with the command post at all times," I say. Then I nod at my supervisor. "The command post will be here in Supervisor Blair's office.

"We're deploying seven officers and agents for each location—except for the clubhouse—where we're going to need additional manpower to accommodate the seizures of what we expect to be twenty vehicles."

A hand goes up beside me. Joe Bernstein. I stifle a sigh, tilt my head in his direction.

"What is it, Joe?"

"Vehicles are to be moved to the San Diego PD impound lot."

"Just in case any of you were thinking of taking a limo home," Frank adds.

He's standing on the other side of the projector, sweating into his tweed sport jacket. His joke gets a chuckle, but barely. There's a serious energy in the room, an intensity that reflects the scope of the job at hand. As experienced as all these people are, it's not every day they get assigned to take down the Hells Angels.

"I think Joe's point is that we don't want anyone parking seized vehicles here at the federal building," I say. "Parking space is jammed as it is."

I hold up a sample file. "You've all got search warrant packets. They contain a detailed description and photographs of the locations to be searched. There's also an inventory of what items are to be legally seized at each location including any contraband."

"Drugs, weapons, stolen property—anything that's illegal to possess under the law . . . take it," Frank adds.

"Anybody interferes with the execution of these warrants, we want them removed or detained until you have completed your searches," I continue. "Any questions come up, call the command post. Assistant U.S. Attorney Barrett will be here to field such questions. Rule of thumb: When in doubt, call it in. All subjects should be considered armed and dangerous. You can expect them to be carrying guns, knives, ball-peen hammers, screwdrivers, you name it. Be sure you do thorough body searches and don't rely on a casual pat-down when you hook 'em up."

Another hand goes up—a burly deputy by the name of Tomlin from the sheriff's department.

"I heard Sledge is back on the street?"

"He is," Frank says. "I ran into him yesterday at the parole office."

I glance across at Frank. It's the first I've heard about it.

"What'd you say to him?" Tomlin asks, smirking, looking around, obviously familiar enough with Frank's reputation to expect some sort of story.

"I told him I was looking forward to seeing him back on the street again."

Tomlin smiles sarcastically. "And what'd he say?"

"Something about sticking my badge where the sun doesn't shine," Frank says, offering a half-smile.

This gets a big laugh.

I allow the chuckling to subside before going on. "When you're searching these premises, you also need to be alert for booby traps. Example: Gonzo is known to keep a rattlesnake under the sink in his Ramona place."

"Name's Lucy," Frank says.

"Lucy's supposed to be Gonzo's surprise for us. Make no mistake, these guys play for keeps and these are all very dangerous search sites."

Another hand goes up. Mike Dove, Squad 7. "I'm team leader on the Ramona search. I don't see any photograph of the house."

"You sure about that, Mike?"

I watch him sort through his packet, then shake his head. There's been such a mountain of paper, the photograph has slipped through the cracks.

"Okay, Mike," I say. "I'll get back to you on that."

"Be careful up there, Mike," Frank says. "Snakes aside, Gonzo also likes to put razor blades in places an officer might want to stick his fingers. These guys like to booby-trap their places just for these kinds of situations."

I nod pensively. "We don't have any intelligence that indicates explosives or bombing materials in any of these locations, but these guys have built pipe bombs before and are no strangers to explosives. Be careful and look at everything before you touch it. If something doesn't look right, leave it alone and we'll address it with the proper personnel. Just call it into the command post."

A voice from the back of the room shouts. "When do we go?"

"This week, most likely," I say. "You're all on standby with your team leaders until we set up the buy-bust. Once the meeting is set, we'll notify the team leaders of the day and time of the meeting and you'll all report to your prearranged staging location near your targets. Everyone wears a ballistic vest and their raid jackets from their respective agencies." I stand away from the harsh lamp of the projector, wait for my eyes to adjust to the light in the room. "Any questions?"

The room is silent.

As everyone starts to file out, I catch a glimpse of Joe the Jew glad-handing and working the room like a politician on election eve.

Chapter 40

Canyon Chaos
Ramona, CA
October 29, 1996

Mike Dove doesn't have a photo of Gonzo's house because I don't have a photo of Gonzo's house. It's a little thing, given all the material we've had to bring together over the past weeks, but it's irritating as hell. I'm starting to regret all the midlevel drug buys we did to prepare Charlie for the big show. These arrests and searches are also part of the overall raid plan.

"Come on, Spence. You've got the address and a description of the place. We don't *need* a photo for the warrant."

I look up from the scattered photographs on the kitchen table and meet Frank's steady gaze. "It's FBI procedure," I say. "Each team leader has a photograph of the premises—an address, a description, *and* a *photograph*. It's a way of avoiding foul-ups. Especially out there in the country. We don't want anyone going to the wrong house."

Frank takes a tight pull on his Marlboro. "Jesus, Spence. We can't hold everything up because of a photograph. I mean, we're ready to go. Charlie's ready to go."

"I'll go up there this afternoon. I'll get Kinney at SOG and we'll take his surveillance van. He can shoot the photo while I drive by. Out and back in two hours, max."

~~~~

Charlie makes the call to Duke just after four o'clock Monday afternoon. Frank, Marty, and I are sitting around him at the kitchen table. It's the first time Charlie's had to do anything since the FotoMat disaster, and I can see that's given him a new edge, a new determination to do the right thing.

Duke, picking up on the third ring, is in his usual cautious mode. Charlie stumbles and stammers a little, forgetting his script, and is reduced to saying that something "really important" has come up.

"Yeah...?" Duke says. "Important how?"

Charlie frowns, struggling for focus. "I think it's gonna be big for both of us, man. That's all I'm gonna say."

"Well, maybe you should come on by," Duke says.

"How 'bout tomorrow morning?"

"Sure. Make it early, though. Ten o'clock. I got a gig after that."

"Ten it is," Charlie says, and he hangs up.

I stand up, pulling on my Oakland Raiders cap. "I'll see you guys later."

Hank Kinney's parked in the alleyway at the back of the house in his brown SOG van. He puts out his cigarette when I climb into the cab, and within minutes, we're on Interstate 8 heading east, Kinney excitedly describing his genius as a photographer.

"That's why I call it the Brown Submarine," he says in his thick West Texas drawl.

Everything on Kinney's face is pointy, elf-like. Nose. Chin. Ears. He's slim and wiry. His brownish-gray, bushy mustache is discolored and yellowing from years of filtering smoke from his cigarettes. And his thin face is Texas-weathered beneath a receding hairline.

"What?"

"The van. You never heard that?"

"Probably," I say, shaking my head, struggling against a yawn. "Because of the periscope? That's why you call it the submarine. That's what I heard."

Kinney looks across at me, grinning. "Jesus, Nick. You look like shit."

I have to laugh at this. Truth is, I haven't had a decent night's sleep in over a month. "Tell me about the camera," I say, initiating what I know will be a one-sided conversation.

"Well, like I say, it's on a little periscope and the camera's attached to the periscope, and when the periscope's raised, there's this little hatch that just barely comes up and opens through the air vent on top. Then it's click-click-click and you can get all the pictures you want—360 degrees."

"You got a big lens on it?"

"Telephoto, up to 800mm. No problem, Spence, we're gonna get great pictures. I got it handled—everything we need right here at our fingertips."

I have to say, his enthusiasm is contagious and refreshing. Kinney's always in such a positive mood.

We wind our way up the eighteen miles of deep canyons and curving roads that snake around the San Vicente Reservoir, not talking much, mainly because I can barely stay awake. Then the town of Ramona comes into view, and we turn north onto Montecito and east again onto the dirt road that leads up to the house. As with Charlie's drive, I'm painfully conscious of the amount of dust we're kicking up.

"Wildcat Gulch . . . ," Kinney says with a chuckle. "I bet they picked this place just because of the badass name. What do you think, Nick?"

"Maybe," I say absently, panning the horizon for a landmark. "Okay, we're nearly there. Pull over here."

We come to halt in a dip in the road. Kinney climbs through the heavy curtain behind us into the back of the van while I clamber across the console and get behind the wheel.

"So it's a dead-end road," I say. "I'm going to drive past Gonzo's house to the next house a little farther down. There's a driveway where I'll pull in. That's where you take the pictures. Okay?"

"Let's do it."

I put the van into drive and head off along the road, taking it a lot slower than Charlie did.

"Shit . . ."

I can't believe it. I see Scooter first, then Gonzo. They're both bent over, working on a bike in the scrubby frontyard. There's two other biker types I don't recognize. All four look up as we go past. "Shit, shit, shit. . . . Goddamn Murphy's Law."

"What's the problem?" Kinney says.

We're past the house in a matter of moments, jolting along the dusty road.

"They're out front. Four of them. It's okay. We're good." We come up on the dead-end and I see the driveway. "Hang on tight. I'm pulling up the driveway. You ready?"

"Good to go."

I steer into the driveway and put on the brake. I can hear Kinney clicking away with his camera. I crane my neck, trying to see Scooter and the others back up the road.

"I got it, Nick. Let's go."

"Hold on tight."

I slam into reverse and roll down the driveway, then make the awkward turn back onto the road. I've driven about two hundred feet when I see Scooter. He's standing in the middle of the road waving his arms. He looks like Charles Manson directing traffic.

"Keep going," Kinney says, peering through the curtain, gripping the seat behind me.

I pull down my cap and the van's visor, trying to shield as much of my face as I can. I don't put my foot down, but I don't slow up, either. Kinney ducks back behind the curtain. Scooter stands his ground, waving his hands and giving me his mad-dog stare, until he sees I'm not going to stop. As I brush by, missing him by inches, he leaps into the muddy ditch.

"Keep going," Kinney says.

"They're going to come after us," I say through my teeth. "They know we're cops. Cops drive vans."

"Just keep movin', Spence."

I'm blinking sweat out of my eyes, gripping the wheel firmly with both hands. The washboard surface of the dirt road causes the van to shimmy and fishtail back and forth as I accelerate. We're about a quarter-mile from the blacktop of Highway 67 when I see a big cloud of dust billowing up behind us from a distance. "They're coming, Kinney."

As soon as my tires hit pavement, I gun the engine and we go speeding off south in the direction of the reservoir. A mile out of Ramona, I hit the first curve a little too fast and the van feels like it wants to roll . . . feels top heavy. I wrestle it down, bracing to stay on the right side of the line as I keep checking my mirror. I'm pushing seventy, trying to get as much distance between us and whoever's coming, before we hit the steep canyons. Once we get there, we'll be trapped on both sides.

Kinney gets back into the front seat, clips himself in. "We're good, Spence," he says, looking back over his shoulder. "We're fine."

"Bullshit," I bark. "We've got eighteen miles of steep canyons and bad road before we're back in civilization."

I've got the pedal jammed to the floor, letting off only as we come into the long S curves. The steeper, sharper curves ahead will slow us down.

Just as I'm thinking I've put some distance between us and our pursuers, I glance at the mirror, see a flash of metallic green. Scooter's green Mustang is planted four-square in the middle of the road, coming like an express train. Behind him, I can see an old, reddish orange Trans AM.

I'm drenched in sweat now. "Was there an orange Trans Am parked at Gonzo's?"

"Sure was," Kinney says ominously.

"Then we probably got four guys after us."

It takes only a couple of seconds for them to get right up behind us, Scooter pushing up to within a couple of feet. I yank around a curve, feeling the wheels on the right side rise off the road before squealing back down on the asphalt.

"Don't worry about those fuckers!" Kinney yells. "Just keep this rig on the road."

I come into a short stretch of straight highway, and Scooter opens up the V8, trying to pass me on the left. I swerve across the center line causing him to jerk the Mustang to the left. He clips the guard rail, and the Mustang shimmies and then straighten up. He downshifts the big engine and I can hear the throaty mufflers backfire as he eases back in behind me.

And then the crunch. A jolt from the rear end. I can't believe this shit.

I lose control for a second, our tires screeching, the van swerving back and forth over the center line. I look back into the side mirror just in time to see Scooter reel up to strike us again.

Wham!

The van lurches with the impact.

"Motherfucker!" Kinney yells. "You motherfucker," he hollers looking in his side mirror. Now he's pissed. Somebody's fucking with his baby.

"Here they come again!"

Wham!

I grip the steering wheel as hard as I can as we lunge into another curve. Our back end fishtails. I steer into the swerve, straighten us out.

"Don't you SOG guys keep shotguns in your vehicles?" I shout.

"Roger that, Nick."

"Well, get the goddamn thing. *Now!*"

Kinney unclips his belt and stumbles into the back.

Scooter makes a surge, trying to get past me. Again I block the way, edging out to my left and straddling the center line. This is bullshit. The steep downgrade, these hairpin curves, and the seemingly bottomless canyons on both sides. We're trapped. And they're playing us like a pinball.

"Come on, Hank!" I yell. "Hurry."

Kinney climbs back in next to me, a Remington 870 pump action with a modified fourteen-inch barrel cradled in his hands.

Wham!

Scooter blasts into our rear bumper again, then makes another big run to pass us, coming up alongside on my left. For a second, I think he's going to make it past so he can pin us between himself and the Trans-Am. But suddenly he jerks his wheel to the right and slams the Mustang against the side of the van. *Whap!* The van rocks violently. The steep canyon looms only a few feet off our right side as I get a stranglehold on the wheel struggling to keep us from launching off the cliff. My heart is thundering as I glance down into the abyss. A car flashes into view. A pickup truck, bearing down on Scooter head-on. Scooter slams his breaks and jerks back at the last second, letting the truck pass by, horn blaring.

I regain control and manage to ease back onto the asphalt without over-correcting.

"Fuck these assholes, Kinney," I bark. "They're not just toying with us, they're trying to *kill* us, run us off the road, make it look like an accident."

Kinney feeds the last of four slug rounds into the magazine of the 870. I reach for the radio.

"705 to Control."

"Go ahead, 705."

I recognize the dispatcher's voice. It's Teddy Rendell, an extremely talented and sharp young clerical employee. I glance at the side mirror. Scooter has fallen back apparently recovering from his near head-on collision.

"705 and 914 are 11-99, repeat 11-99. We are southbound on California Highway 67, about ten miles south of Ramona, heading toward Lakeside. We're in a dark brown Dodge van, California license . . ."

I look at Hank for help, and without skipping a beat, he barks out the license number as I hold the mike toward him.

"Six Romeo, Alpha, Juliet, 485."

"Control to 705—I copy."

"Contact the CHP for assistance. Code 3. We've got a green Mustang and a red, no, an orange Trans Am trying to run us off the road."

"Copy, 705."

"Advise CHP we need to get these guys off our ass. We do *not*, repeat, *do not* want them to mention the FBI. Advise CHP that our adversaries are Hells Angels and to consider armed and dangerous."

"Ten-four, 705."

Scooter's recovered and making another run on us. I swerve across the line, forcing him back, but I'm running out of curves—my only defense. There's a stretch of straight road about three miles ahead with steep canyons on both sides. Between here and there, the road remains steep with very tight S curves. Once we're on the straightaway, without help, they'll have a clear shot at forcing us off the road. I've got to slow this train down to buy us some time before the straightaway.

I take my foot off the gas and coast downhill at twenty to twenty-five miles per hour riding the center line—dodging on-coming traffic at the last second. Scooter's going ballistic behind me, surging to get past, then having to slam on his brakes. There's no way around.

The cat and mouse lasts about ten minutes.

"I've bought as much time as I can, Kinney," I say. "Straightaway's coming up. When they make their next run, I'm gonna let them come up."

I roll down my window. "When they're alongside, blast 'em."

I look across at him. He's got that tough Texas glint of confidence in his eyes and the ever-present smirky smile. "You got it, Spence."

"Fire when I say 'fire.'"

He nods, terse. I glance to my left and see the Mustang making a move.

"Here they come," I shout. "Blow these fuckers to hell. Lean over me as far as you can without touching the steering wheel and get the muzzle at least past my face. I'm gonna close my eyes for the blast the moment I say 'fire.'"

"You got it, Nick," he says, his face streaming with sweat.

I take a heaving breath, both hands firmly gripping the steering wheel. I can hear the throaty V8 howling from the left. We're nearly into the straight, going just over fifty. Kinney racks the slide, chambers a slug round, releases the safety, and leans across me kneeling on his left knee. The 870 is firmly set into his right shoulder as he braces his right elbow against the console. The barrel's close enough that I smell the familiar odor of cleaning solvent Hoppe's #9. Kinney's got the muzzle past my face, barely protruding out the open window. I pull my head back into the seat as far as I can and lean to the right and take another deep breath. We're into the straightaway.

"You ready? I'm braking!"

"Just say the word!"

Suddenly, the Mustang brakes hard and pulls back in behind us.

I can't believe it.

Then I see it in my side mirror, two highway patrol vehicles speeding down the steep grade into the straightaway, red lights flashing, locked onto the bumper of the Trans Am, coming up behind Scooter's Mustang. They both pull off the road in a cloud of dust. Another CHP vehicle with red lights flashing and siren howling roars past us northbound. It's over in about three seconds. One minute, we're struggling for our lives. The next, we're just speeding along the road, heading for home.

"God bless the CHP," I say. "God bless Teddy Rendell."

Chapter 41

Big Buy
San Diego, CA
October 30, 1996

Other than a case of the jitters, I'm pissed off as hell—for two reasons: First, these guys were trying to kill us, and if they had been successful in running us off the steep canyon, nobody would have known what happened; and second, by going up there to get the stupid photographs, I may have put the whole operation in jeopardy. If they were at all suspicious or paranoid after the canyon chase, it may well ruin the element of surprise for our impending raids and jeopardize the safety of agents and officers.

Rendell calls me first thing the next day. I take the call at the PB house, which is in the state of organized chaos that usually precedes one of Charlie's controlled buys or meetings. We're one hour away from Charlie driving over to meet with Duke, and I'm praying that everything's still a go. The only other person on the team who knows about what happened with Scooter and Gonzo is Frank, who, like me, thinks that the less that's said about the matter, the better.

Rendell explains that a follow-up call to the CHP revealed that Gonzo and Scooter were cited for reckless driving and released. They played it as a routine traffic stop . . . no mention of the FBI. I thank Teddy again for his alert handling of this matter and hang up the phone no less worried about the possible consequences of this fiasco.

Looking out at the yard, I see Charlie walking around in slow circles, getting his head straight for the meeting. At least I hope that's what he's doing. He's getting harder to read these days, withdrawing into himself more often and continuing to brood about Bull getting trapped on tape. He's also clearly hung up on the FotoMat debacle. His attention wanders. And, as always, he gets frustrated with all the nit-picking detail.

Today's the first real test of whether he can actually continue to do what needs to be done.

~~~~

An hour later, we're back in the old Econoline—Marty and me sitting in the back, straining to hear what Duke's saying to Charlie.

And it's as frustrating as hell. Despite all our hopes that Duke might start to loosen up, he continues to play his cards close to his chest, scribbling notes, his voice barely going above a whisper.

Then Charlie says, "Duke, I got a guy needs seven pounds right away."

"Charlie," Duke snarls. "How many times I gotta tell you, man?"

"Duke, we're in the fuckin' clubhouse. Who's gonna be listening?"

There's a long silence.

"If you're not interested," Charlie says after a time, "then I gotta find somebody who is. And *pronto*. Don't wanna lose this buyer."

I close my eyes. "Come on, Duke," I mutter. "Give us something we can use."

Then Duke does exactly that.

"Seven pounds, huh?" he says, and this time he doesn't whisper; it's more of a low growl—perfectly audible.

Marty gives a sharp nod, eyes on his dials.

"That's what he needs," Charlie says. "Seven pounds."

"Jesus, that's a lotta product for one buyer, Charlie. Who's this guy, anyway?"

"Duke," Charlie says with a loud sigh. "You interested or not, 'cause I'm coming to you as a..."

"Fourteen thou."

"What?"

There's some shuffling sounds: Duke scribbling on

paper.

"Fourteen grand a pound?" Charlie blurts, nice and clear for the wire, but also sounding genuinely pissed off. "Fuck this, man."

I hear a chair push back. Charlie just got up. Here we go again.

"Now, don't get all riled up, Charlie. Come on. Sit the fuck down."

"Not for fourteen grand I ain't, man. I'm buyin' quantity, Duke. You're talkin' street prices here. You gotta cut me some slack, man."

I hear a big, theatrical sigh. Then more scribbling. Some habits are hard to break.

The chair scrapes, Charlie coming back to the table.

"*Thirteen?*" Charlie says in a disgusted undertone.

Then he must do some scribbling of his own, because Duke says, "Ten? You gotta be shittin' me, man. You forgettin' we got expenses. Overhead."

"Come on, Duke. It's Charlie you're dealin' with here. You guys control the labs. I know what you got into it. Cut me a break, man. We can both make money on this deal."

I hear the snap of a lighter, a long inhale followed by the clunk of the lighter being thrown on the desk.

"The fuck's that?" Charlie asks.

"New lighter," Duke grumbles. "My old lady bought it."

"What happened to the old one, the one Sonny gave you?"

"Lost it, I guess," Duke grunts. I hear the lighter open, shut, open, shut—either Charlie or Duke playing with it.

"I can come up with eleven grand," Charlie says. "But that's it. That's my last fuckin' offer."

"Twelve," Duke says. "I need twelve."

"Eleven-five. Come on, Duke. You know that's a good price."

Another long silence.

"If we can do this deal on short notice, the client's ours,"

Charlie says. "We *own* him. He'll be back for more." The lighter clacks open and shut again. "But it's gotta be good quality shit."

"You know my product is the best there is," Duke says, speaking pretty much in a normal voice at this point.

Marty's nodding, smiling, watching the reels go around as we reel in the president of the local chapter of the Hells Angels.

"Eleven-five it is," Duke says.

"*Eighty grand plus five*," Charlie blurts, sounding more like a banker than a drug dealer. Again, I hear the chair scrape back over the floor. "I'll call you tomorrow morning."

~~~~

As soon as he gets out of the car back at the PB house, I can see his mood has changed, his hangdog demeanor replaced by some of the old excitement and enthusiasm he's shown in the past.

"Great job, Charlie," I say as I start the full-body search. "I mean, Jesus. You finally got him talking."

"Fat fuck," Charlie says in a cheerfully disgusted undertone. He lifts his arms, lets me pat him down. "Fourteen grand. . . . Did you hear that, Nick?"

"Yeah, I did."

"I'm tellin' you, if it wasn't for you guys, I'd a' told him to shove the shit up his greedy fat ass."

"We got it all on tape, Charlie."

"Beautiful audio," Marty says, grinning as he comes up behind us. "It's gonna go over great in court."

"So when's this thing gonna go down?" Charlie says. "The buy, the bust?"

I finish the search and look Charlie straight in the eye. "Tomorrow, Charlie," I say with pride. "Just like you set it up. Everything hinges on you. You're the control guy here. Our quarterback."

"Is it really Halloween, Nick?" he says.

I shrug, nod, and look at my watch. "I guess so, Charlie. I hadn't thought about it. Tomorrow. Why?"

"That's what Duke said when I was driving off," Charlie says pensively. "'Trick or treat, Charlie,' he says." He cocks a brow. "Why'd he say that?"

"I don't know, Charlie. I didn't catch that on the wire. Maybe he's planning a party."

Charlie gives me a blank look. "You think he's planning something, Nick?"

"Yeah," I say. "I think he's planning on treating himself to our eighty grand. But the trick'll be on him."

Chapter 42

Sending Sledge
San Diego, CA
October 31, 1996

The 31st breaks as a clear, crisp, late-fall morning. I stand at Charlie's bedroom window, looking out at the kids going to school dressed as little ghosts and gremlins, tiny Tinkerbells, and miniature Wonder Women. I'm thinking about the innocence of youth and wondering what happens to it all.

"I don't remember there being so much candy when I was a kid," I say, eyeing up the pumpkins on our neighbor's porch. Next to the pumpkins is a tub—maybe a washbasin—full of what appears to be candy.

"I hate the whole thing," Marty says. "Running around in the dark, dressed up in a stupid costume. Trick or treat. I mean it's all pretty dumb, if you ask me."

There's a sharp intake of breath.

"What the hell's the matter with you, Marty? Didn't your mother take you trick or treating?"

I turn from the window, wait for my eyes to adjust to the light. Charlie's standing in the middle of the room with his jeans and underpants around his ankles. Marty's attaching the wire to the back of his right leg with strips of adhesive tape.

"Every time you pull one of those fuckers off, it yanks the hair out my leg."

"Sorry, Charlie."

"Fuckin' hurts, man..."

Marty frowns, reapplies a strip of tape, and then leans back, letting Charlie put the wire into the crack of his own ass. He then starts taping again at the base of Charlie's spine. All of this is by now routine for both of them, but I can see that it's all starting to get to Marty.

"Well, Marty?" I say, trying to lighten his mood.

"Well, what?" he retorts.

"Well, didn't your mother ever take you trick or treating?"

"She said it was a form of begging . . . and we Logans are not beggars."

I decide to leave it at that. Marty's clearly in no mood for kidding around. Truth is, we're all contemplating what's going to be a very large-scale operation—the culmination of months of hard work. But I have to imagine that from Charlie's point of view, as we find ourselves in the heart of the storm, the plan's pretty much the same as we've been running for months. We wire him up for the meet and then follow him to the clubhouse. The big difference this time is that Charlie will be carrying my career inside a big bagful of Uncle Sam's money. Should anything go wrong and we lose the money, the Bureau wouldn't need any more ammunition to fire me.

The money's in a gym bag in the corner of the room—neat little wads amounting to just over $80,000, every bill photocopied as evidence, pages and pages of them on the reams of paper I'm holding.

If Duke fulfills his part of the transaction, we'll have accomplished more than we could have expected on this investigation. The team leaders have all been put on standby. The time for the raid will only be known when Charlie sets the meet with Duke.

"Did you shave your armpit?" Marty asks.

"Course I shaved my fuckin' armpit."

"Because the tape isn't going to stick if—"

"Marty, I shaved my fuckin' armpit, okay?"

Charlie looks pretty tense, but no more than he usually is before these things. Most people would be unsettled by carrying that much cash in a bag, but for Charlie, eighty grand is, of course, chump change.

"It's just like any other day," Frank says. He's sitting on a stool in the corner of the room, lighting a cigarette from the one he just finished smoking.

Charlie winces as Marty adjusts a piece of adhesive tape

to the shaved skin of his left armpit.

"It's like any other day," Frank continues. "And it's important you give Duke that impression. You're probably going to be in Duke's office. You just do the deal, take the drugs, and leave. Drive straight back here."

"He keeps a gun in his desk," Charlie says.

"You already told us that."

"If he thinks I sold him out, he's gonna try and kill me."

"He's not gonna think you sold him out when you show up with the money," Frank urges. "That's all he's gonna care about—the money. You've established your credibility with him, see."

The comment is, of course, out of character for Charlie, and it occurs to me that for the first time he's looking for a little sympathy or a show of concern for his safety. He pulls up his pants. He slips his black T-shirt over his shoulders and turns for Marty to continue his inspection. Frank gets to his feet. We all take a look at Charlie. His eyes are like glass.

~~~~

"This is FBI Special Agent Nick Spence. Agents Marty Logan and Paul Rudnick, FBI, and Detective Frank Conroy, San Diego Police Department, are also present. We are in San Diego, California at 10:05 hours on October 31st, 1996. We are recording a consensually monitored telephone call by Charles Slade, a cooperating witness, who will call Jason Andrew Stricker, aka 'Duke,' the subject of an ongoing drug investigation. The telephone number being dialed is 643-2020."

Frank dials the number, waits for the dial tone to come through on Marty's amplifier, then hands the phone to Charlie. The phone rings and rings, but no one picks up. Charlie glances up at me.

"Kill it," I say.

Charlie hangs up, draws a hand across his face. He's starting to sweat a little.

"You okay, Charlie?"

"Sure."

Paul gets Charlie a drink of water. We resettle, wait about ten minutes, and go again; the evidentiary preamble for the tape, the dialing. This time, Duke picks up on the third ring.

"Yeah..."

"Duke."

"What's up, Charlie?"

"We ready to go, man?"

There's a slurping sound, a soft belch—Duke getting into his morning coffee. "Go where?"

Charlie frowns, and I can see him tighten his grip on the phone. "I got somethin' for you, man. That package we talked about yesterday. I'll bring it into the club."

"Yeah, I got a little problem with that."

Charlie looks up at me. "What kinda problem?"

"Scheduling problem. Today's kinda tight. I got a conflict."

I scribble a word on a piece of paper: "Pressure."

"What the fuck?" Charlie says. "I'm ready to go, man. I got a deadline to meet. I told you that yesterday."

There's another slurp. "Okay, okay. I tell you what. I'm gonna send someone over. I'm gonna send Sledge over."

Charlie looks up at me.

"Charlie?" Duke says.

"Yeah," Charlie says. "You sayin' Sledge is gonna deliver the strawberries?"

"Yeah," Duke says with a chuckle. "The strawberries. That's right."

I scribble a quick note: "Deliver it here. Noon."

"That a problem?" Duke says.

"No, no problem, man. Tell Sledge to come over around noon."

"Okay."

"Good."

There's a lull. Charlie stares at me for further instruction.

"Charlie?"

"Yeah?"

"You forgettin' somethin'?"

"What?"

"Where you at, man? I need the fuckin' address."

Again, Charlie shoots me a look. I nod.

"Got a pen?" Charlie says. And he gives Duke the address of the house.

Duke slurps and burps and says his goodbyes. Charlie hangs up.

Frank gets to his feet. "We got about an hour," he says. "Let's clean this place up."

~~~~

"Sledge buys another one-way ticket to San Quentin," I say. "What could be better than that?"

"Unbelievable," Frank says, shaking his head as we start to go through every room in the house, grabbing up documents, making sure there's no trace of our presence.

"Sledge. He sends *Sledge*."

"Don't tell me you feel sorry for the guy."

Frank pauses, a wad of paper in his hands. "Not really," he chuckles, and crams the paper into the bag.

I grab the phone, call Blair at the command post, and tell him what just happened; tell him I need another agent for backup; explain that we will arrest Sledge as soon as he makes the delivery. Blair's all in. He agrees to send over Special Agent Biff "Bluto" Blutarski, the San Diego office's chief firearms instructor and a SWAT team leader. Bluto's all muscle from head to toe. Just the guy we need to hook up Sledge, who's not likely to go down without a fight.

I give Blair a walkthrough: We'll take Sledge down first, then immediately and simultaneously initiate the rest of the raids, as planned.

A second after Blair hangs up, I hear him on my portable HT radio. "Command Post to all team leaders," he says. "We are on immediate 10-23. Everybody waits until I give the green light. Roll call."

All the team leaders start to call in, acknowledging Blair's message. The lines of communication are wide open—essential for the effective execution of the operation.

Joe Bernstein is at the staging location with the clubhouse raid team. I radio him for a status report.

"SOG reports no movement in or out since our guy made the call," Joe says. "Suggest you monitor channel 10 on your HT."

Paul switches his Motorola over to 10 and we immediately pick up SOG radio traffic. Unless Duke has a secret tunnel, he's still in his office and no one else has left the compound.

~ ~ ~ ~

Bluto gets to the PB house just after eleven, and he's clearly excited at the prospect of taking down Sledge. He sets up with Paul in a van parked down the street while Frank and I sit tight with Charlie, waiting to hear word from Chick Reinhardt, who's up in the Cessna orbiting over the clubhouse.

Charlie's truly disgusted with Duke for sending out Sledge as an errand boy—putting a brother in harm's way for his own personal gain. So much for love and respect.

"Duke, man . . . ," Charlie says, shaking his head. "I mean, what a rat fucker. And Sledge . . . how stupid is that guy? I told you he wasn't very smart."

"Could've been you, Charlie. A year ago, could've been you."

"Not without me helping you, it couldn't."

There's logic to this somewhere, but I can't be bothered to deal with it. I just want to roll . . . to get moving. I watch the seconds bounce around my watch face, aware of how dry my mouth is.

The radio comes to life.

"904 to 705."

"705 ... go, 904."

"We've got a tall, muscular, bald, white male getting into a white Dodge pickup truck at our location. He appears to be your guy, and he's carrying what looks like a large green duffle bag slung over his shoulder."

"Roger that, 904."

"Do you want us to follow him, 705?"

"Negative. Let him go. I don't want to burn this thing. We'll let him come to us. I need you to stay on our primary subject and have your team lock on him if he moves."

"Copy, 705."

Sledge is headed straight for us. I look up at Charlie, who's still shaking his head.

"Stupid fuck," he says, disgusted. "Just gets outta the joint ..."

I get to my feet. "We're going to be in the alleyway," I say with wide eyes on Charlie. "Activate the Nagra and transmitter in your boot. We'll be listening. If anything doesn't look right ..."

"Roses. I know."

Charlie's standing in the middle of the living room as I back away from him, trying to read the expression on his face —a mixture of excitement and anger. Frank and I turn and go.

~~~~

It's hot in the bureau car. The A/C's not working and we have to keep the windows up so the neighbors can't listen into what's coming through the wire or the radio.

Frank lights up a cigarette. "What?" he says, batting away smoke.

"Jesus, Frank," I say. "You're killing me with those

things."

I sit there sweating, once again eyeing my watch. This is San Diego: eighty-degree Santa Ana winds blowing in off the desert in October, and tomorrow, if the wind shifts, it'll be sixty degrees. The radio's silent. Charlie's silent. I'm thinking about the eighty grand I'm not supposed to let out of my sight. It's 12:15 and Sledge seems to be taking his sweet time.

I'm about to get out of the car to get a breath of air when I hear Charlie say, "Right on..."

At the same time, Paul comes through on the radio.

"712 to 705."

"705 ... go."

"The subject is pulling up in front of the house. He's out of the pickup. He's grabbing a green duffle bag from the backseat. Geez, he's a big boy."

"Copy, 712."

I wipe sweat from my face and close my eyes, concentrating on what's coming down the wire. I hear the rarely used front door come open.

"Hey, Sledge!" Charlie bellows. "How's it goin', man?"

"Good, Charlie," Sledge says, his voice coming through flat and slow. "I got somethin' for you from Duke."

"Yeah? Well, that's great. Come on in, man. Come on in." There's some back-slapping sounds, and then the door closing. I picture Charlie taking Sledge through to the living room, and I pray we haven't left anything in sight.

Charlie attempts some small talk about old times and so forth, but the truth is, Sledge isn't much of a conversationalist. He keeps saying what a nice place Charlie has.

"Yeah, you know, it works for me," Charlie says. "It's pretty quiet. You know."

"I do know," Sledge says. "It's a nice place, Charlie."

There's an awkward silence and then what sounds like a zipper. Charlie just opened the duffle bag.

"That the whole seven pounds?" he says.

"It's all there, man. You know Duke don't fuck around."

"Is it okay if I keep the bag? I'll get it back to him later."

"Whatever, man. It's just a fuckin' bag."

"Here's the cash," Charlie says, and there's a thump: the gym bag hitting the coffee table. "Eighty thousand, five hundred."

"Is it all there, Charlie?"

"Sure it is."

"I know it is, man. I know. Just like old times."

"Count it if you don't trust me."

"Nah, that's okay, Charlie. You know I trust you."

There's some rustling, swishing sounds—Sledge getting back up. There's more nothing talk, back and forth, and then the door opens, closes. I can hear Charlie's footsteps. Then the radio.

"712 to 705."

"705."

"Subject's out the front door, holding our bag. He's just standing there on the sidewalk, looking around. He's about thirty-five feet from his truck. Are we a go?"

Frank pops the door. "Let's do it, Spence."

My heart jumps.

Just then, Charlie comes through on the wire. "He's got the money, man," he says. "Why's he just standing there?"

"705 to 712. We're moving on foot between the houses. Wait until you see us—then move in."

I drop the mike and run to catch up with Frank, who's tearing through the neighbor's backyard.

When I come around the side of the house, Frank's slowed his pace, his sights set on Sledge, walking toward him across our front lawn, brushing the sleeves of his tweed jacket. Sledge is just standing there at the back of the truck like he forgot something. When he sees Frank, he gets a sick look on his face.

"Afternoon, Sledge," Frank says. "Remember me? Officer Conroy."

Sledge opens his mouth, but nothing comes out, his

eyes darting back and forth.

"Guess you've come out to the beach to visit my newest best friend, Charlie," Frank says, pointing to the house.

Sledge looks at the house, then back at Frank. He's so stunned, I don't think he even sees me coming up behind.

I hear the van door slide open and see Paul and Bluto jump out to the sidewalk and start running toward us. They're further down the street than I thought—almost a block.

"You know how long it takes to photocopy and record serial numbers on all those bills you have there in your gym bag?" Frank asks.

Sledge holds the gym bag a little higher, his massive bicep coming to attention.

"You're under arrest," Frank barks. "Turn around. Drop the bag. Hands on the truck. Spread eagle. You know the drill."

And whether it's Frank grabbing his arm or the word "arrest" or something else altogether, Sledge doesn't comply and just stands there, glaring.

"Turn around and put your hands on the truck, asshole," I say. "You're under arrest."

Right then, Sledge gets this zombie-like stare and starts walking. He breaks Frank's grip on his arm as he walks slowly between us, straight ahead down the sidewalk, the gym bag still dangling from his hand.

We can't believe he's just walking away from us. Not running... walking.

"Hey!" Frank hollers. "Stop!"

But Sledge keeps walking, goes about ten steps before he sees Paul and Bluto rushing toward him. I guess it's the sight of them that snaps him from his trance because now he starts to run. He gets to the street just as Bluto and Paul throw themselves at him. Sledge lets out this brute, primal yell as Bluto leaps onto his huge shoulders, trying to get an arm around his neck.

Paul has both arms around Sledge's waist, looking to tackle him, but Sledge is just so goddamn strong that he keeps going, making choking sounds now as Bluto gets a good head-lock on him. They all stagger sideways then go down in a heap just as Frank and I pile on.

Frank manages to get one bracelet on Sledge's huge left wrist. Sledge is cursing and trying to get up, all of us on top of him now, and he lets out another yell like a weight lifter about to clean and jerk eight hundred pounds of humanity off his back.

"Give me a hand here," Frank yells, dragging backward with the handcuffs.

Bluto strains with all his might to get Sledge's massive right hand twisted around, and I grab Sledge's upper arm, which is like a boulder, big and hard.

"Cuff him, for chrissake!"

But Frank can't get the other bracelet to close, and Sledge is pulling back against us, trying to get to his feet. Bluto gives his arm another almighty yank, the bracelet snaps shut, and suddenly it's all over. We're just this mass of heaving, gasping guys down on the sidewalk.

Paul rolls clear, and I can see blood inside his lip. Sledge takes a deep, shuddering breath.

"Mu-mutha*fucker!*" he yells, his voice crackling with rage as he sprawls face-down on the asphalt. "Motherfucking mother*fucker!*"

Frank gets to his feet, jams a cigarette in his mouth with shaky hands.

"Jesus," he says. "That was a little more exercise than I needed."

I stand beside him, trying to get my breath. Paul's dabbing at his lip as Bluto examines a big split in his shirt.

"Paul," I say, "you and Bluto take this asshole down to our office and book him. And get the drugs into evidence."

"You bet."

"And make sure the money—"

"Nick. I got it."

I turn to Frank, who nods at me, taking a long drag on his

cigarette. "Okay, Frank. Let's go do this thing."

Chapter 43

Joe the Jew
San Diego, CA
October 31, 1996

I give the go to Blair for the countywide raid at 1:20. At 1:25, Frank and I, backed up by Marty Logan, Joe Bernstein, and six other Squad 7 agents—all wearing our FBI raid jackets and ballistic vests—push in through the front door of Celebrity Limousine Service as the SDPD team is coming through the back. We're greeted by a couple of hulking goons inside the front door—prospects, I guess, obviously there to stop precisely this kind of thing from happening. When they try to halt our forward movement by holding out their arms, demanding to see a warrant, Marty and a couple agents quickly jerk them aside and handcuff them as we press forward directly through to Duke's office.

He's sitting behind his desk. When he sees us barge through the door, there's a look of utter shock on his face. He's stunned by the sudden incursion. Penetration of his private domain is not supposed to happen, given the phalanx of bad-ass bikers he surrounds himself with.

"I guess this ain't a social call," he says.

"And it ain't trick or treat," Joe the Jew shouts as he pushes into the room from behind me, his eyes skittering.

"Keep your hands on the desk where we can see them," I bark, my pistol pointing directly at his forehead. "You're under arrest, Duke."

"Cuff him, Joe," Frank says.

Joe the Jew is just beside himself to be getting this honor —so much so that he knocks over the trash can as he stumbles toward Duke.

"On your feet, Mr. Stricker," he hollers.

Frank and I lower our sidearms as Duke rise from his chair.

"Step back away from the desk and put your hands behind your back," Joe snaps. Duke does as he's instructed. Joe fumbles at his waistband, struggling to get his cuffs out. I'm about to step in when he finally manages to cuff Duke, who's calmly standing there, eyebrows raised in disgust as Bernstein fumbles around behind him.

"You got a warrant, Barney Fife?" he says to Bernstein.

Frank and I stay quiet, letting Joe handle this.

"Absolutely," Bernstein says. "Arrest, search and seizure, forfeitures, all right here in order." He reaches into his blazer pocket and slams a bundle of warrants on Duke's desk. "You might want to take a look."

But Duke doesn't want to take a look. He doesn't even want to look at Bernstein, who's clearly about ready to burst out of his skin with excitement. Duke's eyes are in fact fixed on Frank. It's clear he's humiliated at being put in cuffs by the likes of Bernstein. It's also clear he suspects Frank and I are getting plenty of satisfaction out of this.

"What're the charges, Conroy?"

"Federal charges, Duke. Possession of a controlled substance, possession with intent to sell, distribution of narcotics and dangerous drugs within one thousand yards of a schoolyard, and conspiracy on all charges."

"Fuckin' Charlie," Duke says, and he slumps down on the edge of his chair. "Motherfuckin' rat bastard." He gives a vicious kick to the trash can Bernstein just tripped over.

He's glaring at me now, but mostly at the large yellow letters emblazoned on my FBI raid jacket, and I can see that there are nasty thoughts spinning through his head. "Quite a crew of stumbling feds you've surrounded yourself with, Conroy."

"I only work with the best," Frank says.

"Tell me something, pig," Duke hisses, passing by me as Frank and Joe move him toward the door. Other people are coming into the room—Marty Logan, a couple of Squad 7 guys

—

but Duke's eyes never leave mine as he walks past. "What'd you offer him?" he sneers. "What'd you offer that rat bastard?"

I can't help smiling. "You'll find out at your trial, Stricker."

"Fuck you!" he shouts. "Fuck all of you pigs. And *fuck* Charlie Slade."

And with that, he's escorted to a waiting FBI vehicle, finally in custody after months of hard work.

"I expected more of a struggle."

I become aware of Marty standing there in front of me, grinning.

"If everything goes according to the plan, there shouldn't be a struggle, right, Marty?" I say, and I offer him my hand. "Good work on this, my friend. It's been a real pleasure. You're a true professional."

Marty's grin stretches even wider.

I hear yelling in the corridor and see an officer push a handcuffed and visibly irate Gonzo past the doorway. I follow them back into the light, where there are about a dozen Hells Angels standing outside the main entrance, some handcuffed, some not, all watching with obvious disgust as law enforcement officers search the limos, rental cars, and choppers right there in front of them. If that's not enough to piss them off, a very excited and enthusiastic Joe Bernstein is bounding around the parking lot, directing traffic, whistling at agents and officers to move vehicles, making sure he has all the documents in order before vehicles are driven off for delivery to SDPD headquarters.

I'm standing there laughing. Maybe it's the relief after all the months of strain, but I just feel something inside me let go. The place is secure and everything seems under control. I'm still chuckling when Frank comes alongside. He's laughing, too.

"Duke's on his way downtown to the federal building with a couple of your agents," he says after a time. "They'll book him, but we need to get down there and do an interview, or at least try anyway."

"Okay," I say, wiping a tear of laughter from my eye.

I turn to see a news reporter hurrying toward us in somewhat of a frenzy.

"Officers," the spindly reporter says in a huff, "I'm trying to get a story here for the five o'clock news. The man in charge of this operation over there—the one directing traffic—told me he was too busy to give a statement and that I should talk to one of his men. He pointed at you two."

We both look over and see Joe rattling a large ring of car keys, yelling and whistling at anyone who's paying attention.

I look at Frank. "Looks like our boss has everything under control," I say. "Why don't we head downtown."

Chapter 44

Aftermath
San Diego, CA
October 31, 1996

Simultaneous with our entry into the clubhouse on 35th and Adams, Mike Dove led his team into Gonzo's house up in Ramona, busting through the front door with a forty-pound battering ram. Of course, having Gonzo in handcuffs at the clubhouse made Mike's job easier, but it didn't mean that the Ramona place was unoccupied.

As Mike and his team plowed in through the front, a second team entered through the back. They found Scooter in the bedroom on top of his old lady—apparently trying to patch up their relationship. He was ready to rock and roll with the sawed-off shotgun he kept next to the bed, but when he saw all the raid jackets and an assortment of firearms aimed at him, he made the smart decision to throw the weapon down and put his hands in the air. By the time Dove made it to the bedroom, he found Scooter and his old lady naked spread-eagled against the wall—Scooter screaming to be shown a copy of the warrant as he was being handcuffed. Dove radioed in for a "wants and warrants" check on his old lady. Turned out she had a warrant outstanding for robbery and assault, so she got to ride downtown with her man.

As for the snake, no one went near the kitchen sink. In fact, everyone was hyper-alert to the possibility of this creature, or others, being anywhere in the house. Once the place was secure, a lady from the San Diego County Department of Animal Control—brought along on the raid just for this occasion—was summoned. Lucy was still under the kitchen sink —dead—apparently from lapping up Drano-laced water dripping from a rusty pipe.

Mike's team executed a room-by-room search of the house netting drug paraphernalia, a pound of meth, eight ounces of cocaine, and fifty pounds of marijuana. There was also a pretty sizeable weapons cache, including two AK-47s, a sawed-off twelve-gauge shotgun, an M16, three handguns, a couple of hand grenades, and assorted ammunition. And just to top it off—$300,000 in cash in an old beat-up suitcase.

The other raids carried out that day all went according to plan with no major incidents. The only excitement occurred in the raid on Tink's Bar on El Cajon Boulevard headed up by John Clouser. He and four of his team entered through the front door while three officers came in through the back. Clouser announced that he had an arrest warrant for Spud, a search warrant for the premises, and a seizure warrant for the business. Needless to say, Tink, the owner—a little fireplug of a guy with a shaved head and an earring in each earlobe—was tear-assed at the disruption of business. He was behind the bar, serving a motley bunch of biker types, when the raid went down. He told Clouser that he hadn't seen Spud in several days. Didn't know anything about drugs in his bar. To hear Clouser tell it, Tink was screaming at the agents and officers to get the hell out of his bar or he was going to call the cops.

Clouser ordered his men to search and field interrogate everyone in the bar. While that was going on, two sheriffs' deputies searched the premises, looking for Spud. Within minutes they found him hiding in a storeroom. Crazy as it might seem, with all the cops around, Spud decided to resist arrest and make a run for it. He was in a full sprint when Clouser tackled him to the ground before he could get out the front door. At this point, a few of the patrons tried to come to the aid of poor Spud, but force of arms prevailed and Spud was taken into custody. Three of the bar patrons had outstanding felony warrants and were hooked up and taken to county jail.

~ ~ ~ ~

Throughout the afternoon, there was a steady trickle of bad guys into the federal building downtown. Frank and

I watched Duke being photographed and fingerprinted. Then we sat down with him in the interview room.

We started by getting some routine biographical information from him when he interrupted us.

"Aren't you forgetting something?" he said. "Like, I got rights, man."

"I haven't asked you anything incriminating," I said. "*Yet.*"

"Well, I want my lawyer anyway."

I read him his Miranda rights. When I was done, Duke smiled, his eyes cutting from me to Frank and back again.

"Why'd he do it?" he said after a moment. "You guys got a twist on him?"

"Does it matter?" I said. "Important thing is he's ready and eager to testify."

"'Bout what?"

"We already told you: possession and distribution of narcotics and dangerous drugs; distribution of illegal drugs within a thousand yards of a schoolyard; and conspiracy on all charges."

"Conspiracy? Schoolyard? Man, you guys are fucked up. You got the wrong guy. I ain't been near no fuckin' school."

"And then there's Jacumba," I said, and I slid his Zippo lighter, enclosed in a clear, plastic evidence bag, across the table.

With that, Duke became very still. His eyes took on a sly, hooded look. "I want my phone call," he said.

"You sure about that, Duke?" I asked. "We're giving you a chance to talk here? Now's your opportunity. You won't get another chance to help yourself."

"Fuck you. Phone call."

We both stood up. The interview was over.

Gonzo had to be restrained in his chair. He kept lunging to his feet and screaming every expletive in the book about our witness. When I mentioned the word "Jacumba," he too became still and watchful. "You ain't got nothin'," he growled.

He invoked his Miranda rights, and that was the end of our conversation.

Bull Palac was morose. It was obvious he just couldn't get over the fact that Charlie had turned federal witness. It didn't make him any more talkative, but it was clear that emotions would run high in the courtroom. It was clear we'd have to prep Charlie very, very carefully.

The last guy we tried to talk to was Sledge, but he just sat there, staring at Frank. He didn't even acknowledge that he understood his rights. Didn't ask for a lawyer. Just stared at Frank . . . I guess with visions of San Quentin dancing in his head.

The entire day was a success. We'd carried out twelve raids without major incident and had made twenty-three arrests. At the clubhouse alone, forty-two pounds of methamphetamine were recovered from three of Duke's fleet of limousines. We seized a total of eighteen limousines and four motorcycles. We got $350,000 from a safe in Duke's office and a stolen loaded .45 caliber pistol from his desk. It was a good day's work, and we were confident the cases would stand up in court. All we had to do was make sure Charlie didn't get killed between now and the trial.

Chapter 45

Nine Inch
San Diego, CA
October 31, 1996

After all the prisoners are booked into MCC, the federal detention center, I make the call to the Pacific Beach house from my
desk in the squad room. Paul's so pleased with the way the day
went, he can barely contain himself.

"Charlie's ecstatic, Nick," he says. "I mean, you
should've seen him after we took down Sledge. He was liter-
ally jumping up and down with the duffle bag."

"Which you've logged into evidence, right?"

"Absolutely," Paul chortles. "The drugs . . . money. Bluto
took care of all of that. It's handled. But Charlie—"

"Is excited, yeah," I say. "Well, tell him to calm down. I
want him packed and ready when I get there. Thirty minutes."

"Okay," Paul says, and I can tell he's disappointed by my
reaction. After months of babysitting Charlie, he's obviously
ready to celebrate and kick back a little.

"Listen, Paul," I warn. "We've got to move quickly, so
stay on your toes. We've just upped the ante on the value of
Charlie's life. Duke's on his way over to the Metropolitan Cor-
rection Center. It won't take long for him to get word out
about what Charlie did and where to find him. We've got no
time to celebrate. Pack everything up and be ready to move.
We need to shut that place down ASAP. You understand?"

From this moment forward, the PB house is ground zero
for the Hells Angels. It's the first place they'll target to locate
and eliminate our witness, and they won't waste time or care
about collateral damage. They won't stop until they find the
brother that betrayed them.

I get a taste of just how pissed off they are about ten
minutes later as I'm leaving the federal building. I'm driving
up the parking ramp at around eight o'clock, wiped out but

happy that the day has gone so well. I'm nervous and anxious to get over to PB and help Paul, but as I make a left turn onto Front Street, out of nowhere, a chopper screams up alongside.

At the stop sign, the driver pulls up and throttles the Ironhead Sportster to a thunderous roar to get my attention. I roll down my window and stare into the fiendish face of some asshole I don't recognize. Shoulder-length, greasy orange hair, long, pointed goatee, and a big birthmark on his neck. He sneers, giving me the requisite death stare. Before I can even react, he lifts his hand, points his index finger at me like the barrel of a gun, mimes pulling the trigger, then roars off up the street.

The anger surges through me in a hot wave. I'm irate as I flash back to the canyon chase high above the San Vicente Reservoir. I put a call through to Frank, who's been ordered to Cantrell's office, giving him a blow by blow of today's events.

"You okay?" he says after I explain what happened.

"Sure, I'm okay. Just fucking pissed."

"So who was it?"

"Didn't recognize him. He was alone."

"But you'd know him if you saw him again?"

"You kiddin'? He's got this big, red birthmark on his neck like a—"

"Jud Nagel. 'Nine Inch.' Crazy bastard. A prospect."

"We're not going to put up with this shit, Frank."

"I'll handle it, Nick. You on your way to meet Paul at the house?"

"I'm on my way."

"We need to move Charlie, *now*," Frank urges.

~ ~ ~ ~

I pull up in front of the house at around 8:25 and I'm immediately concerned to see that the house is dark. Normally there'd be a light on in the living room and the drapes would be pulled shut. But it's pitch black inside and the drapes are wide open. For a second, I think Paul must have already moved out. He's stranded without a car, but he could have used the Camaro. I try to reach him on the radio. No response.

A darker thought comes to me—a thought I don't want to entertain at all.

I get out of the car and unsnap the leather trigger guard on my holster. I scan up and down the street, see parked cars, a few trick-or-treaters still moving from place to place, lights in houses, pumpkins aglow with evil faces. I cut through the neighbor's yard to the back alley. It's totally dark and quiet. I listen for sounds coming from the backyard. The house. Nothing. The old, wooden garage door is heavy as I pull, and it creaks on its rusty hinges. The Camaro is there and the engine is cold. Something is very wrong here. I feel my way through the garage in the darkness, tapping the side of the Camaro and the wall to find the small little door that leads into the backyard. I come to a halt next to the weight bench, staring at the darkened kitchen window. The door screeches open, and I draw my pistol ready to fire.

"What the fuck, Nick?"

It's Charlie. He's standing there, smoking a cigarette.

"Jesus, Charlie," I whisper.

"The fuck you sneaking around for, man?"

I instinctively grab his arm and pull him away from the door.

"The fuck's the matter with you, Nick?"

I push him against the house and crouch down. "Get down, Charlie. Where's Paul?"

"In the bedroom, packing up your shit. Take it easy, man."

"Paul?"

I hear footsteps. A moment later, Paul comes into the kitchen, pauses, then pushes open the screen door into the backyard. He peeks around and sees us crouched. "What's going on, Nick?"

We both stand up, Charlie backing away from me like

I've got malaria. I holster my gun. "Why didn't you answer your radio? I called you a coupla minutes ago and got no response."

Paul looks down at the portable radio strapped to his belt. "Must've turned down the volume too far. I was trying to keep it quiet around here. Figured we'd keep the lights off."

I heave a deep sigh. "Good thinking, Paul."

"Phone rang," Paul says. "About twenty minutes ago. I picked up. Whoever it was didn't say anything. Just some heavy breathing. They hung up."

"Okay, let's get outta here. You ready?"

Charlie shrugs. "Where we headed?"

"Somewhere else. Anywhere."

"I ain't goin' back to no fuckin' motel."

"It's just for a while, Charlie. We gotta hustle. A lot of pissed-off people have this address by now."

"Yeah, well, fuck 'em," Charlie snarls. He draws on his cigarette. "How'd it go today?"

"I'll tell you in the car. C'mon, we gotta move, *now*."

I walk into the living room and look out the window at the street again. It's poorly lit, but it looks the same as when I arrived. I get to the car, and without putting the lights on, pull around to the alleyway. Charlie and Paul come out of the garage, toss their stuff in the trunk, close the garage door, and we're out of there.

When we get to Interstate 5 northbound heading for no particular destination, I relax a little knowing we're not being followed.

"Way to go, Charlie. You did one hell of a job today."

"We nailed, 'em, Spence."

"Yes we did, Charlie."

"So what did Duke say?" he asks. "I mean, when you put the cuffs on him."

I glance over my shoulder at Charlie sitting in the back behind the passenger seat, upright like a rail, eager.

"I didn't put the cuffs on him," I explain. "Joe the Jew

did."

Charlie lets out a loud cackle. "Joe the Jew? Fuckin' A, man," he snorts. "Fuckin' Duke, man. Wish I coulda seen the look on his face."

I find a corridor amid the sea of traffic and abruptly accelerate from the number one lane to the number four lane, signaling for an exit, keeping an eye in my rearview for any headlights moving with me. When I'm satisfied no one's following me, I ease back into the number two and keep heading north.

"Joe the Jew," Charlie muses. "What is he? Five-seven? Five-eight? A fuckin' lawyer to boot . . ."

"We were there, too, Charlie. Guns drawn. It wasn't like Duke had a lot of choices."

But Charlie keeps shaking his head, trash talking Duke, unable to believe that he'd allow himself to be handcuffed by a little Jewish lawyer.

Ten minutes later, I get off Interstate 5 and head west toward the Coast Highway, taking the time to fill Charlie in on the raids: who got arrested, who put up a fight, the whole shebang. He wants every last detail . . . can't get enough. When it comes to the subject of Jay Palac, I try to keep it broad brush, but Charlie wants specifics.

"What did he say about me?"

"He was pretty stunned, Charlie. He didn't say much of anything, just shook his head."

Charlie looks out the window into the darkness; falls silent.

Just after 9:30, I pull into the parking lot of a seedy beach motel. Paul pays cash for a room and we drive around the back of the building, park, and walk up some stairs.

Unlocking the door, I can't help remembering the first night with Charlie, watching him shivering in the shower, and I can see by his face that he's thinking about it, too. Of course, a lot has changed since then, especially for him. He was a Hells Angel back then, albeit on the outs. Now he's just a guy that a lot of people want to kill.

I send Paul out for food, make sure the door's locked, then sit down on the end of the bed listening to Charlie move around in the bathroom. I can't even begin to guess what's going through his head, but I know there must be some pretty troubled thoughts. I tell myself that I have to keep him positive, keep him focused on our mission.

He comes out with a half-smile on his face, then flops down on the other bed.

"We did it, Charlie," I say. "We nailed those bastards. Couldn't have done it without you, man. Pete Blair sends his gratitude."

"What happens now, Spence?"

For a second, I don't know what he means. I figure he's probably talking about the big picture—what happens in his life—but I decide to keep to details, keep him focused on tomorrow rather than brooding on next month or next year.

"We have our initial appearance hearings before the U.S. magistrate tomorrow morning, and he sets a date for the preliminary hearings. It's usually scheduled within ten days. During the prelim, we present our case against each defendant and the judge decides if there is enough evidence to believe the defendant's committed the crimes detailed in our complaints. To be honest, I don't think the club's attorney's going to bother with the preliminary hearing when he hears the evidence and learns about the tapes."

"Myron Silverman?" Charlie scoffs. "He'll fuck his mother-in-law if he thinks there's a dollar in it for him."

"He's going to be learning about the evidence pretty soon. He'll see what kind of a case we have."

"That right? You have to tell him?"

"It's called 'discovery.' Part of the pre-trial process. The defense gets to look at the prosecution's evidence."

"So what kind of a case do we have?"

"Rock solid, Charlie. Thanks to you. Silverman's going to see that and he'll waive. You won't have to testify until trial."

Charlie shoots me a confused look. "Wave?"

"Skip the preliminary hearing. He'll either want to enter into plea agreements for his clients or go directly to trial. The big show. Court sets the date for that."

Charlie reaches for his smokes and fires one up. "How long before that happens? The trial, I mean."

I sigh reflectively. "Couple of months. Who knows? Depends on the court's calendar. They have to give the defendants time to prepare their defense. We'll still have to go through discovery first."

"But you've got the evidence, right? Duke's going away?"

"I hope so." I glance across at Charlie, try to read where he's going with all the questions. "We can count on Silverman filing a motion for a detention hearing—to argue for pre-trial release of his clients on bail. The burden's on us to prove these guys are either a flight risk or a danger to the community, or both. That'll all happen in a couple of weeks."

"So, you're sayin' it's possible Duke could be out in a coupla weeks?"

"I doubt it, Charlie. Anyway, I wouldn't worry about it."

He rests with his head against the headboard. "Hey, I ain't worried, Spence. Fuck him. He can come after me anytime he wants. That goes for the rest of 'em, too."

He gives me a vacant stare; his cigarette poised an inch from his mouth.

"I ain't scared of those motherfuckers," he says listlessly.

I'm troubled by what I see in his eyes and hear in his voice. Does he have the will or purpose to go on with his life? As I size up his mood, I honestly can't tell.

Chapter 46

Bad Eye
San Diego, CA
November 1, 1996

The following morning, Pete Blair sets up a rotating schedule using Squad 7 agents for protective security for Charlie—two agents per eight-hour shift. We're going to be on him 'round the clock from now until the trial. We need to keep him under wraps, and we need to keep him alive. Any efforts we've made in the past to protect him pale in comparison to the risks we now face. I'm sitting at my desk, putting together the paperwork for the initial appearance when a call comes through from Michelle, the receptionist.

"There's a gentleman here to see you," she says. "A Mr. McClusky."

I can tell by her voice that she's a little nervous.

"What does he want, Michelle?"

"He says he needs to talk to you." Then, lowering her voice, she whispers, "He's carrying a white flag."

"Mr. McClusky" turns out to be "Bad Eye" McClusky, the vice president of the club, a shambling giant with a massive Cro-Magnon-size head, deep-socketed dark eyes, and a nose that's been broken so many times it looks like a door knocker. He's standing in the reception room like some kind of shamed war chief, wearing his Hells Angels colors and carrying what appears to be a broken broom handle with a white, tattered T-shirt tied to it. Seeing him in the FBI office like this really catches me off-guard.

"You Spence?" he says mildly.

"That's me," I say, looking, I guess, a little perplexed.

"What Nine Inch did last night was wrong."

"Yeah?"

"That kinda bullshit wasn't approved by Duke, me, or the club. We've had a serious talk with Nine Inch about it, and

I can assure you it won't happen again."

"Okay," I manage eventually, thinking that if I know the club, Nine Inch probably needs a doctor right about now.

"Look, you guys do your job and play it straight; you got no problems from us," Bad Eye says. Then he waits, looking like he expects me to say something else.

I just stare.

"So we're cool?" he says after an uncomfortable silence —I'm sure attempting to stave off the wrath of the entire San Diego FBI and SDPD raining down upon him and the rest of the club.

"Hey," I say, shrugging. "You came up here. I appreciate that."

Bad Eye nods, lowers his white flag, and shuffles back out to the elevator.

I glance over at Michelle, who's sitting at her desk, which is enclosed behind bulletproof glass, her mouth agape. I smile and give her a wink as she buzzes me back into the office.

I call Frank as soon as I get back to my desk, telling him about my recent visitor. "What the hell did you do?" I ask.

Franks offers a deep sigh of resignation. "Called out the troops last night," he says. "Paid a visit to Nine Inch out in Ocean Beach. We had a heart-to-heart—think we surprised him and his girlfriend," Frank deadpans. "They were kinda on the couch, you know, when we came in."

"And?"

"After they got dressed, I explained to him we're just doing our job and he was out of line trying to intimidate one of our people. I admonished him not to *ever, ever* do it again." Frank chuckles. "I think he got the message."

I can't help but laugh. "I'm sure he did, Frank," I say. "Your heart-to-heart talks are usually persuasive."

"Yeah," Frank says. "Nine Inch was pretty upset when we left."

"But why did McClusky come here to see *me*?"

There's a pause that qualifies as a "Frank moment." I can

practically see him plotting his next words. "Well, like I said, Nine Inch was pretty upset when we left, Nick. He was yelling something about the Gestapo. You know, the usual: police brutality, illegal entry, no warrant. He demanded we identify ourselves, like he's gonna sue everybody, you know." Again, Frank hits another predictable pause and sigh. "So I gave him a business card."

"Jesus, Frank," I say. "That's just asking for trouble."

Frank chuckles. "Not *my* business card," he says. "I gave him yours."

Chapter 47

WitSec
San Diego, CA
November 8, 1996

Just as I expected, during the initial appearance before the U.S. magistrate, Silverman waives each of his clients rights to a preliminary hearing and files separate motions for detention hearings, which the judge grants and schedules for late November.

For the next two weeks, we keep moving Charlie around, staying in cheap motels. Charlie hates being cooped up, of course, but we try to keep his mind off the surroundings by talking about the trial and what comes after. I'm surprised, but he's in pretty good spirits, all things considered, seeming to buy into the idea that this is a new beginning for him.

The idea only really crystallizes into specifics when we start talking about the Witness Security Program. It's taken him a couple of weeks to accept the reality of his situation and the fact that the WitSec program is his only option.

"I get to choose where I'm gonna be though, right?"

It's a Thursday night in the second week of November, and Charlie and I are sitting in a motel room, talking about his post-trial options.

"It doesn't work like that, Charlie."

"What do you mean?"

"I mean, it's not like *Let's Make a Deal*, where you tell the U.S. Marshal, 'You know ... Florida looks nice.'" I try to flash a smile, but there's no feeling in it. "They have a limited budget. They have all kinds of rules and restrictions."

"You saying they're gonna send me to L.A.?"

I sigh. "They may not send you anywhere, Charlie. They may not even want you in the program."

"The fuck does *that* mean?" he asks, stabbing out his cigarette. "After all I done for you guys."

"Charlie, it's not about that, either. It's about whether they think you can make it, whether you're a good candidate for the program."

I stand up and go over to the open window, trying to breathe in some smoke-free air. The view from this particular fleabag is of graffiti-covered loading docks and Dumpsters and a litter-strewn street patched with broken asphalt. We've moved back south again, hopscotching across San Diego County. Why anyone would've ever put a motel here in this part of National City is beyond me, but it suits our purpose for the time being. Looking out at all this ugliness, it comes to me that I've spent way too much time in places like this.

"Make it?" Charlie says from behind me.

"It's hard to get in the program," I say. "Because . . . well, for one thing, it costs a lot of money to run someone's life for the rest of their life."

He pauses, chewing on what I just said. "So . . . what are you sayin'? Is there a test or somethin'?"

"Several tests," I say, nodding. "Aptitude tests. Psychological tests. You know, to see if you're crazy, or some kind of uncontrollable maniac." I wince as I realize the irony of what I just said. "But it's also . . . their decision's also based on the threat assessments and risk analyses that I'm writing up. In the end, it's the Department of Justice and the U.S. Marshal's Service that make the call—not the FBI."

I turn from the window, look down at Charlie, where he's sprawled on the bed. He looks sad and lost. I feel sad and also lost at this moment. There is a profound sense of gloom and desolation in this dim-lit room. It's the first time since we started with Charlie that I have this overwhelming feeling of guilt. I have to remind myself that what we've done for him is positive. We've used him, it's true, but we've also set him on a different path. If he can just keep moving forward, there are good things for him further down the road. At least that's what I keep telling myself, but in reality, how in the hell is this guy going to make it on his own?

"What it comes down to, Charlie . . . they need to know you're ready to commit. It's hard. I mean, I know you don't have a family, but you have to understand, entering the program, you can never go back."

"Yeah . . . I get that part." Charlie offers a profound nod.

"Do you? You have to sign an agreement, Charlie. No contacts with anybody. And that means no contacts with us. *Nobody* in your past life. It's not allowed."

He sits up on the bed, giving me his intense dark stare, an expression I've come to think of as a mind-reader look. "You mean I can't even call you guys?"

"That's right, Charlie," I say. "If they find out you've contacted anyone—even us—they drop you from the program. Because they *can't* protect you if you start screwing around. And I won't lie to you, it's fucking hard. Not many people make it. You get assigned some stiff-necked U.S. Marshal who's going to basically tell you how to live your life, what to do, and where to do it. He doesn't give a shit what you've done for God and your country. You'll have to get a job; go to work."

Charlie takes this all in as he rolls over on his side and props his head up with one hand. "They don't give you money, Nick?" he says eventually.

"Some seed money, you know, start-up money—at the beginning—something like that. They set you up with a new identity, an apartment, a job. But after that . . ."

I turn back to the window and look out at the gathering darkness.

"You don't think I can make it," he says.

I feel my shoulders slump. "I don't think you have a choice, Charlie. You stay around San Diego, they're gonna kill you for sure. They'll do you in a New York minute. Doesn't matter how tough you are. And you know that."

I sigh, touch my forehead against the glass and try to focus on the positive. "Maybe it's exactly what you need. You know. A clean break. Maybe it's the best thing that can happen. A lot of people would give their right arm to be able to start over, Charlie. A new life. A fresh start."

Chapter 48

Knockout
San Diego County, CA
December 1996

As the days drag on, with motions piling up and hearings in court being delayed, postponed, or rescheduled, we decide to get Charlie into something more permanent, at least short-term. We settle into a little two-bedroom bungalow in Carlsbad back up in North County along the coast. Charlie's relieved to be getting out of the motel rooms, but the truth is, the house isn't a great improvement. Not that the Pacific Beach place was Graceland, but somehow the new place has sadness to it, a hopeless void that we're never able to fill.

Of course, things have changed, and not just the physical surroundings. For one thing, the team has shifted a little. Paul's still a fixture, but Frank is busy with another case at the insistence of Cantrell. And the guys helping with the twenty-four/seven security are more concerned about punching the clock than kicking back with Charlie. But to the man, they all are acutely aware of the dangers associated with the assignment.

Also, the weight of circumstance is pressing down. There's the imminent trial and the looming issue of the Wit-Sec program. Two days before the detention hearings are scheduled, Charlie spends the entire day taking a battery of written and psychological exams with the U.S. Marshal's Service and to my surprise—if I'm being honest—he aces them. He's grinning like a sixth grader when he climbs into the car with Paul and me.

"You know what I did best on, Paul?" he says excitedly. "Math. Fuckin' math, man."

"Course you did, Charlie. You do math all the time . . . I mean pounds, ounces, grams . . ."

~ ~ ~ ~

The detention hearing takes place on a rainy Thursday afternoon. And it does not go well for us. Despite all of Barrett's best efforts, we don't exactly hit a home run. Myron Silverman does a great job painting Duke as a pillar of the community, businessman, friend to celebrities, etc., and the judge seems to eat it up. Either that or she's intimidated by all the Hells Angels sitting in her courtroom giving her death stares every time she opens her mouth. There were Hells Angels from as far as Oakland crowded into the courtroom like a pack of wolves.

Whichever it is, the judge goes easy on Duke, releasing him on bail of $1 million because he has no substantial prior criminal history and therefore, she concludes, he is not a danger to the community. Moreover, his businesses ties to the community show he is not a flight risk. What a sham! Jay the Bull is also released, the judge setting his bail at $200,000. Sledge, Scooter, and Gonzo are denied bail because of their violent and extensive criminal histories.

It doesn't really change much. We already figured Duke was doing everything he could to track Charlie down, and had long enough arms to do it from inside or outside of jail. His being *out* has more of a psychological effect than anything else. Not for Charlie, of course. He really doesn't care either way. He's like one of those old-time Samurai warriors who go into battle already believing he's dead. And as much as I've gotten used to this aspect of Charlie—this simple fearlessness —I still find myself shaking my head.

For the rest of us, certainly, the stress is real enough. We know that Duke and the others are looking for Charlie. Know they won't stop until they find him. I talk to the WitSec people daily, trying to get an idea of how long it's going to take to get a response. They say they can't turn around his application in anything less than four weeks. In the meantime, we have to just sweat it out; take it day by day trying to keep Charlie positive, trying to prepare him for trial, which is a challenge in itself. We haven't even thought about what happens if the marshals turn him down.

He seems to have this idea about taking the stand and pointing the finger, and that somehow it's all going to come out like the movies, where he's the hero. I have to spend a great deal of time explaining to him that it's not going to be like that at all. That there's going to be defense attorneys who will try to make him look bad, insult him, make him out to be a liar, rile him up, stoke his fire, and hope he goes berserk on the stand. I tell him that one of the best ways he can defend himself during cross-examination is to be rock-solid on dates, times, numbers, and quantities. We have all this documented, of course, but getting it into Charlie's head is no easy feat. He's cocky, and as I've often said, an almost clairvoyant reader of people, but the truth is, at times he's a little slow on the cerebral uptake.

As for his character, despite all my best hopes and Frank's belief in his capacity to change, he has in fact changed little in the past six months. This becomes abundantly clear a few days after the detention hearings when Frank, Charlie, and I are walking down the street at night in an upscale business district of Solana Beach, where we're pretty sure we're not going to be recognized. The street is lined with boutiques, surfer bars, and sidewalk cafes, and we pass this bar where a guy is sitting on a stool. He looks like a bouncer or ID checker. He motions with his hands and calls Charlie over.

"Hey, man," he says, seeing Charlie smoking a cigarette. "Got a light?"

We're in the middle of a conversation, so Charlie barely looks at the guy. "Here," he says, and we stop as he hands the guy his Bic. The guy lights his cigarette and then puts the lighter in his own shirt pocket.

Charlie notices it before I do.

"Hey, man," he says softly. "Can I get my lighter back?"

The guy is a big bruiser who clearly thinks he has the measure of the shorter Charlie. He smirks and says, "How 'bout I keep it, my friend. We'll call it a long-term loan."

What happens next is a blur. Charlie hard-stares the guy for a second, mutters "I'm not your friend," and then explodes with a left hook that snaps like a catapult on an aircraft carrier. It pulverizes the guy's face. Suddenly, the guy is sliding down the wall, out cold. One shot.

It happens so fast that neither Frank nor I even get to put up a hand.

Charlie casually reaches in, gets his lighter from the guy's pocket.

"The nerve of some people, man!"

"Jesus Christ, Charlie," Frank says, rushing to get the guy back on his feet. "What the *hell* was that all about? I mean, I know the guy was out of line, but there are other ways, man."

Charlie just shrugs and lights himself another cigarette. "You're wrong, Frank," he says calmly. "People like him . . . they need to be taught a lesson."

"So what're you gonna do when the needle-nosed, pasty defense attorney gets in your face and calls you a liar, Charlie?" Frank says. "What're you gonna do then?"

Charlie shrugs and shakes his head. Clearly he has no idea. Neither do I.

~~~~

A couple of days later, the unexpected happens. The U.S. Marshal's Service expedites Charlie's application in record time. And not just that. They say he's been accepted into the program. The suddenness of this news catches us all off-guard. We're all kind of astounded. There's a sense of finality to everything we've done together for the past several months. We try to celebrate the news of his acceptance and keep a positive spin on it for his sake. We're given a minimum four weeks' notice by the marshals to finish up with our pre-trial briefings and get him packed to move, regardless of the status of the case. Once he's theirs, they'll ensure he gets back for trial.

After the news has settled in, Charlie and I are sitting around talking one night in the sterile and sparsely furnished living room of our newest hideaway, Charlie slumped on the rumpled couch that's even uglier and more uncomfortable than the one we had in Pacific Beach, and I ask him if there's anything we can do for him before he leaves.

He thinks about it for a long time and then says, out of the nowhere, "my teeth."

"Your teeth?"

Charlie nods. "I'd like to get my teeth fixed. You know. So I can smile. I mean, I'm goin' off to a new life and I'd like to be able to smile."

I look at him, thinking he's joking.

"What?" he says.

"You don't seem much like the smiling kind, Charlie."

He stares back at me and then cracks a big wide smile, revealing all of his front teeth.

"You wouldn't smile much if you had a mouth like this, would you, Spence?"

I stare at the brown stumps and blackened gums in disbelief. A thousand tight-lipped smiles from Charlie flash into my head, and all at once it occurs to me that this is the first time he's actually shown any sign of his teeth.

"Jesus, Charlie," I manage after a moment. "I guess not."

~ ~ ~ ~

Putting in a proposal of this kind, especially with such a short deadline—a request that's no doubt going to result in a serious outlay of cash for the Bureau—means drafting a detailed proposal justifying the expenditure to FBI Headquarters and getting the support of Blair and SAC Ziegler.

Like me, Blair's a little thrown by the request at first, but it doesn't take him long to recover.

"No," he says, and he says it with a finality that's kind of discouraging.

I guess I must look disappointed because he raises his hands and starts explaining how he's as appreciative as anyone of what Charlie's doing for us, but that FBIHQ is unlikely to approve such a request.

"We don't even know how much it's going to cost," I say.

Blair raises his eyebrows at this. "A lot. Believe me. I mean, the way you've described his teeth..."

I interrupt. "Look, Pete, I haven't asked for much on this case. We've existed on a barebones budget, lived in shitholes for the past seven months, and rarely got to go home. Charlie's done almost everything we've asked him to do and has asked for nothing in return. I'd appreciate at least a little support from you on this."

I give it a second before adding, "At least let me submit the paperwork. All I need is your signature and Ziegler's."

A week later, I get a teletype back from FBI Headquarters telling me to get an estimate of the cost. It's encouraging news. Not exactly full approval, but at least they didn't reject it. But now I really don't have any idea who to go to with it.

The only dentist I know who'd even consider working on a guy like Charlie is my friend Ben Burnside, whom I've always referred to as "Dr. Demento" on account of his being certifiably nuts in a fun way. The consummate practical joker. He and I go a long ways back. We were in the Navy together, partied together, dated the same girls, and generally raised hell together. He's always been a bit of a risk-taker, but is now a respected dentist and a devoted family man. He runs a successful practice out of a fourth-floor office in the upscale village of La Jolla. He calls it "boutique dentistry," which is why I don't go to him.

So I call him up and give him the whole background, leaving nothing out, telling him that there are security issues, that we'll use every precaution when bringing Charlie into his office. I can tell he's kind of intrigued by the whole thing, like this is some kind of undercover spy operation, and I know he's always ready to spice up his otherwise dull daily routine. So I'm not surprised when he finally agrees to take a look.

As soon as I tell Charlie that I've set this thing up, his attitude changes. I think the reality of having to sit in a dentist's chair and open his mouth comes home to him.

"He's just going to take a look, Charlie."

"Just a look."

"That's all it is."

"No drilling or . . . or poking? Nothing like that?"

"Nothing like that, Charlie. He just uses this little mirror and takes a look around in your mouth."

The next day, Paul and I get him hunkered down in the back of the Bucar, as per our old methadone clinic routine, and we drive into La Jolla. Charlie asks every couple of seconds if we're there yet.

It's after regular business hours when I drive down into the basement parking lot. I leave Paul to stay with the car. As Charlie and I make our way up the elevator, he's completely silent and pretty much white-faced. Before entering the office, he dabs his forehead with his shirtsleeve.

"Jesus, Charlie," I say. "It's gonna be fine."

Demento's hygienist, Cindy, a shy, cute young woman with a cheerleader's wholesome looks, lets us in trying not to stare at what must look like the second coming of Geronimo. She asks Charlie to take a seat in the big chair.

Charlie stiffens. "Is this gonna hurt much?"

"Charlie," I say through a groan. "We're not even at the point where we're going to do it. We're just . . . we're just getting an estimate. It's like taking a car in to see how much it's going to cost to get it fixed."

Charlie eyes me up with little trust.

"Just sit down," I say.

Charlie shakes his head as Dr. Demento himself enters the room. My friend is tall and lean with long, black, slightly frizzy hair. He's a quick mover and comes into the room with a jaunty, energetic bounce offering to shake Charlie's hand and welcome him. It's all a little overdone, and I can see it's not making a very good impression by the way Charlie avoids eye contact and mumbles his replies. The whole thing is, in fact, very uncomfortable, and I, of course, go over the top trying to make small talk to put everyone at ease.

After this less than stellar beginning, we finally get Charlie into the chair, where he promptly refuses to let Cindy put the white disposable protective cover-up gown over his chest and lap.

He opens his mouth. Demento leans forward, bringing his big light down on its gantry, shining it directly into Charlie's mouth, which even from where I'm standing looks pretty horrible.

"Well, Charles," Demento says. "You haven't had much dental care, have you?"

"Name's Charlie. And I ain't never been to a dentist before."

~ ~ ~ ~

Twenty minutes later, I'm sitting in Demento's expansive office looking over the sparkling Pacific Ocean. He pushes his hair back from his smooth, high forehead, looking a little flustered.

"So what do you think?" I say.

"Well," he says very matter of fact, "this is the worst case of dental . . . I don't even know what to call it. Charlie needs some serious work, Nick."

"How much do you think? I mean, how much is it going to cost?"

Demento offers an incredulous look. "You have no idea how much work is involved here. If you want me to do it, it'll take three full sessions with time in between for some healing. It can't possibly be done in one sitting."

"How much, Demento?"

He fixes his close-set eyes on me. "For you, and today only . . . for you, my friend . . . fifty grand."

I almost shit. I jump to my feet. "*Fifty grand?* Jesus, Ben."

"If you went to anybody else, it'd be twice that or more. And no one would do a better job than me. Not to mention finding someone willing to work on Cochise out there."

There's a long silence while I absorb the sticker shock.

"Then," Demento grinds on, "for starters, I have to reconstruct his whole jaw. That's why it's going to be three sessions. It'll be at least eight hours a session, and it'll be *very* painful."

I come out of Demento's office reeling, and just have time to get my normal game face back on before I'm confronted by Charlie, who's standing in the waiting room, leafing through a *Good Housekeeping* magazine. He looks up at me, reads my fake-normal expression in an instant.

"So?" he asks.

"He says he'll do it."

"Is it gonna hurt?"

"A little," I say.

"A little?" Charlie groans. "*A little* . . . like havin' your fingers smashed with a fuckin' hammer . . . I can read you like a book, Spence."

"It'll be okay, Charlie," I say, leading him out of the office. "You're a tough guy. You can take it."

Chapter 49

Cindy
La Jolla, CA
December 1996

It takes a while for the money to come through from FBI HQ, but eventually it does come, and I have to say I'm feeling pretty pleased with myself the morning of Charlie's first appointment. I feel like we're really giving something back to him that's going to help him going forward. Charlie, on the other hand, seems less convinced. In fact, it becomes clearer by the day that he wishes he'd never raised the issue of his rotten teeth. When I tell him how much it's all costing, it only makes matters worse.

"What're they gonna do for fifty grand, for chrissake?" he asks, wide-eyed, I'm sure thinking for that much money, he's in for a world of hurt.

We're sitting in the bare little crater of a backyard at the Carlsbad place.

"It *was* going to be a hundred grand, Charlie."

He turns to look at me, astonished.

"You have no idea, man. A guy like Dement . . ." I stop myself short before sharing with Charlie my friend's moniker. "A guy like Ben . . . he's an artist. A sculptor. Do you realize he takes an impression of each one of your teeth and rebuilds them—only better?"

"Better be better," Charlie says, lighting a cigarette. "Fifty fuckin' grand . . ."

"I'm telling you, Charlie, you're not going to recognize yourself."

~ ~ ~ ~

We drive down to La Jolla on a Saturday morning, Charlie again scrunched down behind the backseat, barely saying a word now that the moment of truth approaches.

"You know, Charlie," I say, "everybody hates going to the dentist. The trick is to focus on what it's going to be like afterward. It'll all be worth it."

I look over my shoulder, meet his dark stare.

"They better give me somethin' for the pain, man. That's all I'm sayin'."

It's Cindy who opens the door with a cheerful smile that can only be uplifting for Charlie. I guess she's figured out since our last visit that Charlie, while pretty terrifying on the outside, is just another human being in need of reassurance. Demento, too, makes a big thing of treating Charlie like any other patient, and is the epitome of professional calm, toning it down from their first meeting. He's got some X-rays and photographs of Charlie's molars, and a couple of schematic drawings to support his explanation of what he's planning to do. There's also a three-dimensional model of Charlie's lower jaw. I know he's only trying to help Charlie by including him in the process, but I can see by Charlie's blank stare that he isn't taking in a word; he's just trying to hold it together for the coming onslaught.

"So, Charlie," Demento says, "take a seat."

Charlie looks like a death row inmate about to take a seat in Ol' Sparky as he slowly eases himself into the big, blue vinyl throne. This time, Cindy insists he wear the disposable gown. For obvious reasons.

"How are you with needles?" Demento asks, realizing too late that it's probably a moot point with a heroin junkie, but he quickly recovers, showing Charlie his little hypodermic. "I'm going to give you a shot of Novocain in a couple of places. You won't feel a thing."

Charlie watches him prep the needle, then closes his eyes. He's gripping the armrests so tight, they make a little squeak. I figure this is my cue to get out of there.

"Look," I say. "I don't need to be here, right?"

"Unless you want to carry the bucket," Demento sniggers through his surgical mask.

"The bucket?"

"The blood bucket," he says, and then he lets out this long, hissing laugh, I guess giving it his best Dr. Frankenstein impersonation. So much for the calm, professional demeanor.

Charlie winces as he watches me back out the door, his eyes bigger than a Mack truck steering wheel.

"You're in good hands, partner," I say. "I'll be in the waiting room, reading *Good Housekeeping*."

I close the door and stand there listening for a moment. It's warm in the waiting room and a little stuffy. It's empty because the office is closed, as it is every Saturday. I no more than sit down in one of the plush leather chairs when I hear this blood-curdling scream. I'm kind of amazed that Charlie can hit such a high note, then realize it's not Charlie who's screaming.

When I burst back into the surgical room, Cindy's pressed up against the wall, her terrified eyes fixed on Charlie, who's halfway out the chair, his right arm tangled up in some rubber tubing. Demento is standing back against the wall, still holding the needle.

"Get this fucking animal out of here!" he roars.

"Jesus Christ, what happened?"

"Cindy turned her back on this perverted asshole and he rammed his hand up to her crotch. Get him outta here *now*, Nick," he yells through his surgery mask.

I grab Charlie's arm and virtually lift him from the chair, escorting him from the room, forcing him to keep walking toward the exit and out into the empty hall, the surgical gown still draped over his neck.

"Charlie, you ungrateful fucking moron, what the fuck were you thinking?"

I slam my finger on the down button of the elevator and it opens immediately. We get in. I'm chin to chin with him, jamming my finger at his shoulder when the door opens on the second floor and a little old lady holding her pet Pomeranian steps in. We ride down to the lobby in silence.

~~~~

"I don't know, man. She's hot. She's right there . . . I . . ."

We're parked behind a Taco Bell on Pacific Coast High-way, out of sight of passing traffic, looking through the bug-specked windshield at the blue Pacific. I can't continue driving, as mad as I am. I'm trying to come to terms with what he just did. And he's just sitting there slump-shouldered, offering some feeble, half-assed explanation with that dark, sullen look on his face.

The facts of it are pretty simple: Waiting for the first shot of Novocain to kick in, watching Cindy's ass as she busies herself with Demento's tray of instruments, Charlie gets it into his head to jam his hand up her crotch. Like he was grabbing a sandwich at the deli.

"What in God's name would possess you to do something like that, Charlie?"

I've had ten minutes to come to terms with this fresh piece of stupidity, but I can't seem to calm down. Charlie, meanwhile, has adopted the beaten-dog look familiar to me from the FotoMat fiasco, a look very much enhanced by the Novocain-induced swelling of his right cheek.

"I don't know, Spence. Like I say, she was right there and . . . and I mean, I've been locked up with you guys all this time. I haven't been with a woman in . . . Jesus, I don't know how long, and . . . well . . . I just did it."

I shake my head in disbelief. "That's the lamest fucking thing I've ever heard you say, man. I mean, that's weak and unacceptable. You've betrayed me, Frank, and everyone who's tried to help you. I just can't comprehend it."

"It was wrong," he slurs.

"You're goddamn right it was wrong. You blew it, Charlie. I spent weeks trying to set this thing up. We could've gotten your teeth fixed. But now . . ." I give him a long, hard stare. "I'm telling you, man, I'm not going back in there to beg for you. That's it. It's done."

~ ~ ~ ~

But, incredibly, it's not done. Two days later, I'm doing the report to return the unused funds to FBI HQ—with a somewhat toned-down version of what really happened—when I get a call from Demento, telling me to bring Charlie back in. I get to my feet, the phone pressed to my ear.

"Are you sure? What about Cindy?"

"Cindy's tougher than she looks. I talked it over with her, and I told her about what you're trying to do for this guy. So . . ."

"Can I talk to her?"

"Nick."

"Please."

There are some muffled sounds—Demento handing off the phone.

"Hello, Mr. Spence," Cindy says, her voice as bright and cheerful as the woman herself.

I tell her one more time how sorry I am for what happened. I say I'd understand perfectly if she never wanted to see us again.

"It's okay," she says. "I mean, it's not *okay*, but I think I understand the circumstances and . . . I, to be honest . . . I feel *sorry* for Charlie. I mean, God, don't tell him that, but . . . well, I do."

"Well, I'm sure that he'd . . ." I start to offer something conciliatory on Charlie's behalf, when she interrupts.

"All I want is for you to be in the room the whole time," she says. "Can we agree on that?"

"Of course. Absolutely. You have my word."

Charlie walks into the room as I'm hanging up. He sees the look on my face and frowns. "What?"

~ ~ ~ ~

I'm in the room for the entire twenty-four hours that it takes to rebuild Charlie's mouth. And "rebuild" is the word. With three eight-hour sessions spread out over a two-week period, I'm pretty well sick of seeing the inside of Charlie's mouth. There are moments I can't believe what Demento's doing. It's like watching a road crew lay cable. And Charlie—ashamed maybe for being such an idiot the first time—takes it all like a lamb: rinsing when he's told to rinse, spitting blood and stumps and chunks of rebar and God knows what else when he's told to spit, and generally behaving himself like a grown man for once.

And a transformation takes place.

The whole time I've known Charlie—from the first time I saw the cockroach crawl onto his bottom lip in the shitty motel room—his mouth has been a kind of dark focus of all that's been messed up in his life, a kind of wound that he's always tried to conceal. And now it's gone.

In its place, there's this new whiteness—not white like plastic—the teeth look *real*. It's unbelievable how natural they look. It's just like I said—Demento, God love him—is an artist. A genius.

And Charlie, too, is transformed. The fact that he can grin without being ashamed seems to work in the depths of him, freeing up all kinds of stuff that used to be blocked. Suddenly, he can't stop smiling. In fact, it gets to a point when the smiling starts to get on my nerves.

"Okay, Charlie," I say. "I've seen enough of the teeth to last me a lifetime."

It's late December, and Charlie and I are in Mike Barrett's small "government gray" reception room, waiting to go in for the last time before Charlie enters the WitSec program. The marshals have really come through for him, getting him into the system before we even go to trial, yet allowing enough time for his teeth to heal.

"Seriously," I say. "Enough with the Bucky Beaver grins.

You're doing it just to bug me. Like I said, you were never much of the smiling kind anyway. It looks weird, man."

Charlie punches me gently in the arm and smiles again. "Can't help it, Nick," he says. "I'm just too goddamn happy. Life's good, man."

Chapter 50

The Address
San Diego International Airport
January 1997

We drive him to the airport on a gray and rainy morning . . . Frank, Paul, and me. It's quiet in the Bucar, with the occasional "you're going to do great, Charlie . . . we're going to miss you, Charlie" kind of stuff.

"Fuckin' Texas, man?" he says for maybe the tenth time.

"Stop it, Charlie," I say. "You're not supposed to talk about it. We're not supposed to know where they're taking you."

"Yeah, but what the fuck am I gonna do down there?"

"You hunt deer," Paul says, flashing his big, wide-eyed grin. "You fish. You take up horseback riding, become a cowboy."

I turn, giving him a scowl.

"You do whatever the marshals tell you," I say. "They're in control now, Charlie. You've signed an agreement with them and you'll have to honor it. They're going to guarantee your safety."

I pull up to the guard shack at the Harbor Police security gate. This is the only gate that allows direct access onto the tarmac at San Diego Lindberg Field and is used only for emergency and law enforcement purposes. I flash my credentials to the guard, who lets us through.

Checking the rearview mirror, I see Charlie staring out at the landing strip. "Charlie." I wait until he turns to look at me in the mirror with empty eyes. "It's what you make of it, man. One day at a time."

"Fuckin' Texas, man. Shit-kickers and cow turds."

Pissed as he is, Charlie deals with it the way he's dealt with every disappointment in a life filled with them: He puts up a screen, scowls, growls. But standing on the edge of the runway with the bags containing the few possessions he owns, getting ready to get on the Cessna Citation II jet that's going to lift him out of his old life and carry him off to the new, he lets go for a second—lets himself let go. Buffeted by a chilly wind, suddenly there are tears in his eyes. Frank offers him a cigarette, which he takes, cupping his hands around a guttering flame. He takes a deep drag, looking like he's trying his damnedest not to cry.

"This can't be it, man."

"This has to be it," I say. "There's no other way."

"But what am I gonna do without you guys? I mean, you guys are family now."

"You'll get another family, Charlie."

"A real family," Frank says. "With a pain-in-the-ass wife telling you to keep your feet off the couch."

"Anyway, you're not finished with us yet," I say. "We'll be meeting up somewhere soon. We got a lot of work to do to prepare you for trial."

"When?"

"A few weeks. A month maybe."

A stern-looking U.S. marshal walks down the small stairs leading into the plane and stands on the tarmac, waiting. Once Charlie climbs those stairs, he's no longer ours. I feel an urge to go over to the marshal and explain how our guy Charlie needs some "special" handling, but I know it's out of our control now.

"Time to go, Charlie," I say, and I'm surprised by a sudden wave of feeling in myself. I expected to be relieved, with this huge burden lifting from my shoulders, but I'm instead awash with emotion and physically drained from the experiences of the past seven months. It's been a nonstop run of events, mishaps, near-misses, and near-disasters. But it's also been an experience I know I won't soon forget. Charlie extends his hand to shake and I take it in mine. I look down at him with curious eyes when I feel something between our palms. Feels like a piece of paper.

He stares at me, I guess expecting me to take it and say nothing. Despite my better judgment, I clench my fist and put it in my jacket pocket. Charlie plays it nonchalant, reaches down into a duffle bag, and pulls out his giant bullwhip, which he hands to Paul. "Here's somethin' to remember me by, Paul," he says. "You're good people. I won't need it anymore."

Paul looks down at the whip, tears in his eyes. "So long, Charlie," he mumbles.

Then Frank steps forward and gives Charlie a hug and wishes him happiness in his new life. It's all done in a brusque, professional way, but I can see that Frank's pretty stirred up, too.

"I'll send you guys a postcard," Charlie says. Then, seeing the flinty glare on the waiting marshal's face, he laughs, points a finger. "Just kiddin', man."

We watch him climb the steps of the Cessna, watch the door close. He's the lone passenger on the jet bound for nowhere. From this moment on, he's somebody else, another person. And we're all just a secret part of his past.

I don't open the scrap of paper until we're back in the car.

"What is it?" Frank says.

I hand it to my partner without a word.

"His new address," Paul says, looking over Frank's shoulder.

I groan. He hasn't been gone five minutes and he's already violated the cardinal rule of the U.S. Marshals Witness Security Program. If the marshals knew about it right now, they'd jettison their cargo out over the Pacific.

Chapter 51

The Plea
San Diego, CA
February 1997

With Charlie gone, we enter into the discovery phase of the pre-trial proceedings. Myron Silverman and whatever eager underlings he's assembled to represent Duke,Gonzo, Bull, Scooter, and Sledge get to review all of the tapes and de-briefings of Charlie, as well as the surveillance logs, investigative reports, physical evidence, and chain of custody logs. It's the phase of the judicial process in which we reveal our evidence to the defense, but in my experience, it's also where we discover the tiny cracks and weaknesses in our own case before spending an uneasy couple of weeks praying that the defense attorneys are either too incompetent or too busy to do the same. That said, in this case, barring major screw-ups, the physical evidence isn't going to be the problem. The problem is going to be Charlie. Without a convincing shot at attacking our evidence and case-in-chief, Silverman will no doubt focus his efforts on tearing Charlie apart on the stand.

We also feel we might have a potential problem seated at the head of the courtroom. Any way you look at it, Judge Sharon Wilson, the federal judge assigned to this trial, is a significant concern at this point. We had a taste of what she's capable of during the detention hearings. Like a number of judges at the lenient end of the spectrum, Wilson's unhappy with the mandatory sentencing guidelines that were introduced a few years ago. Designed to limit judicial discretion and level the playing field nationwide, it keeps judges like "Her Honor" from going too easy on the bad guys; or conversely, in the case of some "hanging judges," from going too far the other way. If anything, she is more lenient than she was before. She has a track record of relying heavily on "mitigating circumstances"—the only loophole of the federal sentencing process in which she has a little judicial wiggle room. On top of everything else, it's become apparent that she's intimidated by the Hells Angels. We know this because she's asked the U.S. Marshals and the FBI to beef up security in her courtroom during the trial. She has expressed fear for her own personal safety and has requested additional metal detectors outside her courtroom.

As the trial date fast approaches, we're all starting to get a little nervous and anxious about meeting with our star witness for the first time since he left.

It's two days before we're due to fly to a yet undisclosed location to meet with Charlie for more pre-trial briefings when I get a call from Barrett, asking me to come to his office. When I arrive, he's putting on a clean shirt, getting ready for court.

"Defense is offering to enter into plea negotiations," he says, buttoning his cuffs.

For a second, I think his mind is on the case he's currently prosecuting then I realize he means Duke's defense—Duke and his associates.

"They all want to cop a plea, Nick," he says, harried.

"What?"

"They don't want it to go to trial." Barrett throws on a jacket and grabs up an attaché case. "Let's walk and talk."

We head back out through the office, Barrett fielding a bunch of questions from underlings who trail us. He seems pretty pleased with the news of a plea offer, as you might expect from a prosecutor, but I can't say I share the feeling. I want to go to trial. I still feel we can win, and convictions mean much stiffer sentences than anything these guys will be willing to plead to.

"Silverman wants the minimum eight years for Duke, contingent on the return of all the limos that didn't contain drugs," Barrett says as we hurry through the bustling U.S. attorney's office, heading for the elevators. He comes to a halt in the middle of the corridor.

"What?"

Barrett turns to face me. "He also wants us to return the $350,000 seized from the floor safe in Duke's office."

Then he's moving again, and all I can do is follow. We step into an elevator. For a second, I'm too angry to speak. Barrett sees the look on my face, shakes his head.

"Lighten up, Nick. We're not going to give him back his money."

"But *eight years*?" I say, and I can't hide how pissed off I am. With the enhanced penalties for selling drugs within a thousand yards of school, Duke should be looking at sixteen to twenty-four.

"And you can forget about Wilson enhancing Duke's sentence on the school issue," he says, as if reading my mind. He checks his watch. "Last two times she sat on similar cases, she ruled that the drug dealers weren't actually selling to school children, so the enhancement rule didn't apply." The AUSA offers a wry little smirk. "According to her *interpretation*."

I grunt with frustration.

"Listen, Nick," Barrett says, laying a hand on my shoulder, "Duke's still looking at eight to twelve. I don't think eight's such a bad deal. No parole."

"What about Gonzo?" I say, feeling a sinking sensation in my stomach only enhanced by our descent in the elevator.

"They'll settle for the minimum mandatory sentence of five years on the dope charges with his one prior."

I groan.

"Contingent upon us returning the $370,000 cash seized at the Ramona residence." He gives me a straight look, then shrugs. "That's right, Nick . . . they all want to keep the cash."

"But what about the ex-felon in possession of firearms," I plead. "I mean his house was an arsenal. He's looking at a minimum of fifteen years on that charge alone."

Barrett shrugs again. "I'm just telling you what's on the table. You know the game."

"And Scooter?" I say, the numbers continuing to tumble.

"With two prior felonies, he'll cop to minimum fifteen. Ex-felon in possession of a firearm. Possession of an illegal weapon—the sawed-off shotgun—and the drug conspiracy all neatly packaged into one deal."

I sigh this time, feeling at least some relief.

"He's going away for a long time," Barrett assures. "Sledge, meanwhile, is bidding his minimum eight."

"What about Jay Palac?"

The elevator comes to a halt on the second floor, and we get off.

Standing outside Judge Jacob Switzer's courtroom, Barrett hurriedly explains. "Possession and conspiracy to sell eight ounces of meth," he says. "His exposure is thirty-six to sixty months. No priors. He wants—"

"Three years," I say.

"The minimum."

Barrett looks at his watch. "I'm late, Nick," he says. "And I'm sorry to be the bearer of bad news, my friend. But I'm just telling you what's on the table."

I nod, frustrated as hell, as I watch him straighten his tie and push through the door to the courtroom.

"Talk to the others," he says over his shoulder. "Frank, Blair, and Cantrell. Let me know what the consensus is."

I stand there in the corridor alone and take a deep breath trying to absorb the news I've just received. I am abruptly conscious of stale air and the distant sound of a gavel hitting Judge Switzer's bench. And I think about Charlie. In my vision, he's brooding on the edge of a motel bed, his head down, staring at his hands. He wouldn't like the sound of any of this.

~~~~

In the end, the consensus is that it's just too risky to go to trial with Charlie as our witness. Any defense attorney worth his salt is going to chip away at Charlie's integrity, get him agitated on the stand, and catch him off-guard. Even if Charlie somehow manages to stay calm, he's more than likely to confuse dates, times, quantities—until the jury sees him as just another unreliable, vindictive informant. And we'd still have the FotoMat issue to deal with. And the knife in Ramona.

It's not a decision Frank and I take lightly, but with pressure coming from Barrett and Blair to settle, and with Charlie safely ensconced inside the WitSec program, we figure it's time to put the case to bed. Not that we roll over on all their demands. The plea we finally agree to doesn't include giving up the forfeited assets or any of the cash. Joe the Jew's made sure of that. Silverman is so beside himself dealing with Joe on the forfeiture issues, he tells Frank he'll do anything to settle the case just to not have to be in the same room with what he describes as "an arrogant, loudmouthed, asshole Jewish attorney."

So Duke loses his business and goes away for eight years with no parole. Gonzo gets fifteen, Scooter twenty, and Sledge eight. Only Jay Palac walks away pretty much unscathed, doing thirty-six months minus time already served. I figure Charlie would've wanted it that way anyway.

With our cases wrapped up, Frank and I are able to move on to other things, including the Mongoose rape case, which we're both keen to see go to trial. Faced with the testimony of the victim and her mother, the physical evidence, and the threat of supporting eyewitness testimony from Charlie, Mongoose is facing ten to fifteen years in the state penitentiary for unlawful sexual intercourse and sodomy with a minor. We'll also now have time to put together the attempted arson of the Jacumba property and the aggravated assault charges in state court against Duke, Gonzo, Bad Eye, and Scooter—if our witnesses can hold together under the ever-present intimidation of testifying against the Hells Angels.

In the weeks following the final settlement with Duke and the other HAs on all federal charges, I manage to get a letter to Charlie through the U.S. Marshals Service, informing him that the case had concluded and that his testimony won't be necessary. I tell him that even though he'd never actually taken the stand, it was because of him that we had such great evidence resulting in the guilty pleas.

"You risked your life many times over by wearing the wire," I write. "And I want you to know how much Frank and I appreciate what you did. And I want to wish you the very best in your new life. It's going to be hard, and you're going to stumble, but like Frank said once, *everybody* stumbles. The important thing is getting back up. I know you always will."

The letter goes out in the early spring of 1997, and with it, I feel a sense of relief. We'd given Charlie the best chance for success and survival. And I truly hope he makes the best of it.

Chapter 52

A Golf Course in Atlanta
1997–99

Charlie starts to call toward the end of May. The phone rings one Friday evening, and when I pick it up, I hear heavy breathing.

"Hey, Nick."

I'd like to say I'm happy to hear his voice, but I'm not. I find my way to the kitchen stool and sit down.

"Hope it's okay calling you at home, man."

"No, Charlie," I say. "It's *not* okay. Not at home. Not at work. You're not supposed to call me at all."

"Come on, man. Who gives a fuck?"

"I do, Charlie. The marshals do. They're trying to keep you safe. But if you start calling..."

"What? You think Duke's tapping your phone? You think Duke..."

I close my eyes, tuning out as he rambles on, talking about how bored he is, how disappointed he was when he got my letter. I try to explain our reasoning for not putting him on the stand, but it's a frustrating conversation in which he seems determined to see our decision as a slight, a lack of confidence in him after all the hard work he had put into the case and all the risks he'd taken.

"You didn't think I could handle it, right? You didn't think I could handle the questions. Fuck that, man. I coulda done it standin' on my fuckin' head."

I try to get him off the subject, try to get him to talk in general about his life, but then I have to keep cutting him off every time he gets into specifics. Eventually, we talk ourselves into an awkward silence.

"I'm hanging up, Charlie."

"You hear about Gonzo, Spence?"

"What about Gonzo?"

"Got shanked in the joint. Dead!"

"How'd you find that out, Charlie? Jesus, you're not supposed to ..."

"I got my sources, Spence. They found him in his cell with a shiv jammed in his neck. Had a dollar bill stuck on the end of the shiv." He chuckles. "Guess Duke figured out who stole the money from the club."

"Goddamnit, Charlie, you're talking to people you shouldn't be ..."

"Take it easy, Spence, I'm just ..."

I slam the phone down before he can finish.

Afterward, I sit there in the silence of the kitchen for a long time, thinking about what I should do, starting with maybe changing my number.

~~~~

The second call comes a month later. This time, there's no recrimination. Charlie just wants to gripe. He talks again about how bored he is and what a bunch of assholes the marshals are. I decide to respond with silence, figure he's going to run out of steam soon enough.

"Nick?" he says after a minute.

"Charlie," I say with a sigh, "I'm going to hang up now. I explained to you that you're compromising me and the WitSec program. You signed an agreement with—"

"So that's it? You're done with me? You're through?"

"Charlie.... You know it's not like that."

"Then what's it like?"

"It's the program, Charlie. You can't just—"

"Then *fuck* the program! I quit."

My heart stops. "What do you mean you quit?"

"I can't handle these people, Nick. I can't do it no more."

"They're just trying to help you, Charlie."

"I can make it on my own," he says, then hangs up.

I get a couple more similar calls throughout the summer, and then it goes quiet for several months.

In October, almost a year from our Halloween raids, Charlie calls. Tells me he's in Atlanta. Says he left the program. Just walked away.

"I can call you anytime I want," he says proudly.

I'm angry with him, but I don't see the point in showing it. "You still shouldn't call," I say. "People are going to be out looking for you."

"Fuck 'em."

"Well, that may be okay with you," I say slowly, "but it's not okay with me. So quit calling. You don't *need* to call me anymore. I wish you the best, Charlie. I really do."

I guess I get angry enough finally for him to take the hint because several months go by without word. I figure he's finally come to accept the way things are, but then he calls again in the early spring of 1998 around Valentine's Day. He met a girl, he says. Her name is Gina.

"That's great, Charlie."

"She's unbelievable, man. She's good people. She's pretty, she's smart."

"Then what's she doing with you?"

We both laugh at this, and for a second it's as if we were back in the Pacific Beach house, swapping stories into the night.

"No, seriously, though, Charlie, that's great. I'm happy for you. What about work? Did you find a job?"

"At a *golf course*, man," he says. "You believe that shit? I'm mowin' lawns, you know, landscaping."

"Yeah?"

"I get up in the mornings. I mean, I'm the first one up. I never used to get up early, Nick."

"I know that, Charlie."

"I get up at four-thirty in the morning. I feel great, man. I go out there with my tractor and I mow the lawn and I listen to the birds wake up. It's unbelievable, man. It's just ... it's just unbelievable."

The last call comes in December of 1998 just before Christmas. The phone rings at six in the morning, Charlie being oblivious to the time difference between the East and West Coast. I grab the receiver from my bedside table. There's a long silence and I almost hang up. Then Charlie's voice, booming, tells me that he's now the proud father of a baby girl. I sit up against the headboard.

"She's beautiful, man. I mean, I can't believe she's mine, uh, *ours*."

It's clear he's beside himself with excitement as he describes every little detail about his daughter.

"What's her name, Charlie?"

"Well," he says softly, hesitantly. "I wanted to pick a name that reminded me of you guys. You know, you and Frank. I told Gina all about you guys."

"Jesus, Charlie," I say. "I hope you didn't name her Frank."

"No, Nick," Charlie says, and I can hear his pride through the line. "I named her Rose."

I smile as if I've just become a proud new father myself. "It's a pretty name, Charlie, but I . . ."

"Don't you get it?" Charlie interrupts. "Rose. Like roses. My lifeline."

I feel a lump in my throat, and my eyes become moist with tears. I'm just so happy for him. *Proud* of him, even.

"Well, she's my new lifeline," he says. "I call her Rosie."

His voice sounds so different, so calm and full of hope. I can't stop smiling.

"I put her in her little crib at night, and the way she looks up at me . . . I'm tellin' you, Nick, it's the best thing ever."

I climb out of the bed and go out onto the deck. The fresh ocean air fills my lungs.

"Nick?"

"Yeah, I'm still here."

"You and Frank and Paul saved me, man," he says. "I owe you my life. You gave me another chance."

I listen through the short silence that follows, feeling myself tear up again.

"And I appreciate it, man."

I open my mouth to speak, but before I can say anything, he says he has to go.

"Okay, Charlie." I say. "Go look after Rosie. Go look after your little girl." And I hang up, praying to God that he's finally made it, that he's crossed the bridge of no return.

Chapter 53

A Harrowing Trail
San Diego, CA
September 2000

Then it goes quiet. A couple of years go by with no news. Which is good, of course, but still I find myself thinking about Charlie from time to time. I see a young family and visualize Charlie with Gina and little Rosie. When I'm at a golf course, I picture him watching birds stir into wakefulness in the first flush of an Atlanta dawn. It's a good feeling, especially in this business, to know that you've helped someone get a new start in life, that you pulled someone out of the depths of despair and self-destruction and set a new course for them to succeed.

Unfortunately, it's a feeling I don't get to keep.

~ ~ ~ ~

For a while, I almost forget about Charlie altogether, caught up in work, mostly an ongoing investigation of the Esposito brothers' methamphetamine operation. The case keeps getting bigger and has now expanded beyond the border into Mexico.

I'm at my desk when Clouser comes into the squad room and pulls up a chair next to me. He looks at me for a moment and I can see he's hesitant.

"This must be good, John," I say. "What've you got?"

"I was at the East County Task Force meeting this afternoon, and guess whose name was mentioned?"

"Hopalong Cassidy."

"Charlie Slade."

I look up from the report I'm reading. "What *about* Charlie Slade?"

Clouser looks down, keeps his eyes trained on my desk. "I guess he's back in town and hanging in the wrong places. He was spotted by our surveillance teams coming and going from one of their targeted drug houses."

"How do they know it's Charlie?"

"Ran the plate on his Harley, I guess."

"Maybe it's a mistake."

"Nick," Clouser says, "I've seen the surveillance photos. It's Charlie."

~ ~ ~ ~

The first shock fades into numbed acceptance as I reluctantly begin to work the databases to track down my old friend. I can't help myself—can't avoid at least trying to find him and make contact—find out what the hell happened.

I run Charlie Slade through ARJIS, and I get a hit on a traffic stop a couple of months ago, in July. He received a warning citation under the motorcycle helmet use law, and it gave an address at 9797 Valley View Road, San Marcos, California. So I run an address check and find that location to be Pleasant Valley Ranch, a religion-based treatment facility supported by a private endowment. A little more checking revealed it is a drug rehab center where people can check themselves in for a fee. It's located about ten miles from Carlsbad, the last place we hid Charlie before he went into the WitSec program. This is all depressing news.

I drive out to Pleasant Valley on a weekend. As the name suggests, the area is secluded and peacefully quiet. A skinny guy with prison tattoos on his arms comes out to the gate and he's immediately suspicious of me, figuring me for a cop, I guess. I explain that I'm looking for someone and want to talk to whoever's in charge.

After about five minutes, an older black man comes out and introduces himself as Percy. He's friendly enough, and happy to talk to me through the gate, but he says he doesn't think he can help me.

"So many people come through here."

"I think you'd remember Charlie," I say. "He was a gang

member. A Hells Angel at one time. Kind of a loner."

The old man's milky eyes go blank for a second, and then I watch him remember. "Charlie," he drawls with a slow smile. "Yeah... Charlie..."

"You know him, then?"

"Yes, sir," Percy says, finally opening the gate. "I met him when I first arrived here. Man, oh, man. I was in a bad way. Charlie'd already been here a couple months."

I follow Percy down a dusty path toward a clapboard building. "You were a patient?"

He nods. "Back then. I was kind of desperate. This place was a last hope for me." He comes to a halt and looks up at me sadly. "I'm a heroin addict. Two years sober."

"Two years," I say. "Congratulations."

"Thank you." He shakes his head mournfully and moves on, walking through to a porch where some wicker chairs have been set out around little tables. "Yes, sir. A heroin addict. A junkie. Just like Charlie."

"You had that in common, then."

"We did. We surely did."

We take a seat and are still for a moment, enjoying the shade and the quiet.

"Like I said, first time I met him, I'd just got here," Percy sighs. "Hadn't even spent my first night. I was checked in and I was just so desperate. I didn't know what was gonna happen to me. . . ." He stirs at the floor with his foot for a while, recalling bad times, I guess. "Anyway, it starts pouring rain and there's thunder and lightning, and I get it into my head to take a walk."

He looks up at me. "I know. Stupid. But it was the *least* of all the stupid I was into back then."

He shrugs. "Anyway, I went outside in the storm and walked down to the creek—it's just down there through the trees." He points in a direction behind me. "There was so much water rushin' down from the mountains. It's like roarin' through here and I'm standin' there, lookin' at all this churnin' dark water when I hear a voice behind. 'Don't jump.'"

Percy smiles. "I turn around and there's Charlie sittin' on a rock in the pourin' rain. He's just sittin' there by hisself, gettin' soaked to the skin. He says, 'Don't jump, man. It's not that bad.' That's how we met."

I nod, liking this image of Charlie on a rock in the rain, for some reason, liking the idea of Charlie doing good even when things must have been bad for him. But I can't help thinking about Gina and about Rosie, wondering where they were. What had happened?

"We became friends," Percy says. "But I think I was pretty much the only one he had. Charlie never associated with people here much."

He's quiet for a moment. I hear a TV come on inside the building. Music. Sitcom. Canned laughter.

"Did he ever talk about stuff?" I say. "His past . . ."

Percy thinks about it for a while. "'I slipped up.' That's what he always said. He said he'd been clean for a long time, but then he 'slipped up' . . . yeah, them's the words he used."

"When did he leave?"

Percy furrows a brow, projects his lower lip. "We'd have to check the records. It's been a while now—a year maybe—jus' guessin'. He went through the program. It's a six-month program and he completed it, participated in all the group therapy and such." He leans forward in his chair and lowers his voice, clearly not wanting to be overheard. "It's kind of churchy here, but he was okay with all that."

"He grew up with nuns," I say, wishing I hadn't said it. The picture of Charlie's abuse flashes to my head again. Unspeakable.

Percy nods, leaning back. "That right?" he says, musing. "I knew he was a biker. But he never said nothin' about no nuns. Nor no Hells Angels, for that matter. He had this big ol' black motorcycle, but he never rode it. There was another guy here, a guy named Biker Bob that Charlie sometimes hung with, a big dude with tattoos and a full beard. I heard he ended up gettin' killed up in L.A. in a gang deal. They dragged him behind a car until he was dead, you know."

"But Charlie," I say, "as far as you know, he got himself clean. He turned himself around?"

"I believe so. He was serious. He'd go to bed early, and he stuck with the program. In fact, he did so well that they asked him to stay on and be a counselor. But about that time, he was offered a job by a guy who owned a landscaping business right up the road here. The man who owned the business—his son was in here, see, as a patient—he gave a lotta stuff to the ranch. He came in here and taught people how to plant and such things whilst visiting his son."

"And this man . . . he gave Charlie a job?"

"That's right. On account of Charlie helpin' his kid. Charlie counseled that boy and told him you gotta get yourself right, you gotta clean up."

"Do you have a name for this man? The owner?"

Percy looks up at me, narrowing his eyes. "I don't wanna make no trouble for no one," he says softly.

"I'm not here to bring trouble. I'm just trying to find Charlie."

"He a friend of yours?"

For a second, I don't know what to say. "There's a connection," I say eventually. "I'd like to help him if I can."

~ ~ ~ ~

Dean Buckley, the owner of the landscaping firm, is a wiry character with muscular hands and suntanned, sinewy arms who looks to be in his late fifties. We talk for a while in his driveway, then end up sitting in a couple of folding chairs in a junk-crammed storage building, each of us nursing a cold beer.

"I knew a little about his background," he says. "How he was a Hells Angel and so forth, but after what he did with Michael, I didn't hesitate to offer him a job."

We've barely gotten settled in, but Buckley gets up again and raps on one of the lime-washed windows that look out onto the backyard. He slumps back into his deck chair and takes another sip of beer.

"He was a good worker. Up early and straight down to it. He'd been in landscaping before. I was sorry to see him go."

A young man comes to the open door, wiping his hands in an oily rag. I'm guessing it's Michael. He's maybe nineteen years old and afflicted with the awkwardness that often comes with that age, but when his father introduces me and tells him what we're talking about, some of the shyness fades and he takes a seat on an old lawn tractor, his skinny legs dangling.

"I was just telling Mr. Spence here about how Charlie got you straightened out."

Michael nods, looking down at his grease-blackened hands.

"Charlie has a way with him," I say, hoping to prod Michael to talk, but it doesn't do much good. In fact, he's pretty much monosyllabic until he relaxes a bit, then starts talking about how Charlie always took the time to listen to him when he was having a hard time.

"What did you talk about?" I say.

"Stuff."

"You want to elaborate on that, son?"

"Was it personal stuff?" I say.

"He never talked much about his personal life. It was more the way he saw things, the way he was."

"Anyway, he worked here six months," Buckley says. "I give him a new truck and all the tools, you know. I put him in charge of work crews, made him a supervisor right off the bat. I figured if he was really a Hells Angel, he wouldn't have no trouble running my work crews."

"You put a lot of trust in him."

"I did. And I'd do it again. I trusted him and I paid him good wages. Hell, I even got him a place to live in the trailer park down the road. He came in to work every day for six months. But . . ."

"But what?"

Father and son exchange a look. Then Buckley takes another sip of beer.

"Well, sometimes I was a little concerned that . . . sometimes he was a little fidgety, you know."

"With the drugs? You think he was using again?"

"I think so," Michael says, nodding at his swinging feet.

"Damned drugs," Buckley says, his face darkening with emotion as he glances at his son.

For a moment, no one speaks—as though his words needed a little reverence.

"Anyway," Buckley says after a time. "One day, I get a call from Ray, the fella who runs the trailer park. He's real upset, you know, and he says, 'You gotta get this maniac outta here. He just threatened to kill my wife.'"

He gives me a look, expecting me to be surprised, I think. When I'm not, he continues.

"So, I said, 'What do you mean? *Charlie*?' He said, 'Yeah, he's threatening to kill my wife.' So I go up there and Ray's sitting there and he says his wife tried to take Charlie some chocolate chip cookies, trying to make him feel welcome in the trailer park, you know. It was the second time she done it. The first time, Charlie said he don't like chocolate chip cookies and just closes his door. And Ray's wife, Angie, she figures it's just because Charlie was shy. So she let it go for a couple of months and then went back to take him some cookies again, you know, trying to be neighborly."

Buckley shakes his head and takes a sip of his beer. "And Charlie says, 'If you don't go away and stop botherin' me, I'm gonna kill you,' or somethin' to those words."

"'Cept he used the F word," Michael adds.

"Charlie did that a lot," Buckley says. "Anyway, so now Ray's real upset, and he wants me to get Charlie outta there. So I go to talk to Charlie about it in his trailer and he . . . he just looks at me like he doesn't know anything about it. 'What are you talkin' about?' he says."

Buckley finishes his beer. "But I reckon he did it. Maybe he was cranky with the drugs or something, I don't know. Anyway, it wasn't a week later that he didn't come to work. We went up to the trailer park and the truck was there. It was completely washed. Spotless clean, inside and out. And all the tools were laid out and the keys in the ignition."

"All washed off and spotless," Michael says.

"And there was a note saying, 'I just can't let you down. I've got some problems to go deal with, and thank you for everything and goodbye.' Somethin' like that."

"Where do you think he went?" I say.

"I heard he was back with his old girlfriend," Michael says solemnly.

"You know her name?"

"Stella? Stephanie? Somethin' like that."

I look down at my shoes. Stacey Ritt. Charlie's come full circle, and I have a sick feeling in the pit of my stomach. "Do you know where he is now?" I ask.

"No, sir."

"He's not in any trouble, is he?" Buckley asks.

"I think he might be," I say, getting to my feet. "But not with me."

Chapter 54

$300
San Diego, CA
December 2000

I come away from Pleasant Valley feeling pretty hopeless as far as Charlie is concerned, but I really don't see myself driving all over San Diego County looking for him. I've confirmed he's back in San Diego, and he's most likely hooked on the heroin habit again. And worst of all, he's back with Stacey Ritt. Even if I find him, I don't have the resources to help him out. I'm concerned for his safety, but the Bureau no longer has an obligation to protect him. The Hells Angels have long memories. It's just a matter of time before he runs into someone who knows someone, and Charlie will be on his own.

~ ~ ~ ~

Two weeks before Christmas, I get a call from Michelle in reception saying there's a Mr. Slade wanting to talk to me.

"Slade? *Charlie* Slade?"

"Mr. Charlie Slade, yes."

I jump to my feet and hustle through to the front of the office. Charlie's standing in the middle of the reception room, straining at a smile, his eyes serious and fixed on me with that dark intensity so familiar. He still has the long hair, mustache, and goatee, and in many ways he looks like he always did. A flannel shirt hangs loose over dirty jeans, the sleeves buttoned at the cuffs.

"Hey, Spence."

"Jesus, Charlie."

For a second, I don't know whether to be angry or pleased. I step back, inviting him into the squad room. He's never been here before and looks surprised when I invite him in. A few heads rise from cluttered desks, but it's not that unusual to have visitors like Charlie in our space. We walk through a back door into a little galley kitchen. Up close, Charlie looks a little dirty, his hair hanging in greasy ropes on his shoulders. He looks like the Hells Angel he used to be, in fact. But there's no swagger to him. No confidence.

"I shouldn't have come," he says.

"It's all right, Charlie. How've you been?"

"Oh, you know. . . . Okay, I guess."

For a while we talk, trying to find a rhythm, talking over each other, getting stuck in awkward pauses. It's clear after just a few minutes that one of the reasons he's here is simply to touch base, to reassure himself that we're still friendly, if not actual friends. He says he's living in Lakeside now, gives me his address and number on a rumpled piece of paper from his shirt pocket, in case I need to be in touch. He starts telling me about Pleasant Valley.

"I know about Pleasant Valley, Charlie."

He becomes still and watchful.

"I went there," I say.

"Why?"

"Why what?"

"Why'd you go up there, Nick?"

"I wanted to make sure you were okay."

The words hang in the air. Then I'm surprised by a surge of feeling, of anger. "Jesus, Charlie," I yell. "The last time we talked, you were in Atlanta. You were telling me all about the new baby. What happened to all that?"

Charlie gazes down at his hands, quivers, then stares right through me. It's a scary look, a hopeless look—the look of total despair—someone who's given up.

"What happened, Charlie?"

"I slipped up, Spence. I slipped up . . ."

We sit down at the little table under a window.

"But your little girl . . ."

Charlie jerks. His face twists in anguish, and for a second it looks like he's going to cry. But then he gets a grip on himself, fumbles cigarettes out of his shirt pocket, and lights one up.

"My little Rose," he says, sucking in smoke. He lets it out on a long, shuddering exhale. "She's okay. They're okay. Better off without me around, that's for sure. Jesus, Spence, I'm such a fuckin' loser." He looks out the window, wipes away a tear with the back of his shaking hand. "I need to borrow some money."

I wait until he turns to look at me.

"What? How much?"

"Three hundred dollars."

He holds my stare.

"You using again?"

He nods. "Can you do it?"

"Charlie, c'mon, man, you can't expect me to . . ."

"Can you *do* it or not? Because if you can't . . ."

I draw a hand across my face, suddenly tired. "Take it easy, Charlie." I paw at my pockets, not really wanting to reach for my wallet, but doing it anyway. I know I don't have much on me.

"You remember the motel?" I ask. "You remember when me and Frank found you on the bed? Is that how you want to end up? Alone in some shithole with bugs in your ass and a fucking needle in your arm? Do you really want to be that fifty-year-old junkie you told us you'd never become?"

He thinks about it for a second, closes his eyes. "I can't fight it, Nick. I tried to fight it, but I can't."

"That's bullshit. I watched you beat it, remember? I watched you get clean."

"I had you guys backin' me up."

"Well, there must be people that. . . . Isn't there anyone looking out for you?"

"There's Stacey. But she's worse than me, man."

"Then you shouldn't be with her."

He glares at me.

"Sorry, Charlie, but it's true. She's just going to drag you down." I look down at the floor, considering options. None of them seems great. "Look," I say with a sigh. "I'll give you the money. And I'm going to help you, if I can. I'm going to get you help. But it can't be here. You need to go back to Atlanta."

I check my watch.

"You need to be somewhere?" he asks.

"Yeah, let me get my jacket." I walk back through to my desk with Charlie in tow.

"What're you working on?" he mumbles.

I glance down at the files strewn on my desk. "Oh, you know . . . the usual."

"Yeah?"

"Well, not the *usual* really. Right now, I'm trying to help Frank with a jewelry heist he's working on. Remember back when we first met, I'd been working the undercover jewelry thing in Phoenix?"

"Sure do."

I pick up the CCTV tape on my desk, tap it once with my finger. "Frank and I have a good friend in the jewelry business. Guy named Mort. He owns a jewelry store here. He just got robbed. So now he's got to make good on a shitload of consignment jewelry. We're talking about millions of dollars he doesn't have. His insurance won't cover all of it, so he's basically fucked. Whole thing was caught on the security camera. But I'm damned if we can ID the bad guys."

"Want me to take a look?"

I raise an eyebrow. "You serious?"

"Sure. Why not?"

I shrug and take the tape into a little room where we've got a TV set up, slot it into the machine, and hit play. So now we're staring at grainy black and white video of two assholes helping themselves to jewelry out of a shattered display case. Forty seconds into it, Charlie points a nicotine-stained finger.

"Guy with the bald spot is Jeff Tyler," he says. "Or Taylor maybe. And the other guy, the guy with the bandana, that's O'Henry. They call him Eight Ball."

I hit pause. "You gotta be kidding me."

Charlie shakes his head with kind of a smirk on his face.

"Was in prison with both those assholes."

I can't believe it. Frank and I've spent the last two weeks trying to put this thing together, turning over every rock, checking with all our sources. I offer Charlie my upturned palm. He gives it a halfhearted tap.

"If you want me to," he says, "I'll come back and look at the video in court and say that's them. I mean, if that's what you want me to do."

He says it like it's no big deal, but I can see the eagerness in his eyes. He wants to work with us again. He needs it. He needs us.

"You're the man, Charlie," I say, choosing to ignore the godawful sadness of it all. "*YOU—ARE—THE—MAN*! Let's call Frank and surprise him. He won't believe this shit. He'd love to see you, Charlie."

"Not now, Spence. Not like this." He sighs, lowering his head. He puts his hands in his pockets and starts to shuffle his feet but doesn't look back up at me . . . hiding his shame. He doesn't offer anything more. I can see he's anxious. He pulls a hand out of his pocket and chews on a ragged cuticle, thinking about leaving now, thinking about his next rendezvous. Again, the sadness of it washes over me.

"Let's get you some cash," I say.

I withdraw $300 from the ATM across the street from the FBI office and hand Charlie the bills. He jams them into his jeans, eyes averted.

"Think about what I said, Charlie."

He looks at me, nods. I offer him my hand and he takes it. When he goes to back away, I hold onto him, squeezing his hand hard.

"You're better than this, Charlie."

He looks down. Tears fill his eyes.

"You're one of the bravest people I know," I say. "And you're a fighter and you can beat this fucking thing."

Finally, I let go. Charlie stays where he is, eyes on the ground. Then he looks up again, a half-smile on his cracked lips.

"What?"

"I was thinking about the time the brakes failed on that fucking car."

I frown, nod.

"What made you think of that?"

He shrugs. "I don't know. Those were happy times. It's good to see you, Spence." He backs away, raising a hand. "Say 'hi' to Frank for me," he says. "Say 'hi' to Paul."

I watch him walk away along the street, watch him go around a corner.

Chapter 55

Christmas Present
San Diego, CA
January 2001

The last time Charlie calls, it's early January, about three weeks after I last saw him at the ATM machine. We've just recovered Mort's jewelry, arrested the two crooks, and are finally able to squeeze the $10,000 reward money out of our tight-assed jeweler friend, so the timing couldn't be better. Charlie tells me he's leaving town and wants to see me before he takes off.

"I got something for you, Nick."

"Charlie. If it's the money, don't worry about it."

"It's not the money. I'm gonna pay you back as soon as I get a job, but I got something else. Something I want you to have."

"Okay . . . ," I say, and I'm about to tell him about the reward money when he goes on.

"I'm going back to Atlanta, Spence."

"That's great, Charlie," I say with genuine excitement. There's a moment's silence. "Charlie?"

"I thought about what you said and . . . well, I think you're right. I . . . I've been clean for three weeks and I'm ready to go back."

"I'm glad, Charlie. But what about Stacey?"

"Stacey's gone."

"What?"

"We had words. Last night. Threw her skinny ass out. Her and her fuckin' cat."

"Oh. I'm sorry."

"Why? I thought you said she was bad for me."

"I did," I say, shaking my head. "I do, but . . . I'm just sorry you're going through all this. That's what I mean."

There's a rushing sound . . . Charlie blowing smoke

against the mouthpiece, I guess.

"It's okay, man. It's all good. It's all gonna be good now. I'm going back to Atlanta. I'm gonna go look after my little girl. You know, get a job, be close. Where I see her grow up."

"That's good, Charlie. That's the best thing you can do."

"Listen, Spence. Can you meet in Lakeside?"

~ ~ ~ ~

It's cold and raining when I pull into the parking lot in front of the Denny's. I look around the lot but don't see his bike, then walk into the glow of franchise neon and the warming aroma of greasy fast food and cigarette smoke. The place is pretty empty, just a couple of truck drivers huddled in the booths. I take a seat by a window and look out at the passing traffic slamming through the rain on Highway 67, thinking about the last time I came down this road after nearly crashing Kinney's brown submarine into the steep canyons of the San Vicente Reservoir.

After ordering a cup of coffee, I sit there nursing it for about twenty minutes. No Charlie. I go outside against the building and call the number he'd written on a crumpled piece of paper along with his address. The phone rings, but no one picks up. I go back to the table and drink another cup of coffee, watching the rain stream down the plate-glass window.

"Come on, Charlie..."

At nine o'clock, I call again. Still no answer.

I drive over to the address Charlie gave me and park on the street. The place is a three-story tenement house with peeling purple trim on the windows. Standing there in the rain, I can see the flicker of TV screens in most of the windows and hear the thump of amplified music coming from the top floor. Charlie's motorcycle is parked under a staircase with a piece of plastic pulled across it, the license plate barely exposed. I walk over to it and put a hand on the exhaust. It's stone cold.

The main entrance door is propped open with an over-flowing trash can. Inside, the buzzing fluorescent light barely illuminates the names on the mailboxes. Scrawled on a piece of duct tape stuck above the slot of 1D is the name "Ritt."

As I walk through the lobby, I pass strollers and a couple of beat-up bicycles parked at the bottom of a stairway, then move on into the carpeted gloom of the lower corridor. Arguing voices and crying babies come through the doors on either side. I make my way down to 1D. My first knock sends the door swinging back a little on the hinges. A bad smell drifts out. A fishy smell.

"Charlie?"

I push the door all the way back. It's dark inside the apartment. I flip a light switch. Squinting in the harsh light shining from a bare lightbulb overhead, I take in a small living room—clothes scattered on a couch, a duffle bag with some clothes stuffed inside, and an overflowing ashtray on a cracked glass coffee table.

"Charlie?"

I continue forward—see a tiny kitchen and open tins of cat food on the floor. Footsteps shuffle behind me. I turn to see someone scurry past in the corridor. I hear a door slam in the distance. Blaring music starts up overhead. For no particular reason, I am beginning to get a bad feeling. I really didn't see Charlie just taking off after asking to meet. And I can't figure him leaving his bike behind. Maybe he's visiting somebody in the building.

Closing the front door, I cross the living room and slowly edge my way into a back room. I see an unmade bed and more clothes tossed about on the threadbare carpet. A bathroom door is ajar, exposing a couple inches of tile. I push against it, but it's blocked. There's something on the floor behind it. I hold my breath, reach inside, and flip the switch. I see the body reflected in the medicine cabinet mirror first.

"Charlie!"

I push harder. I have to step over the body to get in.

He's dressed in jeans and a T-shirt, slumped against the bathtub. There's a needle in his arm, a burnt spoon and his Bic lighter in the corner behind the toilet. His head is rolled forward and there is a crust of vomit on his chest. I squat down, feel for a pulse in his neck.

For a second, I think I'm going to throw up. I stand on shaky legs and lean against the sink; become aware of the dripping faucet; become aware of my own shuddering breaths.

"Jesus..."

Slumping down on the toilet seat, I feel all the strength going out of me.

"Jesus, Charlie."

My heart is pounding so hard, I can feel it in my throat. A wave of nausea surges through me.

"Goddamnit, Charlie! God! Goddamnit! Why the fuck did you come back, man? You had it made."

Then suddenly it comes to me that I don't really know what had happened here. I know what it looks like. There's no sign of a struggle. But just the same, the coroner is going to want to determine cause of death. I'm sitting in what is potentially a crime scene.

Startled, I get up from the toilet seat, take a last look at my friend, knowing it is truly going to be the last. My eyes blur with tears.

"I'm sorry, Charlie. I'm so sorry."

I make my way back out to the living room, sit down on the couch among the strewn laundry, and take a couple of deep breaths. I have to dial Frank's home number three times before I get it right.

"Charlie's dead."

For a moment, neither of us speak. Frank clears his throat.

"How?"

"I don't know. An overdose, it looks like. I'm here in his apartment. He's in the bathroom with a ... with a needle jammed in his arm."

I give Frank the address, tell him to call sheriff's homicide.

"Is there any sign of a struggle, Nick?"

"No," I say. "The place is a shithole, but there's no sign of a fight or anything like that."

"Witnesses?"

"No, I mean there's no one else here. I don't know, Frank."

"Sit tight, I'm on my way."

I drop the phone down.

That's when I see the package. It's on the stove in the kitchen, crudely gift-wrapped. Christmas trees. Smiling Santas. Charlie scrawled "Nick" across St. Nick's face. I pick it up with trembling fingers, tear at the paper, feeling numb, feeling sick. I guess I know what's inside before I see it.

I stare down at Charlie's boxing gloves from San Quentin. And there's a note in Charlie's second-grade handwriting: "Thanks for believing in me, Nick. Merry Christmas. Your friend, Charlie."

The tears begin to swell again, but this time I swallow them back. I pull the gloves onto my hands, bunch them into fists, and press them to my face.

Epilogue

What seems like hours is, in reality, only about twenty minutes before I hear the distant sound of a siren. I stand up and pull off the boxing gloves and lay them back on the wrapping paper. I sit there in the gloom until I hear signs of life outside the apartment. When I go to the door, I see paramedics rolling a gurney down the corridor toward me. I identify myself and show them where the body is.

Coming back into the living room, I'm met by a sheriff's office homicide detective. He says his name, holds out his hand. I shake it.

"You must be Agent Spence," he says. "I spoke with Detective Conroy about the situation here."

I nod, realizing I'm not saying much.

"Thanks for the quick response," I mumble.

"You okay?"

"Sure. I mean, no. Not really."

"What time did you get here?"

I look at my watch. "No more than a half-hour ago . . . say, 9:30. He was dead when I got here."

I watch him make a note, look around at the apartment, look back at me. He asks if I mind waiting outside while he takes a look at the scene.

"Sure thing." Truth is, I'm glad to get out of there.

It's still raining heavily. For a while, I just stand there next to Charlie's bike, getting wet. Images keep coming to my head: Charlie cracking the bullwhip in the backyard of the Pacific Beach place; Charlie boxing with Paul; Charlie driving the Camaro the day his brakes failed; Charlie grinning like an idiot, flashing his new teeth. I look up into the darkness.

"I'm sorry, Nick."

I turn. Frank is standing there staring up at me. His eyes are sad behind the rain-spattered glasses.

I take a deep breath, shake my head. "I don't know what

happened here, Frank."

He sees the bike, pulls the plastic sheet over it, making sure it's covered up.

"I mean, he called and said he'd made up his mind to go back to Atlanta. Said he had something for me. Said he'd been clean for three weeks."

Frank finds a dry spot close to the building and lights a cigarette.

"What the fuck happened here?" I say.

"We'll know soon enough, Spence. Overdose probably. You know as well as I do that guys like Charlie struggle their whole lives." He draws hard on his cigarette, pushes out a plume of smoke. "I mean, how many guys break the cycle of addiction?"

I shrug and come in next to him out of the rain. For a while, we just stand there staring out at the raindrops wafting through the dim fluorescent light over the trash-strewn parking lot.

"I don't know, Frank."

"What don't you know?"

"I feel like we used him."

"No."

"I feel like we used him and then just tossed him aside, like our friendship was just window dressing."

"He wanted to help, Nick. He wanted to do the right thing. And we gave him the chance to do that, to feel good about himself. We gave him a second chance at life."

There is enough truth in this for me to grab onto, but it doesn't stop me from feeling remorse.

"I guess it surprised me," I say after a while. "Charlie surprised me."

"He got to all of us, Nick. He was something else."

"He was good people."

The words just come out, and I realize as I say them that they were Charlie's words, a phrase I'd heard him use many times.

Frank puts a hand on my shoulder. "That's why I needed you on this case, Nick."

I turn to meet his piercing stare.

"Because you care," he says.

The sadness in me seems to rise up out of the depths. I step into the rain and tilt my head back. I feel the cold water run down my neck, inside my collar, and wish that it would wash all the sorrow away. Closing my eyes, I let it wash over me. It is going to have to rain for a long time.

"Every man has his secret sorrows which the world knows not; and often times we call a man cold when he is only sad."

~Henry Wadsworth Longfellow

ACKNOWLEDGEMENTS

This book could not have been written without the support of my loving family and friends. Words of encouragement go a long way when the ones you love have your back. My good fortune during my FBI career was to be surrounded by colleagues whose collective intelligence, intuitiveness, determination, and tenacity supported me, stood by me, and enabled me to perform at my best. Because of them, I have enjoyed many rich and rewarding experiences filled with a lifetime of memories.

Code Word Rose is my first novel and was inspired by a true story. Though the story is a fictional account of events, the real heroes of the story were the tireless partners who participated in the investigation. I include my friends and partners from the San Diego Police Department, The San Diego County Sheriff's Office, The San Diego County District Attorney's Office Investigative Division, The U. S. Marshals Service, and the U. S. Bureau of Alcohol, Tobacco, and Firearms (ATF). They were and are the best.

In certain cases, there are incidents, dialogues, scenarios, and timelines that have been created, modified, or altered for dramatic purposes. Certain characters may be composites or entirely ficticious. In every instance, the names and identities of persons have been changed and are fictional for reasons of privacy.

Made in the USA
Monee, IL
25 July 2025